THE CENSOR'S NOTEBOOK

THE CENSOR'S NOTEBOOK

a novel

LILIANA COROBCA

Translated by Monica Cure

SEVEN STORIES PRESS

New York • Oakland

Seven Stories Press
140 Watt Street
New York, NY 10013
www.sevenstories.com

Library of Congress Cataloging-in-Publication Data

Names: Corobca, Liliana, author. | Cure, Monica, translator.
Title: The censor's notebook : a novel / Liliana Corobca ; translated by
   Monica Cure.
Other titles: Caiet de cenzor. English
Description: New York : Seven Stories Press, [2022]
Identifiers: LCCN 2021057491 | ISBN 9781644211502 (trade paperback) | ISBN
   9781644211519 (ebook)
Subjects: LCSH: Censorship--Romania--History--20th century--Fiction. |
   LCGFT: Historical fiction. | Novels.
Classification: LCC PC840.413.O763 C3513 2022 | DDC
   859/.335--dc23/eng/20211210
LC record available at https://lccn.loc.gov/2021057491

Book design by Jon Gilbert

Printed in the USA.

9 8 7 6 5 4 3 2 1

For my parents,
for Ernest,
for Eliza

"Oh you who sound of mind were born,
search diligently my hidden meaning
beneath the veil of my strange words."

—DANTE ALIGHIERI*

* Dante Alighieri, *The Divine Comedy* (*Inferno, Canto IX, 61–63, Circle VI: The Heretics. Next to the gates of city of Dis. The three furies. The heavenly messenger. The two poets enter the city. The heretics buried in flaming tombs*), Romanian translation by Eta Boeriu.

Contents

Correspondence   11

Preamble   21

Confessions of a Notebook Thief   33

READER NOTEBOOK
Filofteia Moldovean
Literature and Art Division
1974

Justified Interventions   55

Literature Office Number Two   119

Useful Tips from Novels   191

Import-Export   261

The Lodge   327

The Other Beginning   363

The Trojan Horse   419

Translator's Note   477

Notes   483

Correspondence

On 4-22-2016, 3:33 PM, Emilia Codrescu-Humml <em.humml@ xxxxx> wrote:

Dear Ms. Liliana Corobca,

I recently heard about the project of establishing a Museum of Communism, initiated by the institute where you work. I found out that you are the one in charge of the topic "Censorship under Communism" and that the institute would be interested, for the purposes of the project, in "material objects received from individuals and organizations, within Romania and internationally, in the form of donations, in accordance with all current laws" which will constitute the future museum's permanent collection.

My name is Emilia Codrescu (married name Humml), I worked for the General Directorate of Press and Publications, and in 1974 I left for Germany with my husband and now live in Munich.

I would like to donate an item to the future museum—namely, the notebook of a censor who was a GDPP reader in 1974, in excellent condition.

If you are interested, please send me an address where you can be reached. I would not want to send a document like this through the mail and right now my granddaughter from Bucharest is visiting me. She would bring the notebook into the country and meet with you to hand it to you personally.

Awaiting your response,
Respectfully,
Emilia Codrescu

On 4-25-2016, 10:14 AM, Liliana Corobca <liliana.corobca@ ▮▮▮▮▮▮▮▮▮▮▮▮▮> wrote :

Dear Ms. Emilia Codrescu-Humml,

I don't know how to thank you for this surprising donation!

Of course, we would be thrilled to receive this very important document, which surely will become the keystone of the collection of the project division that I am heading. We had no hope of ever finding a notebook like this. In my years of research in the GDPP-CPP archives, I noted the systematic destruction of these documents, considered "classified." I can hardly wait for it to arrive safely!

I work Monday through Friday, 9 to 5, and I can be found at the following address: ▮▮▮▮▮▮▮▮▮▮▮ St., no. ▮▮, ▮ floor, apt. ▮▮, Sector 2, Bucharest (near Romana Square). During work hours, I can be reached at phone number: 021 3▮▮▮▮▮▮▮.

Until the notebook arrives, could you please tell me how it came to be in your possession?

I hope your granddaughter and the precious notebook have a safe trip!

Respectfully,
Liliana Corobca

On 4-28-2016, 11:24 AM, Emilia Codrescu-Humml <em.humml@ ███████ > wrote:

Dear Ms. Liliana Corobca,

My granddaughter, Evangelina Humml, arrives tomorrow evening, Friday, in Bucharest, and she will bring you the notebook at the beginning of next week. You'll also find enclosed a few notes about its journey, including the answer to your question. I wrote a few pages before 1994, when I came back to Romania for the first time after the fall of communism. I had wanted to return the notebook, but it wasn't possible. I added a few notes for you. Please let me know when you've received the notebook.

Respectfully,
Emilia Codrescu

On 5-9-2016, 3:38 PM, Liliana Corobca <liliana.corobca@ ███████ > wrote:

Dear Ms. Emilia Codrescu,

I was gone for a short Easter break and, when I
returned, I found the miraculous notebook on my desk.
I was told that your granddaughter had left it with the
front office. I want to assure you that it arrived safely,
and please thank her on my behalf. I opened the envelope and admired the precious document. I think I'll
also have it photographed, just in case. And then your
notes, they seem straight out of a novel. Thank you so
much! I haven't read through it yet, I didn't expect it to
be so substantial. It's very legible, with the exception of
a few pages written in pencil, I counted fourteen.

I asked the director of the project when the museum
will open and it seems that it will take some time, so
the idea came to me of putting the notebook to good
use by publishing it as well. What do you think? Even
though we will display it in the museum as an artifact, opened to a middle page in a glass-covered case,
its contents are much more interesting than that, from
what I could tell from my quick perusal. It's an impressive object, of course, but I have no doubt that its
contents will be just as surprising and important for a
much larger audience. I've worked on texts in the censorship archives since 2007, I've edited a few volumes
of primary sources, and it wouldn't be hard at all for
me to prepare this notebook for publication as well.
I also hope to find a prestigious press that would be
interested.

I haven't asked you yet: Can I include your name or

would you prefer to remain an anonymous donor? Your confession seems just as interesting to me and I'd like to publish it together with the notebook, if you have nothing against it (if necessary, under a pseudonym).

Respectfully and gratefully,
Liliana Corobca

On 5-12-2016, 10:54 AM, Emilia Codrescu-Humml <em. humml@ ████████ > wrote:

Dear Ms. Corobca,

I'm glad the notebook arrived safely! I must tell you that I had heard about you from a former coworker, he recommended that I write you, saying that if I sent it to you, it would be in good hands. He also told me that you've edited many documents related to censorship, that you're well-published. He also said that it's a shame that she's wasting her talent on these papers and on this subject, and that he can't understand how censorship can be of interest to you. I have nothing, of course, against the publication of the notebook. I also photographed the notebook in the '80s but those fourteen pages aren't legible in my photos either, I think the censor tried to rub them out with an eraser, to write something over them, otherwise I can't explain why the text is blurry. When the book comes out, please let me know and, of course, I would be happy to receive a copy. You may publish my explanatory notes, if you

think it's appropriate, under my name. I wish you all
the best.

Respectfully,
Emilia Codrescu

On 5-16-2016, 4:09 PM, Liliana Corobca <liliana.corobca@
███████████████> wrote :

Dear Ms. Emilia Codrescu,

I must admit that I very much enjoy studying this
subject, but I also write novels on the side. I've already
started transcribing the notebook.
I wanted to ask you something else. A few years ago
I edited two volumes of documents on "the institution
of censorship in Romania" and I found an interesting
brief about you. Do you remember how you managed
to leave Romania despite the interdiction? What happened to you on the way, what the accident was? I read
the notes you sent with the notebook but you don't
mention anything about it.
I'm attaching the document.

Have a wonderful week!
Best wishes,
Liliana Corobca

Attach files

GENERAL DIRECTORATE OF PRESS AND PUBLICATIONS
NO. S. 1407 FROM 21.VIII.1974

(In an upper corner, in pen: "Briefing com. Secretary Cornel Burtica. 26.VIII.1974. I. Cumpanasu.")

BRIEF

On January 15, 1974, Emilia Codrescu, employed at the GDPP since 1959, occupying the position of head of Administrative Services, member of the RCP since 1946, filed a request with the leadership of the institution for the approval of a leave for a touristic trip to France during her time off in June; likewise, in the request she also solicited that the necessary certificate be issued by Bucharest police district no. 10.

The note filed by the Directorate for Personnel-Training on January 31, comprising the favorable opinions of the president of the union committee, the secretary of the branch organization, the secretary of the party committee, and the deputy general director who oversees Administrative Services, was examined together with the request filed by the solicitant with the Executive Council of the GDPP. In the meeting on February 8, the Executive Council approved the employee's requested leave for the trip. The police certificate was issued on February 13. In preparation for her trip, the employee left her party membership card with the secretary of the branch organization to which she belonged.

Per the instructions regarding touristic trips abroad of press employees during this calendar year, the head of the Directorate for Personnel-Training communicated to employee Emilia Codrescu, under orders from the general director on June 6, that the approval given by the Executive Council was retracted and she was explicitly warned not to take the trip. The same day, the employee presented herself and verbally requested approval to leave under exceptional circumstances, given the expenses and preparations already undertaken. The general director of the GDPP rejected the request, maintaining the obligation the employee was under to strictly follow the instructions to forgo the trip and surrender her passport.

On July 6, the sister-in-law of employee Emilia Codrescu informed the institution via telephone that the employee was in the Federal Republic of Germany with her husband and, following an accident that occurred with their personal vehicle, had been admitted to a hospital; under the circumstances, she requests that after her time off ends, she be given unpaid leave.

The general director informed the Executive Council of the GDPP and the party committee of this violation of instructions. On July 8, orders were given for the dissolution of the work contract of employee Emilia Codrescu after the expiration of the period of unpaid leave, a resolution that would have been communicated to the institution after her return to the country, if applicable. On August 20, after more pressing requests from the GDPP to the employee's family members to clarify her situation, we were provided with a letter sent from the Federal Republic of Germany on June 26 wherein the Codrescus communicated to their family their decision to remain abroad indefinitely.

I. Cumpanasu
21. VIII. 1974

On 5-23-2016, 9:45 AM, Emilia Codrescu-Humml <em. humml@▮▮▮▮▮> wrote:

Dear Ms. Corobca,

Reading the document flooded me with emotion! Thank you for sending it to me. Not everything is true, no one ever forbade my trip. Maybe afterwards, because of me, others weren't allowed to go. I think my supervisors got very scared that they'd be punished because of me and they made some things up. Maybe my sister-in-law also added to the story, fearing nega- tive consequences. We arrived safely without incident. Fortunately for everyone, no one knew I had left with a secret document.

I'm glad the notebook is of such interest to you.

Respectfully,
Emilia Codrescu

On 8-08-2016, 11:10 AM, Liliana Corobca <liliana.corobca@ ▮▮▮▮▮> wrote :

Dear Ms. Emilia Codrescu,

I hope you weren't bothered by my long silence, I decided first to finish copying the notebook, to propose it to a publisher, and then to give you the good news. I want to thank you again for making this impressive document available to me! I'm overwhelmed by its contents! I just finished editing it and have proposed it to the prestigious Polirom Press, where I've previously published several books. Now I'm waiting for their response and I'll keep you posted.

I wish you all the best,
Liliana Corobca

Preamble

The archival collection of the General Directorate of Press and Publications—GDPP—can be accessed today at the Central National Historical Archives. The first lists of secret government documents that require incineration or shredding appear in statements toward the end of the '60s. These lists provide the only evidence of the existence of censor notebooks; in the archives mentioned above I was not able to find a single document of this type, and I concluded that they were all destroyed.

By examining the statements, we learn that there were three types of censor notebooks: a "reader notebook," which contained 150 sheets (300 pages) and was distributed to readers in the Literature Division (which in the '60s was Literature-Ideology, after which Ideology migrated toward the Social and Technical Sciences Division); a "field notebook" of 100 sheets for censors in the Training-Inspection Division and Library, Museum, and Antiquities Services, intended for those who did "field" work (outside the institution headquarters), as the title suggests; and a "scratch pad," 64 sheets, for other departments or as needed. I have come across instances when a censor from Training-Inspection received a reader notebook—and a censor from Literature, a scratch pad (See documents no. 94 and 95, pgs. 365–368 in *The Institution of Communist Censorship in Romania, 1949–1977*, vol. I). I am not able to offer a plausible explanation for this.

In the literature on Censorship, a few memoirs and inter-
views of censors (published after their retirement or the
dissolution of the institution, and usually cosmeticized) exist,
though we cannot fully trust their veracity. Official documents
(reports, transcripts, notes on readings) are preserved in the
archives. But what a censor really thought and how they related
to their work, what their unofficial attitude toward censorship
was, and not only that, can be found only in this notebook. Of
course, many moments of interest in the life of a censor, as well
as the life of the institution, are not included in the notebook.
But the aspects that are included here, and they are many, some
of which are completely unexpected, create a new and surprising perspective on the phenomenon of censorship under
the communist regime. We believe that it is very important for
a document such as this one to see the light of publication.

Given the specific character of the document, its being a text
in the domain of censorship, and given that I am a (novice)
specialist in the domain, I have not "come in" or intervened
in any way in this document. The reader can rely on maximum equivalency as regards the original source. I also have
attempted to reproduce the original form of the document as
much as possible. It is written legibly and, in general, without
mistakes (just a few insignificant letters left out and corrected
tacitly), but I have preserved: fushia, beaurdoux, scribbleous,
Morsd, the most demographic, apprenticize, morbidurities,
heterodentical, aestheticizeability, cacaphors, corpsish, schizotude, and other *ejusdem farinae*. Here "God" also appears as
"god," "Zukermann" also appears as "Zukerman." When transcribing the text, I adopted the standard orthographic changes
made by the Romanian Academy after 1993.

I studied it carefully, the notebook being in very good condition, and I didn't encounter words I could not decipher. I had already noticed, in my earlier studies of documents from the GDPP collection, that censors usually have very neat and legible handwriting. Some pages (14) from the first chapter are written in pencil, and they are impossible to make out, a word or two can be deciphered with difficulty, but not a single complete sentence. Thus, 14 pages (7 sheets) cannot be reconstituted, unfortunately. Still, I realized what they might be: censored passages from the novels. Evidently, such passages are quite rare in this notebook. The censor explains at one point that she writes her reports directly, without wasting time by copying the same observations and conclusions twice.

The notebook was divided from the beginning into several sections, but the censor didn't follow through with the proposed categories to the end. Conceived of as a scratch pad, then a journal, then an affront to the system, the notes do not follow a particular theme. The chapter titles belong to Filofteia Moldovean (not the editor). The most official and conventional section, the one dealing with the daily activities of a censor, is entitled "Justified Interventions" and it is the longest section if we include the seven irrecuperable sheets.

The work life of three censors—Hermina Iancovici, Rozalia Toth, and Filofteia Moldovean—is documented in "Literature Office Number Two"; we also glimpse more tantalizing moments in the GDPP, a backstage view of the life of censors, their development. Conceived as an extension of this chapter, the following one, "Useful Tips from Novels," does not differ thematically or stylistically from the previous two, and the so-called tips are neglected slowly in favor of certain everyday observations.

The transfer of censors within the institution was a regular occurrence and, after a long appointment in the Literature Division, Filofteia Moldovean was moved to the Import-Export Publications Division (formerly the Foreign Publications Division), which allows us a greater familiarization with the structure of the GDPP. This transfer also entails, for com. Moldovean, a change of vision regarding censorship.

The most surprising chapter is "The Lodge," halfway through the notebook, sporadically revealing unexpected details about the World Association of Censors. I have studied censorship for many years and consulted countless bibliographies, but I have never heard of this organization. I regret that so little information is given to us on this topic.

The final two chapters were probably written at the same time as the first two, with the notebook turned over, thus offering us an alternative reading (I have not preserved this particularity in the page layout). One is actually entitled "The Other Beginning" and it is rich in biographical details, memories of childhood and young adulthood, confessions of a personal and intimate nature—essentially, many accounts not having to do strictly with professional matters but that nevertheless help construct the typical profile of a censor. The last chapter, "The Trojan Horse," reveals to some extent the professional development of our protagonist but, thematically, it can be considered a more sophisticated interpretation of censorship. The use of the expression "Trojan horse" can be explained by the censor's identification with characters from antiquity (Laocoön, Cassandra) who tried to prevent the cunning and deceitful entry of the Greeks into the fortress under siege.

Thus, our protagonist starts the notebook in the traditional and practical way, jotting down phrases, expressions, passages from censored books, examples of interventions that can contribute to a better and more efficient workflow, but, little by little, she forgoes using the notebook for its initial intended purpose and begins writing things further and further afield from her immediate reality. Which is not at all bad for contemporary readers. The ways in which censorship operated can be seen clearly in the documents we have available to us in the archive. So far, I have published the following volumes: *The Purging of Books in Romania: Documents (1944–1964)*, editing, annotations, preface, Tritonic Press, Bucharest, 2010, 384 pages; *Controlling Books: Literary Censorship in Communist Romania*, Cartea Romaneasca-Polirom Press, Bucharest, 2014, 376 pages; *The Institution of Communist Censorship in Romania, 1949–1977*, editing, annotations, preface, postface, vol. I–II, 400 and 384 pages. But it is harder to reconstitute the thoughts of a censor, their transformations, what surprised them, their development in the field, a biography that can be psychoanalyzed, based on the archive (it is actually almost impossible). That is why we appreciate the uniqueness of this confession and the courage Ms. Codrescu demonstrated in saving a document of this precious and troublesome nature and preserving it for so many years.

A few of the texts are dated, allowing us to know in what period the notebook was written. At the beginning of the very first chapter, the date February 4, 1974, appears, then the dates drop off (two more appear sporadically), but, judging from Emilia Codrescu's date of departure (after June 6 and before July 6, 1974), the notebook was turned in at the end of May, so it represents approximately five months' worth of writing. In any case, the amount written in less than half a year is impressive, especially considering the fact that this notebook does not contain any of the documents that the censor would have had to turn in daily, weekly, or annually in the form of informant notes, briefings, reports, etc. Despite her many other obligations and tasks, she managed to fill up a thick A4-format notebook (it looks like a ledger), writing almost daily there as well (things that often had nothing to do with her professional obligations). The archival collection of the institution of censorship is immense, miles of documents, and that is after a large part (including all the censor notebooks) had already been destroyed. One conclusion would be that censors became truly addicted to writing and could, quantitatively, surpass any writer of that era once they started. If a notebook as thick as this one was completed in only five or six months, meaning two notebooks a year, ten notebooks in five years, etc., and we include all the censors working in the GDPP (between 270 and 350), we can understand why orders were given for these documents to be incinerated so quickly, probably invoking, with reason, lack of storage space. It is very possible that there were censors who wrote even more than comrade Moldovean, but I am glad that hers in particular was the notebook smuggled out by Ms. Codrescu. I do not believe there could be a more unusual and revealing document, one that reconstitutes an inaccessible world in such an unexpected and complex way.

I should also mention the fact that it is impossible to identify the sources of the passages that the censor cites as examples, because the authors are not mentioned at all, which, on the one hand, denotes an attitude of indifference and contempt toward the work being censored. On the other hand, many times they are not signaled as quotes and we understand only from the context that she is citing someone. The task becomes even more difficult when we realize that these lines are censored passages that do not appear in the published works of any author. Very rarely will she cite a title, and it is never one of the more important names of the era. Nothing seems to merit her attention, nor does she appear to have any literary preferences. What interests her the most in books are "useful tips"!

These notebooks, considered secret state documents, intended for incineration, were sealed when turned in, so not even the individuals tasked with destroying them could leaf through them, were they to have the opportunity. The fact that the author of the notebook, several times, in a harsh and defiant tone, addresses a potential reader whom she believes can be none other than a Securitate agent, denotes a certain lack of trust on the part of the censor, who knew that, officially, these notebooks were destroyed but they could still be read should the Securitate expressly request it. This possibility was taken into consideration by the censor, who assumes an enormous risk by writing the way she does. Seen from this perspective, we have before us the notebook of a censor who was potentially suicidal, who surely realized that many of the pages she wrote were actually (self-)indictments of the worst kind. More likely, rather, the notebook seems to be an alternative to censoring. We can also interpret it as an act of desperation and courage. An internal battle. Censoring everything around her for too many years, Filofteia Moldovean tries to avoid censoring herself as well. A way of expressing her freedom and staying sane or easing her conscience, which feels guilty about being a censor who pushes against restrictions to see how far she can go, though never crossing the line. She never gives up on the idea of being something other than a censor. She never gives up on the passages she scatters throughout the notebook, in which the most rigid official language from government reports alternates with the most nonconformist views on censorship.

Returning to Emilia Codrescu's escape abroad, a somewhat similar case occurred in 1975 (so in the same period) when Tomasz Strzyżewski, a censor from Kraków, fled Poland and after two years (1975–1977) of preparing a large number of Censorship documents (seven hundred!) had these documents published in England. His volume, *The Black Book of Polish Censorship*, had a great impact in the West as well as among Polish intellectuals (some of the documents appeared in Poland in self-published *samizdat* versions) and was considered one of the most important testimonies about censorship published before the fall of communism in the entire Soviet Bloc. The documents smuggled by Strzyżewski contained descriptions of the institution of Censorship, rules for its functioning, lists of banned books, lists of the names of censors working in central and local systems, announcements sent to local branches, etc. But nothing about censors' notebooks. We can only imagine the impact the document smuggled by Ms. Codrescu would have had if she had published it in West Germany, for example, before 1989.

I would like to signal one more aspect I was pleased to discover here.

In 2014, I was a fellow at the New Europe College Institute for Advanced Study in Bucharest, with the project "Censorship Institutions in the Countries of the Communist Bloc." For this project, I conducted a research trip to the Open Society Archives in Budapest, where I discovered and read, among other works, *Hot Books in the Cold War: The CIA-Funded Secret Western Book Distribution Program Behind the Iron Curtain* (Budapest—New York, Central European University Press, 2013, 549 pages) by Alfred A. Reisch, the head of the Hungarian section of research and intelligence gathering for Radio Free Europe between 1982 and 1995, about one of the least-known and most mysterious operations during the Cold War—viz., the distribution of books to countries in the Communist Bloc. Launched in the middle of 1956 by US Intelligence Agencies, the operation continued until September 1991, sending over 10 million books to Poland, Hungary, Czechoslovakia, Romania, Bulgaria, and the Soviet Union. The first recipients were cultural and political elites; then books were sent to research centers, cultural organizations, and institutions of higher learning, with the support of a number of Western institutions, organizations, private donors, and ethnic associations (in 1963, a total of 653 institutions were involved in this operation). The content of the books was "adapted" to each country or time period, depending on individual issues. They also sent hundreds and thousands of "harmless" books to lower the guard of censors. One report states that large amounts of "uncontroversial" material were sent to create a relaxed mood favorable to the sending of works of a more politically subversive nature. To countries in the Communist Bloc, they sent works by authors such as Albert Camus (*The Rebel*), Aldous Huxley (*Brave New World*), Czesław Miłosz (*The Captive Mind*, *The Seizure of Power*), Milovan Djilas ("The Crisis of Communism," *The New Class: An Analysis of the Communist System*), José Ortega y Gasset (*The Revolt of the Masses*), Hannah Arendt, Nikolai Berdiaev, Isaiah Berlin, Max Born, Mircea Eliade, Karl

Jaspers, Franz Kafka, George Orwell, Boris Pasternak, Herbert Marcuse, Rosa Luxemburg, Jean-Paul Sartre, Arnold Toynbee, Lionel Trilling, Paul Claudel, Benedetto Croce, Eugène Ionesco, Walter Gropius, Adam Mickiewicz, and many others.

A US intelligence report from 1970 mentions that the program had already proven to be effective in influencing attitudes and inclinations toward intellectual and cultural freedom, as well as in increasing dissatisfaction toward its absence. European intellectuals reading books in common in the East and West created a powerful intangible bond among them, which led to the peaceful end of the Cold War. Specialists conclude that the distribution of books for thirty-five years played a decisive role in the ideological victory of the West over communism. The coordinator of this program and the director of operations in the Communist Bloc, who later headed the entire operation, was George Caputineanu Minden (born in 1920 in Bucharest, a Romanian citizen of British nationality, today unknown in Romania). I wrote about this at length in the article "Hot Books in the Cold War" in *Literary Romania* (27), 2014.

I asked myself how books like these escaped the "vigilance" of Communist Bloc censors when each and every package and all printed material were inspected minutely, in multiple stages. Was there really no one in thirty-five years who found anything suspicious in these massive shipments of books? In this notebook, we have a couple of episodes (brief, but important) where Rozalia Toth notes the titles of certain books that seem to her to be "hostile," and she even communicates this to her superiors, but her initiative is not encouraged; on the contrary, the comrade censor is punished and transferred to the Literature Department. But at least we have convincing evidence that censors realized that something was not right with these books, that their "vigilance" was not lacking, and that, in fact, the high-level recipients had a vested interest in continuing to receive these books, regardless of their content—maybe out of greed (they were expensive books most of the time), maybe from other considerations, without suspecting, probably, that they were dealing with a complex operation whose goal was to chip away at the communist system. We can suspect the complicity of secret powers as well, given certain rather suspicious actions by the World Association of Censors.

I have included, separately and before the notebook proper, "Confessions of a Notebook Thief" (title mine), which consists of the few pages of notes added by E. C., in which she relates how she extricated the book and smuggled it out of the country. The cover sheet affixed to hide the title of the notebook at customs has since been removed, I received the notebook, in any case, without it, the words "Reader Notebook. Filofteia Moldovean. Literature and Art Division. 1974" clearly written in tiny letters on the cover.

In May 2016, I received a fellowship to go to Germany to the Literarisches Colloquium Berlin, where I was able to focus intensively on this project. I'm grateful for the invitation. It was a great joy and honor to be there.

I want to thank Ms. Emilia Humml-Codrescu once again for her generosity in making available to me this exceptional document, one that I consider a true revelation in the field of censorship, a completely unexpected communication from that era. I had long wondered what a notebook like this could look like and what it could contain. I admit that the contents surpassed my expectations. I hope that readers will peruse it with the same interest.

I thank my friends and colleagues who helped and supported me in this period.

I thank my parents, who have always been by my side, for their unceasing love and confidence.

I thank Polirom Press for a continuing excellent working relationship.

L. C.

P.S. The opinions of the censors in this notebook regarding life and literature do not coincide with the opinions of the editor.

Confessions of a Notebook Thief

The infernal racket in the factory was nonstop. My tired co-workers would barely react to my authoritative commands. Usually, besides my girls in Administrative Services, I would also ask people who worked the first shift in national press, who came to work at four in the morning. They were always in a hurry and were, of necessity, the earliest risers, since they were also the ones responsible for newspapers coming out on time (or guilty for them being late), and the last set of eyes on the whole paper when it was still possible to change things if something had slipped (they read it over one last time), checking whether earlier modifications had been implemented, whether what needed to be cut had been cut, whether what needed to be changed was now appropriate and contained nothing subversive. Articles that were changed last minute needed to be reread at the last second. It was a lot of pressure, with equal measures of responsibility and fatigue to go with it. But no one ever dared complain or say no. If they came with me, as part of their job, of course, they knew that in exchange for a few extra hours, in which they really didn't do much, they would get a day off, or at least half a day, which was still something. After all, they were carrying out an important mission, outside the institution and after working hours. Even if it didn't take more than two hours, including the trip there and back (or leaving and then going straight home), they had the right to stay home the next day (for them to have the whole day off, I would take them twice). They all wanted me to ask them to shred documents, they were always more than happy. The ones I chose to help me would accompany me to the shredder; the documents, which we didn't carry, because there were many of them and they were heavy, would be brought over by our driver, usually on a pushcart; we had to be present when they were shredded, then my co-workers were required to sign statements, which I had completed ahead of time, listing all the secret documents and the names of the GDPP delegates who were witnesses and could attest to their destruction. And no one ever reproached me for taking with me people who were tired and in fact incapable of performing any critical task whatsoever. After all, they were just witnesses, they had only to sign a statement that the documents I had listed had been thrown into the shredder before our eyes, that they hadn't been disseminated, lost, perused, stolen, etc. We signed that they were appropriately disposed of, according to the statement. I would usually take the same co-workers and the operation became automatic for everyone. Besides myself, I would take two others (three people were required to sign the statement) and I had already formed a fairly steady team, which I would switch out two or three times, all of us witnessing each time the destruction of our secret documents either by shredding or incineration. It was the most pleasant task of the Office of Secret Documents, which was under the jurisdiction of Administrative Services.

I had no way of knowing that within just a few years our institution would be disbanded, and the notebook I smuggled would be the only proof that such a document ever existed. I kept it, read it, and reread it, marveling each time at what it contained, so many surprises, even for someone like me who had worked in the institution for so many years, and knew the censor to whom the notebook belonged.

I wouldn't say I was very curious to find out why our reader notebooks were destroyed, since they were the only documents that no one was ever required to read, so they were unlike the news bulletins or directives that circulated throughout the entire institution. Censors aren't a curious tribe in general, especially when any regular phrase longer than a line could be deemed a state secret. For me, at least, even the word "secret" upsets my stomach; nothing was ever that secret, meaning our lack of curiosity was basically justified. No one had access to these personal notebooks, scratch pads, besides their owners. They were kept under lock and key, they received a serial number both when they were distributed and turned in (a visa for entry and exit), and a short while later—we had nowhere to store so many documents—we took them to the factory. From time to time, about once every six months, censors received new notebooks and turned in the old ones, but if they had many pages left they could request an extension. I was actually the one who kept track of the notebooks. Usually, most asked for an extension, we destroyed only notebooks that were full, it would be pointless to waste paper. But every six months, I made a list of who wanted to receive a new notebook. Of course, we destroyed a wide variety of documents that contained classified or just confidential information, important data, lists of all kinds, opinions, articles, which we were all aware needed to remain secret. But what could a censor's notebook contain? A censor who didn't work at the Office of Secret Documents and didn't have access to confidential information? I don't remember whether all our workers had or were entitled to have these types of notebooks. Many years have gone by and taking inventory of these documents wasn't among my most important tasks. Censors who were responsible for long texts definitely received them, I suspected that they wrote down examples of justified and unjustified interventions, in order to learn how to censor, to write reports. I think it was harder for those in Literature compared to Technical Sciences, for example. They needed to take notes, to copy passages from manuscripts . . .

A few departments in the GDPP don't show up in the organizational chart, no one knew when they would appear or disappear. There was a kind of consensus of secrecy in our institution. We each guarded our little secret and avoided being too curious about the secrets of others. In my mind, I was sure I knew everything. But most of us didn't even know what all our departments were, or how the institution functioned. They kept their heads down in their individual offices, inspecting the never-ending texts. You had to be a cog in a watch or a gear in the machine, without knowing what bigger purpose you were serving. Who actually needed our work? We did useless things, copied charts, transcripts. Passages from censored books. You'll find them in the notebook you have in front of you as well, that's probably what they all did.

In the Import-Export Division, one of the most aristocratic and widely envied departments, those strange specialists, the "comparatists," came into being. They knew many languages and relied on collaborators outside the institution—critics, philologists, historians whom they convinced, sometimes with the help of pressure from Securitate agents, to offer them all the information they wanted. It made your head spin what they were able to do. They studied foreign literature, poetic eras, brilliant authors, in the original or in translation, some of the most splendid texts of both major and minor literatures (Polish, English, Yugoslavian, Albanian, etc.). Rumor had it that they took things even from the Russians, it was a big scandal. So that our literature would be second to none, the finest works of others were attributed to one of our poets. In translation, you would never know it! The poet was someone trustworthy, usually approved by the Party and the Securitate, talented and with a bright future, cultivated under lab-like conditions, flexible, malleable, and promising. If they didn't agree, they were simply removed from the literary scene. Their book didn't even make it to Censorship, it died somewhere along in the way, in the first stages of the press's inspection. What were our people doing? They were adding texts to manuscripts. They didn't just take out things, they also added them in. You could be accused of plagiarism, you could become a laughingstock, you ran that risk but you became an important poet, without even knowing who actually wrote the splendid poems being passed off as yours—it could be a less fortunate fellow poet, it could be an internationally renowned star. Unfortunately, little information about these mysterious co-workers appears in the notebook. The girls had no way of knowing. I also have forgotten many things. The comparatists were around for about five years and the practice of introducing texts as part of the process of censorship ceased, I believe, at the same time they disappeared. In the '70s, authors were ambitious and talented and wouldn't have accepted their works being patched up with foreign texts.

ONE DAY, I felt like satisfying a curiosity to steal a notebook, read it from cover to cover, and then destroy it. I prepared to do it for days on end, I made a detailed plan so that it couldn't fail. It would've been stupid to lose my job, for example, over such an insignificant act, unworthy of a faithful and devoted party member, such as I was at the time. Perhaps, if I hadn't suspected my husband's intentions I wouldn't have had the courage. In any case, I don't believe it was a coincidence, in the end. I'm sure that the idea of stealing a notebook occurred to me only after I had received my passport and all the necessary approvals for leaving the country, and my husband, in the meantime, had already received the guarantee of work in Germany. I don't know whether I had thought of stealing a notebook before I intended to leave, why lie? I don't think so.

I began practicing. I learned to steal, to remove things, without betraying any emotion. I had never stolen anything in my life. I started with pens, sheets of papers from my co-workers' desks, making sure that they wouldn't get in trouble for anything going missing. Hermina was terrified when her stamp disappeared! She hadn't noticed when I took it off her desk, then brought it back and set it down next to the leg of her table. I had come in with some papers that I dropped on the floor "on accident," and I placed the stamp under the table (a missing stamp was a very serious offense). Then I encouraged her, saying there was no way she could've lost it, it must be here somewhere, look again, maybe it fell down under the table? I already looked! Check again. Ah, there it is, hitting her palm against her forehead. I was so scared that I didn't see it and I had checked there so many times!

STEALING A NOTEBOOK isn't a big deal, you just need to catch the right moment when no one's watching you, take the notebook, and slip it into a big purse. And that's it. That day in June was incredibly muggy. I remember it only too well. It was probably going to rain soon. I remember that a co-worker from the office who knew I was going to the factory asked me to put her name down in the statement, and give it to her to sign that she was present, so that she could go with us almost until the factory—she probably lived close by—but then be allowed to leave, because her child was sick, measles or scarlet fever, she said, very worried. I had never done something like that before, everyone who signed actually came with me. But it almost seemed like a special sign that the moment to smuggle out a notebook had come, especially since we were planning on leaving in a week. She signed, happy and grateful, and we were one less person. I also got rid of our driver. He brought us the documents and then I sent him home because we weren't planning on returning to the Press House and we didn't need him anymore.

It was so hot that I took out a thicker and heavier envelope (I was sure it was a reader notebook) and fanned myself with it. The boy from Press, the other delegate, was also fanning himself with some papers while we waited for the workers to receive the delivery of our documents. I put the statement on top of the envelope and when the workers collected the documents, my co-worker handed over the papers he was using as a fan, while I discreetly put the statement together with the notebook in my purse. That's how it happened.

IN THAT PERIOD, at the beginning of June, all the girls from Lit. Office Two turned in their notebooks, and oh, could those girls write! The smartest of them seemed to me to be Hermina, who wrote a lot, and I had hoped to get her note-book, I think I even dog-eared a corner of its sealed envelope so I could identify it, but no luck. Roza wrote less, she usu-ally turned in her notebook at the end of the year, and back then, in June, she had barely finished the one from the previous year. They were, I believe, the most interesting girls not only from the Literature Division but from among all the GDPP readers, and it wasn't only my opinion. Filofteia Moldovean, by contrast, was more soldierly, more serious, and we had nicknamed her "Ana Pauker" and made fun of her behind her back. She seemed like the prototypical '50s office worker (and censor)—rigid, stern, she spoke to us only very rarely, because she was always reading, sometimes so ostentatiously that we, the others, felt embarrassed, as if out of our entire institution she were the only one reading, and they were paying the rest of us for nothing. When, however, she did open her mouth, she had that monotonous, distinctly enunciated intonation, as if she were reading from a party declaration. She wasn't in con-flict with anyone, but neither was she friends with any of us. Though I considered her, as all the others did, rather obtuse, after reading her notebook, I changed my mind. Even though she included all kinds of ideas relating only to herself, in the general sections that refer to our workplace, I'm sure she wasn't the only one who had those thoughts. I tremble to think what the notebooks of more acerbic, sarcastic, intelligent, talented, and open-minded censors contained. If modest Moldovean wrote the way she wrote, what was in the notebooks of others? We have no way of knowing . . .

The necessity of these notebooks appeared with the Ministry of the Interior's crackdown in the matter of protecting state secrets. It was discussed whether any document, any note, any piece of paper with handwriting on it from us could be considered a secret document. Meanwhile, especially in their first years on the job, our censors would take notes to help them when writing up reports or briefings. If they had to do a monthly summary, they needed to write down what they had worked on in that period and their findings. Some wrote the same thing twice in order to ensure the text reached a satisfactory form. Their sheets could be thrown away, could fall into the wrong hands, be misplaced, get lost, and so they came up with the idea of notebooks that, after they were used up, would be sealed and destroyed. Everything that a censor did, at any point in the process, was also considered a state secret and any trace of it needed to be destroyed. The idea of these notebooks was meant to help our workers not only with their professional activities but also with their extra-censorial, extra-institutional ones, they were allowed to write down whatever they wanted in these notebooks, but not to produce any other kind of document, not a single sheet or note besides what they turned in to their superiors. And from these notebooks, which had a set number of pages that I, at first, numbered and then counted when turned in, censors weren't allowed to tear off even the tiniest corner, however, they could write whatever their hearts desired, everything would be destroyed anyway. The notebooks were sealed officially, I entered them into the chart for secret documents. When I started in Administrative Services, this tradition was already an old one and had been practiced for many years. Depending on needs and specializations, the notebooks were different. I remember that instructors for the

Training-Inspection Division received thinner notebooks than those working in Literature. Of course, after a while, censors got the hang of things—they got more adept at their job and they wrote reports more easily, directly onto the page without needing to use a notebook, but they continued to receive them and write in them.

I LEFT DURING the summer and took my boots with me, also a rain jacket—it could be cold in Paris. The jacket, yes, it was understandable, but the boots, summer, in June . . . not even the notebook, had it been discovered, would've raised such suspicions, since I was a censor with a special press permit, but those boots . . . Now I think, without realizing it at the time, that the boots saved the notebook. They were almost subversive, in comparison with an ordinary notebook onto which I had stuck a piece of paper with the title "Travel Journal" (meaning I was planning on writing down how beautiful Paris was). In any case, no one gave the notebook a second glance, nor did I hide it. That would've been a big mistake, it would've meant I was fully conscious of its hostile contents. It would've been hard to claim, in the terrible event that the notebook had been read and found to be inappropriate, that it wasn't mine, that, oh my goodness, I took it by accident, that they could just go ahead and confiscate it. In any case, I was certain back then that it was highly unlikely for them to find anything in the notebook that was truly hostile. I had looked over the first four pages, a journal with reader's notes, and I felt pretty reassured. I wasn't able to read everything, I didn't have time. I had prepared my most convincing arguments for my boots. They gave me more of a headache than the notebook. What can I say, those boots cost a fortune and you couldn't even find ones like them in Romania! Blue, made of ultra-soft leather, with a small heel and a solid, long-lasting sole, elegant and comfortable. I had received them as a gift from a relative in Germany who had visited us just a few months before we left. We were to stay with her when we arrived and she would help us find work and housing . . . She had brought them to me at the end of the winter season, they were brand new, I hadn't even worn them yet, and I had to leave them in Romania? Perhaps if they had been too big or too small, but they fit me perfectly. I couldn't find it in me to sell them to anyone. The comrade at customs and my co-worker from Censorship were very interested in the boots, of course. "I received them as a gift from my sister-in-law, they're too small for me and she promised me she'd exchange them if I kept the tag."

—What size?

—Thirty-eight.

—Yes, they're too small. I wear size thirty-nine, I would've bought them and your sister-in-law could've gotten you some new ones.

—If I'm not able to exchange them, I'll bring them back and sell them here, I've got co-workers who are just waiting for that.

—Maybe you'll bring me a pair too.

—I'll try, I'll try (and in my mind: "I wouldn't hold my breath if I were you . . .").

The notebook was in a tote into which I threw, for show, a map of Paris, a guidebook published here, a cheap pair of tennis shoes, and a hat. The woman looked at it, opened it—it had a zipper—felt something inside, and zipped it back up. I got through safely with the illegal notebook, and the boots. I don't think the ladies at customs even knew about the existence of these kinds of notebooks, actually. I kept the notebook and the boots up until now. I can no longer zip the boots all the way up, because I put on some weight and my legs got thicker. Delegates from the GDPP and others with special permits passed through easily. It was our people working at customs as well. I had a passport, the hardest thing to get, who would stop me on account of a raggedy notebook?

CENSORS, IF THEY aren't complete idiots, get corrupted (I arrived at this conclusion, of course, after reading the notebook). They're surrounded by temptations that are too powerful and they're too weak. They're the ones who must always be duplicitous, triplicitous, quinqueplicitous. That's how I explain the profoundly reprehensible desire of a devoted and irreproachable censor, as I was always considered to be until my departure, to steal a secret document.

I would never have left, anywhere, had it been up to me. I had a good job, a good salary, I was highly respected by my co-workers, I was promoted to head of my unit, I could've advanced even further. Vacations both within the country and abroad, meals in the party dining hall, medals, bonuses on August 23, receptions and free tickets with my special ID card. But my husband wouldn't hear of it, he was leaving and basta. I knew only too well that if a family member, even one less closely connected than a husband, fled the country, the others would pay for it. I was receiving more and more announcements prohibiting the publication and recalling the works of authors who had merely expressed the desire to emigrate as well as those who had managed to leave and never returned . . . I had never heard of censors with relatives who had left, but I could imagine what fate awaited them . . . Goodbye vacations, bonuses, perks, respect . . . I could already see my co-workers gloating that their uppity boss was demoted to menial work or even kicked out and sent to some questionable institution, with a demanding job for little pay . . . We were chosen very carefully and everyone had spotless files. In the beginning, it wasn't quite like that. We also had among us the more "checkered" kind, from different social classes, especially in Import-Export, where foreign languages were required, an area in which censors with extraordinarily healthy origins encountered difficulties. Then they began sifting them out, selecting them, the new council formed its own personnel. If you weren't pure-blooded Romanian—out with you. Individuals of other nationalities had no business working in Censorship, with the country's secrets. But two Germans, four Hungarians, and two or three Jews remained despite that. And a Serbian, I think, somewhere in the provinces. In any case, in the provinces our national principles weren't so hard and fast.

Well, and one of the two Germans introduced me to a friend whom, after two months, I would marry. I had already been working for many years in Censorship and my dossier at the time they hired me was impeccable. My parents were peasants, no one from my family had left the country. We were all women in the office, I put in long hours, night after night, I was quickly approaching thirty, and I had no one. That my future husband had a sister married abroad, long since settled in Germany, I didn't find out on our first date, but I don't know if it would've bothered me too much, anyway, he had two other sisters in Bucharest who were friendly toward me. Men without relatives abroad and with clean dossiers were probably married ages ago. My husband was a factory engineer at least, without a previous record. My German colleague worked in Foreign Press, my husband was also German, and given the situation at the GDPP, almost all of us were unmarried, so no one said anything to me. We had already been married for about five years, I had traveled before without any issue, both with and without my husband. One day, he decided that we had to leave and stay in Germany. To make it look less suspicious, the vacation package was for Paris. So we didn't put in an emigration request, because no way in the world would it have gotten approved (how could a censor who, officially, has access to state secrets emigrate? How could they escape with our secrets over the border? The mere intention is already profoundly reprehensible!), instead we left as tourists, in our own car, after very discreetly selling off a few things so no one would suspect us. We left the keys to our apartment with one of his sisters. For me, everything was pretty unexpected, while my husband had already arranged almost everything months ahead of time. It was better this way, I was able to work up until the day we left without worrying about the future, I even stole the notebook, thinking I'd read it in Germany, where I'd have more time. In Germany, I found a job, even though I didn't know the language, and even now I don't know it well. But with a German husband and many relatives, the problem was solved, I worked at a kindergarten, so I'd receive a good pension. My husband started working immediately after he arrived. His relatives had made arrangements before we got there.

The stolen notebook was more than an idle curiosity, after all I didn't take the risk merely out of the desire to swipe a secret document, my idea was to have something with me that could count as leverage, something that could be used somehow, I didn't know how, but I gave up on the idea, in any case, after I read the notebook. I had really wanted it to be Hermina's notebook! That beautiful and sensitive woman, who cried when cutting out a more unusual line, had made me truly curious, but in the commotion of the factory, scared by what I was doing, I took one at random, the first thick notebook from the pile of documents. And this one couldn't be used for anything. I skimmed through it in Germany, asking myself many times whether it had been worth the risk, whether I had truly had an important reason for dragging it along with me, whether my "heroic" act would ever been understood and appreciated by someone. Later, after we had gotten more settled, I didn't know anyone there who might be interested in something like this who would not complicate me and my family's existence. I didn't know what to do with it or whom to give it to, and after reading through it carefully, I was horrified and no longer had any inclination to give it to anyone. My husband had a well-paying job, I had something to keep me busy as well— for better or worse, I actually liked my work. I was horrified not by the fact that I had worked in Censorship for twenty years and was only now finding out so many things I had been clueless about, especially given that I would often read the informant notes gossiping about co-workers and revealing a great many secrets—rather I was scared by the dangerous contents of this notebook. Everyone who left the country took a thing or two with them, rare icons, traditional woven rugs, jewelry or other objects of value that could provide them with a means of existence until they found work. If I hadn't had a

German husband, friends who helped us, maybe I would've considered doing more with this troublesome notebook. But my husband started work less than a week after we arrived, and I read through the notebook much later, I simply didn't have the time and it wasn't a priority then, it didn't interest me. If I had encountered problems, maybe I would've offered it to a publishing house, a magazine—maybe I would've at least tried. But I'm more than certain that I would've hesitated greatly and been terribly afraid! With all the precautions in the world, with all the pseudonyms, it wouldn't have been too hard to guess who could've stolen the notebook. I don't think other censors even left the country afterwards, when restrictions were tightened, and I was the only one who had access to the censor notebooks, whose destruction would later be attested to by signed statements. So the desire to be a hero faded quickly. Instead, the desire to remain alive and have a comfortable existence proved to be much stronger. I never published anything, I never connected with people there, neither Romanians nor Germans. Nor did they really want to get to know me, sick as they were of all kinds of heroes with all sorts of expectations. There were hundreds, maybe thousands, of people like me on the other side of the Iron Curtain. Everyone was tired of feeding and taking care of dissidents and protesters. No one knew I had been a censor, maybe it would've interested them. I told acquaintances, relatives, that I had worked as a copy editor at a publishing house. I already felt as though I was always being followed, even without having published or said anything. After all, I'd had access to secret documents, I had fled illegally, and that was reason enough to be punished. To disappear without a trace. My husband was German, an engineer by profession, he was in the clear, but me . . . I feared someone would look through my things and find the document. Thankfully, no one knew about its disappearance, otherwise they would've searched for it. Officially, the object had been declared dead. But the anxiety of keeping it hidden for so many years! Not even my husband read it, though I told him about some notes from work so that he'd help me hide it. He knew where I had worked but he didn't blame me for anything. Then, in 1989, he photographed it, again without showing too much interest. He didn't ask what it contained, I told him only that it was a censor notebook, one of our notebooks from the '70s. On the one hand, it was a burden that I wanted to be rid of, because keeping something like this was risky, but on the other hand, I didn't want it to get lost or stolen, nor to return it to someone who, without reading it, without understanding its significance, would throw it away. It was precious also because I had taken so many risks for its sake, when I saved it from the factory, when I crossed the border with it, when I kept it in West Germany for almost twenty years. And, a few times, I was right on the verge of burning it myself. I had lost hope that I would ever be able to give it to someone safely. I was very disappointed for a long time after the revolution.

After 1989, I seriously considered bringing it back into the country, it was no longer as risky. In 1994, I returned to Romania with the thought of giving it back to its author. I don't know why that's what I thought I should do, to get rid of it like that. I had everything I needed and being a hero among censors wouldn't have helped me in any way. I mean, what business did I have with someone else's notebook? The author should take care of it and do whatever she wants with her own notebook.

But the author, the former comrade censor, was almost blind, she had no reaction, she wasn't surprised or curious, she didn't say: Give it to me. She said: What times those were, and she told me her life's story, her life in the GDPP after I left, how she was transferred to the Cultural Commission, still in the Literature Division, she became head of the department, and, until she retired, she continued censoring. She kept coming back to the subject of her lost son, who in the end found out about his birth mother. Their meeting . . . his mother, a censor, and his father, a Securitate agent. The inner crisis of man burdened with something like that. He also found the document in which com. Moldovean relinquished custody of her son and received (in exchange) a stylish and luxurious apartment near Cismigiu Park, which is where I visited her. Zaharescu gave me her address, I really regretted afterwards not giving her the notebook!

I met with Salvatore Zaharescu-Zukermann in 1991, by then I had read the notebook and he didn't know that I knew. His visit to Munich might have seemed very suspicious to me but, knowing something about their lodge, I wasn't scared of him. We met, as if by accident, one night when I was out walking Puki, my beloved dog, who died, poor thing, four years ago. I believe Salvatore would've liked a contact there, but my reading German wasn't good enough, I didn't have ties to Romanians, and I wasn't useful to him in any way. I didn't tell him about the notebook, the meeting was too unexpected, but later, after 1994, when I didn't have anyone to give it to in Romania, I thought of him. I didn't know where he lived, I didn't have his phone number, or else I would've met with him. He had shared stories about what had happened to our co-workers, he had given me the addresses of a few of the ones who lived in Bucharest, in case I ever came back, which were useful to me during my visit. Salvatore moved to Israel, but I don't know whether he's still alive, someone told me a few years ago that he was very sick. I'm certain that he would've been very interested in the notebook.

AT THE BEGINNING of this year, Filofteia Moldovean passed away. Her son doesn't live in Romania. Back then, in 1994, I had also met with her son, who was visiting. I told him about this historic document, about the inner workings of Censorship. But he wasn't interested in the notebook either, he didn't even pay much attention to what I was saying. If I had given it to him, he would've thrown it away without so much as flipping through it. Nor do I think he really understood his mother's job, he could've at least been curious, if he had insisted, I would've given him the notebook anyway, he was the rightful heir. No, the man had told himself from the beginning: Censorship is bad, the Securitate is bad, they're both criminal institutions, my parents had the most disgraceful professions, but he neither tried to find excuses for them nor tried to find out more about them, especially his mother, whom he met later, when in fact his mother had wanted to keep him, to have him with her, she wanted the family she never had, she never remarried and never had other children. The son had become important, as for her work, she never talked about it, for fear of pushing him away. She had two grandchildren and she was, it seems, a very loving grandmother . . .

I had learned about Hermina's tragic fate from Salvatore, Filofteia repeated what I already knew. After the GDPP was disbanded, H. Iancovici was transferred to the editorial department of a literary magazine in Bucharest. She was much more intelligent than her co-workers, who despised her for coming from Censorship and constantly bullied her. She was fragile, sensitive, alone, she never had a boyfriend, she was also unjustly punished for some articles and, one day, she committed suicide. In 1982, I believe, she hadn't even turned thirty-five yet. Such a shame.

Roza got married two or three more times, she made a name for herself in the State Department, but I never met with her and I don't know what she goes by now after so many marriages. People say that she's doing very well, that she's still beautiful and surrounded by men.

I think the best place for this notebook is a museum dedicated to censorship or communism.

[E. C.-H.]

READER NOTEBOOK

Filofteia Moldovean
Literature and Art Division
1974

Justified Interventions

From today's meeting, Monday, February 4, 1974:
Good to keep in mind, useful for the first paragraphs of the report.

> Since it inherited a heterogeneous staff from the former Ministry of Arts and Information, one generally inadequate from a political and professional standpoint, the General Directorate of Press and Publications had to form an entirely new team from its very beginnings as an independent enterprise. To this end, the Personnel Department aimed at hiring young individuals who presented definite prospects for growth. The mass hiring of the early years was followed by the ongoing process of selecting staff based on their professional and moral-political qualities.

Some expressions to use in self-criticism (in case it's needed).

> Another concern of ours arose in a discussion during one of our weekly meetings covering all recently executed interventions and observations, which allowed each reader to express their point of view, final conclusions being made by the team leader. Here we must remember that in our efforts to do everything perfectly,

certain comrades have manifested at times a tendency to mark—without meaning to change anything—small stylistic issues as well, copyediting and proofreading issues that are, in fact, beyond the scope of our responsibilities. There were also cases—rare, it's true—when certain comrades have demonstrated uncertainty or hesitation in dealing with certain problems or when they manifested unwarranted impulsiveness when discussing work issues. Our weekly work meetings have also been a good occasion to discuss and clarify any work issues that have come up, such as work styles and methods, relations among comrades within the team and outside the team, procedures for dealing with certain materials, etc.

For example:

—I have manifested unwarranted impulsiveness when discussing work issues;

—I have had the tendency to mark certain small stylistic, copyediting, and proofreading issues that are, in fact, beyond the scope of our responsibilities;

—I have demonstrated uncertainty or hesitation in dealing with certain problems.

I hope I won't be needing to voluntarily blame myself for something like that during meetings.

2/7/1974

It's not easy at all to understand, at first, what a "mistake" means and what exactly an author needs to be criticized for: that they're pessimists, that they write about the sad rain in November, or the cold of winter, which makes one think of spiritual coldness, and therefore a lack of enthusiasm for the country's new achievements. A tragic view of the universe, deviationism. The principle of aestheticizeability, a weak aesthetic—it must be denounced, the excess of aestheticism, namely. The denigration of reality. They told us: pay attention to colors! Too much white can mean the void, frozenness, etc., just as too much black—death, pessimism; green—an allusion to the Iron Guard;[1] fancy, extravagant colors with strange spellings, like: *fushia, beaurdoux, beige, turcoise*—bowing down to the West, cosmopolitanism.

H.: And red?

R.: Its days are over. Can't have too much red. Come on, we got rid of the Red Army a while ago.[2]

Me: Really? Did you see something concrete to that effect?

R.: I wrote down the newest provision stating that the latest books in line for the cruel purge are: *The Great Achievements of Communism, Invented in Russia* by Danilevsky; *The Russian Sun* by Orlov; *Socialism's Economic Problems in the USSR*; Svetlov and Oizerman—*The Appearance of Marxism, a Revolution in Philosophy*; *Far from Moscow* by Ajaev; *Homeland* by Karavaeva; *Happiness* by Pavlenko . . . Didn't you all see the provision?

H.: In my opinion, *Far from Moscow* shouldn't be banned. I didn't read the provision, as for seeing it, I think I saw it.

We all chuckle under our breath.

To be clear: if, in a novel, a girl puts on red lipstick, there's nothing subversive there, we leave it alone, but if in a red city red people walk on red streets, casting red glances, the air's red, the sky's red, etc., then I realize I've got a lot of work to do, to censor.

Even a volume about spring where each poem sings of patriotic values can still be criticized for something. There's no perfect book! The secret and the rule is to find something in each text. Knowing what to find is, of course, an art, and whoever masters it is a true censor. But this ability is formed over time, after a certain period. That's why they tell us: censors are formed here, in the institution, we form them. Some learn very quickly, others very slowly, or not at all and then they leave.

We can all learn from Zuki, nicknamed "the walking encyclopedia," who doesn't even bother reading manuscripts, he just gives them a passing glance and reaches a conclusion that not even the most attentive and scholarly literary critics could've come up with. He suggests some formulations that are so charming, we have no idea where he gets them, and advises us not to repeat them too often. For different censors not to all use them at the same time, because everything is sent to the party, where it's all read by the same people. You have to include a little variety, just as the texts we censor are varied. "Censorship must be a pleasure, not a chore," Zuki repeats to us, "you do it lightly, with tenderness, with understanding." He recommends that we think about other comrades of ours (from college, not from here), who were maybe even better than us, and where are they now, in what villages, in what far-flung schools . . . and are we bad off? No. Then: with tenderness, compassion, calmly, courteously, because without naïve and scribbleous writers, how would we earn our bread and butter?

Gosh, we're so lucky to have a colleague like him! I write down all his key phrases, so I can include them in my reports. I think he's the only one among us with an unequivocal vocation for censorship.

Friday 22

No meetings this week, finished the manuscript yesterday, six hundred pages!

Typical themes or reasons that definitely always call for censoring, material for the annual meeting with the delegates from the provinces:

—Any issue related to the operation of our Party, disillusionment regarding the country's achievements, dismissals from the Party, negative characterizations of its members or officials from different domains.

—Negative or satirical portrayals of employees of the Ministry of Internal Affairs, the Ministry of Culture, or even GDPP delegates.

—The literary (and social) fashion present nowadays more in poetry, characterized by the description of states of depression or pessimism, decadence, or even idealism. Pay close attention to mystic states as well!

—Bowing down to the West, along with cosmopolitanism, are issues we come across especially in novels, but also in any cultural, scientific, or technical area; our regime's achievements are questioned or even mocked, etc. Include some concrete examples here.

—"To give the enemy a hearing": one could (or rather, should) observe the excessive quotation, useless and dangerous, of debunked authors, those who have emigrated, and, in general, enemies of our regime. Caution: our authors can also have characters spout hostile ideas with which the main character disagrees and argues against, but the presentation of these ideas and the discussion itself can give rise to an unhealthy curiosity in the reader.

—Erotic scenes, unhealthy love affairs, explicit vocabulary that incites the senses must be monitored closely. To be censored on a case-by-case basis. Here the criteria have changed greatly in recent years, but we stand our ground.

—King, monarchy, the word "Hohenzollern," the name Carol, queen, princess. A positive view of the interwar period.[3]

—Greater Romania, Orhei, Hotin, Basarabia, Bucovina . . .[4]

❧

I feel myself getting better and better at expressing myself.

Memo: At present, 290 employees are working at the General Directorate of Press and Publications headquarters. There were more of us last year.

"I avoid large crowds of people, all alike, threatening in

their mere similarity and uniformity, the starting point, where is it? I want to start somewhere . . ." (example) "oh, majestic ships glide across my line of vision as I write about the heroic Dacians, small blue boats, purple boats, sailboats, ships, rowboats, yachts . . .

The inconsistency of time . . ."

Our comrade writers have paid vacations at the seaside, at Neptune, at the luxurious—from what I hear—Writers' Union villa, they're living large off the working people's backs. They feed them there like pigs. They suck the people's blood, the parasites! and they write about ships and sailboats, with colored sails! And they have the nerve to complain about inconsistency! Well, okay, if they need to write about Dacians,[5] send them off to caves, to forests! For total consistency!

A long passage, well written, without mistakes, where the main character wants to run away from the village and get to the city. That's where he sees his future, life, happiness.

I sigh, I'm sure that my husband thought the same way. My husband wanted to move to the city with same intensity and yearning, probably. He succeeded. I succeeded in certain things as well, but not in everything I wanted.

Examples of subversive texts for ch. 2 "Good Interventions." Monthly work summary for February:

The sun spreading its rays like a peacock,
We're somewhere under its feathers, almost in shadow.

The humble and the proud chased from under its tail, from the mountains,

from ascensions

Relieve my pain in tender procession.

Banned from rose-petal vouchers,

from the caresses of cats,

from vintage photos.

Excluded from the order of the hydrated, from the party of ladles, from Apollonian ballads, from the society of the transparent sails of the private boats on Mars.

I sang of blue eyes elongated neckward and cerulean tresses,

But wily love shot his arrow at a small brunette home-maker, brown eyes she possesses.

I wanted the sea and waves, I wanted liberty, I'm under the woman's heel,

Goodbye, equality . . .

Mannerism, abstractions, questionable experimentalism. Hermeticism—a door slammed in the face of the people, fine, but you can still crack it open for the censor, esteemed sir.

It's been said and it continues to be said that poetry is repetitive, only prose can bring something new, I'm not referring to the subject and predicate, but to the message, not the form, the content.

Why didn't I pass off this stupid volume to Hermina!

Philosoteur—a worthless philosopher.

Philosity—a potato tuber disease!

> A drop splashes and dances,
> another drop splashes and dances,
> as rhythmically as if it were a star
> on the show "Morning Gymnastics"
> An awkward drop dances
> The first drop
> The last drop
> It dances, a queen (allusion to the monarchy?)
> My lively blood
> I give it to you today, so today you'll be even younger
> and more beautiful.
> Catch it, drink it in!

Ugh, this guy and his drop are really getting on my nerves!

Ugh—he wants to send me into early retirement! I'm positive that there's a type of poetry written specifically to give us mental issues, I don't know what effect it has on the common reader, but its effect on the censor is devastating!

From too much tension and stress, our nerves are shot, and worse—we, the valiant workers and servants of the fatherland!

I feel like if I read the poem with the drop again or another one, with a drop identical to it, I'll get an ulcer. I've already gotten acid reflux from all the stress of reading so many texts.

❧

All my enemies are after me.

I kissed the emperor's daughter, I dared, I am happy, but now they are after me, the impudent mortal! Transform me, almighty god, into a fruit tree, she will come, smile, and feast when into her lap I will shake my fruit, my fruit.

Better to become a fruit tree than for people to kill me with their cruel weapons.

I looked at you, my beauty, I took your hand in mine, I grabbed your waist and twirled you, we twirled, heaven and earth became round, I sang for you, I danced for you.

You, amazed, delighted, that to such a wonderful story you were invited . . .

That a mortal had penetrated your high and inaccessible nobility.

Perhaps I stayed too long in your presence and now I must die.

Perhaps I am no longer, never was, never will be the cause of your sigh?

Was I impertinent, irrational?

Or just another knight, banal?

Now death.

God, turn me into a fruit tree, into a fruit tree!

The god listens, takes pity, muscles dry up, the body

diminishes, long branches shoot out, roots, cherry
or apple, sweet tree, awakening intense longing and
yearning in bees . . .

Cool boughs will call you, secretly, fragrant fruit will
tempt you toward me. Now my one wish sincere is to
punish you, my dear.

For the moment, I can't think of how to censor this. There's
definitely a lot to cut out from here. I'll come back to it. Reread it.

To be precise, I don't know what reason to invoke: nostal-
gistic attitude, poor artistic execution, exaggerated traditionist
language, slavish Gongorism?

The concrete measures for permanent growth in the
employees' level of political-ideological preparedness;
the real-life implementation of the task force's plan
of action concerning the development of their professional competencies and moral-political qualities; the
continual strengthening of the GDPP branch organization; and the fostering of an aggressive stance against
mistakes and shortcomings at work, and against a perfunctory attitude and unprincipled displays—all these
have yielded positive results. The work environment
of personnel is healthy, with high standards, the vast
majority of employees are profoundly devoted and
competent. In recent years, there has been no gross
misconduct, violation of work standards, dishonest
actions, or acts of corruption.

~⊸

"I cut, I am my own wing-clipper.

The others aren't as fast as me, they can barely keep up.

I'll reach you and you'll have nothing left to cut!"

Sure, okay, cut, cut away, but you'd be better off having more faith in us. We know that everyone thinks they can be a censor. 'Cause there are born censors, like born writers! You've got people to clip your wings for you, flyboy, there's a stalwart, vigilant army of us, like you wouldn't imagine. If censorship starts with you, what's left? Well, I have to disappoint you, no matter how much you cut out, there's still something left for us, it's our duty as censors to leave a mark on your book. And you write as if you were whistling down the street, anyone can do that. So, dear little wing, seeing as how you're flying in an inappropriate and insufficiently optimistic context, you're using improper meanings, suggesting painful, self-traumatizing experiences, I must declare that you can be sure that you'll disappear from this wonderful volume! It doesn't surprise you at all! You were certain of it, you just wanted me to know that this was the reason why you write so poorly and are so incredibly mediocre in general, because, in fact, you leave out your best writing, and if you hadn't cut it out, you'd be a genius! That's how you all think. You know what, give me a break! Poetry has nothing to do with politics! A genius writes brilliantly even about a duckling, about a leaf, happy children, the beautiful apartment complexes being built, wide roads, the sun overhead! And you're pestering me with your lousy wing! Bug off, out of my sight, you loser! Literature's not for you! Only the strong survive here!

"So much sadness, so much sadness, gray clouds, and existential crises! Do you think, dear sir or madam, that I wouldn't want, with all due respect, to write about the sun, optimism, elemental joys? I see only things that are gray and sad, I am the dark poet, of cold and sad rains."

Your mother's a dear madam, you pathetic man! We're comrades! If you see only sadness around you and you suffer from complete color blindness, with feigned sadness I can come only to the sincere conclusion that you'll see your sad poems published when I'm able to see the happy back of my head without a mirror, or when pigs fly, as the saying goes . . .

"The leaf hurts me, the bird hurts me, the wind hurts me, the ship hurts me, but most of all, illusions hurt me."

Censorable! Pain has negative connotations. Including figurative pain.

Authors in too much pain must be censored!

"I squeeze my hand in yours until the last drop waters the last flower,

With wings like these we immediately take flight . . .

The grateful flower grows her thorn. Come spring, between snows and blood, curiosity and greed will birth the charm of March. When in bloom, in love, someone will steal it and be pricked."

"A boy duck and a girl duck
In the reeds go by,

But the girl duck, like all girl ducks,
Was seeing another on the sly
In vain, in vain, you'd say
That love's sweet like candy,
In vain, in vain, you'd say,
With another she'd bandy.
A tomcat and a girl cat
On the roof go by
but the girl cat, like all girl cats,
Was seeing another on the sly
In vain, in vain, you'd say
That love is forever like candy,
In vain, in vain, you'd say,
With another she'd bandy."

—The poor man . . . This one never even ever read *The Little Ewe*.[6] It must be some newly minted poet from the benches of the capital's Heavy Machinery Enterprise. The heavier the machinery, the lighter the poetry. What can you do?

—What do you mean, what can you do? Censor him. Maybe he never read *The Little Ewe*, but he gets it into his head to promote adulterous relationships: "With another the girl cat would bandy"! What, she can't spend her time nicely and decently with her spouse? Go out to a movie, a concert, from time to time. No, nowadays, lickety-split, in the bushes, on the roof, with other people's husbands! Censored!

[Here follow the fourteen illegible sheets—Ed.]

"I sit in this beautiful forest prison, wood on wood and

stone on stone. I miss stories so much that, instead of grass, I see books growing, instead of the rustling of leaves, I hear poems and songs, the books grow before my eyes, they sprout. Writers, save the forests! Tap-tap, story, tap-tap, tap! The music of my peace. My spirit of solidarity!"

Profoundly subversive, with an allusion to the Morsd alphabet used in prisons.[7]

March 26, 1974

He asks himself where his life went, who's living it, who stole it from him?

I'm living only 10% of my life and that wouldn't be a problem, but I've reached middle age, I've accumulated too much of an unlived stockpile . . .

In fact, I no longer think I'll live that complex, complete moment of fulfillment and beatitude either, the 100% that would compensate for the scarcity and modesty of the 10%. I live 10%, I work 10% (metaphorically speaking, in comparison with my potential, because I'm 150% with my nose stuck in manuscripts!), I'd like to say I also love 10%, but no matter how I try, I can't even muster 2%. I don't love anyone, I don't have time, I don't have the right people around me, maybe Z. fits into that 2%, that's not too much for our talks. Z. is smart and likable.

All of Censorship laughed when, during a meeting, the teams that check the depositories of purged books, describing in great detail the moldy and damp basements, the crafty rats (smart from chewing through so many manuscripts, I imagine them wearing glasses on the bridges of their sharp and intelligent snouts) that scurried across their path, the old dusty furniture that toppled on their heads, and many other things; asked for hazard pay and "milk" as an antidote against the toxins, to compensate for their professional hardships under these harsh workplace conditions. "Milk" was and remains the catchphrase when talking about difficult working conditions. The youngest among us don't understand that it's not a joke, a figure of speech, or a barb aimed at their youth or lack of experience. They weren't here during the first massive purges (I wasn't either, but I have colleagues who were), or the period right after, when the country was a huge depository of banned books and when, as recompense for hard, dangerous labor that could affect their health, workers of those respective institutions received milk. I don't know if the teams from Library, Museum, and Antiquities Services ended up getting the milk. I don't think so. But when an exhausted colleague rolls his eyes and says "milk" when we ask him how it went, we understand. These young snots need to learn.

❦

The playful and tender rainbow. . .

. . . the maiden gazes at the asymmetrical raw apple with a yellow gaze

. . . shoveling with extremities through the pinkish smoke

. . . diluted love, like a transcendent stain

. . . small clouds like fluffy flamingos . . .

I'm sick of flowers and frills, beating around the bush. Can't they write anything decent?
Small lepidopteric wings—
Lepidopteric?

Soft, ductile time—
Ductile?

Where are my dictionaries?
How many times do I have to repeat myself: hands off my dictionaries!
If the jerks from Office One take them without asking, we should keep them locked away!
. . . seasoned with insomnia, the gaze

. . . a bouquet of octopus, a lazily knitted ovum

. . . archeological jubilation, atrocious, thorough

. . . riding horseback on truth, shooting arrows at the essence

Your ovulated cacaphors make me sick!
I'd take some switches to your behinds to teach you all to write, you archeological condiments! As if I don't know that poets are just people like everyone else! Only out of overwhelming vanity, to demonstrate that they're utterly unique, better than everyone and everything in this world, do they write in such a twisted and anti-intelligible way! As if they were determined, at all costs, that no one should understand them, considering this an act of heroism. Decadent worms!

Not all, not all!

You can't make art just by having ideas and metaphors, just by being overly original.

It's so unfair that we're forbidden to communicate directly with authors! Is there anyone these days who doubts our existence? Anyone who doesn't know we exist? Oh, right, censorship doesn't exist in our regime! We don't censor anything, not for a second! What a mistake!

To stay crouched behind concepts and screens, to be ashamed of what I do, to hide where I work. To not be able to come in contact with any writers, and so many other injustices . . .

Censorship doesn't exist in the Soviet Union, not even the word "censorship" exists in their encyclopedic dictionaries.

Does it exist here? R. asks me, but I don't answer, because I don't know whether she's interested in the official answer or asking a purely rhetorical question.

If the Soviets exported as much censorship to the other friendly countries as it did here, it's understandable that they ran out of censorship themselves.

That's a joke, of course. How could it ever run out? Plant a stalk of censorship in the evening and by morning five more will shoot up!

The scene where a clerk goes into the great Lady's office. The Lady's spread-eagle, a man, kneeling, has his head in her crotch, he doesn't even look up, out of either shame or intense concentration, and the Lady nonchalantly says to the confused clerk:

What do you want, he's a go-getter! He wants to get promoted. And she gives the poor provincial clerk, who's about to faint, a brazen and questioning look: Will he take a number too, or not? The Lady, at quite an advanced stage of maturity, with a few rings of fat (a muffin-top) hiding everything she might have below her belt, half covering the head of the unfortunate go-getter, who was trying to perform his work of getting promoted diligently without suffocating. Then the Lady said: If you're not able to convince me, you should know your wife's much more convincing and, since it had to do with her husband's future, she didn't need to be asked twice. Look out the window over there. And the petty clerk saw his wife with two ugly-looking men, as if specifically chosen to be ugly, in obscene positions that the two of them, though they had been together for thirteen years, had never tried.

I hate scenes like this! Am I to understand that our public adores them? That they actually pass for truth? A few negative actions are generalized, and the perverted visions of a degenerate deadbeat writer pass for pure truth? At least he had the good sense not to write "the great comrade!" Great ladies are a thing of the feudal-bourgeois regime and maybe that's how they behaved then.

I cut out the scene, but it's obvious from the context that's something's missing . . . The reader will see traces of Censorship's "scissors" here (I heard the thing about the scissors from Zuki, it comes from a French priest from centuries ago) and that's not good. I write to the editors to replace it with something appropriate, if not in keeping with the party spirit, at least with human decency and morality.

Sometimes I, too, have my suspicions, that scenes like this

could be real, that something like this did take place some-where? Lots of things can happen. But when you publish something, you legitimize it, you turn the exception into a rule. The scene must go! And they all write that way, as if they had an understanding, they should know that things we don't like won't pass either.

It makes me sick not only as a censor but also as a woman!

Sent the passage directly to the Securitate offices! What Censorship's unable to do, the Securitate will take care of. Teach the pervert a lesson.

The faces the girls in the office make when I tell them about the scene! That's how our enemies turn the people astray. How immorally and wrongly they go about things. In fact, worst of all, this passage can actually be taken somehow for realist literature. We can play the goodie-goodies here, the perfect censors, but you think it doesn't happen? Okay, maybe not with two and not exactly with a husband forced to watch his wife . . .

—What the depraved writers do among themselves they attribute to the higher-ups, their superiors, the ones they don't have access to and hate . . .

—It's a mystery here as well how some come to be "censors," Sultana, that girl with the long hair they hired last month, is dumb as rocks . . .

—It didn't used to be like that. You could go see com. Arde-leanu butt-naked and he wouldn't even notice!

—If you want someone to notice your ass, go to Tarnovski, the dirty old man, he'll see your ass right through your coat.

—I've put on a little weight.

—Censorship's treating you well.

—Tarnovski's a decent guy, he's old-school, one of ours. But the team brought in by the new director . . .

—First of all, those guys come from other organizations, that have nothing to do with Censorship, they've got no clue what a censor does, but they walk around with their noses stuck up in the air.

—They all come in as section chiefs, getting paid double what we get.

—Be thankful that they're keeping us, the ones Ardeleanu hired, around still . . .

We're wasting time with these discussions! To work, comrades! Let's read!

Verse about the war. It's the '70s and we're not at war. What business does this have being here?

Must be some naïve first-time author . . .

Summaries or charts of interventions + (turned in)
warnings (never received one)—
notes of approval and notification, with respective
annexes—
reports of interventions +
synopses (not yet)
informational bulletins + (received weekly, put
together by Press)
other kinds of notifications—

Summaries or charts of interventions and referrals are drawn up in specialized units, the unit's management answers personally for their documentation, circulation, and storage.

Notes of approval and notification, with respective annexes, are drawn up at the request of the general director, in two copies. The original, stamped by the deputy general director, is submitted to the GDPP Administrative Office, the copy remains with the section's management.

Reports of interventions and referrals are drawn up in two copies. The original is submitted to the GDPP Administrative Office, the copy is turned in to unit management.

Preliminary inspection—with the aim of preventing the publication, dissemination, transmission, and communication of material that:

> —violates the Constitution of the Socialist Republic of Romania; defames party and state leadership; contains attacks against the socialist order, or the domestic or foreign policies of the RCP;

> —defames party and state leadership; communicates classified information, data, or documents; includes false, biased, or alarmist information or observations;

> —threatens the public peace or poses a danger to state security; encourages the non-observance of state laws or the committing of actions that are deemed felonies; propagates concepts that are fascist, obscurantist, or anti-humanitarian;

> —spreads jingoistic propaganda; promotes racial or national hatred or violence, or offends national sentiments;

—adversely affects healthy morals or constitutes an
incitement to the infringement of ethical standards or
those of communal social life;

—adversely affects the dignity, honor, or reputation of
persons; or proffers insults, slander, or threats to persons.

(They shove these criteria from ten years ago down our throats,
but is anything like that to be found in my novels?)

They compile studies and synopses regarding their findings
and the completion of their tasks and they inform the RCP
periodically.

The GDPP is responsible only for the content of material
given to them for inspection by editors, publishing houses, etc.
At the same time, they monitor whether editors, publishing
houses, etc. submit their respective means of disseminating
public information for inspection (printers and printing presses
providing services, for example, are monitored to ensure they
respect the obligation not to complete orders that have not
been verified by the GDPP).

As regards the political-ideological content, oversight begins
with instructions derived from party documents, from laws
currently in effect, studied by the entire inspection agency, and
from instructions given by the upper management forums of
the GDPP.

I get to page 30 and the novel hasn't even started yet. Doesn't
anyone teach these authors how to write? They waste paper

for no reason and their text isn't even ideologically incorrect, so that I could cut whatever I don't like, invoking solid arguments. I want to get to the heart of the matter, immediately.

I read slowly, taking my time, so I can understand the author, guess what each character, each plant, in the novel wants, why it appears, what it's hiding. Ideally it wouldn't be hiding anything but, even if the author isn't hiding anything, something might still be hiding there for our readers, for a while now readers here have been smarter than writers. We have to watch out for them as well. What did the author want to say? What might the reader understand?

> "The city's architecture looks like it was sketched by a mental patient, lines that are too perfect, precise, and too few curves . . .
>
> . . . Someone in my family made a mistake and I'm paying for it. I don't want anything from life, I expect punishment, stones, blows. Someone didn't consider that every blow given is a blow received. No playing around with fate. The occupier's country melts away, disappears slowly, ruined by an unknown plague. The murderer's descendants disappear, consumed by invisible illnesses. The sinner isn't forgiven anything. Not just like that. You'll receive forgiveness from God, of course, but first you have to make atonement, to pay. A hefty price! . . ."

Fine, I'll cut out the word "God," or make it lowercase if I can't find the right word to replace it. But what did they want to say? What's hiding behind the words?

"Thousands of invisible threads connect us to the past and the future. Who in my past did something wrong . . ."

. . . Even I, to continue with the author's idea, am condemned to this profession of being a doctor of texts, ridding them of scabies, filth, and temptations, of traps and tricky semantics, reinforcing them, improving their message, repairing, reformulating ideas. As far back as anyone knows, no one from my line ever wrote a sentence, I think that many of my relatives could barely even read, and I have to ruin my eyesight with these stupid texts! What twists of fate have brought me here?

I would've made a heroic milkmaid, a valiant onion grower, maybe even an award-winning one, why not, I'm industrious, I like working, or I'd have been the first woman to drive a tractor in my village! And look where I ended up! I think the rotten, bourgeois blood of my father the fugitive is to blame, I knew him only from looking into the scared eyes of my mother, who guarded her love from her sons, hunters of the partisans in the forest. That father who was just mine, whom her sons—my step-brothers (from her first husband, a man with healthy origins, fallen in the war)—couldn't catch, maybe they didn't even want to, out of a sense of guilt for the death of my mother, who was also their mother, not only mine. A father I never knew, and my brothers didn't betray me, so I was an orphan with an ideal dossier, with a father fallen in the war, a poor peasant.

But I feel like my real father is still alive, that man condemned to never know his daughter, to never betray his existence in any way, to live hidden in the forest, like a wild animal. To watch me from afar, but never to come close. Maybe he's trying to communicate with me, but I don't understand? To this day I'm still mad at my brothers for not catching him. At least I would've finally seen him. The existence of my fugitive father troubles me, I would have him safely stowed away for a long term in some penitentiary. I feel his presence sometimes, when I'm reading. He creeps like a lizard between the lines, between all the meanings, he comes to blame me for my mother's death. This enemy of the people who seduced my mother with flowery words. He's not my father, I don't have a father!

Maybe I don't understand anything, I don't feel anything, maybe he's long dead and I'm fighting windmills, maybe he's dying of hunger in some forest or he died long ago. I don't have a father, I've never seen a father by my side, nor a man next to my mother.

. . . Poems, dramas, are on edge. Branches break with a creak. Screams, sounds, meanings. A library, all mine, surrounds me. Don't step on the grass, the branches. Don't tear the books, don't walk through the forest, illiterate fools! If you don't know how to read . . .

. . . Your water comes through pipes, consistently, whenever you turn on the faucet, you're very chlorinated and rather smelly, but you always have the essentials, you can be cold or hot, according to the season or as needed. You're appropriate, civilized.

My water comes from the rains, it's bad during droughts, not a chance, good if many, many clouds, sometimes my water can be dirty as well, but it's never as smelly as yours.

My water comes from above, your water comes from below.

Sooner or later they meet.

It's the duty of every citizen to plant a tree, to dig a well. Our well is modern, urban, with all the waters mixed, homogenized according to the standards, with proper faucets. A shaft 126 meters deep.

. . . We all know what a blow means. Without having hit anyone or being hit, we imagine it one day. When the lover who's been deluded, disillusioned, takes his revenge, he'll leave us . . .

. . . I learn from the waves. What serenity, what peace and, suddenly, crash, the wave smashes into the shore with a smack, you piece of crap! I hate you. A slap across the face! Well, a book shut quickly, forcefully, also sounds like a slap across the face. Self-criticism starts now. You begin regretting all your mistakes, difficulties, heights, limits, liberties, ellipses, incorrigible commas, perishable epithets, mystical phrases, imaginary paradises.

Love, adoration, passion, tenderness! They're words that require a permit, of a high official or a specialized researcher, a documentarian or an archivist. Words shut up in Special Collections, also known as Secret Collections. Lots of boxes there. One is the sealed box of Pandora. Whoever opens it will change the orthodoxy. A revolution and it's still not enough. They're words destined for closed-off spaces that are perennial, punitive, where you receive lessons and thin slices of bread so that you'll forget. And, if you're lucky, survive. If you make it out of there, no one will hire a damp detainer like you. Close to rotting, your sails injured. Because love is specially designated and requires a signature.

Where did these guys hear about Secret Collections? How did something like this make it all the way to us? Do those lazy editors do anything besides pick their noses and other body parts?

Instead of detainee it said *detainer*, as if we were a bunch of idiots and wouldn't understand. The versifiers who don't care to get any farther than Censorship really annoy me. Something beautiful, something for the people! No, they've settled on giving me headaches, I have to sit and copy out, in lengthy reports, all the nonsense I've had to cut.

I arrived at the conclusion a long time ago that it should be absolutely necessary, before being allowed to register as poets, that all these citizens pass a rigorous medical examination, and whoever isn't in possession of their full mental faculties shouldn't be permitted to publish, shouldn't have this right! I'm tired of crazy people!

On second thought, what sane person takes up writing poetry these days?

At college we learned that literature is eternal, poetry is ageless, but I bet my life that what lots of them are writing now will die when the next president comes to power. They allowed them to pulverize the former one, and that's what all the minions are doing right now lickety-split, then another one comes along, someone else needs to be criticized, other literature is needed. Good thing for leaders who live to a ripe old age! Somewhere among these critical briar patches, eternity gets lost, comrades! We, and eternity, would be content if only you, esteemed and brilliant comrades, would be slightly more poetic and less concerned with our country's politics. We've got people to handle that. You, gentlepeople, should observe the first snowdrops, because they should be out by now, the blossoming of first love, since we have to work on our demographics, forget about prisons, atrocities, be grateful that you got out with your life. Enjoy the sun and sing its praises!

Our specialists have come to the conclusion that love poetry stimulates the desire in couples to contribute to population growth. Therefore, if there aren't any allusions to enemies of the people, just to certain parts of the human body, Censorship's in no hurry to make categorical decisions. Careful, however! Too much eroticism is bad and leads to a useless and sterile arousal of the senses. Specialists have determined that too much sensuality and arousal results in fewer pregnancies for women, meaning there's no demographic benefit. So the noble task of determining the demographically ideal limit of eroticism in literature falls to us. A charming mission! Not even god, if he reads our poetry up in heaven, could do a better job of it!

> Comrades, we have to call things by their names, to stress that prattling, gossiping, and discussions that have nothing to do with work, can have grave consequences. They weaken the unity of the collective, the preparedness and vigilance of our comrades, they

introduce an anarchic, liberalist spirit of disorderliness. Where the unity of the collective, its preparedness, vigilance, and discipline are weakened, workplace errors are bound to occur. Our comrades are distracted from their professional concerns, they become less exacting, and this causes them to release inappropriate materials.

Hell if I understand a thing!

. . . Neither chicken, nor egg, nor larvae, nor butterfly, the word like an unshaped, unpolished stone, that says something, but doesn't say a thing.

Weaker still, thinner smaller lighter, more like a puff, more like a leaf, more fragile, more buff, more wind and more fog, from a word—a syllable, and from blood—earth.

I think it's clearly alluding to the fact that people suffered from starvation before our regime, they're that thin, in the sense of physically thin. Let's not forget that in earlier times, folk poetry featured the refrain "beautiful and fat," in folk songs, doinas, this sobriquet referenced health and prosperity. We consider this standard to be valid today as well. But the hero of the poem above keeps complaining that he's getting thinner, this is the refrain that accompanies his entire poem. ("Curvier still, chubbier . . .," I'm also racking my brains trying to figure out the rhyme scheme of this bard of Dâmboviţa county.)

The same word must not be repeated too often. Because you don't know what that layering means.

. . . Toward you, my country, I'm stirred, from word to word.

You've got to show it with concrete actions, not words. We've got enough parasites. Put a factory there, a cornfield, one of socialism's great achievements! The word by itself already had its moment in the spotlight in that sense.

. . . The beautiful fish got away, no matter, at school I learned how to be an optimist. I'll wait for it to come back when it's bigger, heavier, carrying lots of caviar when it returns from warmer countries.

I think that "warmer countries" alludes to capitalist countries, as if the fish were heavier and tastier after returning from there, while here, in the waters of the fatherland, it's small and skinny.

. . . What would you like, my beloved, to receive as a gift? My house as big as a thimble, with a small window that barely lets in any light? closed, inward facing, narrow, dusty; my car like a snowflake, tenderly hard-back bound, that flies more than it spins, and more often in dreams, toward enchanted lands . . .

All these allusions have to go! These guttersnipes have never driven a Trabant a day in their lives, 'cause they can't afford one, but they know how to criticize! The window's small, what nerve!

. . . But I have a dog, without fleas, with all his shots, instead of a bath, he'll lick you, he'll wash you, he'll rid you of all germs, with great alacrity. The dog is rare and precious, many want to buy him from me. Instead of hot and cold water in the bathroom. You release the dog and he'll lick you thoroughly, washing you, cleaning you. When you grow up, my dear, rare dogs will become common, we'll each have a useful dog by our side, he washes, licks, cleans, protects. He heals all diseases, he's also learning to speak. The dog of the future, the new dog. He takes you for a walk two times a day for exactly thirty minutes, he feeds you. The only thing left is for him to learn to sing on command. He'll sing beautifully, valiantly, patriotically. But first he must learn words. Human speech possessed by the dog of the future.

I can't tell: should I send it to the Securitate or just write them an informant note?

The nerve, these ingrates!

. . . To the east, to the west, people live and die, write poems, stories. Everything is circular, like the earth and life itself. Stories, like people, if they continue, return to where they started . . .

Even if the lyrical hero tries not to draw attention to the difference between East and West, the implication that in the West stories always have a "happy ending," while in the East they never "end," that they're swamps, bogs, etc., is already a solid reason for intervening. In general, the word "west" itself suffices for a poem to disappear.

. . . We have the right to write bad poetry, poetry that's scrappy, unfathomably subpar, at the level of regulations. Everything's selected. Everything passes through the machine at the end of the only tunnel. In the West there are scores of tunnels, hundreds of them, you can take your pick, you can find an exit. In the East there's only one tunnel and a single machine. It's economics, you see! We're actually obligated to write poorly and subversively, because the machine, like the sphinx, requires food, texts, poems, ready to be sacrificed, strangled by the almighty mechanism. So that poetry as a whole can keep going, can survive. Whenever it stops in the middle of the road, unsure, terrified, it's pushed forward by others, other texts that want to see the light of day, even by passing through the claws of the sphinx, at the risk of losing something or other along the way. Poetry, like a hunted animal. The hunter's always too quick, but never much of a killer. He just tears something off, a tail, a head, claws off the hind paws, fur, then he releases you, go ahead and show yourself, pathetic beast, to the world, so they can look at you and then ask themselves, what's the point of your existence, what use could a carcass like you be to anyone? To drag your tail and helpless body through the dust, barely breathing, barely, barely, and to ask yourself who needs you? Why should you exist? *Cui bono*? Aren't you better off dead than wounded and torn apart like this?

A futile struggle . . .

The waiting's worse than the machine's claws. Even when in great pain, life's more powerful. The desire to drag yourself along wins out, life wins out. Only those who have everything to lose consider death, we, the ones who are censored, want to live, life's precious to us, we'd give anything!

It's just so touching, if I had a wounded, worm-eaten author in front of me right now, maybe I'd even shed a tear! Corpsish poems have never moved me, they don't make me feel a thing! What era or period was it when they threw anyone handicapped over the cliffs? How generous our regime is toward these deformed creatures! Seriously!

Formulas, patterns, labels.

"iron guard," "fascist"

"imperialist," "spy"

"decadent"

"bourgeois," "criminal," "enemy of the people"

"dangerous element," "saboteur"

Negativistic treatment, misanthropism, fatalism of exasperation, rapid decline, vulgar promiscuities.

I'd do away with the character of the writer—whenever they don't know what (who) else to write about, the great novelists fill their books with writers, the working people don't need characters who are writers. They should profile categories that interest us, a useful intellectual or two, a doctor or zoologist, for example, would work, but not another writer at every turn. These novelists are completely devoid of imagination.

Oh, no, my heart you can't censor,
Even if you cut me into bits, you know,
I won't give up, I won't let go . . .

We don't censor hearts, but if you have a publishable manuscript and you want it to appear, then we'll be handling you. All of you, not just bits, hearts, livers, fingernails . . . Everything, Censorship demands everything. You can't escape . . .

Any allusion to censors and their work is subject to censorship, of course.

Hemorrhaging letters, verbal incontinence, uncontrollable flightiness—those are the qualifications of these brave heroes! They're capable of spending five pages just describing a factory door. I'm not saying that a factory door isn't a necessary and positive point to touch on in a novel as a whole, but in five pages I describe all the novels that have been written in a term, in detail, including incriminating passages! Including plot summaries and sensitive issues. It takes them several more pages merely to describe a sweetheart's nose and the nose is nothing, it's an innocent subject, generally speaking . . . Just like that they emit six hundred pages of literary diarrhea. So that I've got something to keep me busy on Sundays, so I don't by any chance get bored. So the old lady whose room I'm renting gets alarmed, my, how this girl does work, she doesn't stop for a second! Huge print runs, people keep reading, they can't get enough.

Reading, reading, I'm stuck with my nose in their crap! My soul stinks of novels! Even my underwear stinks of books, the stench of manuscripts has entered my bones as well. I'll carry it with me to the grave. Not that I'm complaining, there are worse odors in this country, I'm just stating a fact. To my nose, ink isn't the most unpleasant smell, nor is it the most toxic.

It's as if everyone in the country were writing, cooks write, drivers write, carpenters write, doctors, teachers, presidents, plumbers, they don't eat, they don't sleep, they don't go to work, they just write, they write and they send us their manuscripts, so there's no chance of us running out of things to do and getting paid for nothing. Look who's taking care of us!

—Desire aspire, await contemplate captivate state, sing swing, maybe everything, duration vegetation creation Dacian, shadows impose, ship whip, womb tune . . .
    —And what's this you're working on, dear? A new rhyming dictionary? Just look for death, god, blood, betrayal. Hmph, sing swing! What's there to censor here? Let them sing and swing . . .

—It can't be! Already in just these two lines words like "blood," "sadness," and "pain" appear . . . It's as if the words are specially chosen to give us headaches.

—You asked me if there's any poet I like?
    —I'm not referring to the ones who work for us, but to the great poets, far off and uncensorable. Whom we, with our ideo-

logical scissors, can't touch. The ones who write poetry whose meaning we don't have to think about, you read it and that's it, you like it or you don't.

—Does something like that exist? I'm positive that someone there, far away, is censoring them as well. Because even the ancient classics were censored by someone during their time. A sublime censor presides over everyone, the divine censor, the censor god. He sees all texts, he censors them all.

ৎ৶

"Danko's heart syndrome" means knowing, feeling, that what needs to be censored in one thing shouldn't be censored in another. That everything's relative in Censorship, the criteria are very abstract and if you don't find a way to orient yourself, you'll get lost. You'll make a first mistake, a second, then you won't be able to stop yourself. It's like a drug. But a mistake is a mistake. Not even the sacrifice of a heart cut out and crushed in the right spot can save people like us.

I feel helpless! Just a tiny gear, an insignificant piece in a sophisticated mechanism. If I'm absolutely convinced that a book needs to be banned, that it's dangerous, hostile, no one pays any attention to me. The book appears as if to spite me. The editors at the presses laugh at us, the impertinent and conceited authors laugh at us because, see, they can write whatever they want, they can act out as much as they want! But it's still them, still them, the shamelessness, complaining about Censorship! What Censorship is there to speak of, if hundreds of books appear each year, in print runs in the thousands and tens of thousands? Everyone ridicules Censorship! From the top down, from the bottom up, and from all sides!

Some book editors are also envious authors and they block their fellow writers, but blame us. Many manuscripts that might have appeared, since they're just as bad as many others or just as good, don't even make it to us. The devious editors pretend that Censorship's to blame!

Not that authors are any better. What isn't accepted by a magazine in the capital they send to one in the provinces. They parade their censored works to and fro like holy relics and they don't give up until they see them published.

Who censored X.'s "masterpiece"? Every novel must pass through our hands and no one saw or heard of his book until it appeared. It didn't go through the GDPP? I asked, especially since it's enjoying such great success. If a snot-nosed critic finds something subversive in a text, the censors get blamed, it gets taken out of their paycheck, they get penalized harshly. We read only second-rate books, but everything that's good goes directly to the Party. All the wastepaper goes to us, we get all the blame!

Literature wants to turn me into the weakest creature possible, but I have to remain strong! A valiant woman, not a bed-wetting female. Everything's written to make you cry, suffer, be overcome with emotion, helpless, dependent, sensitive, vulnerable. Never! Not one text will succeed in turning me into that.

Useless, all of them. A waste of time and material resources. Not one person's capable of creating an essential book anymore. A book that's necessary and complete and perfect, done the way we expect, that doesn't require taking out a single word. You're a bunch of weaklings! Diction is degraded with each passing day, it degenerates. Someone's always cutting something out, us or the authors themselves. They cut out life as well. Everything's a second-rate copy. Sometimes outright plagiarized. Useless censorship, worthless literature.

After reading so many novels I'm starting to understand, to be able to guess whether they're being pretentious because of lack of talent, or because that's the best they could do, or to fill up pages so the book is thicker, or whether they're putting on an act so that readers will admire them and appreciate their heroism ("stones for the monument," we call them). I'm also starting to understand that when they intentionally shout out in unconventional ways ("traffic lights," we call them), they're addressing us—*look, censor this*—they have us in mind. There are fewer and fewer writers who truly ignore us. Meanwhile we're tired of being the target audience. But how can we get this across to them?

I couldn't care less about their creations! It's just a way to keep from starving. I've seen these writers, a bunch of potbellied, depraved, lazy drunkards and lechers. And the party coddles them! They give them advances so they can finish their books, they give them prizes, literary grants, summer houses. Where have you ever seen something like this! They don't pay me even one leu in advance, by the time I've turned in a manuscript, I can't even see straight! I have to work, to sweat profusely in order to deserve a modest monthly salary! No one even punishes them for their countless mistakes, while we're penalized for every "god" we miss or every disgraceful "cow" who feels like traveling![8] They cut our pay for three months, with stern reprimands, with demotions! Meanwhile no one pays me in advance, no matter how much I might need it, even if I were dying of hunger, and after any two random slipups, goodbye trips abroad and other things . . . An overlooked mistake (small and insignificant, of course) and the whole country gets wind of it: look, esteemed comrades, what a grave oversight has been committed!, how is it possible for an experienced censor be so lacking in political sensibility! But how it's possible for a filthy writer to write something like that and for it to pass through so many committees and get to us doesn't seem to be an issue! And just like that, censors are to blame. All the delegates from the provinces will receive examples of the unjustified interventions, detected mistakes, etc. I pity these wrongfully punished colleagues of mine.

And, after all this, should I cry when I censor a writer?

Should my nose bleed (like happens to Hermina) for some gem of an uncensored poem?

Never, never!

I hate them.

I don't always know who the writers' ideal audience is, it doesn't seem to be just your average audience, I mean the broad one. I sense that some have other aims as well, ones that are more selective, that certain passages (not the whole text) are intended for someone else. I'm not referring to Censorship.

My target, in case my wonderful notebook doesn't make it to its sole destination (namely, the paper factory, where it'll be burned, like all our notebooks), can be none other than a Securitate agent, who else? The three who come to check that our secret documents are secure come to mind. I choose the most handsome, the most intelligent, keen-eyed one, and I imagine him reading it. He'll be so astounded, he'll be so angry!

I don't care.

Our overly youthful colleagues. All kinds of snot-nosed kids come to Censorship. As if it's a kindergarten, not Censorship, seriously! I understand that the new com. president wants fresh meat, pure minds, but these eighteen-year-olds pee themselves when they finally understand what their duties entail. They pee themselves even before getting to that, the little dears, during recruitment. How do you explain to them what pieces of crap writers are and how you need to hack away at them without mercy?

Ah, gone are the days of the old hens, but what a stew, what a stew . . . The censors of yesteryear, cast off, transferred, retired, but what interventions and what reports! New leadership no longer trusts the old party cadres, they want their own new people. They come in with an entire unit in tow.

Right when I find words to replace the censored ones, some of which fit perfectly, others not so much, after going from office to office, reading the lines and asking: What can I use to replace the words "flesh," "pain," "death"?, right when I have everything prepared, I stop getting poems with those kinds of words, I get other, suspicious ones, harder and harder to replace and what am I supposed to do, start all over again? As if these poets were playing cat and mouse . . . cat and lizard . . . I've never been much for games, even less so now.

. . . Even a banal puddle is luminescent from our love.

Is a turd also luminescent from your love? Just between us! How these things irritate me . . .

According to style, psychological profile, and other elements, writers and their works are divided into several categories that vary more or less dynamically and dialectically.

Those who made caustic allusions aimed at the system, considering censors to be a bunch of idiots, we used to call lizards. You mean to say they thought they could slip through our fingers? What are you up to? I'm reading some she-lizards or he-lizards. I got a lizard and I'm making sure it doesn't leave a tail behind. Afterwards, the generally accepted connotation of "lizard" narrowed to mean just that little hidden expression, but initially it had meant something else for us, with a bit of a different nuance. Lizards gave us something of a headache and they kind of annoyed us. But, as authors, writers like that were rather good and had personality.

Cowards, opportunists, the mediocre ones, the literary padding, were "mice" (if the books were thin) or "rats" (if their work was massive and presented a certain ambitiousness). I was also around back when there was widespread use of gastronomic vocabulary (I got unsalted cheese or I perused some polenta, a mini-polenta, we have assorted salad today for lunch), that sounds downright gentle and poetic in comparison with today's vocabulary. Some say the nickname "mice" for certain authors came not from their cowardice, their mediocrity, or some trait in common with the animal, but from a meeting with the head of our unit, from a few years ago:

—Comrades! Romanian literature is being inundated by mice that chew up everything and ruin our national values! We must be vigilant and exterminate them!

After which he read off the titles of books, short stories, and poems (*The Adventures of a Clever Mouse, Playing Cat and Mouse, Stories from the Life of an Aristocratic Mouse, Kitty-kitty—Leader of the Cats,* etc.) and even a passage from a novel about the life of a group of workers whose factory was taken over by a bunch of mice . . .

Of course, they were all censored not necessarily because of their content, but because of how often the motif was repeated. As if all the other animals had died and everyone felt the urge to write specifically about mice! After that legendary meeting, whenever we received enormous interminable manuscripts that we couldn't describe even after we finished reading them, my goodness!, awful (keeping in mind we weren't like regular readers who, if they get bored, can skip over pages), we called the authors of these manuscript-bricks "mice." We had to read every single page on the off chance that something was hiding where and when you least expected it. Though everyone would've agreed that these deserved the nickname "elephants" . . . They could be as dangerous as lizards. The rodents tried to lull our vigilance to sleep, they'd write and write . . . And sometimes you'd find absolutely nothing, after having struggled through hundreds of pages! We were almost disappointed. In principle, however, we consider that everything might be dangerous. Literature censors who deal with these kinds of manuscripts complain that they're being invaded by mice. But I don't use this terminology, I don't like it.

For a very short while, a poet by the name of Ion Crabgrass replaced mice. He had written an inspidisimous volume, which there wasn't even anything to take out of, and no one besides us had ever heard of him. After laughing at this rather unromantic name for a poet, who, moreover, was a tractor driver in a village, as we later found out, probably eminent in his domain, for a while we said, when we were checking dull manuscripts: we're weeding. A young censor, a newcomer, or someone from another unit needed to be initiated, we had our coded language.

From lizards and mice came extermination. Menial work—extermination.

Extermination means the process of extracting passages liable for symbolic crimes against the system (hostile passages, basically). I don't like this language either and I'll never use it: I'm not a run-of-the-mill washerwoman or exterminator, removing all the lice and trash from books. I like more aesthetic expressions, ones that are nobler and with higher-order connotations. A censor carries out the ideological oversight of publications, whereas pulling weeds, catching lizards, and extermination are done by people who feel worthy of those kinds of occupations.

Careful, the following mistakes are appearing more frequently:

> instead of "historic," it shows up as "hysteric,"
> communist—commonest,
> class—crass,

designation—resignation,

price—prick

"Groups of artists must put on performances at Cultural Centers on the occasion of meetings for the <u>resignation</u> [it should be: designation] of the People's Democratic Front candidates."

Later on:

> "<u>In everything they do, activists must underscore that all the achievements of our people would [missing: "not"] have been possible without the leadership of our seasoned Marxist-Leninist Party</u>."

The GDPP delegate on duty, com. A. Timingeru, reading the material with a great sense of responsibility, detected the aforementioned mistakes, for which we propose a special award in the amount of three hundred lei.

Hey, what's with this?

As far as reading novels goes, this example's pointless for me. It's from the newspapers and it's meant for those working in that domain. What's more, it even received an award, for those three lines. Our people are losing their minds reading novels that are hundreds of pages long and I've never heard of any of them getting an award. It really is unfair. In addition, we have to waste our time copying out "justified interventions" from every field. Not even examples from literature are helpful to me anymore, it's not as if I'm still in my trial period and have to learn the ropes of censorship, and what has appeared in the past usually doesn't get repeated.

You defuse the reconstitution of the contradictory undulations . . . inconsistent illuminations imprisoning the infinite homeostasis . . .

Homeostasis?

How many imagineering equations serving as ballasts . . . the center of gravity verbalizes feverishly, ovulating ovations . . . indescribably, the vocabulary of famished cells . . .

This volume is mind-boggling! In a bad way . . . Feverishly and indescribably! Even if I can't understand a thing, with my hand on my heart I swear that this individual is sinning semantically through the use of cryptic and Western language. I put in just a few examples, the whole volume's like that, the man's sick, obviously, and I'm not a doctor. Let the Party heal him!

Thankfully, intelligible texts exist as well. After that ovulistic garbage, the thing I'm working on now is manna from heaven!

The poem with the mother who threw the child's toys to the pig.

The child asked the pig politely not to eat his toys.

If you want, I'll bring you some cherries that are
    almost ripe,

please—I'll gather some fallen fruit for you and a slice
    of bread that you'll find tasty.

He gave the pig all kinds of goodies and, while it was smacking its lips loudly, he used a stick to pick up the toys that had been thrown into the sty.

While I was reading, I pictured myself, cold, indifferent, toward my own son. Women cry when reading poems about unrequited love, abandoned love, they gave him everything, how they loved him, but he still left them for someone else. Sensitive Hermina cries when reading beautiful poems in general, at everything that, in her conception, relates to beautiful poetry, and to her almost everything seems beautiful, there hasn't been a volume of poetry that hasn't made her eyes tinkle a little. She cries because it's beautiful and she cries because she has to cut it, it breaks her heart and she gets a nosebleed. Roza doesn't usually cry but, when she knows the author's a handsome young man, she blushes when she touches the pages and, if she reads us a stanza, she does it with so much expression and fire that you'd think Eminescu[9] himself would gladly allow himself to be censored by our little Roza.

I don't show my emotions around my colleagues.

I never bought him a toy! I filled my room with teddy bears, puppies, expensive giraffes, thinking I'd give them to him, but he must be big now, he's probably upset with me. I imagine him small, the way I remember him, I give him the toys and he plays, he laughs. I don't have a single photo of my son!

Sometimes we go to events with writers, without betraying our identity. We secretly watch them: they eat a lot, they're greedy, god-awfully depraved, drunkards, lechers, and stool pigeons, as soon as they find out that someone wants to publish something phenomenal, they all begin informing on him, so that he can't enjoy his success in peace.

And we should die of admiration for the likes of these . . . Seriously!

Only a weak censor would sink so low!

This is a censor notebook, it's not a journal. Roza and Hermina claim that they're writing journals. In general, I don't understand journals, as a literary specimen. I don't understand why, for whom, one would keep a journal. Work—home. Censorship—sleep. People—silence. Books—food. And over and over. The rest are pointless words.

I turned in the manuscript, on time, barely.

I still have so many to turn in and so much to do! I don't even have time to write in this notebook!

Dissatisfaction. That I can't humiliate him to his face. That I can't spit in his eyes. That I can't destroy his book in front of him. So he can watch and suffer. He should poop out something with more talent next time. Offer more heartfelt and convincing service to the people and the party, who treat him like a prince. When he doesn't deserve it.

He takes a dump on liberty, values, love. He gets together with every woman poet he meets or who's available, then cusses them out, switches them like dirty laundry, and slaps them with a poem to boot, taking short breaks for a swig of alcohol between poetic rounds.

Degenerates, creeps, sex addicts. But we can't do without

them, so we have to put up with them! Good or bad, they're ours, they're our business. We live off them.

The kind of poems that would suit me would be calm, without all the drama, without excessive stylistic devices, without overly romantic landscapes, but they shouldn't be too gray either, devastating love affairs with constant fighting aren't for me, neither are breakups. I know and it hurts, why rankle wounds? It doesn't hurt when I hear the weather report or about the nation's newest achievements, another factory, a new type of tractor, everything's good and prosperous, I don't want to hear philosophical questions about the supreme good, the first quivers of love make me sick to my stomach, insinuating accusations about the meaning of life, like "so much to do so little time," isn't what I want to read. Something about the fatherland, wholesome and simple, something valiant. I want love, but I want it healthy, appropriate, without hands roving under lingerie, without slimy groping, without useless exhibitionism, as if lyrical heroes got married on account of something like that and not to increase the population. As for making out without matrimonial intentions, what a disgrace!

> . . . I introduce my girlfriend to linguistics, the science of tongues.
> Humanity's gentlest, deepest, most comforting skill. My girlfriend doesn't understand, doesn't believe, and she wants me to convince her. I apply a bit of linguistics to her breasts and she sighs, a bit of linguistics around her navel.
> Civilized Romance tongues, with the present perfect,

Finno-Ugric tongues, that bite, like that, like that,
oww!

She screams, she's scared, my girlfriend innocent in
the ways of linguistics, Germanic tongues, cold as ice,
that prick as lightly as my beard, as lightly as the down
between your legs, Slavic tongues, soft and sticky,
winding lower and lower.

What other tongues are there?

In what language does my girlfriend moan with pleasure?

It must be an Indo-European lingua franca, the
tongue we have in common . . .

When women moan, their tongue is from before the
flood, before all wars, before the fall, the tongue of
women is peace, music.

We, men, lift our spear just like that and stick it in,
complicating linguistics. We want tongues that are
ours alone and women who are ours alone!

What deviants, it's so disgusting I could throw up. Does
anyone really stick linguistics into women like that? Or, drunken
losers that they are, do they just dream of doing it? But given the
kind of women running around with them, I'm sure they really
do indulge in linguistic orgies. And they even brag about it.

A bunch of pigs, these linguists.

In order to work efficiently, you have to understand your
author's essence, to get inside his head, to be able to guess from
close up what he's capable of.

Someone here loves me.
Someone here watches over me.
Forgives me when I don't do as I ought,
Someone here knows my every thought.

These allusions to the Securitate have got to go!
Is someone by any chance reading my notebook?
Someone in Censorship is defending me, protecting me. A man.
But who could it be?

Zuki? Zukie-wookie . . . A total mystery . . .
"Hurry up, time's running toward the brink!"

The phrase about time running out is so annoying! I consider censorable everything related to how quickly life goes by,
what you've left behind, what you've done in (with) your life,
the meaning of some action or other. Our party's taking care of
everything, you all just go about your business and stop asking
inconvenient questions!

"You fan yourself with the poem, because it's hot,
You fan yourself with death and don't know . . ."

Forgive them, for they know not what they say, be magnanimous or indifferent, do your work without getting involved, Z.
would advise me. Look, you have the right, to the fullest extent, to
replace "death" with another word, one you like. The poet knew
that "death" wouldn't make the cut and he's letting you, his censor,
perfect his work, he does it knowingly, because today's poets aren't
stupider than in the past. He's letting you play with his poem. He

thinks he's doing you a favor and giving you the pleasure. You, censor, with your intelligence and poetic sensibility, find what needs to go here, so it'll be good, so it'll be beautiful.

—But if I don't have any poetic sensibility?

—Come up with some. It's your duty or get out of Censorship, if you can't handle a situation as simple as this it means you don't deserve to be here.

—"You fan yourself with the poem, because it's hot,

You fan yourself with . . . and you don't know" . . . With a flower!

—Kind of dumb, it doesn't make sense with "and you don't know"—what, like you're an idiot?

—The leaf of childhood!

—Better, but just as dumb semantically.

—A memory from the future!

—Better, profound even. Bravo! Other options?

—A happy rainbow, a child's smile, an algebraic sphere . . .

—My, my, Z. says, getting wide-eyed, these algebraic, geometric, philosophical spheres . . . See, it's not easy to be a censor! But you're getting along fine.

Z. is so nice sometimes and so patient with us!

I don't think about death at all and I believe it's better this way. Thoughts like that decrease efficiency. If I try to bring up this subject with Z., he says I shouldn't be so concerned with efficiency, someone's already on it. There are words and situations that must be censored categorically, without discussion.

Dying is so beautiful!
More beautiful than loving,

One dies more tenderly, more poetically.
Death won't deceive you, won't disappoint you,
And it never backtracks.
Return to yourself, return,
Listen, your heart beats as if it's knocking on a door,
As if it's walled up, no windows, no exit . . .
The supreme happiness of writing death . . .

Uh, but hey, poet, have you heard about the supreme happiness of censoring it?

The supreme happiness of telling the truth!

Comparable to the supreme happiness of suppressing it.

Supremity of supremities and all is vanity, that's how he should've ended his poem.

I don't understand, how did Hermina end up in Censorship? No, there are, I'm sure, many other things I don't understand. How she, so poetically sensitive, her eyes leaking at any more tender line, reading almost everything with puppy-dog eyes, how this delicate individual is able to censor everything she meets with harshly and justly? For example, I'm a block of ice, there's not a line that can thaw me, not one novel impresses me. I don't like poetry, I don't care much for prose, I don't ask myself, in general, whether I like literature. Literature must be censored and that's it. That's where my mission ends. I know: I like to read carefully, to follow every word, to cut things out, to add, correct, make notes, I do it almost automatically. Without tears, without feelings involved, and that seems right and normal to me. And easy to do. I'd be a nervous wreck if I fell in love (those are her words: I've fallen in love with this poem, I adore it! and every day she falls in love with one poem or another), how could I cut something out of it then, how could I hack away at it? I'd suffer, of course, maybe I'd cry, the way she does, borrowing handkerchiefs from the entire floor! Well, it looks as if she's got nerves of steel! I would've had a breakdown! I don't like literature, I don't prefer a single one of its genres or authors to another, I'm not curious to find out how handsome the man behind the text might be. Or how conniving the woman.

~

Ecstatic! I'm ecstatic!

A scandal broke out when everyone in the press started criticizing the poor writer N., accusing him of everything imaginable. The case had reached such proportions that they began looking for a scapegoat.

So who's to blame for the appearance of this hostile volume? Who? The censor, of course!

Who read the book?

Well, who reads all the illegible wastepaper at the GDPP?

Com. Moldovean!

Hmph, they got all puffed up that, see, I too am a censor who makes mistakes from time to time, like everyone else, as is only human, my colleagues eyed me with contempt/condescension, look, they're going to take our grouch who thinks she's better than everyone in the institution and set her straight. Her, the one who claims she's never made a mistake! (Actually, I've never claimed that, but I've never received, officially, a reprimand or been disciplined for any slipup since I started working.)

An urgent meeting had been called, the entire department came in, solemn. The section chief gave us a long speech in an apocalyptic tone, as if we, not the writer, had made the mistake and were halfway to being enemies of the people. Everyone was in a tizzy and whispering among themselves, I started to get worried too, I felt like something was off, no one had told me what was happening, what the mistake was. It wasn't any clearer to me even when we got to more concrete remarks, and then, oh, how beautiful it was!

I had all the newspaper cuttings with me, actually, we had all received them, to teach us a lesson, people from the party were present as well, to participate in the punishment, more severe and self-important than ever!

So, the meeting started with the order of business, but my name wasn't mentioned. Only after I found out what it was all about did I relax, and then it was my turn to get mad. I proceeded to deliver the most brilliant speech of my entire career, giving everyone from the Party hell, they mumbled three incomprehensible words and quickly left.

They had begun reading from what those jackass literary critics wrote against that dumb ox. But how well I remembered what I had said about the book, what comments and recommendations I had made! Lucky for me, I had said exactly what the critics were saying, you'd have thought they copied off me, that's how alike the ideas, language, and arguments were! I flashed a murderous look at all the coms from the party and at all my little supervisors who were sweating because of how daring I was, and I recommended that they take our humble opinions into consideration from time to time, because otherwise I, for one, feel useless. I make comments, which are ignored, the book appears, and I'm still the one to blame?!

I set them all straight. The party clammed up. My colleagues looked at me with undisguised delight.

You're a firebrand—they said to me afterwards. The Party's going to ask you to marry it, you'll see, they joked. Such oratorical talent!

But I felt like giving someone guilty a kick in the butt.

Triumphant!

My supervisors should be grateful to me for getting Censorship off clean, clean as a whistle, and the people from the party knew that it was their fault entirely! They need to stop blaming us!

⟍⟋

What I can't imagine is what life would be like without these manuscripts, without feeling their weight pressing down on your knees, or in your arms when you take them home and read them in bed (they're not any lighter in the office, but they rest on the table), without smelling their scent, that of a future book, manuscripts at Censorship don't smell quite like books, they have a specific scent, a kind of cheap ink, thick paper, big letters . . . Maybe they have that kind of fragrance only here, and when they're published they probably smell like Censorship as well. That's how it should be, it's only right.

A censor is not allowed to be stupider than the writer—less talented or not at all talented, yes, but under no circumstances stupider.

"And where are you, my soft and warm one? Where is
my youth, where are my wanderings?"

For Censorship, some things are clearly and evidently hostile, and clearly and evidently they must be cut out. You don't
usually find those things in poems. State secrets don't exist in
poetry, so we're clear. That's why certain volumes of poetry are
distributed to and read by the mistresses of party officials, who
can thus cultivate their artistic sensibility, intellectual refine-
ment, and why not? even their vocabulary. I'm referring to the
most dim-witted of our colleagues, who got here through recommendations from higher-ups and all kinds of string-pulling.

A second category consists of matters of interpretation,
meaning nothing's either clear or evident. It depends on the
context, on the time period when it was written or when the
action takes place. Lizards can slip through here, by means of
which authors say one thing, but do something else. Basically
you don't know what he's trying to say, you don't know what
you're supposed to understand. I mean, you know, but it's
not enough. Almost everything is open to interpretation and
it's a true art form to take a firm stand and to defend it with
arguments. When you cut something out, to know why you're
cutting it. When you affirm that something's hostile, to have an
army of reasons and justifications at your side, ready for battle.

. . . and there's one more category. When it's clear and evident that there's nothing to censor, and still you cut something.
In non-censorship language that would be picking on someone
for no reason. The person writes: "I see a white cloud in the
sky," and you accuse them of seeing a black cloud in the sky.
Only when you reach this stage can you call yourself a real

censor. We are few. To be able to pick on anything and anyone at any moment, to make things up almost artistically, like a writer, like a virtuoso, to wield the enemy's weapons and to destroy him with his own arguments is not something to be taken lightly. This third category isn't the most common one, it's not too popular among us, it's actually risky at times. This method must be practiced very rarely, only when necessary or when ordered by a superior. We receive more than enough manuscripts that fall squarely into the first two categories.

In the midst of receiving pompous directives filled with things like "we must unmask cosmopolitanism," "lack of optimism," "mysticism," "where is the truthful presentation of the social-political climate?," the head of our unit bursts into our office yelling: "Watch out for cows! And, in general, pay close attention to animals" ("especially if they have a taste for traveling," he quietly adds). From which I'm to understand that someone high up feels threatened and mocked when a few completely harmless farm animals such as cows appear in novels or poems? The boss leaves, and we talk and talk, and not just about cows.

> . . . and what a rose, what a rose
> sprang up from under your clothes
> your fragrant thigh exposed

. . . continuation of the fairy tale: autumn—your golden hair, russet, my white flowers in spring, your white skin, the scent of apple blossoms, the ripe red apple, your lips, etc. . . . nothing new under the sun. I'll leave the poem as is, what ideological harm can a thigh do? God (and the party and the entire GDPP) help it . . .

"I stand at the edge of the sea and the poem in my head begins its work, what beauty, what stillness, in the poem a giant wave was approaching, I was terrified, I peered into the depths of the sea, look, the wave is as big as a house, it's coming in so quickly I don't have time to step back.

"Every night, the same poem with the giant wave, lavish, overwhelming images, sometimes a mermaid. One night, the wave, exactly as in my poem, rushes in, towering, but it doesn't steal me away, it doesn't drag me to the depths; rather, it leaves behind, like in the poem, a being on the beach. The thought flashes: someone's struggling, a living person has been saved, brought in by the wave. A gift maybe, a gentle mermaid.

"When I approached, I got scared. Maybe it had stayed in the water for too long, or had been floating for a long time, the woman wasn't calm, she was struggling, by the way she was looking at me I thought she was crazy. In short, at first glance, it seemed to be a sea monster. All it wanted, I realized, was to get back to the sea, but the wave had thrown it too far and it was struggling, I couldn't quite tell with what—legs, tails, wings, tresses—to get closer to the water. And there I was, the curious onlooker, who scared it and got in its way.

"Every time I came closer, made any attempt to help it, it reacted violently, as if I were a shark that wanted to gobble it up. I could make out female breasts, a human head, arms, and fingers, but from the waist down, a complete mystery, maybe the fading light kept my eyes from being able to satisfy my curiosity once I had mastered my fear and amazement.

"Meanwhile, reality completely crushed the story. A monster lacking the gift of poetry and speech. Impossible to save. I stood at some distance, waiting for him/her to reach the water alone. I would have liked to have written how I touched her breast and she shivered all over. How I stroked her tail and she shook, pierced (by pleasure). How she spoke to me in the sweetest voice and told me her distressing story.

"But none of that happened. What's fiction and what's the truth?

"Only the inspired reader can judge.
"The mermaid-monster also stunk of muck and rotten fish. It struggled until it got to the water, it waved its tail or whatever it had there and disappeared."

Freedom! you all scream in unison. Freedom! You're free to write what you want, I'm free to censor what I want. No. That's not how it is. You write whatever you want, shamelessly, knowing that I can't censor everything I want. You alone possess freedom, while I'm held captive in a scathing, vindictive, hateful text, from which I can cut just three words and that's all. The writer mocks the censor, laughs at him, the writer's playing around and wins!

༄

Department and service management has endeavored, through its compliance with work standards and methods (the work-flow with readers, the satisfactory and timely completion of items, the briefing of institution leadership and the delivery of the notes and items requested by them, external work relations, etc.), to create an appropriate environment for encouraging each reader toward a more rigorous application of work directives and instructions.

However, we cannot overlook the fact that regarding discipline, performance, as well as the organization of work, the overall training and competence of the reader remains fundamental. Not coincidentally, the best readers read at the fastest pace and conclude the entire process of finalizing the item in the least amount of time. This is why the introduction of certain provisions regarding the political-ideological training of readers, their heightened sense of responsibility and greater personal initiative, has proven to be completely warranted.

It makes me mad when they toy with me, when I'm put in the position of becoming a laughingstock because I see something subversive when there's nothing there. It makes me mad that the author disregards my existence when he writes: "There are clouds in the sky that travel, there are clouds in my soul and they travel me." Maybe he looks up at the sky and sees just this: clouds departing, beaten by the wind, and—at sixty years old—he feels he's gotten older, he's just sad and that's all. But any kind of travel, and especially in such an ambiguous context, could just as easily be a dangerous and hostile allusion referring to our swiftly passing leaders. "They travel him" could actually be an allusion to the fact that even the great, who are inaccessible to us, the powerful ones of the day, are also mortal, in the face of death, we're all equal, weak, and helpless.

If I make these comments not in my notebook, where I can write whatever goes through my head, but in a weekly or monthly report, how am I supposed to know whether they'll give me a prize for vigilance or laugh at me? This lack of certainty kills me. I want criteria! I want clear ideological instructions. Absolutely anything can be interpreted as hostile and sometimes I have doubts, I'm beginning to catch a glimpse of situations in which there doesn't seem to be a double meaning and I'm the one seeing everything in a distorted and exaggerated way. I'm not so sure anymore that there aren't writers who actually enjoy writing, just as I enjoy writing here, I'm beginning to understand that writing can be a release, it can relieve you of all kinds of thoughts, it's like a kind of therapy. I'm beginning to strongly believe that not everyone has subversive and hostile intentions, even when it seems otherwise to me!

> . . . My merciful and infinite God! Forgive me, a sinner! In my immense desperation, in my unbearably painful situation, I see no way to salvation, the air hurts me, my bones hurt me, every smile is gone, even the sun

God, desperation, salvation, hurts.

> . . . My merciful and infinite desire! Forgive me, a winner! In my immense fixation, in my curious situ-

ation, I see no vocation, the air doesn't hurt me, only smiles around me, only the sun I see

???

You're laughing your head off, you loser who doesn't know how to write!

I'll cut out all your desperations, no way to salvations, my gods and all other gods . . .

I'll leave you butt-naked, we'll see who gets the last laugh!

. . . I scream and I struggle, I search, I wrestle!

And what did I ever do to you, that you're screaming at me like this? How's the reader to blame? What does your unhappy experience have to do with me? How am I supposed to benefit inwardly from you? How are you educating me through your book? Literature must offer us something, enrich us, gladden us, propose solutions, show us the way toward peace and wisdom, teach us to respect those who are guiding us so well toward the construction of socialism. What does your scream leave me with? What do I gain from reading you? How can you convince me that your scream is a special one, worthy of attention (and the reader's money, 'cause obviously you're not dumb enough to scream for free), different from that of an anonymous person in a crowd or from that of any calf? After a scream of Homer's, Dante's, Eminescu's, and other illustrious classics, who the hell are you, Joe Shmoe, to bellow at me like an ox? You idiot! You're guilty of semantic pollution! Prison's calling out your name. If not jail time (thanks to the Party's magnanimity and kindness), you deserve at least a hefty fine, to teach you to round your syllables more gracefully, more sagaciously.

Nowadays, everyone allows themselves to pass gas (poetically or otherwise) in all directions, then they complain that they're being censored.

The atmosphere would be unbreathable and suffocating without us!

Literature Office Number Two

Com. S. Albu, in general, handles the tasks he is given with precision. However, he must remain aware of the fact that, maintaining the same level of precision, he is obligated to speak with unit supervisors more attentively and carefully, using a tone more fitting of comradeship in establishing all primary work relations between himself and our institution. Likewise, it is necessary that com. S. Albu exert more effort toward the development of a spirit of self-criticism, to fight against certain tendencies to reject criticism that he sometimes still manifests.

Each one of us should consider ourselves deployed in the elimination of these deficiencies that still persist in our workplace.

Thus, in addition to our assigned modes of party instruction, we will have to raise our political-ideological level through the ongoing study of material published in periodic journals as well.

A prince walked in (a handsome, slender thing!) from Social and Technical Sciences, com. Tudor Mandric, when Roza wasn't in the office, it was just me and Hermina. He brought us some documents about the new stamps and the latest lists of annulments of undistributable information. Actually, he just used that excuse to come into our office, because those papers about stamps needed to go to the Administrative Office, and the documents about factories and tractors aren't of interest to us in general. He starts chatting, of course, and asks:

—Where's your beautiful colleague, the one we all secretly admire, who's so remarkable at correcting the verses of poets and the novels of authors? They say she could rewrite, if necessary, all of literature. She can correct any genius in a way that'll leave you speechless, and she says: As a man writes, so is the man. What an incredible show she put on at Foreign Publications, and no one informed on her. We inform on each other for every five minutes late to work, they'd have thrown her out long ago, with how loose her talk and actions were, dirty in body and soul. We don't have such thrilling colleagues (Technical Sciences heaves a sincere sigh) . . .

—She's out of the office (what, can't you see, are you an idiot, are you blind?) . . .

—Fine, all right, can you let her know I asked about her and take these papers to the Administrative Office?

I swear it made me want to throw up. What an idiot! Hermina and I gossiped about him for a whole hour after he left. Not only is he an idiot, he's also conceited, what an insufferable type of man, first considering just his physical appearance—which we didn't like at all—then, how can you praise a woman like that in front of her two officemates, who are maybe just as good, just as beautiful, etc. We might not have Rozette's boobs, but she isn't better than us. What novels? That's my job. What poems? And no, no one informs on her, because we're censors, not informants, what's so strange about that? We know that she likes to talk a lot and about everything, yes, she's gone from the office for hours on end and she's not penalized. But that's her business! Coming back to our uninvited guest, we're amazed at how an individual as rude, uneducated, and tactless as him is working in our institution! What can I say, a jackass! It's shameful! Truth be told, no one corrects poets' verses better than Hermina! I praise her work with poetry, she praises mine with novels, to get over the anger and disappointment. What did this madwoman do at Foreign Publications? We have no idea. Listen to him, "incredible show," we ape that beanpole . . .

Roza walks in.

—Com. Mandric from Technical Sciences asked about you.

—That idiot?

—Yes, that idiot, we confirm in unison, with emphasis.

Roza's right sometimes.

In light of the fact that the Decree for the organization and functioning of the Committee for Press and Publications (the new title of the institution) will soon be issued, we would like to inform you of our proposal for the production of the following:

– 2 round emblem stamps with the new title of the institution;

– 1 round emblem stamp with the title of the institution for the president;

– 1 round emblem stamp with the title of the institution for the vice-president;

– 2 rectangular stamps, with the title of the institution, for the logging of received documents . . .

If they're making new stamps, it means they aren't shutting us down. Troubling rumors have been circulating about the GDPP's future for some time now . . .

⤸

I can't believe I got away with it. The Securitate coms stopped by again to inspect our secrets, I mean their disclosure, I mean their safety, I mean, I mean . . . I've recovered from the scare . . . They've done unannounced inspections before where few passed the test. You're not keeping your documents in the right place, your stamp's in plain sight, there's no key to your office, your desk, each individual drawer, everything, has to be locked up, protected, hidden, etc. In general, those of us in Literature have nothing to do with their secrets. We've never found a serious and important one, for which we could receive an award, for instance. Those in Press barely find a tiny, scrawny one once every other month and how they pat themselves on the back, how they broadcast it to every floor and all the provinces!

> "In general, the disclosure of numerous classified military garrisons has been observed in local newspapers through the advertisement of military clubs in these localities or through the announcement of the participation of military personnel at various events!"

By "numerous" they mean at most three! In my novels, soldiers, if they exist, don't play in local and regional bands, just to be clear!

Today, around noon, when the silence was deepest, we heard suspicious whispering and clomping around in the hallway.

—My intuition says an enemy's approaching our door, Rozette whispered.

She had just barely opened her mouth, when three scowling individuals appeared in our office (followed humbly by our vice-director). To be fair, they lit up a bit and even smiled gallantly when they observed little Roza's ample bosom. We really lucked out with her! She answered, smiling ear to ear as well and batting her eyes, like a cow in heat, so that the comrade who had just started asking something got flustered. In those few moments, I was able to zip up my skirt and I don't think anyone saw.

Ever since com. Sarossi left, we allow ourselves to undo a zipper, a button—we've all put on weight lately. Okay, Rozalia never was thin, but Iancovici is skeletal and she's also complaining that her skinny-as-a-twig skirts don't fit her anymore, and that's after only two years in Censorship, let's not speak of me, who any day now will have completed two five-year-plan terms here![10] Good food at the Press House kitchen (well, some don't like it, but compared to other comrades hard at work in this country, who don't get to gorge themselves in the cafeterias of the people, we should be grateful), we sit all day with our butt in a chair and read nonstop, other people move around a bit, go for a little walk, some girls go dancing at night, a sports club, a mountain now and then, they've got family troubles, demanding husbands, some devious mother-in-law, an envious sister-in-law, spoiled children, no way for them to put on a little extra padding, but why should I complain? My regimen: books, food, sleep. Reading, sleeping, eating, pooping. That's about it. With dear Pompiliu in our office, even if I wouldn't go out in public with him if he were the last man on earth and the only man in Censorship (that's what we used to say), we would dress up nicely, put on jewelry, even a spritz of perfume . . . But three women in an office . . . Rozalia sometimes has the habit of undoing her bra, everything feels too tight and she can't breathe anymore, sometimes her heart even beats too fast. I believe it! With jugs like that it's hard to find the right bra. Hermina delicately picks at herself, thinking no one sees her, her nose, ears, and wherever she feels like it, she takes her shoes off and her feet smell (when I start squirming, she apologizes and asks me if it doesn't annoy me, if it doesn't bother me), and I undo my skirt, usually. Everything's begun feeling too tight and I can't sit down, I'm afraid my bottoms might split in two. Last month I bought a new suit, jacket and skirt, the right size (I've lost hope of losing weight), but I can't wear it to work every day, to fray it and ruin it here; for now, I'm keeping it for special occasions.

We get ourselves together quickly, the comrades snap out of it too and begin asking us questions: Is the notebook of directives secure? It's secure, very secure, we point, actually I point (I'm the oldest), toward the safe of ours that's been locked for years, only Pompiliu had the key, he'd open it and read something out of that notebook from time to time, I think it was from 1972, we haven't received another one since, some colleagues might have, but they didn't bring us anything. I have no clue what the deal is with the notebook, to be honest. Sarossi had the key for the notebook and he left, taking it with him, or maybe he dropped something off at the Administrative Office, who's to say? He left, called by the State Department, if I'd have guessed, I'd have been flirtier with the man, I'd be sitting pretty now in some embassy, watching the grass grow as the wife of a diplomat or at least a spy. After his departure, no one in the office bothered to get the key back, to ask at the Administrative Office, to request a new key. Hermina's eyes grew wide, because she didn't even know of the existence of a secret notebook in our office, but she was smart enough to keep quiet.

—Would you open the safe?

Oh no, how can we open the safe when we don't have a key, but I didn't say that to them, instead, it came to me to answer in a distinctly enunciated soldierly tone of voice, completely shutting up the coms:

—For reasons of national security and for the heightened protection of secrets, we open the safe only once a week or under special circumstances of necessity, at all other times the key is kept in the Office of Secret Documents.

I figured that there, in any case, they have keys for all the secrets, the Office of Secret Documents is part of Administrative Services, as for the inspectors, whether they had already visited that department, or were going to later, since everyone wants to get off scot-free, the people there will find ways of explaining things so that everything's fine—that is, if the Securitate coms don't somehow forget to ask about our key by the time they get there . . . They're only human too, at the end of the day!

I also added that, given our area, important directives—constituting state secrets but having nothing to do with the subject and content of the texts we inspect—are communicated to us verbally by the comrades responsible for them, to keep us up to date. Which is perfectly true, that's exactly why we don't need an additional notebook of directives that's always lagging behind the new directives.

The other documents we work with, manuscripts, reports, our work notebooks, all kinds of notes that we haven't turned in yet, at the end of each work day, we put them under lock and key, and they're completely secure, exceptional cases where things have disappeared or gotten lost, we haven't experienced that, they haven't happened here. I made a show of opening my closet, in which there were a few sheets of paper and my reader notebook. The comrades took a quick look, convinced and satisfied with the explanations. My girls smiled adorably. Hermina, with her big calm eyes as blue as the sky, watched what the coms were doing through narrowed lids while Rozalia had gotten up and stuck out her chest like a turkey, defying the three guests, two of them were tall, broad-shouldered, but the third—a tiny, scrawny fellow—definitely didn't feel too comfortable next to a mountain of a woman like her. She covered up the window with her boobs and it got dark in the office.

They had nothing to reproach us for and as they were leaving, com. vice-director Tarnovski said to me quietly: "Bravo, comrade Moldovean, you're doing fine work here, keep it up!" and he gave me a friendly, and maybe grateful, pat on the shoulder. I felt like a heroine. After they left, we all breathed a sigh of relief, we undid our skirts, our bras. We have to ask for the key to the safe, who knows, maybe Sarossi took the notebook as well when he left, perhaps he turned it in to the Administrative Office and our safe is empty. I can't even imagine what a scandal that would be! My goodness, we got off easy with the Securitate's inspection this time. The girls looked at me very affectionately.

༄

Promoting women has been a focus of the management of this institution and of other authorities from
its beginnings. While mentioning that this attention
to promoting women is positive when looking ahead,
the activity of cadres must be aimed at strengthening
the collective through the recruitment especially of
men, insofar as working conditions in certain sectors
are harder (night shifts, fieldwork, rotations), work
requirements are very demanding, and the physical
condition of many is inadequate.

We promote, we promote, but how many women supervisors do we have in the GDPP? Only men, always men, women
are subalterns. In general, why do they bring in directors from
who knows where? Don't we have our own personnel, our honorable, responsible censors, who know what the job's about?

Report on the analysis of personnel from last year:
Ensuring an adequate—from a professional, political, and moral standpoint—workforce, one capable of
competently carrying out the responsibilities proper to
the GDPP.
Of the 10 staff members who were promoted, 5 are
women, compared to not a single one promoted in
1973!

Who are they referring to when they say "women promoted"?
Maybe the girls from the Administrative Office or the ones from

the library? Now they're working full time and they are, as such, promoted, isn't that right? Have they remembered that women are people too and that they work ten times as hard as men? And they're also ten times less likely to get promoted . . .

> Characterized by moral traits founded on the ethical and equitable principles of socialism, the management personnel of the institution enjoy the prestige and authority afforded to them by their colleagues.

> Refreshing the workforce
> Along with personnel with valuable experience, younger elements, who show real promise in carrying out important responsibilities, were introduced or promoted.

> There are 142 staff members who know and do work in foreign languages (76—one language, 47—two languages, 19—three or more languages).

Zuki boasts that he reads in seven languages and that he's learning another one now!

> Upper-level foreign language courses through the University of Bucharest. Those who enroll at the request of leadership are assisted in fulfilling their responsibilities.

You mean to tell me that someone's going to read my six-hundred-page manuscripts, while I learn who knows what language? Let's be real! I don't have time to go to the bathroom, and they're amusing themselves with foreign languages! Seriously, I don't know how they do it.

Hence, we conduct only serious conversations.

Roza:

—You know who people who just perpetrated a book or even just a poem look like?

—Who?

—What, to be more precise. Like a chicken that just laid an egg. I saw a movie about chickens on TV. What clucking, what puffing up of feathers, what a dance of self-satisfaction. All to attract the attention of the entire "poultry" (just replace the "ul" with an "e" here) world, the delight of the rooster and the envy of chicken competitors. I'm the best, esteemed associates. Look at the egg I have perpetrated! Not like you, who just squawk for no reason, your beaks drooling after our master, the rooster. I'm the cream of the crop!

—Please, and how would you know? Where do you see these authors after they publish their eggs?

Roza's very theatrical. I immediately pictured her as a fat hen when she showed us how the authors cluck away. We died laughing, Hermina and me both. Our Roza has a wide range of knowledge, including the unrecommendable kind. Censors shouldn't know the latest about a writer's life, they shouldn't concern themselves with the real person behind the text. The reverse is valid too. It's also possible that Roza makes things up here and there, and in certain situations.

Rozy tells us about her love affairs from time to time as well. The girl knows how to tell a story. How she fell in love with a poet while censoring his volume. What poems, what poems, she recites something that doesn't impress me at all, Hermina doesn't seemed moved by the handsome poet's talent either (Roza claims that he's handsome, I've got no clue what the guy looks like). After a book is censored by us, some time has to pass until the book appears, but she started reciting poems to him from his yet-unpublished volume. Oh, what a poet, oh, what verses! With that memory of hers, of a great admirer of poetry . . . Then the book appeared and she continued her glowing recitations, making tender and amorous declarations to him, especially using lines that she herself cut out and which therefore didn't appear in the volume. During one of these trysts, the last one it seems, the poet froze, his face darkened, and he asked her:

—Am I screwing the Securitate or is it screwing me? At least he didn't say Censorship! Our colleague said to him, completely sincere:

—You're the one screwing it!

The poet's mood lightened a bit, but they broke up and he started avoiding her, "then he left and we didn't see each other again," Roza ends her story nostalgically.

We're three women in this office, a delicate blonde one, a fiery brunette one, and me—so-so, older than them and calmer, in my opinion.

The fiery one (R.) almost seems to defend her texts with her breasts, or more precisely, her breasts protect the poems against potential dangers. Her maternal and nurturing breasts cover the texts almost protectively, so that her skillful hands don't find too much, don't cut out too much. But nothing escapes uncensored.

The delicate one (H.) seems almost to asks forgiveness of her texts, for making them undergo such an ordeal, that of censorship, she delicately holds each sheet between her two little fingers, so lightly that they could slip from her hands and float gently through the office. But nothing escapes uncensored by her either.

Our fiery colleague, to not use more exact language for her, with her dark, curly hair, with her enthusiastic heart, loving everything she sees, every time a new volume of poetry written by a young poet falls into her hands, she declares that she's in love with him, she looks him up (though we're not allowed to!), and won't stop until she's spent a night or two with him. She wants to go as far as possible in understanding poetry, to reach the pinnacle, she claims. And the pinnacle that she has in mind is the tip of his proud sword, she declares pathetically!

Then she recounts in excessive detail that delights the public of our offices (Lit. One and Two, she's stopped going to Foreign Publications and to Press, she doesn't get along with them), made up of bored women in general, in uncensored and adorable language, all that's essential in the work of the poet: he writes the way he screws, a bit of prelude in the beginning that makes you think of the Romantic poets, then intensive fertilization that makes you forget about poetic parallels, and, yes, oh!, he's awfully penetrating. For her, poets fall into one of only two categories: non-penetrating (a bunch of backward pessimists!) or penetrating, deeply penetrating, without stylistic evasion or subterfuge, which coincide, no surprise here, with the physiological act.

Did the sweet, poetic, dramatic, etc. message penetrate you

or not? we ask her whenever a new literary star appears on the horizon, curious whether this one (a star of the masculine sex) has also textualized her or not.

Then we ask her: And how exactly, dear, did he penetrate you?

The answer could be metaphorical, so metaphorical that uninitiated listeners wouldn't understand, but we get a huge kick out of it. As is the tool, so is the poetry! would be the shortest answer. Whenever her individualistic and socialistically reprehensible behavior reaches the ears of any boss, she allows herself to be penetrated by the subtle charm of Censorship as well, emanating from some small section chief who defends her to the higher-ups. But we also suspect that the real reason behind this apparent permissiveness is that Roza's precise descriptions are also useful to certain decision-makers, as they are more efficient than any readers' notes bogged down with boring details. More than one of us has been approached by the Securitate with some proposition (the girls would brag about it, but things didn't work out for me in this respect) and there's no doubt that our fiery colleague is working on two fronts, being useful to others as well, because we aren't the only ones interested in writers. So she's never got into any trouble.

She continually tortures pure and innocent Hermina (who always blushes during these moments) by warmly singing the praises of those courageous and salacious poets. Some, however, don't sleep with their admirers, that kind still exists, it seems. They take them on moonlit walks, they read them sensitive poetic texts, walking them back to their homes, without the aim and noble intention of spending a night together.

Some do this out of inner delicacy, others out of communist principles, some are married, others refuse to let themselves be tempted by suspicious strangers, or maybe they take intimacy seriously, theirs and that of others, respectful and shy. They're not all a bunch of assholes, so I completely understand why Rozella didn't turn out to be to everyone's liking. She ends up feeling contempt for them, so these are the ones who go down in reports as hopeless pessimists, decadent, and censorable.

It's been a while now that she's stopped confiding in us about this sort of thing. Either something happened to her or she received some order to leave poetic penetration for another time. Now she seems interested in our colleagues in Censorship, she disappears from the office for long stretches, then she comes back, but she doesn't go into copious intimate details except very rarely.

Hermina's up in arms, the blood rushes to her face from indignation when she discovers poets copying from one another! This girl's got a phenomenal memory! After combing through some manuscript, she gets upset, she turns red, agitated, she looks at us all ruffled and explains:

—A first-time author, usually someone who started late, well over thirty years old and even over forty, publishes a volume that no one pays attention to. Within the already established hierarchy, unknown poetic geniuses, newly arrived outsiders, are accepted only with great difficulty, very rarely, or not at all. Disappointed, the unknown poets, with an acute sense of their worth, with their exceptional sensitivity and intelligence, will publish at most one or two more volumes and then give up on a literary career. Well, then the great literary sharks, conniving and savvy in the ways of poetry, unscrupulously find inspiration in the works of these semi-unknown writers, they take images, metaphors, lines, all the best stylistic devices, and they create new, highly successful books.

I would never be able to split hairs like that, I've got no memory for poetry, I can't retain what I read, or what I cut out, but Hermina sometimes identifies not only one source of inspiration but even two or three for a reigning literary star. It's not part of my job description as a censor, dealing with plagiarism isn't one of my responsibilities. Hermina doesn't do too much in this direction either, usually remaining at the level of indignation. Sometimes we discuss how, having the same literary education, it's to be expected that many will write in the same way, without necessarily copying one another. I'm the peacemaker among us in the office.

If the texts aren't hostile, they can go on repeating the same things forever as far as I'm concerned. It's easier to censor the same book over and over again! They're stealing as if it's their job, if you were to believe Hermina (Roza isn't an authority on this aspect of poetry). I prefer to believe and am even convinced that the majority are actually talented and don't need to steal from each other. I'm sure Hermina exaggerates sometimes. I feel that in a novel everyone sets out to say something, to impose either their own point of view or, with the appropriate artistic means, that of the Party. In the novels I'm given, a stolen metaphor doesn't help and doesn't save anything, as for repeating the same subject over and over, there would be no point.

⤬

They're insufferable, with their reports! They let us look at it for only an hour again when they could've left us a copy! I asked them to, but they answered that the procedure for handling secret documents does not provide for certain classified information to circulate freely, in an uncontrolled manner. We even have to sign, individually, that we have familiarized ourselves with the contents of the document that must not be divulged.

After we've signed, the man leaves and we're lucky if we get an hour to at least skim through the provisions. Sometimes they personally inform us of some boring secret, having nothing to do in any case with literature, so that we can be aware of what we're signing. But usually our comrades with the secrets don't pay us any attention, we sign, we hold the document in our hands for a couple minutes, without bothering about its contents. No one says anything, we don't get upset, we don't get worked up; we, those of us in the Literature Department, don't care. For that hour, for as long as the document is in our office, we can take notes if something seems useful to us, basically no one's interested in what censors do with the document for the span of an hour. Maybe we copy the whole thing and it's no longer so secret. Maybe we leave the building with the notes and someone steals them—a boyfriend, a friend. But that's never happened and no one takes their notes from work home. We take out thick manuscripts, which we sign for but keep quiet about, otherwise we're not able to finish reading everything. I sometimes take out thick novels (to read at night or on Sundays, otherwise I can't hit my quota!), for example, but never secrets. My colleagues jot a few things down, for show, like me, then we return the document. Even if it's totally useless, it's good to have something written down, in case it comes up at some meeting, so we're not completely blindsided. So we can contribute to the discussion with a smart comment or two, as you can clearly see, we're in the know, we're aware of the latest trends in political issues and government secrets.

That's what they're putting increasing pressure on us to know—politics. But it's an utterly useless waste of time! At one point, I, like any censor worth her salt, wanted to enroll in a doctoral program, because we're allowed, even encouraged, to and it opens up new opportunities, the possibility of raises. They suggested I enroll in a doctoral program at the Stefan Gheorghiu Academy of Political Science. A PhD in political science—what good is philology?, censors don't need to know philology, we need ideologists, not copy editors. We ideologize, unideologize, as the case may be, that's our job. Enough to make your head spin! Well, if that's what the country needs, ideology it is. I'll parrot things back, I too will write up reports using the requisite expressions. For the time being, I'll hold off on the PhD in political science. I'm positive that none of these expressions, doctrines, precepts help me in censoring a poem. Whoever drives themselves nuts with ideology won't be able to make heads or tails of a novel afterwards (as in the case of our instructors, for example).

Our brave men from Training-Inspection have the habit of recruiting people who nearly faint from fright at first contact with the respective coms. That's all our ideologist instructors know how to do—to boast about their lofty mission and to inspire fear. But stick a poem in front of them!

Rozy, after saying the author's name, spouts off all the necessary details: she's married to someone high up in the party, they've also given her a well-paid, cushy position, she has two kids who've turned out well, she's sent them to the best schools, and now she's decided to publish poetry with a prestigious press.

Her preface is signed by the most important critic, the press accepts the manuscript on the first try. The manuscript contains nothing objectionable, poems about frail spring, youth is fleeting, birds fly, swallows, swans, gratitude for beloved parents, love for the husband who puts bread on the table—from an ideological standpoint there's nothing to cut. But it's worthless from absolutely all other points of view. Our comrade has suddenly felt the need, right before menopause, to make a tender debut in poetry.

Or maybe the guy, her husband, has some young secretary and the wife wants, with all her might, to demonstrate to him how accomplished she is in every respect, including intellectually-poetically, and we all know how young mistresses compare in that delicate department . . .

I bet she gives the mistress her book, with a withering dedication. Such a waste of paper . . . How many readers will be forced to buy a worthless book bundled together with one they want![II] And we, here in Censorship, this powerful establishment, have our hands tied. Under what pretext could we suppress the book? What could be the rationale? Could we write in the report that it's aesthetically null? No, we can't, that's not our assignment, not in this case, not now, basically not as long as her husband is a party member (because in other situations it wouldn't be a problem). We do that (aesthetic censorship) mainly when it's a new edition or if they specifically ask our opinion about those issues. But no one's asked our opinion about the book we have here in front of us. These namby-pambies with poetic aspirations rile me up more vehemently than any poet who fills a volume with innocent obscenities and vulgar trash. At least there my skills as a censor aren't wasted, while here, it snows rains sun clouds, foggy wind, dawn swan . . . crap with flowers added on . . . it weighs on your heart, seriously . . . We all suffer because of it, not just me.

My girls are lovers of good poetry and when you hand them something like this, you're killing them . . . I'm strong, I can get anything down, I've got an iron stomach, but my poor colleagues who adore brilliant verse get sick. Look, I've got red spots on my neckline, says Rozy. Shy Hermina complains, too, that she has slight palpitations, maybe it's her nerves (she doesn't get a bloody nose or start crying at the sight of this poetry, of course!). A dame like that with party connections and poetic dreams can put you in a bad mood for a week.

Comrades, the era of tractors and cranes is over, gone is the era of collectivization in literary circles. Now they're writing literature! It's on a higher level, the standards have changed. Your jaw drops when you read what's being written and getting approved these days. The little lady raised the young'uns and fixed her hubby's stew, how could she know? These madams who have succeeded in life and in their profession confuse vegetable borsch with poetry. They send you into early retirement. When you think that an intelligent person will read the first page of the book and then throw it across the room, that it's clear to the reader what kind of author wrote this, and we're required to carefully study all the poetical rantings of every pig and sow. How many talented men and women are out there, how many real poets have been waiting for their turn on the publisher's roster for years, and for a critic's preface they'll never get! Too bad the Party didn't marry the ones who were more talented, better educated, instead of all the idiots and schemers. Who, even when it comes to poetry, stick out their elbows and push to the front, wanting to be first in everything, even here.

We don't have many of those all-too-common types working in Censorship, our reputation for hard work precedes us. Basically, we fall into the third category of employees, the least desirable one.

The first category—we pretend to work, you pretend to pay us—is the majority and it's welcomed in the enterprises of the socialist field.

The second category—we pretend to work, you pay, you pay out the nose—is for the chosen ones, higher up, we know who they are.

The third category—we work, we break our backs working, you pretend to pay us—there are desperate folk like that, either because they have no choice or out of loyalty and zeal. We belong to this category. But at least we're not the lowest paid, with some seniority, and as a bonus for foreign languages our salary goes up 20 percent, it's actually decent for not being a supervisor. But compared to the work we do, the sleepless nights, the considerable demands, reading overtime, sometimes even on Sundays, compared to our comrades in other institutions who do only about half of what we do, it's not enough, and many leave citing the low salary, with good reason.

ᥫᩛ

Everyone's sitting quietly, busy with their own work. Usually we're reading when Z. comes in like a tornado and, looking straight at me, asks in that voice of his, like a scholarly tomcat wearing glasses on the bridge of its nose:

—What has our gentle and poetic killer been up to?

I get riled up:

—I wouldn't hurt a fly! I'm no killer!

This is followed by our colleague's speech about the murder I commit when I cut something, no matter what, from a text. Murderer, killer, our comrade bombards me and I can't, I'm not even able to, open my mouth, he doesn't let me get out a single word. Weapons with trip wires, delayed-action mass destruction, national bibliocide, censorship terrorism! I remember him repeating: you put the gun to its temple and pull the trigger. But you do even worse than that, you destroy more! A murderer, that's what a censor is!

The censor—a murderer? Because I recommend that 0.5 percent of a work that's 70 percent criminal be cut? All these sinful books that usually don't so much as kiss the Party's ass (gone are the days when you learned the alphabet and became a writer with a "bada bing, bada boom, the flowers are in bloom") and all the poems about bountiful hips and sadness, all the novels about love and passion, all the trash, regardless of whether the tone is correct and damning, they all fall into the hands of readers! What can I say? It's not something that began yesterday! Z. sometimes brings us a spicy passage from centuries ago, antiquity even, goodness, "ars amatoria," for example— they were corrupting readers even back then!

We have our hands tied, there's nothing we can do. Censors have never been as insignificant as they are under the communist regime! At most, censors can censor themselves! We're reduced to simple readers who give their opinion, anonymously, covertly. Censors used to be respected, they were treated like gentlemen! Their word carried some weight! They had their own ministry! While we're a publications directorate that operates clandestinely, we're just tools of the party, even less important than writers. But they're all complaining now, much more than in previous times, that censors are taking away their freedom. When have they ever had so many rights and privileges?! When has freedom ever been at their beck and call the way it is now? When has freedom meant the ability to insult your country and its values?

I want to bring up these arguments to Zuki the furious, I think of convincing comebacks, I have retorts, I wait for him to take a breath so that I can, finally, open my mouth, but he doesn't stop, he's not silent for a second, he doesn't let up until I start staring absently off into space with a frown and I'm tired of it all, just waiting for him to finish already and leave!

When he notices I've stopped listening to him, he becomes serious, he puts one of his big, heavy paws on my shoulder and says, slowly and distinctly:

—You're this institution's best censor, comrade Filofteia Moldovean! and leaves.

Even though there are three of us in the office, apparently I'm the only murderer and killer. He keeps the girls from their work with his ridiculous tirades, meanwhile they're glad that all his accusations are pointed at me and he finds no fault with them. He's the only one who calls me by the name on my ID. I've told him a thousand times that everyone calls me Dina or

Diana. Everyone's called me that since childhood. No, com. Z. declared himself smitten with the name Filofteia and that's the only thing he calls me, to tease me, to the general amusement of all. If someone were to call after me using that name, I wouldn't even turn around; the name feels strange to me and I don't like it one bit.

Z. says ecstatically:

—Not only are you a censor, your name is Filofteia to boot. Brilliant! and he laughs.

He told me how in France in the seventeenth (?) century, I don't know what kind of censor of theirs (religious?) was depicted as an old woman with scissors—Anastasia. It comes from the name of a bishop, Anastase, who had authority in that domain and was overzealous. And Filofteia is a better name for a censor than Anastasia, not etymologically, just naturally, phonetico-humanistically. A model name for a censor. All our censors should filofteia themselves. What kind of censors are these: Dorina, Ioana, Cristina, Stela, Carmen? No, we want Filofteias!

Look at Roza, how her eyes haven't moved from the page, how she's fidgeting, but she's not saying a word! I thought she'd fallen in love again with another manuscript, but I was wrong. Finally, after a long stretch of silence and intense concentration, she begins an unexpected discussion, copying away from a party report and dictating it to us so we can write it down as well. It's nice of her, we all chime in with arguments. In short, about:

What dazzling intelligence and refined sensibility would be ours if we had only our manuscripts to read! (An idea unanimously accepted!) But political training, party meetings, bureaucratic obligations, studying the directives, etc. are killing us. Or to be more precise, they're making us stupid, they're completely tiring us out and I can feel how they're turning us into a bunch of indifferent, docile little soldiers. Maybe that's what they want; who needs smart, mentally acute censors? On the one hand, they ask us to become well-rounded, to go to shows, to sports club, to learn foreign languages, nice, sounds great!, and on the other hand, all kinds of party instructions, precepts, duties, obligations, responsibilities, secrets, documents, all dry, lacking in real content, they don't communicate anything, but we're required to assimilate them. I feel like I'm turning into a stupid parrot (again, we all feel it and concede it unanimously). They tell us that this aspect of our growth in Censorship is very important, because we're in close, intensive contact with the ideas of the enemy and the Party doesn't want to lose us, they won't let their good men (women) be tempted to cross over to the camp of the conniving imperialists. We could get corrupted if they don't keep a close and strict watch over us . . . Especially those in literature? Why us? Gosh, we're only reading our own people, those in Export are much more exposed . . .

Here you go, the new proposal for the Action Plan for the Enhancement of Educational Efforts among the Ranks of GDPP Workers. We write as she dictates the proposal, commenting a bit here and there.

Objectives:

1. The formation of well-rounded intellectuals, with well-defined goals and innovative tendencies (I've got nothing against this, but it's easy to say, hard to do!);

2. Familiarity with socio-economic realities for the fostering of partisanship in the appreciation of daily phenomena (it doesn't make any sense, we work with the phenomenon of literature after all!);

3. The cultivation of a collective spirit and interest in public issues (that doesn't help me at all, but as a waste of time it's perfect!).

Good thing there are only three objectives.
But wait, it keeps going:
We have a first chapter about "party instruction." What do you all think that presupposes?

I. The current instructional year
For all the forms, an analysis of the roll-out of the program of study will take place so that

a) all responsibilities within the form can be carried out (what does "form" mean here?)

b) the degree to which the case studies correspond to levels and training categories can be determined (censors aren't trained anywhere, "the problems" are so general that the application of "knowledge" doesn't help us in our actual work)

c) a list of topics is generated from which each reader must prepare a presentation, on the basis of individual study (that's never been a requirement before—I,

for example, have never proposed a presentation and
nothing's ever happened, they've never taken it out of
my paycheck)

II. Preparations for the next instructional year
1. The reorganization of the program of study. The
basis of which will be constituted by individual study.

a) According to the specialization and level of participants, specialized groups will be formed in which they
will discuss case studies periodically (I propose a study
group on penetrating contemporary poetry, led by Roza).

b) Popular organizations together with department
management will establish a schedule of papers to be
delivered within the departments so that they can be
integrated into the topics of individual study.

c) According to department needs, the readers' gaps
in knowledge, and their level of preparation, a chart
will be drawn up with upcoming themes to be recommended to readers (by department) for individual
study.

Roza: Girls, we won't make it!
Hermina: Don't read any more.
Dina (me): How many pages do you have left there?
Roza: I've barely started. I've only read party instruction
to you, we have the chapters "Well-Rounded Briefings for
Readers" and "The Collective Spirit, Interest in Public Issues,
Encouraging Patriotic Sentiments" next, sixteen pages in all,
with details of the particulars that must be respected.

In addition to this, we also have:
Work issues:

1. Following up on the implementation of H.
regarding the reading of required publications:

a) the analysis of the reading of these publications

—in departments, the committee of the Union
of Communist Youth, and the trade union committee (trimesterly)

—the party collegium and organization (semesterly)

b) the introduction of monthly charts regarding the
projected dates for the discussion of material from
required publications

. . . girls, I'm going to skip a couple pages . . .

—We also have the responsibility of drawing up a presentation chart with a record of readings and sending it to the
departments.

—Not us, that'll be the job of some unfortunate person in
the Administrative Office.

The descriptions of foreign writers drawn up at the
train station will be copied and transmitted to all
departments.

—Oh, no, that's definitely going to fall on us.

—Do that many writers come? That task doesn't seem too
hard to me.

—No one is "too" hard, but to me there seem to be
"too" many!

General problems:

Participation in the contests "Cheerful Trails"
"Be a Book Lover" . . .

Drafting a program of future events for the Red
Corner, to include:

> —gatherings (literary, musical, etc.);
>
> —circles (music appreciation, creative writing,
> foreign languages, amateur photography, etc.);
>
> —professional issues (exchanges on different
> themes, the presentation of reports that depart-
> ments found exceptionally valuable, etc.);

c) suitably furnishing the Red Corner.

I'm not finished yet, I'm not reading everything. A few things
from the last chapter, the patriotic one. Copy them down for
yourselves, so you can choose the activities you want. Otherwise you'll be put in a group automatically and it'll be too late
to have a say.

Here we have:

1. Well-rounded development of athletic activities:

a) each reader who meets the physical health conditions will practice a certain sport (not one of us meets
them, we'll bring in a doctor's note!)

b) sports clubs will draw up a prospective plan for
well-rounded activity (including gymnastics, volley-
ball, bowling, women's handball, etc.)

Bowling? Who proposed this project? Girls, if this gets approved, my days are numbered!

2. Activation of the organization the Volunteer Association for the Support of Homeland Defense:

a) the inclusion of non-member employees

b) the progression to combat training and the handling of weapons for all VASHD members

c) creating radio, wireless telegraph, and research circles

3. Engaging employees in volunteer work activities

4. The ongoing organization of excursions (Really? But wait until you see where!):

– to industrial enterprises (monthly)

– to socialist agricultural units (every other month)

– to historic places outside Bucharest

– to picturesque places (that's better, but who knows what "picturesque" means in the conception of the author of the project, next thing you know you're at some pond in the Baragan—how picturesque!)

Meetings featuring artistic performances. "Our View" will organize an ample discussion on the theme of education . . . and so on . . .

A deafening silence has descended on our office . . . I don't say anything, but I'm thinking it's more important to work on the manuscripts we receive, and to get more involved only if you want to and can, from time to time, in something like this.

The project's awful, of course, but no one's overzealous when it comes to extra-censorial matters and at the end of the day it's just a proposal. Let's hope it won't get approved in its current form. It's written up this way for show, for people in general and for the party.

Roza breaks the silence:

—Hey, and "the handling of weapons," will that be our responsibility too? It's not enough that we handle manuscripts!

—As if you didn't know that our departments and services are called "units" in imitation of military structures. And if a state of emergency is announced, we consider ourselves to be already enlisted!

—You mean the "U" in the corner of documents means unit? I never would've guessed! (says Hermina, surprised)

—Yes, except in the beginning there was U. 10, U. 11, U. 12, two years later, something of the structure had changed and, at the same time, the numbers of the units also changed, now they all began with two and three, U. 20, U. 29, U. 30, U. 31, those were also before my time, com. Mirare, who retired before you got here, told me about them. Then the numbers changed again. For a few years, all the units began with the number five. Our number in Literature was U. 54, then Ideological Services merged with the Literature Division and we switched to number eight, what it was when I came in, and it hasn't changed since then. Except that Ideological Services disappeared, and Literature merged with Art and we became the Literature and Art Division . . .

—Ideology, poof?

—What do you mean "poof"? It was transformed into Social Sciences, then merged later with Technical Sciences!

❦

Com. Codrescu from the Administrative Office comes into our office when I'm not there. When I return, Roza, with that nasty mug of hers, lets me know and is just waiting for me to ask, "Okay," and "what did she want?" It annoys me that she's stringing me along, she could say whatever she has to say from the get-go, not wait for me to ask her, but since she's not saying anything, I give in and ask:

—Okay, and?

—She opened the safe.

—And?

—There was nothing in there, no notebook of directives. And she grins triumphantly.

—Mhmm, what a predicament.

—Since coming to this office, I've never seen the safe unlocked. Today was the first time, and I've been here for almost two years.

So Sarossi left with not only the key but also the notebook.

Roza and Hermina came into this office at the same time, I remember, it feels like just days ago, the years have gone by so fast . . . Hermina was transferred here because she bothered the people in the main office, she unsettled the other censors with her tears. In our office there's no one to unsettle, Roza isn't moved by womanish tears, me even less so. Roza's been shuttled around the most out of us, first she worked in Press, just a short while, where some said she couldn't really handle the work, then in Import-Export, where, upset that she couldn't handle the work in Press, she was overzealous and they came close to firing her, now she's at Literature. They didn't fire her, because she knows too much and it's better to have her here where they can keep an eye on her instead of who knows where. I had worked with Sarossi and com. Mirare, who retired, she'd been here since the first days of Censorship and, sometimes during breaks, she'd tell us some stories about how it was at the beginning, stories that left us, the younger ones, with our mouths agape.

—And what did com. Codrescu say?

—She was surprised. She said that someone had to have two notebooks somewhere, because right now she doesn't have a single spare one.

—Let's hope the coms from the Securitate won't be back any time soon. In any case, we don't need that notebook. Did she leave the key?

—It's right here.

—Fine, now we have a key, but we don't have a notebook . . .

At first, I, too, thought that Hermina suffered on account of being a censor, she suffered because she has to cut out a beautiful line or an illicit word. She cries at the drop of a hat, she reads and cries, she censors and cries. I kept racking my brain: how is it that she doesn't make any mistakes, no one criticizes her, and she handles everything impeccably? Later, I began to understand her: she cries when a line is beautiful. The beauty of the text moves her. She doesn't shed a tear when cutting something out, the censorial intervention as such doesn't affect her. She doesn't pity the cut-up text, she doesn't cry because she's cutting it. Reading and censoring are two different operations. You cut out wrong ideology, but you leave beauty alone, it gets to stay. It's regrettable, of course, when these two happen to meet (ideology and beauty, not censoring and reading). Without the latter (Hermina quietly declares), censors would die. Beauty is the lifesaving blade of grass that keeps the ant from drowning. I don't at all feel as if I'm on the brink of dying, regardless of much beauty I do or don't cut out from a book. I feel even less like an ant.

My conclusion is that we've all got something of the madman (madwoman, as the case happens to be) in us. But Hermina, making these kinds of statements, has more than a little in her. I don't tell her my opinion, it's better to hold back. If I'm not paying attention and I ask her something while tears are trickling down her face, she ignores me, she pretends she doesn't hear me and she continues crying, if, accidentally, I repeat myself, she shoots daggers at me, turns her back toward me, or hides her face in the text. She doesn't answer. There's no point in insisting. There's nothing left for us (Roza caught on as well) to do except respect her moment of tearfully savoring the beauty of the text.

Censors have their quirks too.

It's too bad that we're not given some details about the authors along with their manuscripts. So we can get an idea, so we can know what else they've done, what else they've written. Books by known authors don't contain bio-bibliographical info either. We turn to the *Dictionary of Contemporary Writers* from 1971, good thing it exists. At the GDPP there are two copies, we keep one for ourselves, the second is for the other literati. We don't lend it to anyone, whoever needs it can take it from the main office.

But sometimes not even the dictionary is enough. Hence our Rosalinda is invaluable. She has no idea when the writers were born or where they went to school (that can be looked up in the dictionary), but only she knows who's been with whom, the identity of the muse (man or woman) inspiring the poet (or poetess), what real experiences formed the basis of a poem, a story, or even a novel, who will win a prize, whose "imprimatur for celebrity" the party has signed off on, who will represent the country abroad at some festival or contest and why, who is writing what exceptional, astounding new thing, my dear, there are, I won't deny it, enough crapheads publishing to supply the people with beautifully scribbled-on toilet paper, because a fresh book is better than a tattered newspaper,[12] and if you happen to be constipated, you can also experience some poetic revelations there, in the thick of it, but we've got some amazing writers too! What writers! What books are coming in!

To my astonishment, our seductive younger colleague also knows which of us from Censorship will be assigned to read the wonderful masterpieces that were just released this year. Sensational books that even censors quote and actually recite passages or memorable lines from . . . She knows rather a lot for a young and fetching censor . . .

Of course I felt like making a fuss about it, maybe expressing justified disapproval, because I see that, even though I'm unanimously considered to be a very good censor, with experience and seniority, last year I also received the Worker of Merit award—so my efforts and competence were officially recognized—even then, I never get those kinds of wonderful manuscripts! "Serious" works, belonging to well-known authors who are studied in textbooks, are never or only very rarely assigned to me . . .

Rozette, who gets the manuscripts of poets, even the best ones of recent years (according to her), is quick to explain to me how things stand: the best writers no longer need the best censors (she pronounces the words softly and slavishly, like a fox that wants to get the raven's cheese)! Good poets are just as good, maybe even better than we are (sometimes) at censoring, otherwise they wouldn't have gotten to where they've gotten and they wouldn't be enjoying what they're enjoying. Idiots are given a chance by the party, who's generous with literary folk; it's only in their case, in order to save something from their work, so it won't all be thrown straight in the trash, that censors are needed . . . The good and very good ones have already been read and reread by the time they get to us, at the highest levels, the party takes care of them, and the Securitate knows what volume they'll write before they've put down a single line. A very good writer has a censor alter ego inside who's just as good. We give these works, so that the party, up there, doesn't feel stupid, a perfunctory reading rather than carefully censoring the volume.

The party is also a reader and consumer of literature, I'll have you know, over there they read not only our readers' notes, which actually, in general, I rather doubt that they read (we all doubt it, but we keep on writing them!), not that they wouldn't be of interest to them, but there aren't enough party members to keep up with all the notes we write! Even if they were to read them 24-7, it would take them more than a lifetime to be able to even skim all the wastepaper (well, I wouldn't use a term as harsh as that) we issue. But there's a vested interest here, they've got an opinion as well and we can't cross them, we don't contradict them when the fate of the book has already been decided and it doesn't depend on us anymore, when all the decision-making entities and authors have come to an agreement, our mission being merely symbolic. Ah, yes, if the volume happens to be criticized, we'll be the ones to blame, and if it's praised, then the party will ask itself rhetorically whether these censors are really necessary, when our writers no longer need to be reviewed so many times in so many stages (which are useless and bureaucratic, as we all know!). And an assortment of semi-illiterate lackeys who can't stomach Censorship will repeat this in unison over and over again.

And you're too good, you know that, you wouldn't write a flimsy report, you wouldn't hide its mistakes, you'd point them out, you'd intervene, propose things, you'd make arguments and it could become evident that, up there, those who are reading and approving things are either stupider or more careless than they should be. We're not discussing now whether or not it's possible for you to be in this position. But, if you were to write a report like that, you'd risk putting our supervisors in an awkward position. Our supervisors are chosen by the party, approved by them up there, you see? Who are you, smarty-pants, to make them a laughingstock? They'll start up again: that we're stuck in a rut, backward, bureaucrats, that we don't understand the changes in society. Meanwhile the poets will take advantage of this and their writing will become more sophisticated and more vehement. When the party decides that they've crossed a line, only then will they turn them over to us, with clear orders, when they need to be stopped. In this way we'll know ahead of time, it's a game here and we're not the only ones thrown into it, we're in with the Securitate, who also adores giving us orders. Meanwhile, the Party is kind to everyone, but when someone needs to be punished, then censors and Securitate officers are bad. In a situation like this one, we'll be the scapegoats.

⁓

I think I'm careful not to offend anyone. I try to be as thoughtful and sweet as possible to my officemates. But what kind of liberties do they take? Why are they laughing? Me, a robot? The square head in that poem isn't me! They've bombarded me with all kinds of insults. Look at what the girls recite to me!

RONDEL ABOUT A ROBOT
—by Cicerone Theodorescu
retitled "The Blockhead's Rondel"

A square head made of tin,
The automated guard robot,
Considered himself, with a grin,
The keeper of every thought.

. . . Fine the work—and hard—for him
Watching, even in his blind spot!
But woe to us, a shame and sin,
When he sees us and we're caught.
A square head made of tin.

Blockhead—a stubborn person, a stupid individual (good thing I didn't ask the girls)

Tin—low-quality metal, object made from sheet metal (as if you have round heads embroidered with golden threads, oh, rhymesters!)

I once said that it isn't hard to work with poetry and that it's a greater and more complicated responsibility to concentrate on novels. I still think so today, I haven't changed my mind. And I think that I'm issued mostly novels precisely because I have more experience and they know they can rely me. How many readers does a novel have? Tens of thousands, maybe even hundreds of thousands, while poetry has a much more modest, limited audience.

My young and arrogant girls who, since they began working here, haven't received more than two mediocre novels at most, the rest have been only slender volumes of poetry, are retaliating. They're doing their hair during work hours and dying of boredom, while I'm reading novels even on Sundays. They've told me that poetry is harder than novels, because in novels all you have to do is cut something out and no one misses it and no one suffers, while in a poem sometimes even a punctuation mark matters . . . When you cut out a word from a poem, you have to replace it with something, sometimes you have to change the whole line, change everything, but in such a way that the reader won't guess what was wrong and what was changed. So that even the poet who wrote it will be amazed at how beautiful his poem looks and sounds, after passing through "the fine sieve" of Censorship. If it were possible and if they were honest, they'd acknowledge that, sometimes, it's even better.

So, if you don't have any affinity for and any sensitivity, attraction, or calling toward poetry, then how can you bring a crippled poem to a healthy state of improvement, as healthy as it can be?

"Gobbledygook, gobbledygook

Someone's caught a fish on a hook" (instead of censored this book).

They recite contemptuously, but I'm hearing it for the first time, something like that has never passed through my hands, I don't understand why such a phrase is being attributed to me in that tone of voice! You have to be a bit of a poet to make an intervention, not just a censor who hacks away blindly left and right. Sure, they know lines by heart and I don't, they fall in love with the poets they censor, while I couldn't care less who they are, I don't want to get more involved than I am, and I'm sure I'm right. Those lines about the square head don't refer to me. There's no point in wasting my breath on the girls, but it bothers me!

After this discussion, I decided not to ask for, and not to accept, poetry manuscripts anymore. I was upset with the girls, but deep down I know they're kind of right. Either I should've been born a man, harsh and ruthless, or I'm a cold and insensitive woman who won't allow myself to be moved by anything.

When it comes to a manuscript, I'm first and last a censor and I fulfill my obligations as best as I can.

We've had discussions about widening our horizons. A censor

must be one step ahead of writers and know about everything going on in this country in as many and as widely differing subjects and fields as possible. Otherwise, how would you know what's hostile, what should be banned? Even if you were to memorize the notebook of directives, it still wouldn't help you, faced with a poem you're vulnerable and defenseless. It's also necessary that you be a good psychologist, and have good intuition, and be, okay, a bit of a poet, you have to understand current politics and, if possible, future politics as well.

I came into the office today with a tote bag full of books which I took out and noisily plunked down on the table, so the girls would see and die of envy, they, the sensitive poets, who, besides knowing about a couple poets with dimples, don't know anything. They stared at my stack of books, probably trying to make out the titles, but they didn't say anything, they didn't ask anything, they didn't betray any curiosity, not even for show, to be polite.

∽

I can tell who among my colleagues hesitates. Hesitation is the most reprehensible trait a censor can have. If he doesn't believe in his mission, if he isn't eager for self-sacrifice, it also means he's not fortunate enough to be fit for the lofty mission bestowed by the Party. You shouldn't get caught up in small problems; the party's also made up of people who are only human, some make mistakes from time to time, but our mission's greater than human mediocrity, it's an ideological mission, of the utmost importance, and you're not allowed to become discouraged, to hesitate, to fail, to lean toward a better-paying job with fewer responsibilities, you're not allowed to dream of publishing books yourself, to be in the spotlight, to stand out, to secretly hate the institution, to despise it and criticize it behind closed doors, to complain about the hateful human condition. The burden is too noble and too great. That's what I believe!

I was there during the good old days, when we were called just Literature, then Literature-Ideology, now they've merged us with Art. It's a change in name only, just like the other ones, it doesn't change our processes or activities, and I, for one, am not affected in the least by it. But something's happening now, I can feel it in the air. You have to have a nose for intuiting the future, Zuki always tells us. Let's learn from authors, like the birds they can tell when the winds are changing. We, here, really should be able to predict things even better than they can, to point them out, to redirect them. These new directions will be imposed on us as well—yes, but when you're spoon-fed you lose the ability to guess on your own.

You be the ones to change literature, don't wait for it to change you. Evolve! Move forward! Transform! (Zuki makes wide gestures, like Lenin in the textbooks, but I don't tell him, because it would upset him.) The best ones here are in Export, you should be in closer contact with them, read a newspaper of theirs from time to time, especially one of the ones they hold back from subscribers and the public, and see what kind of reader's notes they write, what's being said and how things are being viewed in the world. You, here, have been bogged down with lousy manuscripts, that bore even you and don't help you to grow at all. If you stay like that, in this state, your services will very quickly become unnecessary, everything evolves now, and very quickly. Don't get stuck in a rut in a narrow profession and leave it at that. Don't become complacent with the idea that you've learned the trade and now you're in business. Whoever said that a censor has to be well-rounded was no idiot. Political acumen, foreign languages, interdisciplinary studies, communist mindfulness—do you think those are empty words? If you don't feel how thin the wire you're walking on is and what chasms are beneath you, you're wasting your time in Censorship!

I don't feel the thin wire, nor the chasms, but my colleague Zukerman manages to set me on edge!

᭙

Roza knows the names of all the censors in the institution. It was that one, from Training-Inspection—handsome, serious, seems smart . . . Ah, Dumitru Milatinov, married, one child. They're all rather handsome, slim, young, we also have a few who are older than forty, but only a very few. Only Z. is not young, nor that handsome, nor slim, but there's something seductive about him, attractive, and when he speaks to you and on top of that smiles at you, he wins you over. He has a gentleness in his voice, there's something comforting in the way he pronounces his words. I've realized that, while I don't know the names of other people, I don't communicate with them, not a day goes by without my talking to Z. Grandpa's back again for you, Roza teases me, though he talks enough to her as well.

Or: he's coming to talk to you, but he's also keeping us

from doing our work. He's definitely got a crush on you. He's smitten, Roza says, and I don't know whether she's being sarcastic and contemptuous or not.

In moments like these, I'd like for him to be just a bit more handsome, just a bit better dressed. Thinner and less bald, there's no point in wanting that. When, at some meeting, he explains something condescendingly, he asserts his point of view, and our little bosses sit and listen without making a peep, everyone either is silent or agrees with him, I'm happy, I'm glad, I'm not embarrassed for him.

❧

Roza makes her rounds through the offices and, after about an hour, she returns victorious with the latest institution news and she solemnly declares:

—Crap has appeared in Romanian literature!

We've come to expect anything from her mouth, but we are not prepared for a statement like that. Surprised and confused, Hermina and I get caught up in speculations:

—Another awful pretentious first-time author . . .

—No, real crap, four letters long, in the novel of a great writer.

—Well, how many times have I censored four-lettered crap until now, I begin, and Hermina nods her head approvingly . . .

—Well, exactly, you censored it, you made it disappear, you cut it out, you delicately wiped it off the face of the earth, but this one comes with approval from high up, from the party, and it can't be censored. They're trying to come up with solutions.

—Goodness, what are you saying?! we exclaim, riled up, even more surprised. How is it possible?! This is very serious . . .

—Yes, and all of Office Number One of the Literature and Art Division is busy studying, analyzing, proposing, laying out, breathing in, breathing out, perspiring, stinking, crying, laughing . . . They're all circling around the problematic little piece of crap . . .

—And?

—In the end they arrive at a conclusion . . .

—To change it . . .

—No, the people at the publishing house could've change it . . . But the author requested (he ordered, what have we come to, what nerve!) that no one touch his crap, to leave it there, not to censor his delicate expressions.

—How exactly does it show up?

—In the expression: "You're a piece of crap!"

Yes, it's a precise expression that's hard to replace. The meaning is "you're a worthless person" and it's a given that the Party and the Securitate are aware and have given the publishing house instructions to indulge the author. So we're dealing with high-level, or to be more precise, uncensorable, crap. Of course, when something stinks, the Party and the Securitate wash their hands of it and leave us to rack our brains and befoul ourselves with the literary excrement. The party handles swallows and little flowers, censorship handles crap. The first suggestion was to leave just the first letter: "You're a piece of c." But "c." could mean cake, caution, cardboard, conscience, creation, clarity, candy, etc. It got shot down. The proposal that was accepted and voted for unanimously was to leave the first and last letter, and put a dot between them for both missing letters: c dot dot p. If you put in more dots or fewer dots, it might make you think of other words again. Riiight, they'd have been better off leaving the crap there in all its splendor. It seems funny, but this situation will turn out to be the crappiest for us. For better or worse, at least we censored something, we changed it a bit, we were able to chase two rabbits and catch both. I'm glad that I wasn't the one assigned to the crappy manuscript. If I weren't a censor myself, I'd die laughing.

Now all of Censorship's in an uproar. Riled up, as one, from Press, from Sciences, even from Small Publications. Helpless, all out of ideas. Yes, it's a historic piece of crap. A huge turning point in the history of literature. And of Censorship. If this "piece of crap" is released, I have a feeling that very crappy times are to follow for Romanian literature and not only that (namely, also for Censorship). I mean, if authors go with all their crap straight to the party and they give us orders, not this, this yes, don't touch this, don't cut that, if they catch on that this is how it works and they can pull it off, what role would we continue to have? Okay, writers are writers, they're always demanding and don't want anyone to touch their masterpieces, but the publishing houses? After keeping manuscripts in their depositories for years, to the point where the authors have lost all hope of ever seeing them published, they're ready to file a complaint that Censorship's one month late and it's because of us that books aren't being published on time, we're holding up editorial production! Listen to them! They've shoved their crap down our throat on purpose, to humiliate us and to demonstrate to the party that they're right, they're adept and useful, while we're good for nothing.

—You were very young, I hadn't started working at Censorship yet either, but I know from Mirare about the time love was released! It was the beginning of the '60s . . . That's what the censors would say then. We're going to release love! After that, literature changed radically, true poetry was born, lyrical, emotional, profound . . .

—Exactly! It's one thing to release love, a positive and uplifting emotion, and something totally different to release crap! Just one decade later! And what will we release another decade down the road? At this rate, and the way things are "evolving," in a decade we won't even exist! Censorship will be released—from our responsibilities! Can you imagine what will happen then? What is our party thinking?

—That's evolution and we can't stop it.

—At least if things evolved, but they're devolving, they're getting worse, and I don't understand why. Where did we go or are we going wrong? What are we not offering enough of or not doing well enough or maybe doing too much of, what? What can we do to have in front of us on our table our long dreamed of manuscript? In which there's nothing to cut out! The ideal book! So I can leave Censorship, so I can quit and become a beekeeper! Instead, we get crap. That's what's coming out of the mouths and pens of these writers! That's their great socialist achievement! Not one of them has nothing to cut out, they've all got something or other to censor, not one of them can do without our polite adjustments.

—Come on, we're not overflowing with politeness.

—Has someone ever said "thank you"? Spend some time with them and see what they say about censors. They don't even try to hide it from Securitate officers, they come right out and say what they think. How can our relationship not be reciprocal?

—So it's contempt, not politeness.

—I don't hate any of the writers, I don't despise them. I think of them as people who are able to do something I can't. They have talent, they have the willpower to complete a work of sizable proportions. I write a two-page report and I'm sweating from all the effort and exhaustion, but them, look at what bricks they're sending us. (What's right is right, even here, in this notebook, I don't write more than two pages a day and only if I don't have to turn in reader's notes or reports.) Well, and two pages a day times thirty days equals sixty pages a month, in three or four months the novel's done . . .

We're all in a bad mood and butting heads because of a word. I'm not going to debate with the girls anymore. It's a waste of time.

∽

Three women in the office who are still young. Sometimes men, all young, come by and they sniff around us, they study us. Or rather, they come to see Rozinda. They start out, for example: "Girls, I'd like to invite you out dancing tonight," and they're staring intensely only at her. She answers, just for herself, of course: " I can't." Then it sometimes happens that the men want to try their luck a second time as well. Hermina, I'm not sure whether she feels offended that she wasn't their first choice or she never goes out on dates or to those kind of events, maybe she has other reasons as well, always refuses abruptly, without giving any details. A third attempt, meaning a situation in which someone invites just me, is never tried, and the men politely excuse themselves for bothering us and leave. Meanwhile I can hardly wait for one of them to ask me out as well, so that I can give the good-for-nothing a withering "no" for asking me out after eyeing those stupid, snot-nosed younger women. Well, the men might be younger too, it's definitely possible, and I'm not upset anymore, after all that.

One came in today as well, from Social (and Technical) Sciences. As soon as he entered, I thought he'd make a perfect match for Hermina. Both of them blond, shy, sensitive, etc. Come in, come on, and don't get lost in Roza's cleavage, she's out of your league. He comes in and gets flustered, he even starts stuttering. He'd memorized some line and had kept repeating it until he got to our office door and, when the door opened, out of nervousness, he must have forgotten it. He also made a move as if he were going to go back out the door (out of fear or shame) and we were very surprised. Still, in the end, he issued the banal invitation: "Let's go out to a movie, girls." Kind of stuttering, looking off in the distance, not at the seductive neckline. Then he got scared at how daring the phrase sounded and stopped strategically next to the door, actually next to my desk. Roza, spoiled by men, cut him short: "I'm busy." Hermina and I felt that the cleavage was far from his mind and that this time the young man had addressed his invitation not only to Roza. I restrained myself from commenting, I felt bad for him, I left him to Hermina. The boy, however, didn't repeat his invitation, but just stood there overwhelmed by the busty one's refusal, as if he'd been refused by all the women in the GDPP and the entire House of the Press, as if the sky and the ceiling had fallen down on him, he was silent, helpless, and somewhat pathetic. He didn't have another response memorized and he was, probably, trying very hard to think of what to do and what to say. He stayed like that for a while, then, finally, he began explaining something to us, but it was so disjointed and stammered, that Hermina and I could barely keep from laughing, while ill-mannered Roza had covered her face with a manuscript and was laughing so hard she was crying.

—We·at So-social Sci-sci-iences don't have e-extra-institutu-tional activities, our bo-boss reco-co-co-mended that I take the girls from Literatu-ture to a mo-movie, that he'll add points to my record. And in the main off-office there are too ma-many girls (about eight, we know, and here it's just us three), so I thought I'd invite you three to a very good mo-movie.

—All three of us?

Even Roza seemed surprised, but it would've been pointless to ask him if he would've preferred just one of us. I think he was so scared that he was seeing right through us. Roza already said she wasn't going, he's not my type either, maybe Hermina might like him, but, out of shyness or because she's embarrassed in front of us, she'll probably say no . . . The boy finished his round of explanations and breathed a sigh of relief, looking hopefully at each of us in turn. His eyes pleaded with us as if he were a beggar or someone dying of thirst asking for a sip of water. There was nothing deceitful, nothing flirtatious, nothing manly in his gaze, this guy's definitely never kissed anyone in his life, if we don't accept his invitation, he'll go to the bathroom and cry until quitting time.

—What movie were you thinking of inviting us to?

The young man searched his pockets, he took out a half sheet of paper and started reading:

—At the Vasile Roaita movie theater they're playing *The Ki-king's Je-jester*, at the Tudor Vladimirescu *Swamp Dog*, at the Constantin David *The Hu-hunchback*, the Al. Sahia *The Man with Two Fa-faces*, the August 23rd *Operation Co-cobra*, the Grivita *Fi-fishing in Troubled Wa-waters* . . . I heard that *The Ki-king's Je-jester* is very go-good . . .[13]

Roza burst into such uncontrollable laughter that it scared us at first, then we all started laughing. I looked at Hermina and then said to him:

—Thank you for your invitation, we'd love to go with you to a movie, to see *Je-jester* at Vasile Roaita, tonight at six!

—Give this list of films to comrade Mastora, I'm sure he won't feel like laughing at all when he sees it . . .

Neither of the girls objected anymore. We set a time and place to meet up. The child was overjoyed! How he's going to brag about his triumph! Censorship will be in an uproar! How many snot-nosed kids are dreaming about our little Roza and maybe also Hermina! And look who he's going out with! He was so happy that it made me glad I was able to help a person out. The girls were also smiling. We should all do a good deed now and then. He's a good kid, but he's so shy, how did he end up in our institution? After he left, Roza filled us in: that was comrade Wolfe, he's actually really good at what he does, he's shy and scared just when it comes to girls, etc.

Com. Mastora, the head of Art Services, wrote a note about the list of movie titles that, from a political standpoint, shouldn't be matched up with the names of movie theaters and awarded comrade Wolfe three hundred lei for his vigilant attitude. We half-jokingly, half-seriously suggested that he split the award with us because he never would've caught on by himself.

Roza, after the movie, among other impressions:

—He's a good guy, too bad his name is Wolfe! He'd make a comrade named Hurd very happy! Don't we have a Hurd who's lost her way somewhere in our institution?

According to Roza, the last name Moldovean goes with Ungureanu, so I need to look for an Ungureanu, Iancovici goes with Johnson (shush, someone might hear you, where would we find someone with that name here, fine, then with a Petrovici). And Toth goes with Vass.[14] Why Toth and Vass, I don't know, maybe she's got a new boyfriend? I tell her that, actually, my maiden name is Long and she predictably replies: You need to get yourself a Short. Opposites attract. Ha, and com. Limb from Press should find himself a Boddy somewhere! It's a tree limb, not a human one, so it would go with Reed, Bush, or even Flower. I bet he'd like Flower. Com. Flower dash Limb! Laughter and good cheer in our small little office.

Though I'm the only one with a Romanian name in our office, my colleagues consider themselves to be the most Romanian out of everyone in Censorship. What, you mean to say Iancovici isn't a purely Romanian name? How could you think that? Hermina says, honestly appalled. Wasn't even our great national poet Eminescu originally Eminovici? Roza doesn't claim that Toth is a Romanian name, but it's not her maiden name, so three 100 percent Romanian women here.

⚬᷄

If Wolfe took us out to a movie it means that he had a very low rating, otherwise he wouldn't have put himself through that torture, the poor guy. This week our comrades are contesting the ratings "good" and "satisfactory," which would mean goodbye, medals, goodbye, bonuses, goodbye, promotions, for more important and more monetarily rewarding jobs. Management goes back over profiles, makes changes to reviews and comments, if need be, but keeps the ratings the same, for those contesting them. There are three ratings: very good, good, satisfactory. I'm an A-level Reader, which is the highest level you can reach and I don't want to become a supervisor, so I don't really care about these. But we're all at "very good." An exemplary office.

Our office is privileged. We don't have a section chief in the main office, I'm the closest thing we have to one here. Com. Molho, the executive director of our division, told me she trusts me, she asked me to take care of my younger colleagues, to guide them when necessary, to help them out, so months pass without her stopping by our office. Even if we had someone decent, you can't really say everything you have on your mind when your supervisor's right there, you can't really visit with other colleagues, and you can't be that late. Sometimes someone drops in to give us the latest news.

About our delicate, sweet E. T. (Emeric Tulpan, where did a name like that come from?): the com had been attending the university writers' group for some time. Rather handsome and kind of out of place in that environment, he was noticed by a young student. They liked each other, the story goes. So she's a student, and he's, what? He also had to say where he worked or where he studied (we're not allowed to reveal where we work).

He ended up saying that he worked as a copy editor at some obscure magazine. The girl looks into it, she lets her group of friends know, they do some serious investigating, the magazine, yes, exists, but no good-looking copy editor by that name works there. The girls' friends decide that he's a filthy Securitate officer. The group actually was full of Securitate. But the kind that's deep undercover, innocent ID-card-carrying students or even ambitious poets. And what did they do to him, the poor guy, when he went there? Word is they got a kid to pour water on his head and pull his beautifully curly hair. They probably also spit on him as he was leaving. He's still in a state of shock . . .

While we were stunned and pitied him, our blonde one shoots back:

—Good thing they thought he was just Securitate, they're everywhere, everyone's gotten used to them, but if it had occurred to them that he's a censor, he wouldn't have gotten out of there alive! For a poet, a censor is ten times more nefarious than an average Securitate officer. The officer meddles in your life, but the censor meddles in your work. And the dog's life a poet leads—what does it mean to them? Nothing. Instead, their work is all that's best and most meaningful in their life, the whole point of their life, their sacrifices, their trials and frustrations, from which you, cruel and heartless censor, cut out whatever you feel like.

I never expected such a realistic outburst to come from Hermina! To which our pillowy Roza adds a few more observations:

—Those scumbags from the publishing houses cut things out left and right, to the point where there's nothing left for us to do. Yeah, sure, poets are all riled up against the GDPP, they imagine we're the whole of Censorship, if their volumes don't appear, the GDPP's to blame, it blocks, it cuts things out. And how often is it that their masterpieces never even get to us, the publishing houses block them, we don't even hear about them. Who proposes the publisher's roster? Us? Never. We don't draw up the lists of books to appear each year, ever, we don't even approve them, no one shows them to us. We know they exist only because our secret sources have told us! Everything that comes to us is approved. If a volume gets to the GDPP safely, it will definitely appear, and quickly. We here get fined if we keep a manuscript more than a few days. Not like at the publishing houses, where it's months, years . . . I mean, I recently received a volume with poems dated 1966, 1967, 1968. They stop at 1968 and now it's 1974, the text's good, there's nothing objectionable about it, where has it been all this time? We don't have access to the first version of the authors' manuscripts, we can't track what in particular was selected, whether a good book was blocked, whether it didn't get approved, what exactly happened and why. Proposals are discussed at the Division of Publishing Houses, with which we never cross paths and don't have any kind of relationship. And a book editor is allowed to hold up an author for two years or more, he makes him change and revise the content, asking him to keep taking things out, to cut out more, because, you see, "this won't make it past Censorship." By the time they get to us, some manuscripts are so different from their initial form that the author could claim he's written a different book, and, to top it all off!, after so many cuts and additions, no one can be sure that the volume is in better shape than it was in the beginning. Pretty much all editors toy with their authors, and we have to save appearances, to put on an act. But the most disgusting editors are the ones who themselves write. There are many such editor-writers (they need to put bread on their table too), mediocre and jealous. Sometimes a new genius falls into their hands, and they destroy him, pulverize him, the guy's feathers are flying everywhere, he forgets his own name, that's how scared he is of being brutally censored. And there's nothing we can do about it. Only Securitate agencies that have access to the original manuscript could still intervene. For example, if the editors completely overstep their bounds, they can be punished. Usually those hellhounds come to an understanding though and it's still the writer who stands to lose. Whichever way you turn it, in the end, editors are the good guys, and the monster who's to blame is still the censor. No one cares about the future of literature. We're the only ones who lose any sleep over it, it breaks our heart, we offer support and assistance, and still, in the eyes of writers, we're the worst, a bunch of criminals. Us, the destroyers of gems, of masterpieces! We're the ones they hate, not the editors, not the Securitate officers. It seems unfair to me.

It seems unfair to me too. Who's to know whether the publishing editor didn't steal some brilliant line of poetry from the volume that he blocked, banned, edited to death. What wouldn't I do to have access to the raw volume in its pure, untouched state!

—To some editors you have to come with presents, invitations to dinners at restaurants, cakes, flowers. How fast your future book gets published and how much is cut from it depends on them.

—Can you imagine something like that in our case? Okay, maybe not flowers and cakes, but at least a sincere thank you . . .

—Don't hold your breath . . .

❦

While everyone's engrossed in their reading, I don't know what gets into Rozella, who begins philosophizing:

—Maybe poets aren't trying to provoke us, they aren't tempting us, they just awaken something dormant in us. Maybe they're not a bunch of rotten, arrogant parasites who don't want to work. Maybe they're courageous to risk being different, to yell certain truths without which we'd be headed back toward living in caves, toward the monkey some say we all come from, and censors should cut things out lovingly, because, without writers, how could we earn a respectable living? So, long live the writers, may they keep writing.

Speeches like that get on my nerves, it's completely tone deaf when it comes to the manuscript I'm struggling with right now, which is giving me a headache. I haven't written in my notebook for a week. Hermina doesn't react to the hard-line enthusiasm of our colleague either.

Nothing moves me in their texts, neither crude passages, nor romantic descriptions, nor mysterious scenes, sensual poems don't excite me, nothing touches me, I'm cold and objective, I have a clear head and I never fall apart, I never lose my cool in tricky situations.

❦

I calm my colleagues down. They're unhappy that we have to read all kinds of documents that are of no interest to us, that have nothing to do with literature. Hey, we'll be enriched, we'll expand our horizons, we can't refuse . . .

Rozy never admits it and says, "I don't know," if I ask her something, then, while we (Hermina chimes in as well) try to come up with an answer and rack our brains over some issue, what could it be, what should it be, she jumps in: Yes, that's what I wanted to say, that's what I was thinking too, but you took the words right out of my mouth!

—Mr. Giurgiu from Press came looking for you . . .
   —What did he want?
   —He didn't say.
   —If he needs something, he'll be back. I've got no business with Press.
   —If it were up to us, we'd have no business with anyone. But I've lost count of all the times we've had to go from one division to another . . . There are many circumstances and situations, you know, when we're the ones having to run to Press, and to Sciences, and to Export, and they have to come to us too, though I'm sure it gives them no great pleasure.
   —I hope what happened last year doesn't happen again, when two of the short stories cut from a volume that came to the Lit. Division appeared in a newspaper inspected by the Press Division. In a well-known and widely read newspaper (if it had at least been a monthly literary journal, where things wouldn't have been so urgent . . .). What a scandal! How would Press know what we receive and suppress? In the reports that circulate we put the title or at most a fragment, both of which can be modified by authors and submitted for publication else-

where. Moreover, it's very hard to coordinate with the provinces as well, so that what we suppress in the capital doesn't appear, soon afterwards, in another city.

—Especially because the people in Press read everything last minute and, many times, they have to turn in the publication without a second to spare. They get things at eleven o'clock at night and have to turn them in at four in the morning. How could you know what the situation is?

—Yes, I don't even know what to say . . . Maybe the story wasn't that subversive if the censors from Press didn't consider it to be hostile enough to cut from the newspaper. I've heard that over there, in Press, they've got the best, the most intelligent, the most competent censors. We can pore over a text for up to two months, and it can take up to a year for it to appear. But those guys have to go through newspapers and magazines at lightning speed . . . If they make a mistake and they get the order to pull an issue, it's almost impossible to salvage anything, because newspapers sell like hotcakes in the early hours of the morning, while canceling the print run of a book can be proposed even a month later. A couple thousand books might sell in a couple of days, but the remainder of a print run can be successfully pulled from the shelves and sent to the incinerator. They're usually able to get back nine-tenths of a print run. But these are rare cases for us, because we're not in a hurry to publish things; by the time a book gets to readers, it passes through so many commissions, departments, and all kinds of other checks, that nothing slips through the cracks. Not like at Press, where everything has to be taken care of immediately, where night and day are irrelevant, and the institution's minibus takes one group of censors home at midnight and on the way back picks up another group to take over . . .

—Gosh, I wouldn't survive!

—Few people would, and their salaries are the same as ours.

—That's why it's good to circulate examples of interventions, so everyone can see how you censor correctly, what the methods and newest trends are, for one thing, and for another, so we can become familiar with the content of censored works and prevent an author who's been censored in one place from appearing somewhere else.

—Press censors might be competent, but ours in Literature aren't idiots either. Seeing as how things in Press move quickly, those who work there don't have time to go into details, that's a point in our favor and there's more. The story could be hostile not just in and of itself, but in a specific context or set of circumstances, so we have justified and well-founded reasons to suppress it, with approval from all the directors and heads of services. The order was sent to the publishing house, the editors, and the author. They were all aware that those stories were banned, thus they aren't authorized to appear. In any case, at that point the reason doesn't matter anymore, whether it's of a harmless or hostile nature, just the fact that the author dared to defy Censorship, to defy the decision of the highest committee, he decided to lie, to play us, to overstep his bounds. If it were only that, it wouldn't be so bad and treacherous. He wrote something, he worked hard on his text and he wants to see it published, it's understandable. But what if he's testing our competence and vigilance? What if he's saying to himself: You might be clever, but I'm even more so and I can fool you, I'll get my way! Seen from this angle, it's inadmissible that a text that was banned by one division be approved by another. Don't they realize that in Press, as well as in the provinces, they're all censors, they're all one of us, everywhere! You fool one of us today, you manage to slip through, but it's not the last story you'll write in your life, you're not giving us your last book now, and next time, you'll still end up with us. We can't punish him, because the fault is ours, we slipped up, nor can we, for the time being, condemn him. But the fate of a brave hero like that is sealed and, if it's not God himself submitting his stories to us or at least a party deputy wearing epaulettes (but we already know who these are and we have a special relationship with them) then woe betide the hero and his books! If you don't like being censored, don't publish! Write on clay tablets and bury them for future generations to find, so the Securitate has something to keep them busy as well. But don't take Censorship lightly! The ones who are above us in the chain of command, the Party and the Securitate, may laugh at us and criticize us, but they'll all back us up when it comes to the bastard who made the mistake of playing with fire. When push comes to shove, the ones with the most power are on our side, they support us and the author's punishment will be even harsher. What a simpleton, we don't even need idiots like that in the literary world.

We discuss such witty expressions as "you're as dumb as a small publication!" and "you're behaving like a small publication!"

—That Ciufecu guy from Training-Inspection is as dumb as a small publication, Roza says, clenching her teeth. I explained to him three times how to record the statistics of interventions and he came back again . . .

—Girls, stop making fun of the Small Publications section, because if you don't get married within the next five-year plan, that's where you'll end up!

—Why?

—Well, everyone gets married there. All kinds of individuals stop by, some of whom are handsome, single, they bring in some poster, a business card, or some other trifle. And you have to stamp it. You do, because there's nothing hostile in that poster or that brochure. You start chatting, the poster's for a concert, for example, and, oh!, you're so interested, he might invite you, maybe you also go out for coffee together. He's no good, you don't like him, tomorrow, three or four others will cross your threshold. With a college education, with a clean dossier, some younger, some more mature, engineers or clerks, you choose according to whatever criteria and expectations your heart and mind are set on. You don't offend him by censoring anything because, usually, there's nothing for you to censor, and no one hates you, they don't look at you as if you're an enemy of the people, you don't ruin his life, you don't crush his destiny by cutting out a comma, you don't mutilate his life's masterpiece, etc. Small Publications has the responsibility of approving posters, flyers, brochures, programs, educational public lectures and conferences, cards and invitations, rules and institutional lists, packaging, tags, name badges, forms and anything else that needs to be printed . . . And that's not all. We're not allowed to come into contact with authors. No one knows who exactly cut something from a text, we work under special codes that are strictly secret. They're not supposed to know our names, or our faces, they're not even supposed to know we exist.

—You think they don't know?

—Editors are more in the know and they blab. Word gets around. But, officially, no one should know anything about Censorship. The only exception is Small Publications. Precisely because they don't truly censor anything and it isn't dangerous for our people there to see and be seen, to consult and be consulted. You're not always dealing directly with those who ordered the individual printing, but also with serious representatives from institutions, enterprises, committees, directorates; you always have different people coming through. Mostly handsome young men, like I said. Management has taken note of this fact and assigns unmarried young women there. After a few months, the ones who have gotten married are transferred back to their previous departments. Other ones are sent to Small Publications, because there are lots of us unmarried women. So, they're looking out for us.

—What are you talking about, lots of unmarried women? I only know a few, the rest are all married. We've got more men than women in Censorship, Roza says.

—So I shouldn't be afraid of dying a spinster, Hermina jokes.

Though the prospect of working at the much-despised Small Publications doesn't thrill her at all.

⟿

The last simplification measures were applied through decree no. 22 from February 1968 when Library, Museum, and Antiquities Services was disbanded, and its responsibilities passed over to the Literature Division. From the same unit, the institution's library passed over to Administrative Services.

In the same decree, besides the elimination of the position

of head of Library, Museum, and Antiquities Services, two deputy head of services positions were also eliminated: from Science and Technology Services and Administrative Services, after they concluded that the amount of work necessary for the management of the two services could be completed without these two positions.

☙

I've been dreaming of stacks for a week. Roza tells us about an interesting dream, with young and fertile poets, of course.

. . . The beloved poet throws a stone, and another one—she gets scared, she ducks—then another one, Roza thinks he wants to hit her, to kill her, because he hates her. But instead, he dedicates an ode to her, a paean of love and gratitude, he acts out that poem in stones, he builds a lasting monument to her. Pushkin? Yes, Roza says, confidently (of course she has no clue what I'm referring to!).[15] She wants all the poets to love her, it hurts her when Censorship is criticized. Only the party's allowed to criticize Censorship, not writers. Writers should adore us, they should thank us for existing! They should dedicate poems to us and build us lasting monuments!

Roza doesn't even get that I'm being sarcastic. She agrees, repeats after me.

She brags about her wonderful manuscripts, she's positive that all that's best in literature gets assigned only to her. I don't know how it happens but she really does get handsome poets often. Maybe others do too, except that no one, besides Roza, cares about this aspect.

She asks me: When was the last time you felt satisfied?

I want to laugh the question off, then I think about it: When was the last time I felt truly satisfied? When? She's expecting me to name a book, to brag about some successful author, maybe some lover, though we're not close enough for me to share those kinds of intimate details. But no, no, I know when, being completely serious:

—One night recently (two days ago), when I killed a mosquito that was keeping me from sleeping. It was incredibly muggy out, almost ninety degrees, you could barely breathe, I needed some air, I opened the window and in came a little beast that bit me, it sucked my blood and, now that it was stuffed, it started buzzing energetically. After scratching away at the bites, I had to listen to it buzzing around my nose. There was no way I could fall asleep! To think that the next day I'd be at work, sleep-deprived, exhausted, my vigilance at rock bottom! I got up, turned on the light, looked for it, couldn't find it, turned off the light, buzzing again, turning the light on again. Found it! And, with the manuscript that was next to me, when I whacked it, man! When I smashed it! My blood and its blood transformed into a red flower on the white wall! That's satisfaction! That's the ultimate victory! Even if I had just made twenty cuts to a page it wouldn't have felt as good! There's no author who could be a greater enemy to me than a mosquito who won't let me sleep!

When any new colleague starts working in our institution, our Rozette already knows when he was born and where, what he studied (if and when), brothers-sisters-parents-relatives (high-level or just ordinary). One of the young censors turns out to be the son of a gynecologist and it's clear that he'll be our colleague's chosen one, so it would be good for us to steer clear of him, because no one messes with her. If she at least stopped at just one. For a while now, she's become quite well-known in the institution for being popular with the men. She can't get enough, a bottomless pit, all the poets, all the censors, the entire party!

One day anemic Hermina also turned up with a guy from Sciences, she probably wanted to brag too or maybe the man just wanted to chat, well, and after five minute the science com had forgotten who he came to see, what he wanted, he was standing transfixed-bewitched-completely whipped by little Roza's cleavage, drinking it in with his eyes, or to be more exact, drinking in her generous bosom. She happened to be wearing a low-cut dress, she doesn't dress up that flirtatiously every single day, but that day happened to be one of them. I was right there, in front of them, but I couldn't say how exactly she attracted him, she didn't say anything out of the ordinary to him, I don't think she asked him anything special. I don't think she even paid any attention to him. I felt, and I think Hermina did as well, that the two found a common language and they attracted each other like a couple of magnets. We felt invisible in our own office, ugly, and old. I'm over thirty, but Hermina's barely twenty-five, and she looks even younger. She looks as if she just got up from her desk at school, that's how slender and delicate she is.

Only Z. doesn't fall under the sway of Rozella's charms. When he addresses her, he doesn't call her comrade Toth, her actual name, but com. Tod (emphasizing the "d"), which in German means "death." Com. Toth doesn't have a foreign background, apparently she was married briefly and that was the name of her first husband, while she's a pure-blooded Ionescu. She can't stand Z. either, she says contemptuously: as if it weren't enough that his last name's Zukermann, his first name's Salvager! Or was it Salvadore? she says sarcastically; in fact, his name's Salvatore. I really like his name a lot. Our Savior, we say to him fondly when he helps us and gets us out of tight spots.

I'm amazed at everything Zuki tells us, he knows everything about censorship, I take notes so I can impress the provincials at the next seminar. When it's necessary! I've been told that I was chosen for the refresher course for the delegates from the provinces, I'm glad, I'm proud.

The most censored book in the history of censorship and our civilization is the Bible.

The most efficient, longest-lasting, harshest censorship (books and authors burned at the stake, torture, etc.) was religious censorship. By comparison, what we're doing here is child's play.

The cruelest form of religious censorship was practiced by the inquisition. It's written with a capital "I."

1391—the first revolts against the Jews in Spain, many leave, many convert to Catholicism.

1478—Sixtus I don't know which issued a papal bull that allowed the establishment of the Inquisition.

Boil?

No, a bull, a type of decree.

How nice, a bull is a decree! That joke with the bull in a china shop . . . We'll leave that bull for another time . . .

Among other things, in the Spanish territories where

Judaism had just been outlawed, the Inquisition was charged with wiping out fake or less-enthusiastic Catholics. And they really went all in, they were always finding someone or something that could be persecuted.

They pursued converts—*conversos*—the descendants of Jews who converted to Christianity and didn't seem that convincing, they didn't demonstrate exceptional self-sacrifice and devotion when it came to practicing the faith, there were also *moriscos*— the descendants of Muslims who also converted to Christianity.

Some were forced to convert.

But there were also cases of autodafe for older Christians, pure Catholics, who didn't have Jewish or Moorish ancestors.

Auto-da-fé—the indictment of heretics and their execution by being burned at the stake.

Relajados—those who are sentenced to death.

Later, the Portuguese also established an Inquisition.

"The Witch Hunt"—a respectable censor absolutely needs to know about it!

It extended through countries such as Austria, England, France, Germany, Holland, Sweden, Scotland, Switzerland.

The burning of books is something much older, it was first practiced long before our era. Athenians in the fifth century BC burned Protagoras's works, the Romans proved equal to them, as did overzealous Christian ministers even up to the present day. In 1508, Cardinal Ximenes burned a hundred thousand Arab manuscripts, and in 1510 the emperor Maximilian ordered all Jewish manuscripts to be thrown in the fire, with the exception of the Bible.

Czarism, the poet Nicolae and the czar Pushkin . . . no, no, the other way around . . .

Peter I, Peter II, Catherine the Great, Alexander I, II, III, and all the other czars . . .

French censorship Napoleon and one more . . .

Slow down, speak slower, we beg Zuki. We can't keep up. He complies with our request and speaks slowly, he's almost dictating to us, I write quickly and look up at him and what do I see? Com. Zukerman had stuck his fingers in Roza's curls, her tangled hair prevented him from extracting his digital extremities as quickly and as inconspicuously as he would've liked. He ended up pulling her hair, she grimaced in pain. I leaned over my notebook, pretending that I hadn't noticed anything. Hermina was focused on her writing, she didn't see anything! So it's like that! So, comrade Tod! While you're making a show of complete indifference, you're getting your hair pulled like that by the comrade! Com. S. Z. has also grabbed my hand or my shoulder during his oratorical flights. He'd come up so close to me that I could feel his breath on my face, he'd come up so close it was as if he wanted to communicate something to me with only his eyes, without saying a word . . .

I can't concentrate . . . it's nothing, I'm fine, Zuki isn't my husband, I don't care whose hair he sticks his claws in . . .

Not just religious censorship . . .

The most general and applicable, universal and eternal criterium is morality, even the ancients were censored according to this criterium, before the spread of Christianity.

Ovid, the poet, banished to the wild shore.

Which shore? I didn't catch that.

Tomis, Tomis, our Constanta. (Big deal, what a thing to brag about, probably all our lechers are descended from him!)

But this criterium is also the one that fluctuates the most, from being a narrow set of rules, it loosens up, very rarely vice versa (in certain regimes) . . .

In their time, Flober and Bodler, *The Flowers of Evil*, what a scandal.

Zuki leans over me:

—Is that how it's spelled? Flober and Bodler? And you claim you took French, I was positive, comrade Moldovean, that you didn't know how to write it correctly. Fla-u-bert and Ba-u-de-la-ire . . .

I didn't answer back that I write how and what I like in my notebook. What a scandal when they appeared, then their works, considered classics, were published in pocket editions, widely accessible to everyone, they're even taught to kids in school. Then others come, they're more radical, fit to be sent straight to court, other books are confiscated and the previous ones become classics, the criteria become laxer, they change . . .

Voltaire, Diderot, you'd be hard pressed to find a respectable classic that wasn't chased down by censors and didn't suffer because of them, and now they're canonized in textbooks.

Decadent lecher! I should've asked him how he likes sinking his paws into the tresses of our officemate right in front of us . . . Zuki continues talking, not a muscle in his face has twitched, he hasn't betrayed one shiver from having touched Roza. Roza, however, is looking at him with undisguised hatred and blatant disgust. Well, that's good. I'm glad! Our Roza doesn't give the time of day to every potbellied fungus, rotting capitalist! That bastard of a censor! The hairy caterpillar!

Give us a break with your insane emperors!

Of course, it's easier to burn a book and its author than to scrub it clean of errors and impurities! The savages!

Once again, I'm convinced that our regime is generous and extremely civilized! When authors make mistakes, and they're always making mistakes, in every book, they're forgiven each time, their delicately corrected books are published in thousands and even tens of thousands of copies, authors live like princes, they're allowed the use of luxurious villas, writers' residences, grants, special restaurants. I don't even think they realize all the honor they're being given, maybe they think they deserve it all, I don't know what it was like and maybe still is like in other places. You don't know how to write—to the stake with you!

Zuki should give a talk on the Inquisition to those other lunatics as well, so they can see what real censorship is, so they can appreciate our magnanimous regime, so they can be grateful for us!

Useful Tips from Novels

Door hinges won't creak if you rub oil or dust or a simple pencil on them. From a volume of children's poetry.

We exchange tips like that, after analyzing them, of course, to make sure they're not just fabrications, next thing you know you're applying some passionately touted hair mask, after which all your hair falls out.

Going barefoot—very healthy for the nervous system and for vision especially.

Head massages are good. In general, you do it for your loved one, but whoever's alone should massage their own head. Relaxing, you fall asleep quickly.

To improve your memory, it's good to learn a small (short) poem by heart before bed.

In the short story "A Day at the Grandparents," the grandmother recites the poem "The Curly-Haired Puppy" to her granddaughter—the grandmother knows it, the granddaughter doesn't. One's memory has to be developed at any age.

For sedentary work, walks are recommended. Wear low-heeled shoes.

Goat milk—for coughs.

Carrots on an empty stomach—for intestinal parasites.

For deep sleep—

Constipation—

In the winter, don't put objects such as cotton, sawdust, and other materials that absorb humidity in between double windows, use small jars of kitchen salt to keep the windows from fogging up or freezing.

Slightly dirty wallpaper can be cleaned if, after sweeping the dust off with a broom, you wipe it down with a dry cloth, dipped from time to time in oatmeal flakes.

Dirty spots on wallpaper can also be cleaned by brushing a piece of dry bread across it from top to bottom, top to bottom.

Women with shorter hands should not wear opera gloves. To be copied onto small notecards and taken out of the institution: they do not constitute state secrets!

For personal use.

Those nitwits from Office One really get on my nerves, every other second they're coming to ask you whether it's okay to cut out a word, whether it's justified for them to intervene in a given context. I understand when you've been saddled with a couple beginners who've got no clue what we do here, you teach them, because you're obligated to, you've got orders from higher up, you show them, you turn them into censors in two months and bye! Adios, dear comrade! Going forward each person has to figure things out on their own as best they can. But the girls who've been working here for years and come to ask you questions at every turn are dangerous. They, in fact, don't want to assume responsibility for their own work.

Next thing you know they're writing reports where they mention that they've cut out what they've cut out and they've intervened where they've intervened only after consulting with com. X. (Moldovean, for example). If the intervention is criticized, considered inopportune, the girls can't be punished, they wouldn't have made the mistake, they wouldn't have intervened, if com. Moldovean hadn't insisted, if they hadn't been led to do so. They're never to blame, they're perfect! What assholes! I better not catch them in our office! I wouldn't be surprised if they're also writing informant notes on us in which they describe in great detail how, in an especially difficult case they ran up against, they asked for the help of an experienced censor and he (or she) balked and didn't want to help, to get involved, which isn't collegial, comrades, it's not in keeping with the spirit of our institution! Com. X. is giving proof of petty-bourgeois egoism, of individualism, their negative behavior must be discussed at the branch meeting. If X., the son of a bitch (or the bitch), is also a party member, we have the right to be shocked, to ask ourselves how he (she) got to be one, in light of his (her) lack of collegiality, patriotic spirit, and many other things. It's clearly a vicious circle! Thus we ask that he (she) be punished!

So keeping in mind that both situations are to be avoided, when one of these hussies with questions approaches you, try to get yourself out of the situation as honorably as possible without getting too involved. "I'm busy right now, the case you present is, indeed, difficult, give me some time to think about it, I'm not specialized in this area and I couldn't give you an answer immediately, I've had a migraine for three days now, I need to go to the bathroom . . ." Let them complain in their notes that I didn't help them, because I was hurrying to the toilet! Disgusting cows! Though it's not good to think like that about our wonderful colleagues. I'm with my girls in the office and all day long we're exchanging lines of poetry, words that are high flown (or merely strange), polysemantic expressions, each more subversive than the last! But it's your business what you do with your manuscript, we read texts to each other, we get indignant, we're amused, we trade a recipe or instructions for a hair mask every now and then, but each one decides independently what she does. I don't ask anyone what I should cut from my manuscript nor do my officemates ask me, sometimes it happens that we leave in an ass, a death, a god, and it's never caused the Press House to crumble! We take responsibility for them all. Of course, whenever you decide to cut something or leave something, you're armed with arguments and you can give reasons for your choices. If you're a man, or woman, who's too stupid to do even that, what the hell are you doing in Censorship?

I don't brag and I don't tell anyone that I was part of, albeit for a very short time, the Personnel Advancement Section. I had my finger on the pulse of the entire department, I knew who was late and by how much, what problems each of them had, how fast our readers got through manuscripts, what they did well and what they didn't do as well, what they did when they declared that they needed two weeks to read a book, when, in fact, it took them at most a week, how they filled up that free time, who bought the latest coat, I would also notice who stood in line at the nearby grocery store during work hours, who stepped out at noon to breastfeed their child . . . I would note it, and if necessary, measures would be taken. I knew everything. We receive the same salary, why should I work like a horse, even on Sundays, while others snooze in lines? Back then, that was my job, I was part of a special section of Censorship, that's what I was supposed to do, officially, even if my colleagues didn't know. It was an important mission, I was chosen to fulfill it for a year and that's it. When the section was disbanded, if it was disbanded, doesn't matter to me, I think the people in Administrative Services now have those kinds of obligations. I don't worry about what others are doing anymore, I don't care to think up petty schemes, to demonstrate to someone that he's better or worse than me, I don't rat on anyone to my superiors out of overzealousness, that's not part of my job description. I don't harm anyone gratuitously, like these disgusting colleagues. And watch them even move up the ladder! Despite not knowing how to read a text properly, they dream of being supervisors, the nitwits. How else could they shine, when their mediocre work wouldn't get noticed in a million years? So they start informing on some colleague or other, in the hope that just maybe their efforts will be rewarded.

Announcement regarding the respecting of work hours, situations of tardiness, requests for time off for doctor's visits and for personal reasons during semester II, 1973.

During this period, tardiness and time off has amounted to 1,569 hours of which: 28 hours are for tardiness, 923 hours are for doctor's visits, 618 hours are for time off for personal reasons—this, over the course of the entire semester, would amount to almost 200 work days. Of the 1,574 hours, 724 hours appertain to the first trimester of the year and the other 850 hours to the two months and three weeks of the second trimester.

These numbers indicate a slight upward trend in tardiness and time off in trimester II compared with trimester I.

That's basically what I would do too, so the structure's changed, the section has disappeared, but their surveillance of us hasn't. The report is public, so everyone knows! I remember that, in my time, announcements like that weren't made to employees during their meetings, they were confidential.

I'm in a meeting and I'm amazed. At first, I'm bored, then I'm amazed, in that order. Everyone's buried in their books, note-books, sheets, notepads, and I don't know what they're jotting down with such concentration, they're writing, eyes glued to the page. We have typists, stenographers, who take down every word spoken in a meeting for us. We get all the good interven-tions, newspaper cuttings, everything that's important and that will be helpful in our work, handed to us, so it isn't necessary for us to conscientiously record, down to the smallest detail, everything that's said. Then what do they keep writing? I can only guess what each one is busy doing. Some are copying rec-ipes, others, tips on how to keep your feet warm: from sitting so long, we have poor circulation, we start getting unsightly varicose veins, back pain; others gossip in their notebooks or ask themselves existential questions, just like me. Even our sensitive Hermina is writing something, looking through her sheets, focused, I doubt that she hears what this guy is telling us about the party, about the newest trends and the latest cri-teria. When some supervisor asks us something, we all look up, taken by surprise and incapable of reacting or answering. Until he repeats the question, distinctly and slowly, no one makes a sound, which means no one is listening.

What's the point of my always writing down in my notebook

all the objectives, all the topics, principles, criteria? Either they change, more quickly all the time, or I never come across anything useful, because, along with the principles, the texts we're given to correct change as well. When we finally receive orders to suppress all nostalgic attitudes, who cares to write like that anymore, when cosmopolitanism must be stopped, there's not a text like that to be found, it's as if the writers know our criteria even before we do! By the time we catch up with the newest wave, I'll have gone through this notebook and received a brand-new one. I can start over again once, twice, but seven years in a row of the same thing . . . Anyone would get bored. I'm not putting down anything else, I'm tired of incessantly copying what we need to censor from one notebook to another! In any case, I'm experienced enough that I can kind of guess, improvise a little. Writers aren't that dumb, editors don't lag behind either. There's not much left for us to do.

. . . prepared with objectivity and a sense of responsibility

. . . one-sidedness in the presentation of some aspects, a certain stereotyping

. . . raising the level of professional and political-ideological preparedness

. . . enacting the Party's policies

. . . eliminating deficiencies and improving work quality, raising the general level of knowledge, sense of responsibility

. . . Among certain personnel there still exists a reticence in critically analyzing one's own deficiencies, and this demonstrates that more persistent political-educational efforts toward this end continue to be necessary.

No matter how good you are, you're regarded more highly if you're skilled at applying self-criticism. I've become convinced of this, I have to invent all kinds of shortcomings, otherwise you're not considered a real communist, nor a real censor in the true sense of the word.

Why do they make life difficult for us? Two months ago we had to sign that we've been made aware of the fact that, until the respective objectives become operational, nothing can be disseminated. Now we've had to sign again that we've been made aware of the fact that the activation of the respective objectives may now be broadcast and the following information is no longer secret. How many poems and how many novels will we get having the visit of King Hussein Ibn Talal of the Hashemite Dynasty of Jordan to our country as a central theme? Pfft, I hear hemming and hawing! We, the censors from Literature and Art, really should be spared from these useless/bureaucratic procedures and obligations. That kind of information never makes it into our texts. All of us agree, but no one does anything, if I were to propose something in a meeting, all the supervisors would jump on my case . . . 'Cause the defense of state secrets, 'cause ideological purity, 'cause the GDPP's mission . . . I know it all by heart, they've crammed our heads with their directives.

> January 29–30: King Hussein Ibn Talal of the Hashemite Dynasty of Jordan pays an official visit to Romania.

Nothing bad about Jordan then.

February 14–17: President Nicolae Ceausescu visits Lebanon and is awarded the title of doctor honoris causa from the Univ. of Lebanon.
He also visits Libya, Syria, and Iraq.

The following no longer constitute state secrets and information may be broadcast about:

—The precast concrete enterprise in Timisoara, which began production in January (and may be broadcast)

—The bearings enterprise in Alexandria (it's already up and running, or will be soon, in any case it no longer constitutes a secret)

February—in the Galati shipyard, the first 18,000 dwt. *collier* has been launched. And what might that be? (Some of our colleagues in Technical Sciences enlightened me: a ship for the transportation of coal.)

I imagine poems about the marvelous, the smashing, the dashing Galati collier of our surpassingly proud fatherland. Come, poets, saddle up, to all things carboniferous! Onwards!

Roza feels like chatting and she's started telling me of her brave exploits, after Hermina left with comrade Codrescu for the factory. I listen carefully, it's interesting, rumors have been circulating about this topic, though I think she's exaggerating in some places:

—Our comrades, leaders in the party, directors of key

institutions, receive extremely expensive books from some suspicious sources, luxury editions that can't be found even in the catalogues of the largest European libraries (books with inadvisable content, at least). I discovered by chance that one of these sources doesn't even really exist, I remember a return address with a Pluyer Street in Paris, others do exist, but in response to our thank you note for the package they sent, they deigned to answer dryly that they hadn't sent any books to the address mentioned. We wrote them specifically to see who they are. We didn't solicit these books, we didn't so much as know of their existence. Some are even translated into Romanian, but we mostly receive books in French and English, foreign languages that are studied here and that it's assumed our highest-ranking officials know. Not a single minister or party member who receives such books knows the sender personally. So that I wouldn't find out more, they transferred me here and they have to nerve to talk about "the party's policies," and our "ideological training"!

She's told us about this before, and at the time it was the talk of the institution. Roza worked in Press first, then in Import-Export, in the office and in the post office, depending on the tasks she was given. They also had censor notebooks, just like us. She wrote in a scratch pad, not a reader notebook, as she does now. The scratch pad is in a much smaller and thinner notebook format. Well, and our little Roza, who's the farthest thing from dumb, would make note of all the new books that came through the mail that seemed suspicious to her. She'd write down where they came from, meaning the sender, and who received them, meaning the addressee. On occasions when she was allowed to open the package, she'd write down additional information about the book. She had at her disposal the list of institutions to which we were obligated to send anything that was addressed to them, regardless of contents, we're not supposed to make any judgments about these publications. But we're allowed to keep a record, so nothing Roza was doing was illegal. In the post office, she worked with a sharp and rather handsome Securitate officer, they got along wonderfully (Roza sighs) and she asked him to try, taking advantage of his position and connections, to see whether the foreign senders existed, whether they were real or whether the books were sent using a fake address, whether all the institutions and associations listed on the envelopes were actually active or whether the books were being sent by someone else, hiding behind them. And what did she discover? It isn't hard to guess: not one institution existed! Sometimes not even the street mentioned existed, though usually the address was real, only it belonged to a private individual who had never heard of association X or Y and had never sent anyone a book, had no connection with the book, and, usually, didn't know what it was. But Roza didn't stop here: she observed the pattern in which the books were sent and connected it (the pattern) with their themes: at the beginning of the week absolutely inoffensive books were sent, end of the week, inoffensive—break—beginning of the month, inoffensive—end of the month, dangerously offensive.

—What does inoffensive mean?

—Scholarly books, in principle. Sometimes expensive and useful.

Twice a month, on Wednesdays or Thursdays—absolutely hostile ones, hidden among totally inoffensive ones—then

again inoffensive and expensive, inoffensive and cheaper. Based
on this scheme intended to lull the censors' vigilance to sleep,
she could've proven that someone, to this day we don't know
who, was sending these books with a specific goal in mind and
that we should be careful and take precautions. She was able to
predict what books we'd receive and she was never wrong. Her
boyfriend ventured into this pursuit and calculated that only
25 percent of the total number of books were truly harmful,
while the rest were manna from heaven for our specialists and
other important addressees. He recommended that she not get
too worked up about it, because she didn't have the backing
(he'd probably already gotten an answer from his superiors).
Rozel, however, didn't understand what he was saying and filed
a report with the GDPP, our people immediately took notice,
they were scandalized, they informed the Party, they tried to
take action, but the Securitate blocked it, and they sent the
smarty-pants censor to us to teach her a lesson.

She says she got off easy. Our upstanding bosses were made
to understand, I don't think in a very polite way, that if they
stick their noses where they don't belong, the inspection of all
publications will be moved under Securitate, and not another
censor will step foot inside a post office. Imagine, for a small
parcel weighing half a kilo or for a regular envelope, an army
of parasites are getting paid a salary. They open the package
or letter: private letter?—that goes to Securitate; newspaper—
it's the censor's job; book, printed volume—the censor again;
scarf or coffee—Securitate; audio cassette—censor . . . Some
write up declarations sometimes, the others send the packages directly to their destination, others sometimes steal things
from them. Shouldn't the operation be simplified? Of course

it should, it's just that Censorship considers that everything coming and going through the mail should belong to them, control of it, I mean, while those in Securitate think the same thing, except that everything should go through them, not Censorship. The ones who have the power to decide who's right and who should be in charge of mailed imports and exports haven't decided yet, they probably have more important things to do. So the issue remains unresolved . . .

The Import-Export Division has many skilled workers and many responsibilities, if it were to be taken over, the acquisition should include the employees, because who'd be able to find competent people overnight? Inspecting publications that come through the mail isn't the only thing they do, by far. Meanwhile, they've been alerted, if they're too clever and they've got a big mouth, like that grouchy individual (our Roza), they'll be demoted—that is, if the comrades are feeling generous, meaning that's the best-case scenario. If not, some spaces just opened up in good prisons for persons acting against the security of our country. They threatened us! They showed us who's boss here! Our people all clammed up. They understood what they had been refusing to accept over the last few years but had become increasingly clear and embarrassing for us. They had started up at the same time, the Securitate on one side, Censorship on the other, we had started out on the same rung of new institutions, we, censors, considered ourselves to be just as important as them. But very quickly, they climbed higher, and higher, while we fell far behind. If the Securitate were to snap their fingers, in a few months our entire institution would become just a regular department within their domain. If that hasn't happened, it's because they don't consider it to be necessary (yet), but I'm expecting that moment to come, that prospect wouldn't surprise me.

"The woman was swaying, was swinging her . . ." I'm not reading any more . . .

Z. comes and he kills us with all his passages. Following his example, from time to time we read a spicier short text among ourselves, then we comment on it afterwards.

What shamelessness, what perverts!

Z., wily and devious: But a poet is cheaper than having to take a trip to a clinic![16] All he does is turn you on, it doesn't cost anything! It turns you on, doesn't it? Yes or no?

I look down and don't answer. Me, no, but I'm thinking of the readers.

—We censors are above that, we're immune, Hermina very bravely tries to answer, but she doesn't know Z., who doesn't even let her finish before destroying her.

Among other things, censors are human too, they're vulnerable, corruptible (read: already hopelessly corrupted), hard-headed. It's difficult for them to understand important things, instead, they rush to react to all kinds of cheap little tricks (like the vast majority of our readers, unfortunately).

—Want to know what the world thinks about censors? Zukermann continues his harangue.

Why would we want to . . .

—You're the only ones, in your office with flowers (so we've got a geranium on our windowsill, it's scrawny but always in bloom, it makes us happy and we're proud of it), who consider yourselves to be important and respectable ladies (I, for one, consider myself a commendable comrade censor, not a bourgeois lady, but there's no point in saying anything)! But you want to know what you mean to the weakest and most naïve first-time writer of literature? Do you think your readers are a bunch of idiots? False, false, a hundred times false—and he keeps going like that, totally unrelated to the dirty lines that sparked the discussion.

He's never been so violent, he almost spits on us with all that yelling, in any case he's not yelling only at me, this time I don't feel as if I'm the main target, so I calmly watch him out of the corner or my eye. I can't tell whether he's being serious or joking, whether he's angry or he's only pretending. He recites that stupid poem with the square head and reproaches us, as if we were the ones who wrote it. I know the lines as well, they're old, and the poem's not about censors, but about party workers. Some author's book was hacked up at a publishing house, it hadn't gotten to us; the man, incensed, sent a magazine a batch of furious poems in which someone with a square head doesn't understand his message and how talented he is, the magazine featuring these poems did make it to us, but the volume suppressed by the publishing house never did . . . The story's old and irrelevant . . .

Fruit compote is tastier and needs less sugar if you add a pinch of salt.

You can clean silk lampshades with a small brush soaked in gasoline (Hermina has a lampshade at home, I don't, neither does Roza).

An old pair of nylon stockings (with lots of runs) is ideal for cleaning mirrors and delicate porcelain or crystal tableware. I could've thought of a use for old stockings on my own, but, okay, not cleaning porcelain . . .

You can seal window frames for the winter with paper soaked in fresh milk.

Knitted dresses and suits go well with jewelry made from wood or metal, and ceramic jewelry.

Older people prefer soft-hued fabrics.

How is it possible for them to write so many novels? How is it that they're all so similar, so long, so predictable? I have the impression, actually I'm certain, that only censors truly and carefully read everything that's written. Writers—a bunch of parasites that just write and write, with all the abundance of incontinence they're capable of. Readers, the poor things, read what's published, what they're offered, but they nonchalantly and with indemnity skip over all the passages that bore them, a sign of mental health, of course. If I weren't a censor, I'd do the same, I don't even think I'd read, actually. As a literary species, the novel should've died out long ago, but it doesn't even show signs of aging, in fact, once every fifty years, when there's a somewhat more radical social change or even a small one, it starts over again, the same themes, the same forms, as if none of it had ever been done before. Poetry's not far from this model either. Literature, in general, is repetitive, but it seems that readers are capable of endlessly reading the same things over and over. There's a great need to hide and find refuge in books. Which is lucky for freeloading opportunists who shake their pens and get rich off it!

Preparations for the National RCP Conference and the twenty-fifth anniversary of the Republic have mobilized the entire nation for the completion of the

five-year plan in just four and a half years for the accel-
erated development of the country's economy, the aim
of which is the more rapid growth of the material and
cultural well-being of workers.

In this context of creative effervescence, we include
the ever-increasing contribution of our institution's
workers in staunchly defending the ideological purity
of the materials being published, as well as in handling
them with maximum efficiency. This obliges us to be
more demanding, to ask that each of us demonstrate
a greater conscientiousness in fulfilling the tasks for
which we are responsible.

Fulfilling the fundamental requirements of our work
as readers has necessitated the radical improvement of the
system of communication among institution personnel.
Increasing the volume of work, the communist education of employees . . .

Direct labor, a spirit of collaboration . . .

Necessary guidance and help may be granted in a
differential manner, according to the complexity of the
problems that need resolution . . .

I just finished a 408-page novel and I didn't find a single
practical tip, something wise, about how to be eternally
youthful, how to keep your husband from leaving you (well,
even if I don't have one right now, I still think it doesn't hurt
to be as informed as possible on this topic), a novel this thick
and nothing good in it. Roza has some stupid poems and she's
been reading what she's found to us for about two hours: jump,
graceful doe, through the morning dew and the vision of an

eagle will be yours, allow the sharp stones to touch your soft heels and no sadness will be able to reach you (in our practical translation: walking through dew is good for your vision, walking barefoot on stones relieves depression). Tips in poetic form, I guess. Hermina never plays along with our innocent, and after all, I think, useful, game. Roza writes down in her notebook what I read, I do the same whenever she finds a thing or two and reads it to us, only Hermina ignores us utterly and with a tinge of contempt. We couldn't care less!

Before working in our office, Hermina worked in the main Literature office (no. 1). She says her nose bleeds a little the day before she gets her period, but it also happens that she cries (very rarely, she claims, and only at the beginning of her career as a censor) if she reads poems that are too emotional. I can imagine what a spectacle that was with everyone watching. Something like that can leave a negative impression on young, newly hired censors in our institution, but also on the faint of heart and those who are easily scared. It's not for nothing that they moved her into our small office.

I can't say I prefer a particular literary genre, I like the act of reading, the reading itself of a manuscript, which fills my life with meaning. And what I cut out, my interventions, the more important they are, the more they motivate me. I adore the responsibility, having the fate of a book in my hands, having its final form depend on me. I really am thinking of the poor readers, people who are busy, who are tired, and who want to spend their free time reading books.

Like in a marriage. Soulmates, the book and its reader. An

amorous coupling that lasts just moments, but at maximum intensity!

When I take the tram on my way to work, I look at people and imagine them reading books. I put a book in each of their hands, they flip through it, I try to guess what kinds of things they'd like. I spot some who I guess are rebels, nonconformists who would enjoy reading exactly what I cut out. In my mind, I assign the correct book to them, of course. Some are already holding books in their hands and I make out the titles, I take the trouble of considering whether they're appropriate for them or not really . . .

Too many books are being written, too many are getting published, and they don't realize that not all books are good fits for them. And so many books have passed through my hands that I could draw up a portrait of each one's ideal reader. I'm not complaining that I have too much to read; if not enough volumes were sent to us, we'd be out of a job. But I have to mention that when I was hired, there were many more of us in the department, I worked in the main office, but there were fewer tasks and we all had less to read, about half of what we receive now. So the volume of work has doubled, tripled, while the number of GDPP employees is shrinking by the day. Who can imagine the amount of work we do! Who can imagine how many hours of overtime we put in, we work Sundays too, we stay up late and we're barely able to hit our target!

Now everyone's afraid of making a mistake, you can get kicked out because of a single slipup if it's considered very serious. Before, you were allowed three, you were warned, harshly admonished, your paycheck was cut, now they can hardly wait for you to mess up, in any case the issue of reducing the number of positions has been raised officially in meetings. Punishment is much more frequent, you're quaking from fear that you might miss something, and then it's over—kicked out of your beloved Censorship!

Some have families, they have sick parents they're taking care of, they have children they've got to take to daycare or school and they still have to get everything for work done. If it were only the responsibilities that strictly pertain to our job! Yeah, right! Patriotic service, public activities, cultural, educational, always more! It's enough to make you faint just looking through that plan of activities. But I'm single and I manage it all. Nothing scares me! I think about my son less and less. I mean I think about him every day, but I don't know whether I want to or can have him by my side, whether I want to take him to kindergarten, to cook for him, I'm positive he's doing fine with his dad and that educated and doting woman. My son has already started going to school, but I can't accept the fact that he's growing up. For me he's still the two-year-old boy I left in my home village when I went away to college. For me he's the little child who still needs to be taken to daycare. I can't just skip over years like that, and take him straight to elementary school, even in my imagination. I think he's already been going to school for a few years now . . .

I'm careful not to teach the young bloods all of what I know, they're ready to wipe us, the older ones, off the face of the earth and, especially, from Censorship. I understand that the new director is dreaming of a new team, made of people who don't even know the name, or the worth, of the former director of this institution. Young newcomers have lots of energy and enthusiasm, but rather little knowledge, and you can learn how to censor only here and only from those who are more experienced. You'd have to be stupid to teach them, only to be thrown out of the institution afterwards like trash. No, we let them make mistakes, to demonstrate to our bosses that their training will take a while and, until then, they can't dispense with our help. Perhaps they could put up with us until we retire . . .

Milk doesn't turn sour as quickly if you boil it, adding a pinch of sugar or baking soda.

To avoid burning milk, rinse the pot with water beforehand.

To spread butter on bread more easily (when it's cold, straight from the fridge), dip the knife in hot water.

Aloe vera—for stuffy noses.

For the duration of a cold, if you have a stuffy nose, put fresh aloe vera juice into each nostril every 3–5 hours: 5–8 drops for adults, 4–5 drops for children ages 3–16, 2–3 drops for children under three.

A good way of fighting against bee and wasp stings and insect bites is a mixture of onion juice and chopped-up coltsfoot leaves.

An efficient way of warding off moths is with walnut or tobacco leaves, dried orange peels, as well as peppermint.

Hold a frayed broom for a few minutes over a basin of boiling water.

Of primary importance, prefiguring the radiant character of revolutionary humanism . . .

An atmosphere of charged emotions, the complete affirmation of human personality in our society.

We pay tribute to you most fervently for your inestimable and decisive theoretical and practical contributions.

Revolutionary insight and boldness . . .

On com. Ceausescu's birthday, a beautiful and heartfelt greeting card was sent on behalf of the entire GDPP. I would've liked for my name to be on that card too, I had contributed one of the sentences. We'd really love for him to come visit us as well, to see the work we're doing, how we're striving to exceed the plan, how devoted and responsible we are, to witness how seriously we're taking the fulfillment of the tasks drawn up by the party! He visits all kinds of little factories and plants, but us he avoids and, even worse, supposedly he criticizes us and wants to shut us down. The people around us all bad-mouth us, but if our beloved leader could see with his own eyes who we are and what we're like, if he truly got to know us, he'd stop believing what they say and wouldn't hold it against us.

Our men are such unbelievable pigs. They address us using only censored lines that they've memorized. I have to copy out an example line two to three times and I still can't memorize it, it's a good thing we have notebooks where we can write down examples when we need to, while they rattle off lines about spread-apart legs, sweet thighs, and not just thighs but boobs, asses, slender waists, the girls giggle, how shameful, how horrible!

I don't even know Eminescu's poems by heart, I've forgotten everything. They memorize things not only from the
books we receive for inspection but also from the reports we
all receive with examples of interventions. Unfortunately,
they don't marry us. They run from women censors as if we're
the devil! Whereas I'd be thrilled to have a male censor as my
husband, especially one from Import-Export or from Training-
Inspection, someone tall, with blue eyes, an enigmatic drifter.
I wouldn't have to hide where I work, to be ashamed, to lie to
him, etc. We'd understand each other just with a look, we'd be
a team, a real family.

For many outside the institution, Censorship's a kind of hell, a
nefarious and condemnable business, a ton of men hate Censorship and avoid us. Men who are otherwise educated and
well-mannered, who have university degrees and jobs, hate us
out of principle, without knowing what we do here, and they
don't really care to either. Engineers, doctors, whom we tell that
we work in the Press Division and who have no clue what that
means and aren't interested in finding out, we barely ever meet.
We hardly ever meet good men, in general, nor do we have time
to leave the perimeters of the Press House. While we're wasting
away from loneliness, we're past twenty-five years old and we're
tragically pushing thirty, our men find women in the blink of an
eye, meaning very quickly. Even if they find out who they are and
where they work, their darlings don't run from them, they don't
leave them, they're not afraid that they're censors. It's unfair.

Recently we've started a textual war (or just a friendly exchange
that later proved to be belligerent) between the colleagues in

our office and those in the bigger one next door. We choose a so-called adversary and send him what we think might impress him (strike him down, wound, vanquish, or, if we come in peace, what might delight him). We try to guess each other's tastes in texts. It's a risky operation and I don't think anyone is overly open about it. No one gives themselves away, of course. A convention, to communicate with each other more. Whose idea was it again to play this stupid game? Don't tell me Roza felt like having some fun? My colleagues send me poems, with rhyme and meter, appropriate, intelligible, about our beautiful country, the radiant growth of socialism, clear skies, sun, optimism. They're probably laughing, they're sarcastic, but really, I'm savoring them and I don't know where they find them, because it's been a long time since I've gotten something like that. Poetry has to have rhyme and meter, so you can sing it if you want.

In general, all the poetry being written nowadays annoys me, all the novels annoy me too, and the plays make me want to pull my hair out! Good thing there's a special section for those and they're not shoving dramas down our throat too, with the additional obligation of attending premieres. I'm really amazed that some people like that sort of thing.

The comrades from the insignificant former "Art" services, now merged with us (what joy!), are the least likable out of the entire institution, a bunch of bums actually, just like the playwrights they regulate. As conceited as they are sanctioned by all the authorities. We read a text and the average reader will read it exactly as we do. We read more carefully and even take a thing or two out if it seems questionable to us or prone to different, discouraging interpretations. The people from Art also have texts to read, just as we do, so far so good. But they're dealing with plays put on by people who speak/recite the text that's already been inspected, only actors' voices, gestures, pauses, moments of silence can't be inspected, they can't be anticipated. Actors can emphasize innocent words, arriving at the most illicit allusions, which the poor Art censors have no way of guessing in order to ban them and they're almost always discovering them when it's too late, after the premiere attended by all sorts of comrades with their ears pricked . . . On saying the word "ear," regardless of the context, the actor stretches an ear out to the audience to show that he's playing it all by ear (alluding to the portrait of our beloved leader, photographed in 3/4 view), on "shoulder," he begins shaking his shoulders, sometimes also pointedly putting a finger to his lips, as if someone were secretly listening to him (watch out, Securitate!). To shake, they don't even need the word "shoulder": they start the shaking after any line they want to load with nonexistent dirty meanings in the text inspected so carefully by the poor censor . . . Someone's traveling and he halts like a donkey, so everyone gets what kind of travelers he's alluding to. At a birth, they come with allusions to abortion—recently banned—something extremely subversive crops up from who knows what.

It's to the point where even in a classical play written a few centuries ago, like *The Bourgeois Gentleman*, there are two main characters—a couple—the actor bows—so that you all understand who I'm bowing to—he pauses, draws out his words. It's no longer done on opening night of the play, when all possible officials are attending, from the Party, from the Committee for Art, and from our department as well, but afterwards, when there's less pressure from authorities. At premieres everyone's listening, watching, the officials might have an insubstantial objection or two, but only after all the approvals have been granted does the real show start. Even though Censorship's the least to blame for this, we take all the heat, we play the old and tired role of scapegoat in exemplary fashion. Then the people from Art crouch down, humiliated, until the storm blows over. They turn our department into a laughing-stock. No one had any issues with the Literature Division until they shoved them down our throat. Okay, fine, where else could they have stuck them? Foreign Publications, no, Technical Sciences, no, Training, no, the Administrative Office, no, drama is literature too at the end of the day . . . I really don't want to work with them. Lately, because of the differentiated interpretations, they now have the obligation to attend not only the premiere but absolutely all the theater shows, to see the same play thirty times if need be. My stomach would turn at the premiere alone, but then to have to watch the same twisted show dozens of times! You could really go off the deep end! For this reason, lately the authorities are promoting and investing more and more in cinemas, where everything can be controlled and the most insignificant lizard dies along the way.

Imported feature-length artistic films are screened by the GDPP under the authority of the CCES and receive approval for viewing after having been approved by the Commission. To avoid the acquisition of films that will be rejected for domestic audiences, we propose reintroducing delegates from the GDPP into the commissions that acquire foreign films. The other categories of imported films receive approval for viewing after being screened by GDPP agents. Concerts, popular music shows are inspected during dress rehearsals (which are attended by representatives of relevant agencies).

Classical music concerts are not inspected.

The annual report from last year came out:

Report On Volume of Work By GDPP Division 1966–1973

		Volume of Work			Number of Employees		
		1966	1972	1973	1966	1972	1973
Social and Technical Sciences Division	Titles	5,491	22,445	25,016	42	37	41
	Pages	1,009,000	1,670,000	1,639,349			
Literature and Art Division	Titles	2,215	3,422	3,360	37	33	31
	Pages	432,400	572,600	532,600			
	Feature Length Films	352	426	327			
	Short Films	319	630	611			
	Exhibitions	–	–	396			
	Shows	–	–	75			

—Girls, that can't be right! How's it possible that we have so few pages read in comparison with Sciences?

—They get everything other than literature, from all

areas, from history to medicine, including both pam-
phlets and brick-volumes, and most of them don't contain
anything ideologically hostile, you go through them very
quickly, they don't have polysemy, lizards, decadence, senti-
mentalism, eroticism . . . And there are more of them than
us . . .

—Still, I thought that we put in the most work.

—Everyone knows that what we do is critical and very hard,
that we're working on slippery and dangerous ground . . .

We don't have offices for all the sections, so I've heard we have
colleagues who are mixed in with others. There are only two
Literature offices, might there be colleagues of ours who work
with people from other areas, might some of our people be at
the publishing houses as well? Seriously, I don't know of more
than fifteen people in our department. Art has about seven. A
few supervisors, two to three. But the others? There are thir-
ty-one of us! I don't know, people in Press used to work in
the editing rooms of periodic publications and they were on
GDPP payroll, so why wouldn't people from Literature be in
other places, places that are less familiar to us . . .

> March—N. Ceausescu, with his wife, visits Liberia,
> Argentina, Brazil, Guinea (March 9–11, where the
> Romanian-Guinean Treaty of Friendship and Collabo-
> ration will be signed).
>
> Take out every single oink from poems!
>
> March 28–29—the office of President of the Republic,
> who is also the head of state, will be established.

Sometimes poetry and prose can be gotten through without too much effort, we've been spared theater since the Art section was established, they take care of it, but the volumes of literary criticism still fall on our shoulders and they drive us crazy! I've never encountered anything as useless and hard to read in my entire life. How can you torture a censor like that? Why don't those kinds of books get to skip over Censorship? Let the comrades disregard us! They wouldn't be the first! And it wouldn't bother us (this time). The authors of these kinds of books are, in any case, party members or trustworthy people, they know better than anyone (even us) who to promote, who to praise to the skies, and who to criticize, they can censor better than us, and if they're not working in Censorship, it's because they have a bird's-eye view of everything, they're the ones choosing what books to read and pay attention to (we can't do that, we're not allowed to choose), they consider themselves to be independent, superior, us they treat with great disdain, they often lodge complaints against us with the party.

Critics that rewrite novels in summary form or translate poetry into prose, making "raffiné" observations to demonstrate their erudition, are insufferable. In the end, I can stand even them. But deceitful mangy dogs who take on ideological mistakes, incompetent and incapable of writing two lines themselves, digging through what we've painstakingly inspected in order to beat a dead horse, get on my last nerve! The good-for-nothings! An army of censors are allowing their souls to waste away reading and combing through for ideological mistakes or subversive content and some scalawags come out of nowhere and disregard us, thinking they're smarter!

When they discover something in an author's work and

destroy him, declaring him an undesirable enemy, on top of that, they criticize the censors who didn't suppress his book. Don't try to fight them: not one of our censors, not even all our censors put together could come up with as many arguments to demonstrate how a manuscript is guilty. Critics find proof in anything, where you'd least expect it, they could even turn a party manual into a national threat if they wanted to. We don't move a muscle, we don't respond, we don't defend ourselves—it would be pointless and they'd crush us with their devastating arguments. They're monsters. Z. says they're an insecure bunch, capable of killing a good writer out of plain envy and promoting a mediocre one who takes them out to a restaurant. Because he knows what kind of fights go on behind the scenes, that they've got their own little cliques—these ones are yours, these ones mine—and if one group praises someone, the other one destroys him, nitpicking every little thing. And we censors are stuck in the middle—scapegoats, as always. Our bosses can't stand the sight of them either. For me, a mere mortal censor, I find it very difficult to read and write a report on the volume of a literary critic who writes about books. Some of them imagine themselves to be the center of the universe, think they can do no wrong, they anthologize authors who have been banned, enemies, members of the Iron Guard, or exiles. They present their new vision of values, disregarding all the efforts made before them, they present what they consider to be true literature, as if they understood better than the party what's true and what's not.

All good, we're just waiting, no worries, let them get cocky, let them cross all the lines and then we can complain to the party as well, with proof and arguments, just like them. But, usually, to not make matters worse, we don't do anything, we don't take things that far, we let the party take measures, without intervening in any way. It's not that we don't know what critics are thinking, not that we don't know they're not allowed to promote those who are ideologically question-able, but if we permit whatever their hearts desire to pass, if we don't censor what we should in the works of these critics, they might arrive at the conclusion that censors are people too, decent ones, even, and one good turn deserves another, we also make mistakes sometimes when we let someone questionable slip through (on accident!), someone any novice critic could destroy, they make mistakes too, but we don't jump down any-one's throat and we don't make it out to be a party tragedy.

Of course, texts can be criticized in such a way that we aren't the ones punished, but others are—the author, for example, or the publishing houses. Critics can do that and, when we come to an understanding with them, everyone's happy. Why go through all the hassle! In any case, when the gall of critics gets to be too much, the vigilant Party is the only one who decides who is guilty and to what degree. And the Party's always vig-ilant. There are thousands of zealous petty informers capable of inexhaustible output, they're everywhere. They're against everyone. You can't defend yourself against them, you can't escape being snitched on by them. Critics can't escape either.

Thus, I read everything carefully, I note everything that needs to be noted, mistakes, issues, so I can't be accused of lacking ideological sensibility, but I end the report with "I agree with the publication of this volume." If there's any problem in the future—I'm covered, I found the mistakes, I pointed them out, it's not my fault if others didn't want to take them into account.

Useful things from novels:

Washing your hair with gasoline makes it soft and shiny, gets rid of any lice.

Instead of spending money on expensive creams that don't work, make this mask at home:

Mix together the inside of a baked apple with a tablespoon of oil and a teaspoon of honey. Leave it on for fifteen minutes, then rinse your face with warm water.

A mask made with potatoes that are boiled and crumbled (mashed), one egg yolk, plus a dash of hot milk. Wash it off with hot water after 20 min., then rinse your face with cold water.

A face massage—extraordinary effects: take a silver teaspoon (ideally, two), warm it up (ideally, dip it into a cup of herbal tea), use it to lightly tap your forehead, cheek, chin.

My heart's too full, how can I say what I feel, how? It's as if you were to gaze at a willow for a long time, a willow for years on end, and you become a willow. If you're a bad censor, then there's a lot you don't understand and you don't censor well; if you're a good censor, you understand too much, too much builds up in your soul and your enemy the text and your friend the text transform you. Love and hate converge! Censorship can't be a long-term career. It can't even be a long-term state of mind.

I'm a censor! It's a lost battle. I'm not the one you should be fighting, I'm not your enemy.

You start thinking that your egoism is natural, your confusion is natural, your sky becomes more important than the party's sky, with its sun and all its values put together.

Esteemed comrade Moldovean! How many times have I told you to stop beating around the bush in this notebook?! It was given to you to take notes for summaries and reports. That's it. Write down passages from manuscripts you have doubts about, write down the more important points from our unit's weekly meetings (I do that sometimes, but they're useless!) or the monthly general ones, to help you later in your work, write down the directives that everyone has to keep in mind, the new decrees that would also be good for you to recall, and, if your memory's not great, copy them carefully into your little notebook. The more important things you've censored, an opinion about some more considerable work, an alternative way of commenting or types of interventions and that's enough, little Didina! Enough!

Imagine if your colleagues were to read what you write!

Imagine if the head of the division were to read it (she's a decent comrade, she doesn't stick her nose in things, she wouldn't read this notebook even if she were obligated to!).

But the best thing would be for you to imagine those tall and handsome Securitate officers who inspect our offices reading your writing. Since they're so interested in how we're storing our secret documents. Imagine them coming to ask you: What kind of document is this? What does it contain? And how will you answer, and what will you do?

You search for subversiveness in others, you look for their ideological mistakes, but you, here, now, what are you doing? For shame! You deserve to be thrown out of Censorship!

We know, comrade, what a censor notebook looked like before com. Codrescu took you to burn secret documents. Yes, comrade Codrescu took me to the factory, I watched, I signed the declaration, she takes us in turns, but she likes Hermina the most, she goes almost every week. When little Didina saw for herself how everything's burned, destroyed, shredded, you throw in GDPP documents, our secret directives, notebooks, envelopes, entire files, and out comes cardboard or rolls of toilet paper in minutes, everything's whirled around, it's burned, it's chopped up, and not a trace of our work is left. Nothing! When little Didina saw for herself that everything's destroyed, everything disappears, she got the courage to write what she wanted, what she hadn't even dreamed of thinking . . . But I'm censoring day and night, I search and search through texts and I need to think and write a little in here, to organize my thoughts, to put them in order!

My supervisors tell me that my reports are impeccable, that they use them as examples for all the novices and the delegates from the provinces, but in the beginning it wasn't like that, it was hard for me until I got to this level. I teach others to write, to think, and it wouldn't have been possible if I hadn't written down a phrase or two every day, something. Improvement through reading and the correction of manuscripts makes me feel happy, satisfied, fulfilled, but only writing regularly, regardless of what I write, organizes and sharpens my mind.

In order to be able to think better, be more acute, have fresher thoughts, not only do you have to read what others write, but you also have to put some lines down, to write something yourself. The assurance that everything will be burned, that it's been that way for years and that's how it'll always be, gives me a feeling of freedom that not even the best interventions in manuscripts can give me. There I have to be careful, always ready with explanations, justifications. Here in my notebook, I don't have to justify myself, defend myself, control myself, they're my private notes, unconstrained, bound for the fire, I can make mistakes, exaggerate, leave out punctuation. But I put in all the punctuation precisely to be organized, to be better. I'm careful about syntax.

This notebook is my little bit of privacy, otherwise I think they know everything we do.

—It's no secret that "the location of military units constitutes top secret information of national importance," I'll never find something like that in my novels. That might be a secret everywhere in the world, but they're empty words.

Roza cuts in:

—Hey, it's not quite like that, you know. When I was in Press, I came across: the choir from the military unit in the neighboring village came to the fairgrounds . . . so we have the disclosure of a secret! Or about this year's harvest: if before a hectare barely yielded a few cartfuls of corn, now times have changed and the crops have tripled . . . another secret!

Hermina:

—I also have a difficult case to solve: in the novel *Burebista's Treasures* it says that there's so much ore and so many mineral deposits in the Carpathian Mountains that they could be mined for thousands of years . . . And he takes up three lines naming them . . . Okay, I can cut them out, but what if these rich guys are making up the names of these minerals, look, this rock, piezooptic, what if it doesn't actually exist in reality, we'll make fools of ourselves if we cut it out. Mineral deposit of something or other. Novels are fiction, authors have the right to invent whatever their hearts desire! Why don't they give us something, a notebook, a list of all the names, with instructions that could help us? What am I, a zoologist or specialist in mineral deposits and precious stones?

I put in my two cents in a wise tone of voice:

—In principle, we have to cut out all the real mineral deposits, but, if the authors are making them up only to put the country's history in as favorable a light as possible (basically, look at how rich we are and what treasures we have!), I don't think that should necessarily be cut. The real mineral deposit constitutes a secret, not the imaginary one. And like idiots we'd be cutting out who knows what metal "alvabut" or the precious stone "mastofact" . . .

—I bet they all exist, and that because of this Popescu guy's stones, I'll be slapped with a three-month pay cut. Plus a reprimand. And if it's very serious, goodbye, beloved Censorship!

—I haven't gotten something like that until now. These ones, with poetry, what do they know about state secrets! What good times we're living in! How many books are being published and what ungrateful and impertinent authors. The minute you let the little old men move their nibs . . .

A domain in which Roza excels:

—Ugly poets use many beautiful epithets. The more pitiful and scrawny, bald or paunchy, the more delicate, the more tender is the woman in the poem, sweet little wings, graceful angel, darling heart flame, golden and mysterious child. In order to compensate. Handsome poets write differently. Right now there are all kinds of young dragon slayers, who look like Prince Charming from the fairy tales. Youth conquers on its own.

Roza observed this long ago. She reads us a line or two and we guess: Is he handsome, is he ugly? But what exceptions! An ugly one writes as if he were the center of the universe, as if all women belong to him and he doesn't have to lift a finger to win them over anymore, he's tired. So Roza's theory only partially holds up.

You can get rid of oily hair by rinsing with the juice of one lemon, vinegar diluted in water (1:1), a few teaspoons of alcohol (beer, wine) plus half a cup of water.

Vinegar—

A lady teaches her servant good manners.

How to dress tastefully. How to match articles of clothing.

Young women are forbidden to wear exotic violet.

The man enters a restaurant first.

If a man grabs your waist, it means he wants to invite you to dance . . . (too much context).

If he puts his hand on your rear, his intentions aren't serious.

Baking soda is a very effective and very cheap way to combat perspiration, I found this recipe in two novels . . .

Nail polish will last longer and dry faster if you dip your hands in cold water.

Clothes come out cleaner if you soak them overnight in citric acid, from a historical novel (did they have citric acid in Stephen the Great's time?).

Ioana washes the window, then she wipes it with brandy. How shiny, you could eat off it, you'd say it was brand new!

Full-figured women look better in clothing with geometric patterns—tree patterns, stripes, plaid, large circles, small circles, fabrics in subtle shades with small prints are preferable.

Big-chested women should avoid large spherical jewelry—earrings or beads.

Do not wear more than two articles of jewelry at the same time!

Sportswear should be worn without earrings.

Masks of curdled or sour milk are good for your hair. Wet your hair thoroughly with sour or curdled milk and after twenty minutes rinse with hot boiled water mixed with baking soda (1 teaspoon per cup of water). Your hair will become silky and have a nice sheen.

Take care of a wig as you would hair. Wash it, comb it, and, if you like, you can curl it.

Treat rough skin on your elbows and heels with lemon peel shavings after a bath.

A large mouth will look smaller visually if you don't apply lipstick to the corners of your lips. (This is for Roza.)

Mosquitos won't bother you if you apply a mixture of unrefined sunflower oil, eau de cologne, and camphor, diluted with petroleum jelly, to the exposed parts of your body.

There are, of course, many categories of books that drive me out of my mind, but the worst category is—the ones from which I have nothing to cut. You can't pick on absolutely anything, it's so impeccable from all aspects that only a censor could have written it, or a filthy editor. But our censors don't write literature, they're not allowed to at all nor do they have enough free time. Meanwhile, no one's keeping editors from writing, they've even learned better than others what will pass and what won't, what will be cut and what will stay. About half of all editors have literary aspirations, what's more, they have the power to censor others, they can say to some take this out, it won't work, and they can add it in themselves. A bunch of cheats, we know all about them. They should be kicked out, the thieves!

Some authors are truly murderous. They attack the central nervous system. Those who puff themselves up with their genius, their talents, and their limitless good luck make their less fortunate fellow writers, as well as the average reader, fall into a state of depression, let alone censors! A reader can skip over a page if he doesn't like it, but we have to gawk at every letter. Stop with all the happiness! Put something tragic in the biography for the common good! Some infidelity, a disobedient child, an adulterer, a broken rib, a small accident, something. What a joy it is for everyone to be able to enjoy the chosen one's unhappiness! Genius is by definition unhappy. That we can stand. Gifted, but alcoholic. Beautiful, but unmarried. Talented, but ugly and hunched over. That's more like it, that's how we want them!

There's nothing surprising about novels. They start from a predictable pattern and when you summarize them, one summary can work for ten. Language makes them different, some prefer verbs, others nouns, others overwhelm you with adjectives. Long monotone sentences or shorter ones. Dialogue or description.

The volume *Quiet Waters*. Poems, about sixty.

The author sits at the edge of some body of water, that's where the poem's action takes place, ships go by, boats, a heron appears, seagulls scream. He could've said—the Black Sea, where the bums receive free vacations in luxurious villas, with good food and to-die-for views. Or the Danube—also ships and seagulls. But I can't officially, in writing, criticize him for something like that. The birds aren't screaming hostile things, the ships don't have capitalist or antidemocratic names, like the Queen Mary or King Ferdinand. The sails of the ships aren't black or gray (I could've accused him of inclinations toward pessimism), nor are they white (too much white would also give rise to interpretations, for someone not too long ago it was a symbol of spiritual coldness, of absolute nothingness, thus deserving of our attention), none of all that, the sails of the ships are beautiful and flutter in the swirling of the pleasant wind, a warm breeze, not a cold and biting gale. The flora is poorly represented, considering the preponderance of the maritime landscape. A small tree somewhere and no flowers, but flowers don't grow on the seashore, maybe they grow on the banks of the Danube but the lyrical hero is attracted by other objects and he can't be accused. It would've been totally different if he had written, if he had taken a vacation, the poor thing, at Peleş Castle, in the forest, in Sinaia. That's some real flora and fauna. Of all the animals and birds, those most satisfactorily represented in the volume are preponderantly sea birds, which fill the landscape in almost every poem. But we also get pairs of swallows, him and her, twice, sparrows five times, a stork once, "circling timidly and amazed," the heron mentioned above, related to the stork, appears with fragile legs, strolling from left to right and back, looking for a frog to eat. The frog itself doesn't appear, but it's mentioned.

Ha, if a lizard had appeared too! Or not just a simple decorative seagull, but a dangerous, hard-to-define bird that knows everything about you and follows you with its wild eyes, its feathers glimmering like epaulettes, and tears at the flesh of your poem—allusion to the Securitate and Censorship. If some animal with a square head appeared grinning fiercely—allusion to the party workers, bureaucratic officials. Or at least some storms, tempests, inclement weather that correlates with the psychological state of the lyrical ego, too little concerned with the achievements of socialism . . .

Nothing. We also get some flies and mosquitos at night, buzzing melodiously, five times. Small clouds in the sky—six times, fog—two, rainbow—two, evening—five, moon—two, sun—six. The sun compensates for the excess of night and rain, the poet gazes, thinks, rejoices, waits, starry-eyed and confident, many times. Smiles and sadness appear in equal measure, four times each, he goes (strolls) from one end of the road, path, I think, to the other, moments of calm. The writing can't be accused of being worthless, because his writing is convoluted, with stylistic flourishes, but he doesn't take it too far: "a lively sun winks hurried waves!," "I touched the large, cold stone, then a wonderful bird in flight appeared," "tweet tweet, the spellbound sparrows admired the sea's calmness."

I read it to the girls and add staunchly:

—I've got a good nose, ear, feel for everything ideological, I pick up any trace of hostility, I bark, I shake my tail, I say, joking, and I think it's a pretty good one. But no . . .

—So you're an ideological bitch, Roza jokes.

You obese lazy seal, I think and write . . . Better an ideological bitch than a bitch in heat like you . . . but I refrained from saying this to her. She's more popular with the bosses, with all the men. She sometimes banters even with Zuki. I can't brag like her that I dropped my boob over the director's head. With boobs that big, she could've crushed our beloved director, or at a minimum given him a stroke. If the other one had dropped on top of him too, it definitely would've killed him!

Freshly hired, she went one time to the director (not the new one, the former one, Ardeleanu) to get some signatures. When she bent over to have him sign the papers, a boob slipped out of her bra, then her dress, or rather she was braless, with the clear intention of tempting her superior (maybe she was dreaming of a lightning ascension?). She was there with her boob over his head, if it actually touched him while he was signing, we don't know, then she struggled to put it back and it's impossible for him not to have seen, because she was really pushing it (I mean, that's what everyone says, but maybe it wasn't exactly like that). But the comrade director, no reaction. You can't find bosses like that today. They're a dying breed.

Even though fiery Roza seems like a movie star the moment you see her, blinding you with her sultry beauty, the blonde (Hermina) is more beautiful after you get to know her better. The fiery one is animalistic, the blonde—more human. Hermina becomes beautiful when she reads texts, I can almost tell what she's reading by looking at her face.

The story of the diamond, full of censorable undertones:

A precious stone that shone, with perfect facets, fell into the kingdom of mud and got lost . . . Who are

you?—a shiny diamond. The mudballs were envious,
they wanted him to be as ugly and insipid as them
and they dragged him down, as deep as possible, into
the miry ground, until he disappeared completely
covered in muck and he couldn't be seen, he couldn't
be heard . . . They buried the diamond in the mud
and they said to him: you're mud, you're dirt like us.
And one day, the enemy of the kingdom of mud, king
scorching Sun, came and declared: I will let you live
only if you can give me a diamond, I've been searching
everywhere, this is the only place I haven't checked!
Then all the mudballs, frightened by his threat, pulled
the diamond out of the depths, here's your diamond!
Ha, the scorching king laughed: a diamond shines,
and this is a hardened mudball, an eyesore, a bit of
filth! Say who you are: I'm a mudball, like everyone
else, a mudball, a mudball, no, I'm not at all a diamond, I don't shine at all, I'm a hardened mudball!
Aha, death to you all! king Sun burst out furiously and
he pounced with his blistering rays on the kingdom of
mud and dried it out, all the dried mudballs cracked,
disintegrated, but as the diamond rubbed up against
the other mudballs, the mud fell off him, he spun
twice on his own and immediately he shone! The Sun
yelled: my Son!

In the only way out of a situation, we wait for the only
kind of effective lifesaving medicine, the only remedy
against old age, the only remedy
A single way to love and be young

The only way to answer correctly

The only song and the sole concert

The only ray that reaches us, day and night, moon and
sun in a single body, dressed up, two pieces, a suit. The
cosmos aligned to the higher order, the only whole.
The only king from the only story left in the only
pages puts on his only mantle, in a way that's unique
(and comic), upset at his only cheeky lady servant who
lied to him, after she saw his sword gone rusty, the
fallen member of a forbidden party, once the one and
only, now grown elderly. She laughed at him. The only
old king, now beggarly. And the last. The only fairy
tale that's still left unread, after the only flood, don't
be misled. While the only unmistakable voice from
the building across the street ruins the symmetry and
rhythm. It shouldn't be heard, yelling, complaining,
screaming, and preventing the wonderful singular
ending of the embalmed king.

The Poem of the Coin

The coin is very sad. Found by a child, after it was
lost by a drunkard who kept rummaging through his
pockets for no reason. Another child, stronger and
surlier, takes it from the first child and runs to the
store. He'll buy himself a kite, but we don't have kites
a stick of chewing gum, wrapped in pretty foil—we
don't carry that a small toy, a little boat—we sold the
last boat long ago and it cost a fortune, not a coin
then a bottle of fresh water—also too expensive

give me a wing, so I can take it to my mom to cook it,

a biscuit—but that also cost more than a coin.
We have nothing at all for a coin, was the reply.

The child walked out annoyed and threw the coin in
the dust, which is sad, because it was warm and cozy
inside the pocket, but it would've been better in the
store, next to its sisters and brothers, or even distant
relatives. Who'll pick it up from the dust if it isn't
worth anything . . .

Profoundly subversive, you'd think that our store shelves
were empty, or that anything left would cost a fortune! And
that kids are in need and collect small change off the ground.

The most poetic are the corners, the wooden beds, the
stone walls that are in so many poems. All of literature is scratched out on our walls, whispered in corners,
between morning tea and afternoon soup. Poetry is
tapped rhythmically, tap—taptap—t-ap—tap—tapta
long tap-tap allegro. The poetic walls are becoming
poetry by the day, by the day, overnight, until they learn
the alphabet, until the limits of suffering are annulled.
The plank is poetic too, and the bread, and the soap we
play chess with.

Allusions to prison poetry.

How boring . . . what a worthless book! This is how I'm
wasting my life away. How many times do I end up asking

myself the same thing, I think about what else I might have become? I wasn't at the top of my class in college, ha, not by far ... So I definitely would've received a modest post as a French or Romanian teacher in a faraway and chilly village. At least here, when I don't like a book, I don't have to come back to it, I turn it in and I forget all about it. While as a teacher, not only would I have to drive hundreds of kids crazy with literary nonsense, but I'd have to do it every year, dozens of times, always the same thing, the same text. The same stupid books, year after year. Here, there's always something new, unexpected, and it can actually happen that they're not all stupid, over the last two years even novels have gotten better, more complex, polished, there's stuff worth reading. Some I actually really get into and I'm sorry when I've finished them. Sometimes you find a recipe, a hair mask, sometimes you're also handed volumes of poetry, which are easy to read and are becoming more surprising. A censor's life isn't so bad. It doesn't stink in the office, you don't catch lice or the flu from sick kids who won't stop coughing. I met with a former colleague who had long silky hair, who told me she washes her hair with gasoline, because the kids keep giving her lice. Meanwhile, I'm only reading about this kind of thing in novels where minorities are oppressed by paunchy bourgeois men. Having two officemates, sweet and discreet, doesn't compare with having twenty-five to thirty kids jumping up and down and screaming. I'm not terribly beautiful, so I don't see myself getting married to or being courted by someone decent. Especially when I've already been married. Girls wilt like flowers in darkened schools and on top of that they're single. At least I can brag that I was married once. Not all our girls are married here in Censorship either.

Our girls, beautiful, with a well-paying job, some even have their own studio apartment, now they're past twenty-five, they turn thirty and they're still unmarried. Some don't like the job, they're bitter and dissatisfied, who'd want them, while I really like it and think this occupation suits me. I can't even imagine where else I could work, what else I could do. You brighten up the institution! Z. says to me. You come here as if you're on a holiday. I have to agree with him there.

Back to reading. Enough with the stream of consciousness and aesthetic reflections.

Write, write, write, read, read, read. Cover over all your senses, your thoughts, with letters and words. Don't lift your eyes off the page. I don't lift them. I curl myself up around the life-saving sheets. I buried him completely in letters, I pounded the ground over him down with heavy words, so he couldn't escape, I hid him, I killed him. And he, dead as he is, sticks his hand out from under the pile of words, slowly, unhurriedly, and reaches it over the pile. He searches around, feels the air with his fingers, as in a graceful dance, he searches for my hand, to caress it. My hand is far away, he doesn't find it and then he imagines it next to him and traces the caress in the air. I see his hand, separated from his buried body, shaking off texts and caressing me. Imperceptible touches, but so . . .

Concentrate. The texts are where you left them and they're waiting for you. The hand disappears, good, it melts away, it gradually dissipates, slowly, without ceasing its caresses, dancing with the same tender gestures. Some of us love each other only in dreams, as of lately, in texts as well: after the decree of 1968, we've all become platonic . . . I mean, everyone with light wallets. It's not a problem if you have the necessary connections, money, trustworthy lovers, little Roza assures us, as if she were encouraging us. To be able to hold in her arms a sweet, tender, romantic, enchanting poet, who whispers verses of unquestionable aesthetic merit while he rides her, she has to accept two or three generous high-level comrades as well, who behave in a civilized way, they give her gifts, they feed her well. Then she also has to accept two or three Securitate agents who sometimes aren't content with just her gift of faithful retelling and so the road to poetry is long and filled with obstacles. But it's worth it! she yells, startling us. I don't think she knows, either, whose child the next abortion is, because they all hurry to help her, only the poet says: Keep it, it's a human life, it's a shame, he'll look like you, he'll be handsome, he'll be happy. But she goes to the doctor and gets the child taken out. She tells us about it in great detail, though we don't ask her to, we don't insist, and we hunch over, busy ourselves, noses in our manuscripts. At certain stages you might feel like throwing up, I'm referring to myself, because, given how delicate she is, it's hard to imagine what Hermina goes through. I can handle it, but I pretend I'm not listening in the hope that maybe Roza will break off her confession. She doesn't stop talking, she keeps going and going. Finally, after she's described all the stages to us, the slightest, most insignificant desire to allow a man to get within three feet of us disappears. My belly rejects even the idea of a man. And all the manuscripts!

The literature of the future will be pornographic or nothing at all! our fiery colleague claims, reading verses to us about certain parts of the human body about which it's forbidden to express too much or too shamelessly poetic of an opinion.

To fuck with the mind! Forgive the expression, esteemed Securitate readers! But that's how Roza put it, not me.

—These writers fuck us with their minds! 'Cause otherwise they can't, they're impotent, unhappy, dissatisfied, petty and vengeful, with their pointy and aggressive, slippery, moist, and seditious texts, they're fucking us, the valiant citizens. They fertilize us, they inseminate us with their ideas! They impregnate us!

—And the party? (I risk asking, because I keep hearing the expression: the party keeps fucking us over!)

—The party too, day and night, relentlessly, now *there's* a member that can't be accused of impotence! But who believes it anymore? Who lets it get past the orifices of their ears anymore? Do you have the party in your heart? But you'd definitely like a sweet, moist cock in you, young communist darlings! These ones want poets, to create the illusion of the absolute cock (that's what Roza said, verbatim)! To read them and wet your undies, so your nipples get hard, to rip the crotch of the only pair of pantyhose you got off the black market in search of ideological mistakes! To pee yourself from searching so hard, to search until the roof of your mouth is dry, and you stick out your tongue to moisten your lips, dry from so much concentration, reading about desires, passions that are more explicit, more suggestive, more brazen, more direct. You search for mistakes even in your m.'s p. (excuse me, that's exactly what Roza said, spelled out, without the dots)! That's our profession, like border guards, we rifle through everything, because these ones hide things even in their heinies (Roza used the shorter variant: "ass!"), hidden meanings, dangerous, subversive, hostile metaphors. What they can do with three letters, let alone hundreds of letters, it makes your head spin! So, girls, stay vigilant and moist!

Thus, all that's left is for us to fuck with our minds, in the words of the poet and Roza (who's slimier!). To look ferociously into each other's eyes, to sling fiery snide remarks at each other, to shoot venomous arrows that raise any desire above sea level. What heights abstract desire can reach, and what a clear sound, what a sharpened knife! All that's left for us is poetry, comrades! That is, if we're not driven by the desire of immediate reproduction. For some, only abstract desires, while other men or women, sometimes under tables, sometimes under desks, are concerned with more concrete and pragmatic matters. Suckable love takes on important patriotic fervor, new and extremely varied perversions are discovered. More children still aren't born. Increasingly unexpected solutions are found, whereas before everything was simple and clear. Even capitalist-bourgeois customs flourish, despite all the precautions, interdictions, and weapons of Censorship and other authorized agencies. They intended the best, and the worst is happening. Even the notion of love itself is degenerating. Some say it's degenerating, others, that it's evolving. It can be seen in literature as well. Words can't be aborted anymore either. You say everything, you give birth, you commit a text. You procreate a poem, a novel, work, literature. Literary demographics, flourishing! If this demographic growth is what they had in mind, then they've succeeded! Any day now you'll hear writers numbering the children-books they gave birth to. We have room for children like that, after the purges of past years, they don't need to be fed. Long live our literary party!

"I'm a writer and my love life's a mess . . ."

I'm a censor and mine's no better, we're in the same boat . . .

Interestingly, whose love life isn't a mess? No one loves each other in this country anymore. That's why literature's so constipated too. Everyone's terrified that they might get their concepts wrong. The only thing they care about is for it to work for the Party, so they don't get their ears pulled. Who is the Party? A building? And what kind of readers do they have in mind? The Party takes a dump on their novels, and our souls are wasting away from continually trying to save them, to bring them to an acceptable form . . . The Securitate does its job and sometimes trails a couple of scribblers, inventing hostile intentions for them . . .

Dear Securitate officers, sometimes I get mad when you barge into our office with your unannounced inspections, but still, you're to be pitied, I hold no grudge against you, I just say things sometimes. We're fighting on the same side of the barricade. Of course, Censorship's not heaven on earth either. But how hard and unpleasant it must be when you're obligated all the live-long day to listen in on people's phone conversations! I see what gets to Censorship, where we know how many filters a text will go through and how many prior readers it'll have, and I can imagine what these people say to each other when they pretend no one's listening to them, disregarding our devoted

agencies and sullying the ears of respectable agents with all possible kinds of filth. Such shamelessness, such a lack of respect,
what assholes! You could bug their phone right in front of them
and they'd still talk as if no one were listening! A bunch of pigs!
They get to us somewhat cleaner and more brushed up and still
we've got a lot of work to do on them, some rather improper
expressions, words, but in comparison with what our Securitate has on its shoulders, what gets to us is a piece of cake. How
hard! I'm sure that they're receiving milk for such difficult and
psychologically assailant activities. And our man—still unsat-
isfied and ungrateful! He'd end up penniless and feeding at the
pig's trough without us. We help him become civilized, speak
properly, be careful what he writes, behave politely and respectfully to those who want, ultimately, all the best in the world for
him, but the seed of uncouth peasants is hard to root out. Full
of weeds, our people! We've got a lot of work ahead of us.

This week, besides Z., not one man came into our office. Z.
doesn't work in our department, he's not our supervisor, he
doesn't step into too many offices, and when he comes into
ours, he has so much to say, criticize, praise, convey, comment on, he eats up so much of our time that, after an hour
or two, we can hardly wait for him to leave. We get thirsty, we
get hungry, but he stays and stays and keeps talking, there's no
way you can go to the toilet, there's no way you can bury your
nose in manuscripts, where does he get all that energy, how
does he know so much? Just get him started on something. If
the subject is the act of censoring itself, then he starts with the
Inquisition, mentioning that censorship starts even before then,
but we'll leave its beginnings for next time. If we read a more

sophisticated poem to him, he tells us that poet, the author of that poem, isn't "discovering America" with that style of poetry, given that the ancient, classical, pre-classical poets already . . . On that occasion, he might also recite something to us from a similar classical standard, from Ovid especially, or one of the ancient Greeks, translated recently and superbly, superbly! (by some exterminator, only those guys know their way around the pre-classics), so that we can observe the similarities, which we don't actually observe, but we don't tell him . . . On I don't know what occasion, he declared that prostitution is also an art, practiced officially, and he gave us a solid introduction to the subject. I admit, we listened with our mouths agape. Whether it's all true or he makes some of it up, he knows how, when he wants, to tell a very interesting story. He doesn't scare me and he doesn't shock me with these dirty themes, but my office-mates! Hermina pricks up her ears and tries to look as busy as possible with something else, I think her delicate little ears are wilting from so much filth being spewed by the minute, while our passionate Rozie-Posie is licking her dry lips and she can't seem to sit still, she'd tie up devious Z.! The more unperturbed and contemptuous I look (though I'm listening dutifully!), the more Z. increases the quantity of words intended to stun us. I realize it's just a way of tempting us, a game of seduction, a mode of domination. The girls are easy prey, I understand that I have to resist, to not give in so easily. I look at his hair that flies out in all directions once he starts talking. He doesn't have enough shirts, probably, and some have gotten too small for him, they're squeezing him, his stomach's almost popping out. I stare either at his bald spot or at the waves of flab on his stomach, disgracefully outlined in his ill-fitting clothing, at any moment his buttons are about to pop, at any moment his shirt might split. I learn how not to listen to him. To concentrate on, to think about, something else. With his determined tone, he wants to put us in our place, he wants to conquer us, to demonstrate his superiority. Well, you won't win, sweet colleague! Sugary man that you are, Zukermano! I learn how not to hear him. Let him say whatever he wants, scream, throw his hands up in all directions, spit while he talks. I pull out my notebook and begin taking notes, let 'em think that I'm taking notes on what he's saying because, oh!, he's telling us such important things! Sometimes I really do write down what he says, because he knows a lot and knows how to tell it, other times I don't. At all. I do my own thing. I don't know what the girls are thinking, but they begin writing too, following my example. Z. gets tired and leaves.

Then months pass without com. Z. stopping by. When he runs into us, he's very courteous and kind, he invites us into his office. I'm not sure what exactly his title is, maybe he's a section chief somewhere, if he's got a small, comfortable office all to himself, without the headache of other colleagues. He helps us in any way he can, he brings us books, materials, he counsels us if we need it. We almost begin to miss him. It's desolate in our office, no one comes to visit us, we feel lonely and abandoned, we're almost missing Zuki. With him, you can talk about a thing or two, we find out the latest news in the institution, who's coming, who's going, who's with whom, who's against whom. Vacations abroad approved or not, for whom exactly, nominations for the August 23rd bonuses and medals are already being made, our work is being analyzed in order to determine who'll receive the awards, there's a list of censors being proposed for postgraduate studies and foreign languages. What notable mistakes have been made recently . . . How relations between the GDPP and our higher-ups have been developing and he taps his forehead, he taps his shoulder, so we catch on about who he means. He's very nice when he wants to be, com. Z.; he can read romantic verses to us from Eminescu as well, not just our contemporary miscreants. But the other things Eminescu wrote too, girls, we have no idea, what a scandal, he's also got passages that aren't quite fit for children and some of our examples come from him. Us: really? Oh, no, not Eminescu too! Without Censorship, not even Eminescu would've become a national classic! Without us, the face of literature would've been uglier, cruder, and incredibly dirty, the comrade grins . . . Then he complains that he's old, he's single, his belly's getting bigger, his hair's falling out. We assure him with complete conviction that he's the handsomest man in Censorship. But how many things would have to be censored for what we say to be true, he says (he's got a sense of humor and a sense of reality!). Belly—censored; bald spot—censored; and tongue, ah tongue, ce-en-en-so-ore-d, he sounds out to a dancing rhythm and he moves as if he were doing a folk dance, hop-hop. Then, to make me jealous (or maybe just because, like that!), he teases my colleagues, he praises them, fawns over them, they blush, fidget, blink, stutter, he reads their radiant futures in their palms, little damsels, beauties, the pride of the institution etc., etc. But it's really all the same to me, though I'd prefer for him to do it when I'm not right there. I don't ask myself what this man wants from me. I know, with the exactitude of a soldier: he wants me to be an even better censor, better and better, to know more, to develop a greater sensitivity. Love helps you travel faster down a very long and winding road, like yours, comrade Moldovean! You burn through stages, you sharpen yourself, you grow. I don't understand. You can't ram love down my throat. I don't love anyone!

Nothing. Around me, nothing, in books, nothing, in my heart, nothing.

Com. Zuki claims that the heart is just a muscle that pumps blood, up-and-down, side-to-side. The head is responsible for everything we feel and everything we love. Love has nothing to do with the heart at all, not a smidgen, not an iota, it's all in the head, that heart that we claim to love with is also located in the head. I sigh, though I have no reason to doubt what he's said.

We need negative characters in novels too. A complex novel, now, when our public has become more aware, more advanced, pickier, a complex novel contains a vast range of characters, two or three disgruntled intellectuals, worthy of pity and contempt, can appear in secondary scenes or even central ones, but why writers of all things, always writers? That's why it was good when they would organize trips to industrial areas, meetings with workers in factories and plants, with farmers from progressive cooperatives, otherwise, authors imagine that our country is populated only by writers and that this category represents all that's most important to us. False, of course. Unfortunately, you can't always intervene using this observation. You can't suppress the entire novel because of one character. Especially when the author is a party member, because now, as of late, they've all fallen in love with the party and you can't censor them any-

more like you used to. You can cut out a line of dialogue or two
and content yourself with that. You, a miserable censor, dare to
come and teach them, experts in the field, how and what they
should write? You dare overstep the qualifications of your job
for which you receive your generous (that's how they consider
it!) honorarium? I think of all these comebacks, I figure them
out, I predict them and I prevent them, I don't cut anything,
but I don't agree with it. I've got arguments too, but I'm not
going to fight against windmills. I'd have to be a stupid censor,
but I'm not and I want to survive. I think I can guess who's in
charge of Mentorship. Without adequate mentoring, without
a serious education, writers, even with all their talent, go bad.
Their environment is not at all conducive for the true socialist
novel. However, it's been proven that the authors born and
raised in what are considered adequate environments are much
weaker than the bad ones. Most of them have potential, regardless of environment, they intuit what's the best way to write,
we support them too, give them a chance, because maybe what
they didn't manage to say now they will say next time. We pay
them well, feed them well, take them out, get them some fresh
air, but most of the time it's a waste. I'd abandon them and
invest in others, I'd raise a new generation. A new school of
literature! But it's too expensive.

> April—in Constanta, the construction of the dry
> docks for the production of large-capacity ships is
> being completed. It can be written about.

> April 16–20: The spring session, in Bucharest, of the
> Inter-Parliamentary Union, with the participation of
> over four hundred political figures from sixty countries.

April 18–29: The XXXIX-th Session of the UN European Economic Commission takes place in Bucharest.

The Institute of Mathematics in Iasi, the Institution of Numerical Analysis in Cluj, the Center for Mathematical Statistics in Bucharest of the SRR Academy are now under the authority of the Ministry of Education and Learning.

Okay, and?

Ugh, I think it's the height of injustice that we're the ones who have to purge the library (we did it until our souls starting getting moldy too!), we have to monitor the status and the finalization of requests regarding Special Collections, and, at the same time, in order to be able to consult any ordinary volume, we need to have the validation of all kinds of little pieces of paper in order to be allowed into the Central University Library. "We ask that you allow com. Popescu, section chief in the GDPP, to borrow, in order to consult within the permitted time frame, books from the Special Collections necessary for personal and professional research. We would like to add that com. Popescu is a doctoral candidate at the Stefan Gheorghiu Academy. His doctoral thesis focuses on the theme of economic and social-political thought in the Romanian communist and social-democratic movement."

Romanian Romanticism, Dimitrie Popovici, 1969

The Romanticism of the Revolutionary Hero, Silvian Iosifescu, 1956

German Romanticism, Ricarda Huch, 1974 (it's already out!)

Romanticism in Romanian Literature: Bibliographic Contributions, Henri Zalis, 1967

Romanian Romanticism and European Romanticism, Alexandru Balaci and Yvette Nafta, 1970

Romanticism in Music, Ada Brumaru, 1962. A colleague from Art brought me this one.

And that's not all of them, but it's enough for a report. In any case it's just for "internal use," there's no need for personal and original analysis and observations. I have to look through them all, some I have to go through thoroughly, some I have to outline, and do this when? Besides the hundreds of pages I have to turn in on time, I offered to enrich my colleagues, talking to them about Romanticism! Who cares that it occurred to you, of your own free will, to present reports in meetings in which your colleagues either fall asleep or become exceedingly bored, same as happens to me when other zealots and goody-goodies present their reports. I regret choosing this theme, but none of the others were any more satisfactory. You didn't have much to choose from. I had avoided getting roped in to useless patriotic work as long as I could, but when the boss asked: "Who's never presented a report to their colleagues?" I was the only one and everyone was really surprised, what, such an exemplary comrade, such ability and nothing, not once? I quickly said yes, with pleasure, yes, I'd be very glad to, yes, I'd be more than happy! What wouldn't I do for my beloved colleagues! But on the inside it was the exact opposite.

I've started on my report of Romanticism. My bibliography is squared away and I've gotten down to work. When I started reading the first book, I discovered I had the tendency to look for ideological mistakes and oh! how many I found and how many things should be changed, and, in general, I don't understand how a volume in such a state could have been released! It came out three or four years ago, almost four, so it definitely came through our hands, not mine, but someone from out department handled it, of course. And look what it's like! Anyway, I don't intend to squeal on anyone now and, anyway, a thing or two changes from time to time for us too; what's one mistake more or less in a monograph about European or Romanian Romanticism, which not even the devil himself would read cover to cover, who cares! But, besides the mistakes, besides what shouldn't have appeared, besides what should've been censored as a matter of course, I couldn't focus on anything else. I said, fine, maybe this book's full of mistakes, let me pick up another one. I tried not to notice the mistakes anymore, just the main ideas that I was going to put in my report, chronologies, concrete uncensorable facts, when and where the phenomenon began, representative figures, trends, main aspects, but the mistakes kept jumping out at me. The more I tried to ignore them, not to think about them anymore, the more they overpowered me from all sides, as if on purpose, subversive phrases, hostile words, dangerous polysemantic lizards, leaving behind their poisonous tails in every line. Horrible! Everything's censorable! I lost any desire whatsoever to keep reading. I would've never guessed that I couldn't hold a book in my hands in any other way than as a censor, that upon finishing college (junior year of college, actually) that's the only way I would read! The girls sometimes flip through a fashion magazine under the table, the people from Export sometimes forget a dirty novel on their colleagues' desk, filled with depravities and sex, that our people secretly read, I know all about it, but it's their business! I don't, I don't, I don't read anything besides what I'm assigned to read, it's enough for me, I'm not even able to finish that and then I have to take the longer novels home. In all these seven years I've been working here, I've read an enormous amount, novels, poems, monographs, criticism, and many, many other things, looking for mistakes.

As a simple reader it's a totally different matter. A different way of reading. They relish the most beautiful poems, the most exciting, passionate passages in novels. I relish passages, poems, expressions, words that are incorrect from an ideological standpoint, hidden, ugly, wrong, hostile. I relish identifying them, finding them out in the pile of words, understanding them and extracting them from the whole of a book, cleansing the book of all that would corrupt the future reader, I relish cutting things out. I read intently, I read attentively, and oops! there you are, too sad, too dead, too rebellious, too mystic, too belligerent, too desperate, decadent, cosmopolitan, nationalistic, too Hungarian, too little socialist, too not at all enthusiastic, too too much, too too little, the mistake is hidden among innocent words, hands folded in its lap, painted sweetly, as if it were just like the other words, as if there wasn't the slightest reason, no reason at all, for me to intervene and cut something out, to take something out of the whole and throw it away. When this happens, and it always happens, I revel in it, I exult in it, I love it! Only like that.

It's slow going with Romanticism! I'd prefer to be working on a reptilian manuscript!

May—in Resita, a 4,000 hp engine is being built, the first one this powerful built in the country.

May 12–19—the first edition of the International Fair of Consumer Goods "IFCG 74" in Bucharest, with the participation of ten countries, with national pavilions and twenty-four foreign countries, with independent participants.

Nothing's being sold, it's just for display? They are selling things? Yes, but it's beyond our reach. Is anyone going Sunday, on the last day at least?

Hermina considers that it's very important that our work, no matter how intensive, not leave visible traces in the text, that the reader can't guess where and what we cut out. I agree. We should be as invisible as possible. I've known only one person who was able to tell you exactly where you'd intervened, no matter how hard you tried not to leave a trace. The fantastic Badrus, my former colleague. After the poet left her, she stayed behind in that godforsaken village. She was the only one in the history of Censorship who, after reading the books that arrived at the modest village library, sent us notes in which she would indicate the exact nature of our work there. Not maliciously, but collegially, out of boredom. She'd tell us with (terrifying!) precision what we cut out, what the initial version looked like. She could feel the lack of continuity, she'd show us when our intervention wasn't the happiest solution, she knew where it was missing coherence. She was so well-trained that she was taken back and made a supervisor. A talent like that scared our guys! I can't even tell you what it was like in the institution when Badrus would send us her wonderful notes!

I really hoped that only she was like that, I hoped that the other (regular) readers were concerned only with the content they had in their hands, not with what it was initially. What a nightmare it would be for a simple reader to show us exactly where and what we cut out from a text! Badrus wasn't just anyone, such cases had never happened before . . .

Of course, now the girls ask me about Badrus. They've heard all kinds of stories, they keep bugging me to tell them my version (I knew her personally, we were colleagues and we worked together in the main office) . . .

No one leaves Censorship willingly. Or very, very rarely. It could happen that high-level institutions might want to hire you. But those ones summon you, they choose you and request your superiors to send you over, sometimes without asking you. But for you not to want to work here anymore, to say, Enough, I'm leaving, is unheard of. One case, yes. An exception.

I remember her, I was still a student, newly hired in Censorship. Com. Badrus was considered (already!) the smartest woman ever to step foot in our GDPP, she was a star, not, however, because of her intelligence (she was also beautiful, but even that wasn't enough to make you a star here in Censorship), but because of the poets who fell in love with her. She was also the head of the Literature department—the most demanding and difficult one. Her work was continually praised, she was never criticized, and she slid in alongside the party, she entered into the good graces of people there as well, she made a career for herself. But she also had weaknesses, the story with the poet wasn't the only one. What must that man be thinking about her now? He abandoned a lowly censor then, and now he wouldn't even dare to dream about her, that's how high up she is. Whereas he remained a poet as he was, just some guy, still a slave to letters, dependent on the good humor of a bunch of party officials and zealous censors. She came back from that village changed, she had cut her long hair, had lost weight. I only met her after she came back, when she was in the office with us. She kept us all on a short leash, she inspired fear without raising her voice or frowning at us. In the beginning, I, too, was scared of her. Then I understood her. Yes, it was good that she moved on. Those who are too talented, too beautiful, too smart, too ambitious have no business being here.

She had wanted to consult with me once. I'll never forget the time. Regarding a young poet, but another one, not hers. She was emotional, affected, but, in the coldest and most disdainful tone of voice she could muster, she proposed that I bring up some objections as well and make a couple changes to that volume, if needed. Back then double readings were customary. Two censors wrote reports on the same volume. I don't mess with poets unless I'm obligated to, I'm not crazy about them and I was rather afraid of making my opinions public, especially side by side with Badrus's. However, I had no choice, I wrote the note quickly and gave it to her. She read it, I remember her sad eyes, like a kicked puppy, I think she realized this place wasn't for her and she was already thinking of leaving. She said in a tone that was meant to be neutral: "You're a good censor." I don't know what else happened to that volume . . . I don't even remember the author, that's how nervous I was. But it's unhealthy, condemnable to allow yourself to be affected by the object of your activity, by some beautifully arranged letters, filled with meaning, that fog up your mind and cloud your discernment. If a line makes you emotional and you're afraid that you'll miss its dangerous meaning, imagine that the poet was scratching his butt while writing it or something like that. But she was the boss, how could I give her advice? I've never been a boss nor ever will be.

Florentina Badrus, an energetic brunette, tall, strong, proud, etc. She also studied philology and would get all snotty and soggy at the university literary circles where the young poets went to prove themselves. One of them, who stood out a bit more, a good poet, as it happened—we still get books of his—made her fall head over heels. And the reverse proved to be true as well. She was probably also recruited when she was a student. Our people are recruited from college classrooms, when they get to Censorship, they're still students. She accepted. Naïve as she was and very young, she had thought that censors were the enemies of poets, the enemies of literature, in general. That's probably what her poet told her, and she heroically agreed to infiltrate the enemy camp and save the poet's work from their deadly clutches, the work of her gifted boyfriend. That was the rumor then in Censorship, we have no way of knowing the truth. But her boyfriend didn't know what the young student, his classmate and admirer, was doing for work. How would he know? The poet was really very talented, we, meaning the girls in our department, liked him as well, but we had no idea this story was happening at the time. When they hired her, no one knew about her love for the poet. It didn't appear in her file. She was studying I don't know what exotic languages and they sent her to Foreign Publications, to translations. Our little savior experienced a prompt let down, she didn't receive a single poem, she didn't censor, for the most part, anything. She translated, from Polish, I think, articles where the word "Romania" appeared. She was disappointed, she wanted to get here, to Literature, to poetry. A strange thing for a beginner, whoever could tried to get away from us as fast as possible, because it was hard, a lot of work, all of it demanding, they could get on your case even a year later if they spotted something in a volume you were responsible for. They let her learn the trade, she learned to cut honorably, they praised her in meetings and even gave her as an example of perseverance and devotion.

Eventually, the poet completely lost himself in his love for her, he declared that he wanted her by his side for more than just a few nights, in fact for eternity. He insisted, he pleaded vehemently for her to be his wife. How they became husband and wife remains a memorable page in the history of Censorship. He was to go to a village and she would have to accompany him. Both of them would be teachers, instructors in the village school. If she accepted, she could no longer save his poems from the enemy's clutches. They say that a beautiful and poetic dialogue took place between them in which he pressed her with his blind and crazy love, while she tried to warn him that it would mean poetic death for him, her refusal only attracted him more, she responded dryly to his increasingly fiery declarations. Her enigmatic way of being would've driven even a more level-headed poet mad, let alone a poor lovestruck, young and shy first-time writer. She poured more gas on the fire of their love, she tied him even more to her. He, more and more ardently, declared he would die without her. Abandon poetry if you love me. But my poetry is you, I write the way I breathe, it comes to me without my asking, it comes like that, like you. But I'm your poems' murderer, I receive a paycheck every month to clip the wings of your passionate poems, and to kill them slowly, wouldn't you rather die by yourself, of your own choosing, without me? Carried away by emotion, com. Florentina told her boyfriend what she does. I'm a censor, my dear poet! The poet broke down, then he said: I can give it up if you also give up this profession. She gave it up, she left us, she went to the small village, they got married, they wanted to forget everything, but he couldn't stop writing. He was wasting away, growing thin, there was nothing left of his former youthful enthusiasm. I thought it was over for him, with or without her. That he'd give up. He couldn't abandon her, he couldn't hate her. He was so gentle that he couldn't even be mad at her. He was as delicate as a flower and she was like burning lava . . . But he didn't stop writing. They say that's when she started writing as well . . .

—Poetry penetrated her until she became a poet herself! Rozette comments, as was to be expected, in her characteristic style.

One day, the poet ran away. He left her. Badrus worked as a teacher in the village or as a librarian (she was bored, pining, and she sent us her reading notes), while he returned as an editor somewhere, in the capital. Our people forgave her, they called her back, she came, she became head of Literature, she was my boss for a while, the period in which the stories about her and the poet circulated. Then they summoned her to the Party. An example of a successful career, an intense life, courage, and insanity. She could've been punished for saying where she worked, poets are blabbermouths, he might've spread the word, but the poet has a decent career, the censor has her career as well, the mistakes are forgiven. Others are thrown out because of a line of poetry, while Badrus is higher than we can even see. But she's also as smart as a whip, and very talented. People say that she, too, would've become a great poet if she hadn't become a censor. Now there's nothing keeping her from writing, but if you're a censor, it's strictly forbidden. Others say that she is a great poet, but she hides her real name. If she's now a party councilor, as I heard, in Culture, among the big bosses, her books would enjoy recognition and success. I think that the minute she imagines her manuscript falling into the hands of com. Craca, a colleague of hers in university days, or mine, since she knew me better, any desire of having a poetic career vanishes immediately. Or is she actually writing under a pseudonym? Is she publishing under a fake name, so we won't know, so no one knows who she is? I'm sure it hurt her that she was a censor, just a censor, she was ashamed, she disdained colleagues who loved their jobs, who were proud of having gotten here. I know this from personal experience. She wasn't proud of it, this wasn't her place. While working alongside her colleagues, she felt it was they, the ones who felt comfortable in their skin as censors, who truly belonged here, whereas she didn't, at all. I'm actually really glad she left. The two of us would never have gotten along. She loved poets and poetry, I love the fatherland and censorship. I was very young when she worked here, but I still understood a thing or two.

Ask Zuki, he's positive that she's writing under a pseudonym. He has outside sources that claim that Badrus, when she lived with her poet, became aware of her irrepressible calling as a poet, destructive, like an avalanche, so powerful that it was as if everything she had experienced alongside her poet transferred over to her—including his talent, including even his desire to live. After she returned here, she went from poet to poet, she couldn't stop, poets fell like flies in her web, they became incapable, sterile, after such brilliant beginnings, while she seemed to feed off their lifeblood, as if the poets, at the same time as their sperm, spilled all their poetry into her. The more they wilted and drooped, the more she blossomed, triumphed. What a career she's built, what talent! About her occupation as a censor, not one word! But Zuki wouldn't for the life of him say what she's called now, and I don't know a single poet who writes that brilliantly and enjoys the astounding success he claims. Maybe Hermina knows, poetry's her thing . . . In any case, if it's true, her later career among the poets was still made possible with the help of other institutions, because officially we're not allowed to publish anything, even under a pseudonym, not even book reviews.

Many rumors are circulating about her, she's become a legend in Censorship! What degradation, from a censor to a poet! How shameful! But everyone has their own destiny and it's very possible that a young college graduate might sooner dream of having a literary career than one here in Censorship. Censorship is also an art, you also need a vocation for it. Badrus didn't have it and merci au revoir. She looked a bit like Roza, also a brunette with an ample bosom, but I don't say this to Roza, so it doesn't go to her head.

When I asked Roza where she read that you should douse your head with a kilo of oil, she said: "It's from one of your novels, you read it to us, don't you remember?!" In a very ill-advised moment I must have read it. Her curly hair shines from all that oil, but for Hermina and me, it throws our noses completely out of joint. I've got oil at home too, but it doesn't stink like that! At least if she washed her hair Saturday evening, so that by Monday that strong odor coming from her head might have dissipated. But no, I'm sure that from some other novel of mine Roza must have found out that you should wash your hair once a week, exactly on Thursdays, so for two days it reeks of oil in here, Zuki figured out the secret too, and he visits us only on Tuesdays and Wednesdays. I've said before that these tips should be applied with great caution. Only once did I, too, want my hair to shine, so I oiled myself just a tiny bit, two drops, and I rubbed my modest braid, my hair stuck to my scalp and looked dirty, I washed my hair three times after that and it still felt like rancid grease . . . I arrived at the conclusion that not everyone was meant to shine and, after all, it's not only a person's hair that should shine . . .

Import-Export

A political activity par excellence, the work of the GDPP cannot be done by anyone other than people deeply attached to our regime, with excellent political training, conscious of the responsibility our work bears.

The education of people in this spirit has been a guiding precept in the operations of this institution's leadership, of the party's organization, throughout the years. The most valuable result of this effort is the fact that the majority of specialized workers have been in our institution for over ten years. The presence in each work collective of a group of veteran readers, with a great deal of experience and prestige, has ensured a healthy work environment, as well as their prompt intervention when needed.

The GDPP ensures the inspection of all editorial products:

Social-political publications:

– Editorial works (in the original and in translation) from the field of social sciences, party propaganda; works of a synthetic nature; lessons and plans for schools, brochures, documentary materials, et al.

– Publications for religious groups.

Literary and artistic publications:

– Editorial works (in the original and in translation) of
literature: poetry, prose, dramas, theory, criticism, and
literary history.

– Editorial works (in the original and in translation) in
fine arts and musicology, for specialists and a general
audience.

– Editorial works of a philological and linguistic
nature.

Technical-scientific publications.

Publications of a didactic nature.

These Exportsers are so pretentious, as if they were at the
top of the pyramid and they were the ones doling out slices of
the pie. For as long as I can remember being in the institution,
that's how they've been. Any birdbrain from this division feels
entitled to boss others around and offer us free advice, that no
one's asked her for, ever. There's no point in saying that what
they do in Export is a piece of cake compared to what I used to
do in Literature, my former department. Who pays any attention to their opinion regarding a book? When have they ever
been punished for approving the import or export of a publication? It's child's play.

In general, I've observed that each department in Censorship
is characterized by a prideful attitude (not always founded) and
they all consider themselves to be more vital than the others! I
admit: in my opinion, there's no department more important
than Literature and Art, where I come from. Without us, there
simply wouldn't be a reason for the institution to exist—fine,
us and Press. Books and newspapers! But if you were to listen

to the instructors, who work with those from the provinces, or if you were to listen to these fredericas from Export! They told me their names and I recalled only one, "Frederica," and when I need something, I start with "comrade Frederica" and they all wrinkle their noses, as if I were offending them. Maybe they'd prefer Freezeria-Diarrhea? Especially after one of them said: "Give comrade Filharmonia these notes to read!" One of them is definitely Frederica and I haven't butchered her name yet, I've politely refrained. They all look alike, all skinny, all wilted, indeterminate ages, sour faces. I already miss my girls! I nit-picked them, but compared to my new colleagues, my former ones were a couple of angels!

They've given me the spot by the door. I'm next to the door, what can I do, that's never killed anyone. As if I had the intention of running away, as if any day now I'd move somewhere else. For now, this provisional state doesn't bother me.

They've dropped the department's archive from the last two years on me, to read their boring notes and learn their trade. Some trade!

> Rules of conduct for employees of the General Directorate of Press and Publications in relation to foreigners.
> The inspection activities performed by the General Directorate of Press and Publications are not public and involve no direct working relations with foreigners. According to the regulations in effect, employees are required in any discussion held outside the institution (even with Romanian citizens) to refrain from any ref-

erence regarding the functions, attributes, and concrete aspects of the task of reading within the institution.

The work of inspection occasions GDPP employees to know an array of information and facts from different areas of activity that constitute state secrets or that without being secrets are not intended for dissemination. This increases their accountability and requires them to demonstrate the highest levels of prudence, in order not to divulge the information, facts, etc., as such, as well as the circumstances in which they came to be informed of them, since this affects the interests of our state.

Situations also exist in which GDPP employees fulfill tasks that put them in contact with foreign individuals, within the country as well as abroad. Employees should not be introduced to foreigners nor should they allow it to be understood that they represent the GDPP.

In order to provide support for employees who come in contact with foreign citizens, the regulations provide that the limits of the dialogue with the aforementioned that is set to take place should be established—as precisely as possible—beforehand; as is only natural, the discussions, however, at a given point can broach other subjects as well. The content of conversations held outside work cannot be determined ahead of time. For these reasons, the obligation is included of faithfully rendering in the requests for information, which must be drafted within twenty-four hours, the questions posed as well as the answers given, and different observations made concerning the attitude of the foreigners regarding Romanian citizens, regarding our country.

All this does not result in the recommendation of prohibiting contact with foreign individuals, but only that of respecting certain measures of security against those who would seek to obtain through indirect channels certain facts, information, opinions, etc. that could serve their hostile purposes.

It is asked of each employee, according to their training and areas of responsibility stemming from the political work they undertake, as a citizen of our socialist fatherland, that through the discussions they hold with foreign citizens they contribute to their interlocutors' comprehension and affirmation of the policies of our party and state, toward a better understanding abroad of the achievements of socialism in our fatherland.

When you have a problem, a question, a complaint, you go to your immediate superior in the chain of command, you don't run to the head of the institution or to your relatives in the party.

I've had it up to here with your documents! Every day I'm handed some "the most important document" or other without which my existence in this department would be unimaginable! I'm here copying things down like an idiot!

Sheets with themes inadvisable for import

– works of a nature obviously hostile to our country and communist regime;

– books that promote a foreign and hostile ideology in relation to Marxism;

– books of an idealistic orientation;

– books for children that contain elements of bourgeois morality promoting outdated values;

– the works of counterrevolutionary authors (who're they?);

– the works of Romanian authors in exile;

– religious, mystic literature;

– adventure, detective, and society novels that propagate crime, violence, immorality;

– literature published by religious societies, regardless of content;

– literature by prisoners;

– books that praise monarchical regimes.

While I'm wasting away reading and copying out all kinds of documents, one of my colleagues assures me that in Export, in fact, the work's not so hard, you read a book and write a note. You pick on something in almost all the books and, in conclusion, in the last sentence, you don't approve the translation, you don't approve it for import.

—Not one book corresponds, in fact, to our socialist standards, Frederica assures me in a pedantic tone, and after I've found two or three incriminating passages, I don't even bother finishing the book. If I say that I don't approve, I'm not taking on any risk, the superiors decide what they need to do. They'll

approve as many books to be translated here as the foreign countries are prepared to translate into Romanian. As many as they
approve, that's how many we do too. The title selection doesn't
depend on the opinions of censors anymore. The work isn't hard,
but what a nest of vipers, what a stifling environment!

Some news, I already knew this back when I was working in
my office. It isn't hard work, but I moved here a week ago and I
still haven't received a single book in French, as I was expecting.
I've spoken with Zuki, apparently for us, in Lit., it's a disaster
without me: two comrades have come in my place, Ciufecu and
Turcu, fine boys, praised, considered censors with great futures
ahead of them, but they've proven to be completely unprepared
for the new occupation. I don't know whether Rozy's cleavage
also contributed to the turmoil and confusion of the new colleagues. I don't really think so and secretly I'm glad. You find
out who the true censors are only in Censorship. Hmph, more
than half the institution's employees have never truly censored
anything in their lives! They don't even have a clue what it is.
But they've got their noses stuck up so high in the air you can
barely see them! I'm going to rub it in the faces of these idiots
in Export too, but for now I'll sit quietly and behave myself.

The two boys came from what used to be Training-Inspection,
seeing as how the number of censors is dwindling, there aren't
really any more openings, no new positions are being created,
meanwhile in the provinces they're doing massive personnel cuts,
who would they be recruiting, who would they be training? So
they transferred the boys here, in order not to kick them out.
They've had it pretty good up until now, they were gone for
weeks at a time, since they were coms on a mission, and they'd
come back carrying some scrawny student in their teeth who was

fainting from fright, positive that he'd fallen into the hands of the Securitate and if he didn't agree to collaborate, prison awaited him. Our guys would act like bosses and put fear into people. But faced with any ordinary text, they are completely thrown for a loop. Instructors don't exist anymore, they've made them Local Press. Ha ha, instead of the famous Training-Inspection Division! They don't have anyone to instruct anymore, poor things, and they sent them to us, to censor poetry.

The names of other divisions have been changed as well, but the job description and the makeup remain the same: Press is now Central Press and Radio Broadcasting; Export-Import is Import and Export Publications, for us, after they stuck Art onto us, they didn't change our title again. The girls here discuss that we (meaning the Literature and Art Division, where I come from) and Technical and Social Sciences (they've stuck several departments onto them as well) are now the biggest departments in Censorship, after the latest transformations.

The attitude of my colleagues here toward Zuki astonished me. Very respectful, and they don't call him anything other than "comrade director." What kind of director might my Zukerman be? And what side-eye they all gave me when I said to him, in a familiar tone: "Zuki, you promised me last time . . ." I'll wait a bit and then get it out of these prigs . . .

> A note referring to the list of inclusions in the editorial plan for social-political books for 1974:
>
> —25 titles were approved by comrade Cornel Burtica, secretary of the CC of the RCP;
>
> —11 titles represent works that will appear on the

occasion of the World Population Conference, they were approved by the decision of the CC of the RCP;

—2 titles were included as a result of certain obligations in collaborating with institutions from other countries;

—7 titles represent works approved by the Presidium of the Academy of Social and Political Sciences (the positions are indicated).

The visit of comrade Nicolae Ceausescu in the Federal Republic of Germany

The visit of comrade Nicolae Ceausescu in Latin America

The visit of comrade Nicolae Ceausescu in the United States of America

M. Berzea—*Romania—The Promoter of Peace in the Balkans*

C. Popovici—*Physical Labor and Intellectual Labor in the Process of Forging a Well-Rounded Socialist Society*

L. Serban—*Alienation in Contemporary Capitalism*

A masterful exposition by the secretary general . . . A contribution of overwhelming importance in the well-rounded development of Romania, ensuring the well-being and happiness of the people, the forging of the new man, with a heightened revolutionary consciousness, a devoted builder of socialism on the precious land of the nation . . .

I've decided to stop getting worked up and upset that they give me these kinds of documents to read. If this is Z.'s handiwork here, I'll find out what his intentions are. But I'm very disappointed and I consider it a travesty to make a censor with this kind of potential, such as myself, copy out a bunch of nonsense!

We inform you that over the course of 1973 the following associations were constituted, as reciprocation for the associations for friendship with Romania active in different countries: Romanian-Chinese, Romanian-Korean, Romanian-Mongolian, Romanian-Egyptian, Romanian-Italian, Romanian-Peruvian, Romanian-Chilean. In 1974—Romanian-Indian.

The list of works from the program for export for which "P"-stamp approval is requested

The "Ion Creanga" Publishing House

N. Nobilescu, Gh. Zarafu	*Bark*
N. Nobilescu, Gh. Zarafu	*Meow*
N. Nobilescu, Gh. Zarafu	*Squeak*
N. Nobilescu, Gh. Zarafu	*Quack*
N. Nobilescu, Gh. Zarafu	*Chirp*
N. Nobilescu, Gh. Zarafu	*Thump*

The Technical Press

A. Strambuleanu	*The Industrial Flame*
C. V. Negoita, D. Ralescu	*Vague Crowds*
D. Moraru, I. Dimitriu	*Humidity in Production*
I. Oprean	*Romanian Cooking*

The SRR Academy Press

I. Fagarasanu	*Liver Surgery*
Sala Marius	*A Historical Phonetics of the Romanian Language*
Beles A., Soare M.	*Elliptic and Hyperbolic Paraboloids in Construction*
Vaicum Lydia	*The Biodegradability of Detergents*
Dan Dascalu	*The Unipolar Injection*
Keintzel Schoen	*Family Names of the Transylvanian Saxons*

The Medical Press

E. Aburel	*Genital Tuberculosis in Women*
P. Lepadat	*Intestinal Infarction*

The volumes have already been approved by several committees of specialists.

Oh my goodness, I'm dying over here! Humidity, tuberculosis, infarction! Where are my books of poetry, where are the novels about our wondrous life?

I know why I've ended up in this horrible department! I mean, I suspect. I once told Z. that, from having read so many novels, I've begun seeing the frame, mechanisms, concept, first floor, second floor, what the author wanted to do, to say, and how it actually turned out, and, at a certain point, a new perspective opens up, something opens up that makes me understand the author's potential for being either hostile or innocent. Those without the potential for being hostile or subversive usually don't have any talent and they're not writing prose. The intention of writing a novel in itself already contains a certain subversive potential. Some poets can be innocent and benign, a very few essayists or literary critics are. But critics, too, aren't critics unless they throw into their canon some capitalist dog or someone merely nostalgic for the former feudal-bourgeois regime . . . Of course, there are also good, trustworthy critics . . . But to stick to my main idea . . .

I began understanding what might come of the author's raw material. Meaning what he seems to intend to demonstrate and how it evolves . . . and we don't always arrive at what we should be demonstrating. Our intention might be honorable and unanimously approved, but the means don't allow us to carry it out. Characters that die halfway to their destination. Or the character who, after being brought to life, can no longer be controlled by the will of the author, he obtains a kind of personal independence and evolves in a roundabout way, and the author doesn't have the strength to take him where he should. Somewhere, someone stumbles, he gets lost, and because he doesn't have the privilege of following the story as only a censor can, he ruins everything. Authors don't read novels noticing technique or concrete things—the worst of it is that they don't think geometrically and they don't really read, in general, and instead spend their time writing. Of course, art doesn't conform to strict rules, but the construction of a novel presupposes some rules and naïve authors miss them, I feel this with every fiber of my being! In poetry, when two plus two equals six, it can be wonderful, original. But in prose it's a catastrophe! Mathematics should be a required course for those who are contemplating bombarding us with miles-long prose. A math class before every novel. So they know not to start with a love story unfolding at the height of collectivism, only to be derailed afterwards by fundamental questions about the meaning of life. They get lost along the way, become didactic, saviors of the nation . . . I'm really tempted to show them where exactly around the bush they lost it. But no, I'm not allowed to leave a trace. I can make notes, suggest what passages should be cut. Novels have an indescribable architecture . . . I was discussing this with com. Zukerman, who I remember listening to me with great interest, even if sometimes with an ironic glimmer in his eyes. I think that's when he first said to me: "A bit of experience in Import-Export would do you a world of good, com. Moldovean." I didn't understand what he meant at the time and, to be honest, I still don't. Well, going by the look on his face, he seemed to be saying: You've gone off your rocker and you need a break, but I hope I'm guessing wrong. It's a kind of break here, for sure. But I'm tired of copying out nonsense!

One of the Fredericas teaches me the ropes. I listen to her, it's more interesting than endlessly copying their documents. She talks to me about the mail. Half of the colleagues from Import-Export aren't in offices here, like us, but at customs offices, in train stations, airports, post offices, and they inspect the publications coming in or going out. We handle the books that arrive, through special contracts, for translation. We approve or don't approve the translations of volumes in foreign languages (she's referring strictly to what people do in this office).

We hate the Securitate, those pigs, especially since they've started coming by here constantly, constantly checking up on us, considering themselves superior to everyone else in this country. But when it comes to the mail, we pray that we get intelligent, curious, ambitious Securitate officers who might be interested in our books and give us something in exchange. Share their goods with us. The rotten imperialists aren't stupid. They know what it means to go through the mail, the inspections, the transfer of goods! You put something in the package for the customs officers, because they're people too, if you want at least some of the package's contents to arrive at its destination. If there are three or four boxes of coffee or three scarves in the box, then for sure one will get to its recipient, at least out of appreciation for the sender's generosity. But if you get stingy and you put in just one, then bye! We didn't receive it, it didn't arrive. All the goodies fall into the hands of the Securitate, absolutely everything, we're left with only the inedible publications, unfortunately.

With books it's simpler, if it's for the Party, we send everything, we don't even open it, usually. For important figures in various domains, as the case may be, at least 50 percent, usually, get to them (we have precise instructions and lists). But your average mortal, some poor sap on Furnicilor Street, why would he receive foreign literature that might be, because of its content, hostile? And it's a rare book from abroad that doesn't fall into this category. In cases when the package contains about ten to twenty copies of each volume, what can we do, especially if we decide that it's unsuitable for reading and there's no need for it to arrive at its destination? Officially, you send one, okay, two, to Secret Collections but the other copies have to be destroyed. What a shame for such expensive publications! Sometimes books with pictures, in foreign languages, hardcover, on glossy paper, valuable. Well, and if we're lucky enough to have a more curious Securitate officer, we'll hand him a book or two, in the hopes that he'll have the decency to give us something from his miraculous packages. It's safest and easiest to offer banned books to Securitate officers. Because they're the only ones checking up on us and they're the only ones interested in what happens to banned books. No one can punish us if we give them books. And it's not out of decency or courtesy when an officer happens to share something with us. Well, at first that's what we thought too. People sometimes find out, whether from letters or in other ways, that they should be receiving a package, sometimes they know exactly what and, when they don't receive it, all the blame lands on us. When the disgruntled person is a more important figure, investigations are made, they try to find out who's guilty, they find out, but nothing ever happens to anyone, and just like the dead never return from the grave, neither does the coffee from packages. We can't do anything because, officially, we don't even exist. As you well know, esteemed comrade Moldovean, in our communist regime, censorship doesn't exist! To pretend that the Securitate doesn't exist either would be too much. But the Securitate officers pretend with complete aplomb that Censorship, even though officially it doesn't exist, goes crazy for—we don't know why—coffee, chocolate, tights, and soap, the imported kind and exactly what happens to be arriving in packages for comrades through the mail! If they're going to blame us anyway, we do what we can to ensure that a coffee bean from the missing package, a bite of chocolate, or a measly pair of tights finds its way to us too. But nothing's for free. So we do an exchange. In general, even the stupidest Securitate officers, who've never read a book cover to cover in their entire lives, allow themselves to be seduced by the sight of an attractive book. They won't read it, but they can sell it somewhere, or give it as a gift to a superior. They have an extraordinary nose for business and they rightly consider that one of these thick books, written in an unknown language on white paper, is more expensive than the trifle from their package that we're dreaming of. Meanwhile we're happy with even the smallest trifle, because no matter how expensive it might be, the book would still have to be destroyed if we didn't trade it for something. What commercial exchanges take place at our lookout posts! All censors dream of making it to the mail!

If I had ended up in Securitate, I would never have referred to them as "those pigs," I wouldn't have called them stupid, etc. They would've been the best. As it is, censors are the best! And as for Securitate officers, I adopt the point of view of Censorship and of other humble readers.

> Comrade Major General Nicolae Bucur, Minister of Internal Affairs
>
> We are sending, attached, the following materials which were discussed by the GDPP Leadership Council in a meeting on April 15, 1974:
>
> Summary regarding the infiltration of libertinism, vulgarity, and pornography in certain publications from the West.

Summary regarding certain materials from Bulgaria, from the press in Soviet Moldova, certain problems regarding Romania reflected in the press of the People's Republic of Hungary.

Problems discussed in Czech and Slovak press.

Announcement regarding certain problems referring to our country that have appeared in the Polish press. Announcement regarding certain aspects of Romania's domestic policies reflected in publications arriving from the USA during the period of March 1, 1973—March 1, 1974.

Please note that all these materials of a strictly confidential nature are for your exclusive information, and we ask that you return them to us as soon as possible.

Signed Director General: Ion Cumpanasu

Most of the readers in the Foreign Publications Division (currently Import-Export) work with newspapers and magazines in foreign languages that arrive in the country through private or state subscriptions, solicited or unsolicited. Periodic publications are read carefully and if they contain information that could be harmful to our readers, they are recommended for suppression, a noble and honorable occupation. If some article is of interest to the party or other high-level institutions, they translate it partially or entirely, upon request, usually everything referring to Romania. Sometimes the party reads the newspaper before Censorship and a request for translation comes in at the same time as the request to inspect it, regardless of how good or bad the material is, orders aren't questioned. In such cases, Import-Export readers find themselves more in the position of foreign language translators than censors, and for years, all their activity is reduced to translations. In fact, they've never shouldered the responsibility of censoring, they've never had to cut something from somewhere, you can barely consider them censors, meanwhile what colleagues in other departments do doesn't matter to them, it's of no interest. They don't really come in contact with the others, if they work from customs offices or post offices, we don't see them for months on end, even I don't know what their faces look like. They excuse themselves from participating in meetings, if attendance isn't required, always citing their large volume of work. As if they were the only ones working in this institution. The girls explained to me that, as opposed to other colleagues, to ones dealing with books, like you (meaning me), they have to turn in the publications immediately, to make a judgment from one day to the next, they work with important state institutions, ministries, high-level subscribers, who pay for expensive subscriptions and you have to have extremely well-founded reasons not to put them at their disposal or to delay their delivery too much, especially in circumstances when you have to inform the party and give it time to decide. Speed's of the essence there and it's a huge headache.

The Romanian Bank for Foreign Trade subscribes to a series of specialized periodical publications abroad among which we mention the newspapers: *Agence Economique et Financière, The Financial Times, Handelsblatt, Le Monde, The Times*. These publications are strictly and urgently necessary in order for bank leadership, as well as executive Party and State agencies, to be informed as efficiently as possible on the latest regulations, and economic and foreign currency financial developments in capitalist countries, as well as regarding the up-to-the-minute situation of monetary and foreign currency exchange markets, the precious metals market, etc.

Insofar as the newspapers mentioned above reach us as a rule with a delay of approximately three to five days, sometimes even greater, thus annulling the value of certain news items in making decisions designed to protect our economy's interests, we ask you, in the spirit of good collaboration, to analyze this problem and to arrange for the respective publications to be received by the Romanian Bank for Foreign Trade as a matter of priority.

Lately, we have received numerous complaints on behalf of certain institutions and important figures in the scientific and cultural-artistic world concerning the nonreceipt of certain foreign publications to which they subscribe, either within the country or abroad. Please note that the majority of complaints refer to publications suppressed by the GDPP on account of their inappropriate contents.

One of the Fredericas, spiritedly:

—One day late and so many people up in arms because of one thing or another. We don't give them their treasures, what bureaucracy, what a tragedy! While the book you (meaning me, when I worked in Literature) are censoring now or that you censored last week or last month, if it appears two years later, the author and everyone else will be happy. You read quickly (they've heard as well!), however some hang onto a skinny little manuscript for even two months, you saw the problem was brought up at the last meeting.

I also know the nature of the manuscript the unfortunate person had: it contained the names of precious stones, and their publication might constitute a violation of state secrets. The poor censor had read the directive that stones of a certain category are to remain secret, but, practically speaking, who could know which ones, and what a scandal it might cause if it's later discovered that something from a certain category shouldn't have appeared . . .

Now we get down to discussing the directive:

Reserves of mineral wealth are secret as pertains to overall data, as well as for individual deposits.

The greatest attention should be paid to:

—nonferrous, rare, and noble metals;

—rare soils;

—scattered elements;

—piezooptic minerals;

—radioactive elements.

For any censor, the fact that the minerals or metals that belong to each group aren't concretized constitutes a difficulty. In order to understand what a "scattered element" is, we have to consult several academic papers, to write up files as documentation listing them with their definitions, which steals time away from our reading and leads to the retention of the manuscript.

In situations like that, it would've taken me a while too, I would've sat on the manuscript. But two weeks with an itty-bitty brochure just a few pages long is a lot in any case; I also know there are colleagues who have a manuscript on their table officially and sci-fi novels under their desks, some are lazy too, and irresponsible, also those who aren't as well-trained, who don't know what they should be doing, but they don't ask for help either . . .

In general, what gives us the most trouble are unsolicited publications, especially ones sent for propagandistic purposes (commercial, touristic, cultural, political) in a large number of free copies. They're sent by magazine editors, publishing houses, different enterprises specializing in disseminating publications, to the addresses of institutions, publishers, and especially private individuals.

> Unsolicited publications are divided into two categories:
> —those that don't raise political issues, which are forwarded, usually, to the addressees, regardless of the quantity in which they come and who sent them;
> —those that raise political issues and that, through their content, infringe upon art. 67 of the Press Law Act. If they arrive for private individuals through the regular mail, they're confiscated; through regular mail or customs from capitalist countries, they're confiscated or returned; from socialist countries, they're confiscated. If they present documentary value, they're handed over to Special Collections. If they arrive for important figures and specialists, it's resolved on a case-by-case basis.

Publications from the USSR are not subject to our inspection. Our division reads issues of the main publications from the Soviet Union only as a matter of information.

Each year we receive a list of the beneficiaries of "special shipping"; the political figures, institutions, publishers included on this list receive foreign publications without passing through our inspection.

(Where is this secret list? Do you all have it as well?

Our colleagues in Mail, where the publications arrive, have it. We don't need it.)

Religious publications are confiscated—with the exception of what arrives for institutions and figures from religious organizations included on a list communicated periodically by the Religious Affairs Department.

Publications in Romanian and Hungarian arriving from Israel, regardless of the recipient to whom they are addressed, whether institutions or private individuals, are confiscated (exception: head rabbi Moses Rosen).

The most wonderful moment of the year.
    The censors' annual meeting! I've been waiting for so long. What diversity of species! The complexity of our profession

is never so clear to me as when we have the censor-delegates from the provinces with us. Day after day, months, years in a row, we sit in our offices and carry on with our work, each with his own. If it wasn't for our weekly meetings, we wouldn't see our boss for months, and if it wasn't for our monthly general meetings, we wouldn't meet with our colleagues from other departments for years. Before, we'd all eat at the lower cafeteria, everyone meaning most of two or three departments, because many people work in newsrooms, in customs or post offices. Some we just say hello to—we know they work here, we recognize their faces—without striking up a conversation. Maybe the heads of sections, or services, or divisions meet up more often, they go to gatherings or party meetings from time to time, but we readers lead a static life in the office, without unexpected events. With the exception of the general conferences of censors from the entire country, a real event in Censorship! It's the only situation when hundreds of us censors gather together, not only to exchange experiences but also to attend extra-censorial activities of a cultural, social, etc. nature, concerts, films, plays, banquets in restaurants, etc. Guests from the provinces are divided into smaller groups for specialized seminars, discussions, and conferences. I'm always one of the people who's given a group to coordinate. During this time, for the span of a few days, I'm looked up to as a god, a goddess, none of them can take their eyes off me, both men and women, they take notes while I talk about my experience in Censorship, about the mistakes I've uncovered, about general trends, and, of course, about professional secrets in tracking down the enemy. I feel very important, I even feel very beautiful, and I really like teaching them. I need this, especially now, when they've moved me here. (I feel like saying: as a punishment! I consider myself a convict, an innocent prisoner!)

I like being surrounded by a crowd of censors, we feel wonderful together, we feel like a powerful, invincible army! I'd like to be around even more censors, I'd like to be surrounded by thousands of censors; three hundred some, our actual number, including the provinces, isn't enough for a country as big and flourishing as ours. Not enough and it shows . . . I like encouraging them, giving them advice, helping them. I try to answer as best I can all their challenges and questions. Some of them are phenomenal, born censors, I barely start speaking and they've already understood what I want to say, they guess immediately what needs to be cut out when you present them with a sample text. There are, however, unfortunately, also those who aren't too bright, but are conceited and stubborn. They'll never admit they've made a mistake, they don't show any flexibility, they don't want to grow. I think strings were pulled for them to get here, because it's supposedly nice, easy, not stressful, and not too much work. If only it were really like that . . . They're lazy and they don't want to break away from that pattern. It's impossible to teach them anything. If it weren't for the good ones with a true calling, the future of censorship would sadden me. The future that's been disturbing me for some time now anyway.

I'm troubled by the "transfers"—a subtle euphemism marking our gradual disappearance, I hope I'm wrong, but I'm afraid they'll "transfer" all of us until the entire institution disappears. Censorship must have powerful enemies if that ends up happening. Whom does it bother that we exist and do our jobs? I couldn't say. But I feel a great deal of uneasiness and I think it's impossible to live without censors. How will books be published? How will television, radio, newspapers, magazines survive? No, we're not talking here just about the enemies of censorship, the enemies of the entire nation want to destroy us, they want to destroy our country. I don't know who these enemies are. Maybe poets, writers? Maybe those whose works we cut, maybe them? But they're helpless and cowardly, they allow themselves to be trimmed and clipped without even making a peep. It must be someone more powerful, higher up, someone who's following us closely and who gives us only as much power as he desires. He maps out tasks for us, he gives us missions. Then when he thinks that there's nothing left for us to do, there's nothing left to censor, our mission's over, it ends here, we're no longer good for anything, he "transfers" us, in friendly fashion he sends us to other institutions. As if you could transfer censorship! As if censorship were ever really ours. Too many people practice it, they've stolen the tricks of the trade, maybe they can do it better than us and we don't even know and that's why we've become useless and transferable. These days, even a snot-nosed first-time writer begins his volume with "Ode to the Party"! There's nothing left for us to cut, the lesson was successfully assimilated. This is as far as we were meant to go.

The Fredericas from my office talk of nothing else. I'll return to this.

Up until recently I hadn't even heard about transfers, before last year I hadn't noticed so many people leaving. Whereas, starting a few months ago, there's not a single meeting where we're not informed of new orders concerning "strategic employ-

ment transfers." I was also here when they'd give out orders with
spreadsheets of comrades "requested" by other institutions, the
most prestigious ones, usually, where many of us never even
dreamed of reaching, such as the State Department, the Council
of Ministers, and other prestigious ministries. Those times have
passed, *hélas*. Some colleagues would be content and happy
with just the position of cultural councilor somewhere or as a
teacher in an educational establishment or as one of the editors
of a newspaper. Most of the censors from the provinces actually worked in similar fields before receiving the offer of working
here. Usually, many of the censors from the provinces are or were
employed here part-time (some even with only a quarter of the
normal hours), working simultaneously as editors, professors,
party activists, cultural workers, etc. They wouldn't even notice
the difference. But me? I've been working here since I was a college student, starting junior year I've been reading manuscripts
nonstop, improving the state of texts, I've never done anything
else in my life and I don't at all wish to. I never want to be transferred, anywhere, all I want to do is censor texts, that's all I know
how to do, until my dying day that's all I want to do.

After each weekly meeting, the girls in my office whisper among
themselves, agitated, worried. From what I gather, they're firmly
convinced that people from Import-Export are transferred to
areas that have nothing to do with their actual work.

The girls claim that readers from Ideology, Press, and Training
are transferred to institutions of higher learning, the general
administrative offices of the Council of Ministers, the Committee
for Radio Broadcasting and Television, prestigious presses and
newsrooms, People's Councils, the National Tourism Bureau, var-

ious ministries, the Board of Education, the Romanian Institute for Foreign Cultural Relations, the SRR Museum of History, the Institute for Systematization and Construction Design.

By contrast, those from Import-Export, our wonderful colleagues, are transferred to:

—The Center for Health Statistics and Numerical Analysis,

—The Association of Beekeepers,

—The Wholesale Hardware Products and Construction Materials Enterprise,

—The Bucharest Clothing Industry Headquarters,

—The "Ilie Pintilie" Ink Factory,

—The Bucharest Sewing and Knitting Factory,

—The "Red Flame" Industrial Enterprise,

—The Popesti-Leordeni Industrial Center for the Processing of Rubber and Plastics,

—The "Klement Gottwald" Electric Car Factory,

—The Baneasa branch of the Enterprise for Radio Components and Semiconductors,

—The Bucharest Dairy Factory,

—The Chemical Equipment Plant in Ploiesti,

—The Fruit and Vegetable Enterprise of the City of Bucharest . . .

It's a disaster! Unfair! You don't even have a choice, it's an implacable order, no one asks you. To top it all off, officially they're called "strategic employment transfers." How can it be strategic to move a good censor, with job seniority, with so much experience, to a random plant? They're toying with us, they used us for as long as they needed us, they stole or ruined our youth and health and now they're throwing us out with the trash, they're stomping all over our hearts . . . The girls rattled off the names of transferred colleagues, but I can't recall them . . . Some will get an increase of 10 percent, others just 7 percent. Some will start receiving bigger salaries, two hundred to three hundred lei more than they received when working here, but not everyone. Why? What are the criteria?

I've got no way of knowing either.

When I arrived at Import-Export, someone had just been transferred and a spot opened up in their office.

You're lucky, the Fredericas said to me, they transferred you from one department to another, a sign that they want you to learn about censorship (as if I don't know it well enough! I thought, but I kept my mouth shut, so they wouldn't think I was stuck up), they want you to know as much as possible. If they had really intended to move you, you would've ended up at some plant. However, it appears that they're preparing a team of long-distance censors for themselves, while the others will be dispersed into other activities. When I heard "a team of long-distance censors," I imagined a herd of scrawny old nags, pulling heavy carts packed to the hilt with manuscripts, panting, Hey, keep going, hyah-hyah!, while sheets from the cart are flying, falling, cascading, scattering everywhere.

What a scandal, what a commotion! Now it's because of commercializing bibles. Check out what that guy decided to commercialize! At least pornographic novels are understand-able, but bibles, brought from England . . . We're caught between structures that follow our every move, we create tons

of documents for every little thing that goes on in our institution and all of it gets sent along, all of it is deposited for
hundreds of years to come, the truth is what you put down on
paper. I don't think just Sabadeanu's to blame—a single person
can't do it alone—it's an entire network with people from the
mail, maybe with the Securitate officers there too, a bunch of
bad eggs who've rubbed off on our people, etc. It's possible that
our com might not be guilty at all, but with the Party and the
Securitate out in front and with who knows how many others
implicated—so that the entire department or someone higher
than us wouldn't be found guilty, so that even worse things
wouldn't be found out, with which by comparison the selling
of forty-one bibles is just a drop in the bucket—Sabadeanu,
who got wind of what was being attributed to him, zealously
applied self-criticism, and it was proposed that he be kicked
out. In keeping with team spirit, my, how everyone jumped on
him, what a good friend, what a trustworthy comrade, what
a communist, and, oh my goodness, how was he capable of
doing something like this! They condemned him unanimously
in exemplary fashion! To the satisfaction of the party member
who was looking on, bored. I'm not saying he wasn't guilty, it
was clear as day that he was a smooth operator, but the way our
people treated him showed me how risky it is to be a boss. By
the way, a cushy chair and a good salary await com. Sabadeanu
in any case, I'm not worried about him. Those whom he didn't
betray will express their gratitude.

Today's agenda:
   —Discussing the case of workplace regulations violations
committed by com. Petre Sabadeanu, supervisor on duty.

Comrade Ion Cumpanasu informs us that ten days ago leadership of the institution was alerted to the fact that local authorities from the city of Bistriţa confiscated forty-one bibles from a citizen living in a township in that county. This citizen declared that she had received them from Petre Sabadeanu. Bibles, in Romanian, edited in London, were sent into the country and retained by the division for imported and exported publications. Com. P. Sabadeanu, on being asked by institution leadership and by other members of the Executive Council whether he gave the bibles to that respective citizen, categorically denied it. He sustained his contestation of the deed in a written declaration as well.

In order to establish the truth, two members of the Executive Council (deputy general director com. A. Sandescu and director I. Banyai) were tasked with traveling to Bistrita, where they spoke with the citizen who was found with the bibles. She made a written declaration in which she indicated that she had received them from com. P. Sabadeanu, at his domicile in Bucharest, with his recommendation that she sell them at two hundred lei a copy. Faced with the evidence, com. P. Sabadeanu admitted the deed.

In light of the extremely serious breach of workplace regulations and communist ethical standards committed by P. Sabadeanu, the ratification of the termination of the employment contract in accordance with legal provisions (Labor Code, article 130) and internal regulatory documents was proposed to the Executive Council. Com. Cornel Lupea, the secretary of the party committee, then took the floor and presented the committee's report concerning this problem to be discussed by party branch organization no. 3 with the motion that Petre

Sabadeanu be sanctioned along party lines with a "resolution of censure."

Comrade Ion Cumpanasu gave the floor to com. P. Sabadeanu, who in his statement admitted that he is very much to blame, but maintained that he didn't take the bibles in order to commercialize them . . .

That's what happens to you when you don't want to split the loot with the right people. I'm just saying.

The girls from Export address me: you all in Literature, as if I weren't working with them here. They say that lots of people pass through their department, for a change of scenery, to get a feel for what's happening in the civilized world, but few stay. It's their opinion that I won't stay long either. I'm not on the list of the new department, so I'm here for just a temporary experience exchange. Knowing what fate awaits them given this frequency of transfers, it doesn't even bother me, I can hardly wait to leave this office.

> Frederica Maksutovici (the skinniest and tallest one, quiet, doesn't engage in conversation)
> Nely Iordan (the kind woman at the window, on the left side)
> Erica Galambos (chubby and pretty, friendly)
> Magdalena Hilsenrad (hair dyed a shade of violet, sits with Erica at the same table, they're friends, it seems; whenever I've spoken with her, I've called her Frederica)
> Veronica Oberst (works at the mail too, rarely comes in, short hair, big boobs, Romanian)

> Georgeta Spafiu (more olive-toned, brunette, in
> charge of newcomers, it seems, killing me with
> important notes and documents)

There's so many of them in the office! And I'm always forgetting their names, they get mad sometimes, but I just got here.

Notes, notes, and more notes, they're not even recent, as far
as I can make out. They've got a gigantic cabinet here, out of
which Frederica (actually Georgeta, I think) takes out some
files, placed there as if specially for me, waiting for me. The
next stage, she smiles at me mysteriously, "begins with these
mild ones." As if she had other ones as well that weren't so
mild. As far as I can tell, the difference between Import-
Export and Literature is that in the former you don't censor,
usually, anything, the most you can do is point out some passages harmful to proletarian morality and not recommend
it for import. No one asks whether you've read over every
page, while in Literature they'll send your feathers flying for
each subversive word crouching in a forest of innocent words,
in which birds are singing sweetly, little flowers are peacefully blooming. You're obligated to intervene, naming all the
words, pages, passages that need to be cut out, you write long
reports, short notes, and again reports, and again notes, with
everything that seems inappropriate to you and it's preferable for as much as possible to seem that way, otherwise you
risk missing something and being punished. The more you
point out, the fewer your chances of being punished for any
new and unobserved mistake. If you've made about twenty
objections, the other seven you didn't catch (but which were

caught either by other authorities or by some especially vigilant colleague friend) are forgiven and you'll get out of the
three-month pay cut.

In Import, you write a two- to three-sentence summary of
the book and you act like a big shot in the conclusion with "I
propose or I do not propose it for import/translation." Here,
no one, in general, dares propose something. After reading
the manuscript a few times, after we pick on every comma, it's
not something that's within our power, we're not the ones who
decide whether a book appears or not. There's an injustice to
that. But, if it were up to me, I wouldn't allow a single book to
appear, especially not ones about love . . . I feel as if I'm here
only as a visitor, just to see what other people are up to, but my
place is in Literature!

> *Paris-Match*, no. 1135, an article by Raymond Cartier,
> fragment: "The Chronicle of Current Events." It
> doesn't have an official address or an administrative
> director. Its first number appeared on April 30, 1968,
> and the following ones appeared successively at an
> almost consistent interval every two months. It belongs
> to the type of clandestine literature called samizdat that
> circulates secretly in the Soviet Union, typewritten,
> copied by mimeograph, passed from hand to hand,
> often rented out for significant sums, like the works
> of circulating libraries. Modest and fragile, constantly
> threatened with suppression, this small magazine will
> certainly remain a testament of our era. It's the stifled
> voice of intellectual freedom and human protest under
> the regime of communism.

—Now I understand, finally, why (even for us!) all our type-writers are registered.

—Is that all you finally understand?

I didn't answer, because I wasn't sure what exactly the comrade meant by that.

Confidential.

Le soir. No. 21. Political daily from Belgium.

Published on page v is an interview given to the newspaper's special correspondent in Paris, Yvon Toussaint, by Jean-Paul Sartre, in which is said, among other things:

Y. T.: What you're describing is a perverted democracy, just as we find that socialism is perverted in Eastern Europe. Might this mean that there's a fatality to it, that power automatically perverts any ideology?

J.-P. S.: That thought has never occurred to me. Democracy has never been perverted for the simple fact that it's never existed . . .

Y. T.: Socialism doesn't exist either?

J.-P. S.: No, it's never existed either . . . It could've existed . . . There's China . . .

. . .

Y. T.: So, in each camp, either there will be a multitude of local revolutions simultaneously or there will never be a true revolution?

J.-P. S.: Exactly. And I'll add that this multitude of simultaneous local revolutions is possible . . .

Tomorrow there could be multiple revolts in the camp dominated by the USSR. In that moment we'll find ourselves in a crisis situation.

Proposals: No—private individuals.
Yes—everyone else.

Note for the volume *Open Letter to Europeans*, Denis de Rougemont, including:

"By refusing the unification of Europe, either you or your children will discover that one day you're no longer French, or Czech, or Swiss except as an honorary title . . . because you will be Americans or Soviets through mandatory economic, social, ideological compliance . . . You will be colonized one by one and unwittingly warped by the dollar or your communist parties, as you were before, not long ago, by National Socialism," p. 10.

The problem of all problems. Selection:

"Even with all their differences of character and outward aspects, there isn't a Gierek problem and a Gomułka problem. A single problem exists, the problem of communism. Does communism have a chance of succeeding? Or does communism have to begin thinking about giving up on itself? This is the problem of all problems.

They can strut across the deceitful and illusory screen of propaganda with very different faces! Nagy and Kádár, Dimitrov and Ceausescu, Beria and Brezhnev, Gomułka and Gierek. They're all acting out one and the same drama: a communism that believes it exists and which won't actually ever exist.

Because here's the situation: after twenty-five years of communist governance, Poland, which before the world war was a large exporter of agricultural products, can't feed itself except by importing, year after year, more and more significant quantities of American wheat, Canadian wheat, capitalist wheat. After twenty-five years of communist governance, in order to be able to eat, you have to stand in line in front of the collective stores that give out meat, bread, eggs, and margarine on the basis of rations cards. After twenty-five years of communism, the majestic paradise that was promised is nothing other than a bitter purgatory where boredom reigns, or a hell in which workers, when they express their indignation, are answered with tanks, guns, and attack dogs . . ."

In place of a conclusion:

"Is communism still possible?

"Is it still possible for a country to be a vast national prison?

Is it still really possible for a farmer to cultivate the land without the drive of personal interest?

Is it still really possible for a writer to write without freedom?

Is it still really possible for a historian to be required to gather testimonies under coercion?

Is it still really possible to maintain the farce of a state economy that conceals nothing other than the most terrifying speculation and the biggest economic racket that has even been known?

And is it still possible to parade around the former prisoners of Auschwitz when you risk opening the way for those who want to create a new Auschwitz?

. . . Gierek won't change anything compared to Gomułka. The only one who's right is Solzhenitsyn, when he uncovers, with his relentless gaze, the system's cancer. The metastatic cancer will get worse."

The sky's falling down on me!

Now I understand why those from Import-Export are "transferred" to clothing and dairy factories!

Who is this Solzhenitsyn?

Zuki, where have you brought me?

"The muzzle continues to be tightly secured. In many countries censorship of the press hasn't changed very much":

"The generally somber aspect of press censorship has hardly changed at all over the years. In many countries in the East and West, the collection, transmission, and broadcasting of news and commentaries is still subject to certain serious restrictions. Censorship takes on various forms, from the knowing suppression of information by authorities and administrative agencies—a method also practiced by countries traditionally having freedom of the press—to the existence of certain special censorship officials using indelible pencils and exercising authority.

The Soviet Union respects the rule in effect since Khrushchev's time, according to which direct pre-censorship—the inspection of the manuscripts of foreign correspondents before they were sent—was suspended. Subsequent censorship remained, the minute analysis of materials written by correspondents in Moscow that appeared in foreign press. Repeated notices of certain unpleasant matters leads, as it has up until now, to expulsion. In the last year, three Americans have had to leave the country.

The Polish press appears to have become more lenient toward criticism after the events that took place in December. However, foreign journalists can continue to expect the revocation of their term of accreditation. The Czechoslovakian government has clamped down even harder in the last year, the country's press has become even more one-sided, while the issuing or extension of visas for foreign journalists functions in an even more arbitrary fashion. In Hungary, however, there have been some concessions. At the party congress in Budapest, numerous foreign correspondents were accredited.

At the beginning of December, a serious concern arose among foreign correspondents in Greece when the impression was given that the punishments in effect until then only for Greek journalists—up to a year in prison, as well as hefty fines—would be applied also in the case of foreign press agents who publish 'false' information that could shake the confidence of the population. The government vigorously refuted this measure. In Spain, as well as in Portugal, the press is subject to 'self-censorship.' The publication of certain news items and commentaries that are upsetting from a political standpoint can result in the arrest of or fines for the editor.

'Blind' surveillance

Strict censorship in the majority of countries in the Near East has remained almost unchanged. Beirut, where restrictions are laxest, has remained the principal base for foreign correspondents. In Egypt, foreign press telegrams are subject to 'blind censorship.' This means that the respective correspondent doesn't know which parts of his material were erased or whether the material was transmitted or not.

Israel continues to practice strict military censorship and, due to the current critical situation, there is little hope of restrictions for journalists being lifted. Detailed news articles from Morocco, Algeria, and Tunisia are no longer subject to censorship. Foreign correspondents are sometimes denied entrance visas, however, expulsions are very rare. Press in Sudan was nationalized on August 26, 1970. In Ethiopia, foreign correspondents who relate negative aspects about the country are summoned to appear before the minister of information. Kenya expelled three European journalists who worked for newspapers within the country. And in Zambia, sixteen foreign correspondents were arrested on the eve of the Non-Aligned Nations Summit conference. In South Africa, censorship doesn't exist, however, entrance visas and residence permits are severely regulated. Censorship doesn't exist in Rhodesia either, yet despite that fact, a significant number of native journalists have been barred from practicing their profession.

Cold comfort

The International Press Institute (IPI) has determined, concerning the situation in Latin America, that freedom of the press is being undermined by extremist attacks from both the left and the right. In Argentina, the situation has improved noticeably since Levingston took on the role of president. The Association of Newspaper Editors, who had declared in March that 'in Argentina freedom of the press doesn't exist,' observed a noticeable improvement in August.

In Uruguay, references to the activity of those from the Tupamaros organization have long been prohibited. Various dailies were, on account of violating these restrictions, suspended for a period. Close monitoring of adherence to the 'laws concerning freedom of the press' issued on December 30, 1969, has led to a reduction in comments critical of the government.

In the Brazilian press, self-censorship is combined with the 'directives' drawn up by the government. For example, accounts of terrorist acts, the arresting of members of the military, and comments about controversial clergy are prohibited. Officially there is no censorship of foreign correspondents. However, these journalists find themselves increasingly subject to pressure from authorities."

Not one word about Romania!

What things are being written, what things are being published out there! Such preoccupation with censorship! I'm much too astounded and overwhelmed and nervous and frightened and . . . !

ᕀᕀ

Note for *The Boy Market*, Gallimard Editions, 249 pgs.

The novel presents the life of a certain category of French young men, kept by women, whose only care is the cultivation of their physiques and the different ways of meeting women. In the book there's a series of older women who keep these young men; they try to get their hands on as many boys as possible, turning this pastime into a real sport. The hero, Rémy Chasseau, lives the same kind of life as the other young men of this category, at the age of only seventeen he's in a sexual relationship with a thirty-five-year-old woman. Ultimately, he becomes disgusted with this way of life, he retreats to a small provincial town and gets married to a young woman, but he doesn't find the love he's been seeking for so long. Several passages in the book relate in detailed fashion the sexual encounters of the hero with his various lovers (pgs. 42–47, 126–128).

We do not propose it for import.

Half a Man

A pathologic case in which an adult man has a serious inferiority complex after disappointments in love, the consequence of certain errors in what he was taught at home. Psychologically traumatized, the character is represented exclusively as being dominated by his sexual obsessions, in a permanent state of erotic crisis, observing couples in love with an unhealthy curiosity, secretly watching an episode of sexual intimacy between his brother and his brother's girlfriend, etc.

We do not propose it for import.

The Housekeeper

A man who was left impotent as a result of the bombing of Hiroshima lives alone and is obsessed with his ailment. His housekeeper, who knows of his illness, eases it discreetly and devotedly on two occasions, in which the protagonist arrives at the knowledge of sexual satisfaction. Several episodes portray diverse aspects of their sexual relationship presented in a licentious manner, the entire novel consisting of a series of the most blatantly erotic scenes. Then the man becomes jealous, assuming that the housekeeper hadn't been only with him, and leaves town. Upon his return, he finds the housekeeper has died as a result of an extrauterine pregnancy. A morbid, pathological atmosphere dominates the entire book.

We do not propose it for import.

Paris, Paris

A young striptease dancer in Paris wants to have a child by her lover. As he doesn't want to marry her or complicate his life, he asks a friend to become the father of his girlfriend's child.

Offended, the girl accepts, however, out of a desire to make her boyfriend jealous, and the strategy works: the young couple now becomes conscious of the depths of their feelings.

The uninstructive content of the acts and scenes of sexual intimacy does not recommend the volume for import.

Guide for Married Men

After twelve years of normal family life, Raul Marning decides to cheat on his wife, an act his good friend Jack encourages him to do. In spite of thorough preparations, arranged with the help of his friend, not one attempt is successful. Raul remains the same faithful husband, since the difficulties of adultery, the effort it takes to lie, and the fear of consequences seem insurmountable to him. Numerous obscene and vulgar episodes, uninstructive message.

We do not recommend it for translation.

The Love of My Life

After several years of sexual intimacy, a young unmarried woman become pregnant. She hesitates between getting an abortion and letting the father-to-be know, out of fear that she might drive him away. In the end, it's implied that the young couple will get married. The theme of the book—responsibility in romantic relationships—doesn't present any issues. The subject however is loaded with love scenes narrated in abundant naturalistic detail.

We do not recommend it for translation.

The School of Life

In a girls' school in England whose director is the mistress of a minister, the students' behavior is libertine, and their dress code is disagreeable. Intended as a critical depiction of a world situated at the edge of English society, the novel is more of an argument in favor of a life free of any "prejudice" and removed from the tyranny of any norms of behavior. The message lacks any educational value.

We do not recommend it for import.

No One Can Take What's Yours

Having at the core of its plot a young woman who desires to succeed socially, the action of the novel is littered with numerous episodes in which sexual intimacy is presented in an extended and detailed fashion. Moving up the social ladder is considered possible only through making compromises of a sexual nature. The numerous episodes permeated by excessive eroticism and the fact that to a good degree social decadence is presented as an attractive way of life give the entire novel a profoundly uninstructive tenor.

We do not recommend it for translation.

The Ideal Wife

The book aims to be a foray into the psychopathology of the modern woman, attempting to depict an example of a marriage that fails due to unfulfilled sexual desires, to sick sexual curiosities, a clinical case of masochism. The erotic scenes and the ones imagined by the main character confer an immoral character to the volume from cover to cover.

For Special Collections.

Eve

A woman of loose morals falls in love with a doctor, who also loves her, but, convinced that she's unworthy of his love, she leaves him and returns to her free and easy lifestyle. Exceptionally vulgar are the scenes which describe the woman's ingenious methods of capturing a man. Lacking in any cautionary intention, with a heroine whose motto is "pleasure, freedom, and as many lovers as possible," this book is a string of episodes depicting real orgies, erotic scenes, etc. Detailed passages abound in which he sticks his tongue deep into her mouth when he kisses her; he rubs his finger between her legs, for example, then holds it up to his nose at length; he lightly slaps her butt, until her butt-cheeks redden; she leans over, she bends down, she pretends to sink her little teeth into his mighty and stubborn penisterone. He, pretending to be scared and waiting for her to blow him and so on . . . (pgs. 14–18, 23, 29–35, 38–41, etc.). The writer of this note cited all these passages to demonstrate that there's no need to import this book . . .

Oh, no! Oh, no! I wasn't expecting this, I never would've believed it!

Damned depraved capitalist pigs! Disgusting scumbags!

We want nothing to do with them and their foul and immoral literature!

If in this very moment I were to meet with any Romanian scribbler, I would stroke his head, maternally, paternally, I'd kiss his forehead, maternally, paternally, and again maternally.

Fine, sometimes it happens that we, too, are sad, sometimes it rains down some reptile or something sharp here, we love each other sometimes, and we, too, feel attracted to the much too covered-up body of our other half, we imagine the hidden parts of our ideal partner's body, we unintentionally make mistakes every once in a while, but otherwise, what worthy comrades, what honorable citizens, what loyal and understanding friends of the people and the party our writers are!

By comparison!

I'm horrified! I want to go back to Literature! Back to my manuscripts about factories and plants, about searching for the meaning of life, about valiant communists and platonic love. I've seen and read so much since becoming a censor (our people proudly call themselves "readers," I made it to senior reader level I—what else could I possibly want! We have level III readers, level II readers, and level I, but I like to call myself and be called censor—senior censor one. I'm a true censor, what's that, a "reader"? Is your job researching linguistics? Do you have an appointment as reader in a mathematics department? Too abstract, everything's too veiled. While the only meaning of "censor" is censor and there's no room for ambiguity, it's honest, it's blunt and determined . . .), I've had my fair share of books to read, I repeat, many manuscripts have passed through my hands since I began working here and how many hostile ideas, how many reprehensible, subversive passages, perverse lines, etc., etc. have I had to censor! How many times have I had to intervene harshly, feeling myself wronged not only as a censor (don't authors know into whose hands their manuscripts end up? Then why do they send them to us in such a state?) but also as a true citizen of our fatherland and as a moral woman who believes in communist ethical values, in the conduct and integrity of the party . . .

But this week in Export, in these few short days, reading the notes made by my colleagues, on a tiny page, with just an overview, with at most two or three short fragments from the work, a few impressions from the reading and, at the end, the recommendation of translating it or not, of importing it or, instead, sending it to Special Collections, these turbulent days have completely and fundamentally changed my view of the world and of censorship! It's turned my soul upside down!

I didn't believe things could go this far! I didn't know, I had no idea, in all these years of censorship I've never run into a danger like this. Not one of the sample-reports that circulate for everyone throughout the institution includes a note like the ones I've just read. The girls told me that not everything's like that, they specifically picked out something for me that I've never read before. Just one of these notes is enough to turn your world inside out! Now I understand why com. Z. kept repeating to me that you can't call yourself a true censor, you can't ascend to this honor, if you don't go through Import-Export, to come in contact with this poison and to remain in your right mind, to get close to it, to breathe it in deeply and intensely, to go through everything carefully, and not to become infected by the putrefaction and corruption in the books you read, to plunge into the swamp but survive, to not drown and to keep your dignity and values intact. To remain as good a communist or even better than before, this is a censor's hardest mission! Not to let yourself be tempted, to go right up to the devious Lorelei, without plugging your ears up with wax, without tying yourself to the mast, without precautions, without the guarantee of survival, to listen to her fiendishly disturbing, powerful, dangerous, poisonous, however you want to call it, song, to listen to it once, twice, to take out your pencil, to write a note, to copy out the most delicate fragment, to put together a report on the book, then to leave. As you leave, you can spit in disgust or step away proudly and dismissively. This is a censor's hardest mission! To be able to distinguish between a nasty bedwetter, behind whose verses are only prissy feelings, and the true Lorelei, the dangerous one, lurking, savage and hungry, lusting after tall and slender spirits. Who feasts on weak and stupid censors for lunch, breakfast, and dinner, singing more and more beautifully. While the censor is punished by having to listen, to endure, to suffer, and at the first wrong move, to be quickly guzzled down (or transferred to a plant!). To not have the right to protect one's vulnerable soul, to not have the possibility of refusing contact, of running away, of getting out of danger's path. If before, the people in Export seemed just a bit odd to me, now they seem like monsters. How can they stand it, how do they go on living?

Now I understand why capitalists don't have censors as we do—they've all died. Who can endure such psychological pressure (Z. contradicts me good-naturedly: You wouldn't believe what censors they all have! There's no such thing as a country without censorship!). Weakened, dizzy, reeling, I returned the pages. The girls, sympathetically, told me that I have to get over the first shock, it's hardest the first time, then you're past it, you don't even look at what you're reading, you learn to be indifferent and not let the poison get into your blood. Yes, poison in my blood, that's what I feel right now. A poisoned censor, wounded, helpless. Small, weak. I'm so glad that there are people with the strength and competence to ban such readings. I'm so glad that we exist! A sensitive soul, a feeble heart, an unprepared mind would doubt, would fall, would perish . . . I ask myself, though, what kind of people are they who read something like this? Those who consume this kind of literature? They're only human too. How do they go on, how do they love, how do they build families, go to work, have fun, grow old, die, reading such books? What kind of society and what kind of values? How are authors permitted to awake all the worst, all that is most putrid in readers, to give lessons in disobedience, suicide, insubordination, anarchy, disrespect for one's country, contempt for love, glorifying theft, pornography, depravity, despair, and all the other sins.

Each society has the writers it deserves, they write what everyone around them feels, they're the nation's conscience. How has their society not collapsed? Fine, how has it not only not collapsed but is still producing things that we're missing, clothing, music, appliances, culinary delicacies, that our people are crazy for? Other than literature, everything seems to be going very well over there. Something in this world isn't logical. Something's not adding up. I don't want to ask Z. again, or my new colleagues. I want to search on my own and find the answer.

One of the notes nauseated me, another one made me moist between the legs, I slept poorly at night, had dreams with rapes in them, these writers are mocking the Communist Party, they're predicting its downfall! Horrific apocalypses! Women at thirty-five running around with seventeen-year-old kids, everything described in elaborate detail. I might not be the most "orthodox" (I'm thinking of upright and moral) person in the institution, I don't go to church at all, but after reading such things, I arrive at the conclusion that they, over there, are without any God (it's written with a small "G," but here, in this context, the big one works). They're merciless, cruel, bad, and for what reason? What's the purpose? What are they trying to do? I've aged more this week than I have in the last five tranquil years. Don't tell me I've even gone gray. I shouldn't get so worked up. I shouldn't allow the text to get to me. You run or you fight back. Defend yourself, save yourself. It would be a shame to die next to Lorelei, while she goes about her song without giving you a second thought. Wanting to swallow you up, to destroy you. Would it be easy, would it be hard? How can someone get past this? What secrets do these darling, scrawny Fredericas have?

I can't read any more. I feel as if I don't have an elephant's thick skin, which can't be pierced by the hunter's sharp spear. But it's a test I have to pass, as far as I can tell. I'm headed I don't know where without the certainty that I'm strong enough. The hardest test of censorship. To get through the poison safe and sound. I'll pass, all right, I'll pass. There's no other way, I have no choice.

After readings these notes, the trial period (the girls say), the trial by fire (I bitterly remark), I arrive at the conclusion that there are two different ways of doing literature. Ours and theirs. Our literature and their literature. Literature under communism *versus* literature under capitalism. To put it simply and without too much explanation, here we write for education, for the fatherland, we write well, beautifully, inspiringly, triumphantly, to help people be happy, grateful, good citizens. Here we sing praises, there they criticize. There, literature's like the process of defecation, you expel all that's worst in you, all that's going rotten and stinks, the most pessimistic, the most sordid aspects, you're on the lookout for any small mistake made by the state or your neighbor, and you point your finger at it, you exaggerate it and criticize it. Now, that doesn't mean that we don't also have our crappy writers and our critical ones, the people need them too, but in the background; here, the stench of their works has a small, and harmless, radius of action. Only the poor importsers-exportsers have to take in the same filth day and night, reading only this!

I would ban readings like these, but there are so many things I don't understand (I'm told), like bilateral agreements, like Romanian-French friendship (I work in French, France being where most of the novels like these ones come from, what a disappointment, I had such a good opinion of French literature—formed in the college classroom, admittedly), where you translate three of ours and we'll do three of yours. Do you expect Romanian literature to appear in Parisian bookstores by batting your eyes? They don't care at all about our beautiful and brilliant literature, exactly the same way we don't care about theirs. Politics is everything, even in the tenderest poem of amour. In the poem itself, no, but if everyone begins to read it, praise it, translate it, it gets transformed into politics. By the way, books like these are popular with our audiences no matter how much you censor out of them, but I'd ban them, because they set a bad example for authors. A writer shouldn't criticize the state, the authorities, our beloved party, he should praise its achievements, not be on the lookout for mistakes. To contribute tactfully to the undoing of conflicts (because they happen sometimes, no one's perfect!), in a prudent, poetic, constructive way.

While the literary motivations and processes are different— the impetus to birth something beautiful or to defecate literarily—the state and its literary needs have been, for centuries, the same everywhere. The state looks to literature for support. I've also discussed this with the coms from Export, who are much smarter than they seemed to me at first. How many tens of thousands is the press run of a book of ours? A beautiful, optimistic one that makes your heart sing when you read it—multiple tens of thousands! You have to stand in line to buy books, they're sold under the counter, authors are heroes, respected by the party, adored by workers and farmers, paraded at gatherings like holy relics, etc. In how many hundreds of copies is the sad, pessimistic, sarcastic, depraved little book of a capitalist author sold?—in a few hundred, and the author is viewed as a miserable clown, a beggar, tolerated, surviving on subsidies for alcoholics and unemployed people, getting thrown, out of pity, small change. Prince or beggar. What do you choose to be?

Everyone gets corrupted in our Censorship. Corrupted politically, corrupted morally, corrupted ideologically, mentally ill from so much newness. Terrified not so much by texts as by the fact that somewhere, we know where, someone, we know who, knows what we're reading, what we're finding out, what it is we do. As if we're to blame for everything in the world that gets written? As if we wouldn't want to read only what's useful and advisable? We end up becoming the biggest enemies. We possess, accumulate depositories of, hostile and subversive ideas, day after day, year after year. Day and night (literally—Press works more at night than during the day), ceaselessly, we touch all kinds of filth, sullying ourselves. Who cleanses us of it? Has any special program been laid out in the provisions? Is anyone looking after us? Who cares? The party? We're profoundly affected, exhausted, nauseated. We're unlucky witnesses who didn't chose to find out about the extent of human pettiness and can't escape the inevitable punishment. They should keep us in special cages, completely forbid us (but really, not just as a formality) to communicate with the worthy comrades of this country. With so much poison in us, even the mosquitos in the park would die if we breathed on them a bit harder. More dangerous than Securitate officers, more hostile than the inmates in prison. Any day now, any day now, phrases, words, diversions. Behold the censor putting on the shiny and slippery garb of a lizard. The censor is the lizard! I drag my tail through texts, through books, I leave it somewhere, so I can escape, survive. From hunter I become the hunted, from executioner I transform into the victim. You'll shut down the institution and massacre us. Disinfestation in Censorship! All that we'll leave behind will be informant notes and reports, the justified interventions and the less justified ones . . .

Invisible, murderous, I can't assure her in any way that I'm innocent, a well-behaved little censor who'd never do anything bad. No, the mere fact that I got close to her is more than sufficient reason for me to be killed. Like with Genghis Khan, who was buried in a hidden spot and whose witnesses were killed afterwards, so that no one would discover his final resting place. And I'm not only a witness, I'm also a soldier. I serve, I'm under certain orders. Someone's watching our every move, untrusting, unyielding, unforgiving.

I don't even have to write down anything in my notebook. I write it all directly in my report. I don't have any misgivings, it doesn't happen that I lose control of a text or I don't understand something. Truly, it's nothing complicated, it even seems too easy for me . . . All the mistakes march right out in the open. What lizards, what "giving the enemy a hearing"! Their writers seem dumb to me actually in comparison with ours . . . Ours have passed through the fire and the sword in their efforts to hide things, to make allusions, our writers have reached such pinnacles that sometimes you have to fry your brains for several days and you still don't understand what they meant to say and how much subversive potential their message holds. Some write just for the love of writing, but not many of them, their writers are professional degenerates, from the youngest to the oldest. You couldn't find a novel without sex scenes and since the author has to bring something new to the table, to not repeat the same things, he doesn't know what else to come up with, so that, in the end, you could extract a pornographic anthology out of their books, a manual of positions. Jail would be the place for them if they were writing here! A bunch of degenerates, profligates, who corrupt the nation. What good is arousing the senses, what good is the representation of ruined souls?

A book or two like these would be good as an example from time to time for our audiences, as a demonstration of the decadence of capitalism. What ruin, what depravity and decay! And how beautiful, how wonderful it is here!

Zuki came into our office, I was tired, staring blankly, absently, I didn't feel like opening my mouth. I turned in the report. He didn't say anything either, but he gave me a long look, then he put his hand on my forehead, as if he wanted to check whether I was running a fever, then he addressed the Fredericas: "Our literati is hanging in there." The girls laughed, then Z. added: "Censorship is a delight," and he left the office. For some it's a delight, for others it's a fight. A strange episode, I'm still thinking about it even now.

After he shut the door, I started to pump the girls for what they know about Zuki.

—You mean comrade Zaharescu? Zuki is what his girlfriend, one of your former officemates, calls him.

A suspicion flashed across my mind.

—Roza?

—Exactly.

—Com. Zaharescu was born in a village near Braila. A houseboy serving in the home of a noble family, supposedly exceptionally intelligent even when he was little, the nobleman taught him how to read and speak foreign languages, he educated him, he cared for him like his own child (he didn't have children of his own). In 1945, when he fled the country, he wanted to take his beloved servant with him, but the young man thought that he could have a better future here. He thought right. Supposedly, in the first years he presented himself as Mr. (and then comrade) Zaharov, to get in good with the Russians. He stood beside the great figures of the era, his experience as a houseboy served him well. But being smart, he held back on climbing the ranks when he saw that those who lifted their heads too high didn't end up so well, even with their impeccable dossiers. Supposedly, he even knew Lucretiu Patrascanu,[17] whom he later visited in prison too. He had adequate social origins and, with his extraordinary intelligence, he could dream of getting far. He stood out in any case with his brilliant mind and many didn't care too much for him. They say (he told us the story) that a wise man once told him that if he wants to die of natural causes, he should come here to Censorship, because it's more low-key. I think he came in with the people from the Press Division, carved out of the Ministry of Arts and Information. The fate of certain higher-ups affected him so much that he never accepted important positions (I mean, section director isn't a big deal), even though here no one would've asked for his head for this. When he saw that there weren't any Russians in the GDPP, and the director and almost all the supervisors are (were, because most of them have left) Jewish, he decided to change his name again.

—Our director is Jewish?

—The former director, Mr. Ardeleanu, comrade Adler Dome. Hungarian Jew, supposedly he didn't even speak Romanian well and he stacked Censorship with Jews and Hungarians, but when he saw which way the wind was blowing, fearing that his job was in danger, he disposed of them. He kept about two for seed, for show, but what great censors they were, and they were kicked out just because they weren't Romanian enough! In return, the director himself was able to save his own skin, he survived. A good director, that one. And a good guy, he knew us all, he was like a father to us. He knew each of our problems and how much we could handle. These people from the new team have been here a year and they don't even know our names, they avoid us, they barely open their mouths in meetings . . .

—And Zuki? How did he go from being Zaharov to Zukermann?

—Supposedly he met with some Jewish friends of his and they all racked their brains to find him a new name. They suggested he choose between Zukermann, Zukerberg, Zukerstern.

—Why necessarily Zuker?

—Well, it means "sugar," the root of his name. Sugarman, a mountain of sugar, a sugary star. Zuki turned his nose up in disgust at all of these, but his friends told him that it's not good to deviate from his true name, meaning to keep the root of Zuker, regardless of suffix. They were dying of laughter, but they helped him. Zuki took advantage of our regime's benevolence toward all the paupers and down-and-outs and he got about three college degrees, then he enrolled in a doctoral program as well. They say that he's in the process of defending his thesis for another one, his third, even though he's up for retirement any day now. Then, all the Jews, I mean almost all, who wanted and were able to stay in the GDPP, changed their names, our Censorship became full of Popescus and Ionescus, each more Romanian than the next, only Zuki kept a Jewish name. You can bite his head off, but he didn't want to go back to Zaharescu.

—Well, doesn't everyone know the truth?

—Ha, "knows" my foot. He's so smart that no one doubts anymore that he's a real Jew, especially with his glasses and his beard and something of a bald spot, every bit a Jew!

—I was also positive he was Jewish.

—But Zaharescu can be a Jewish name too, what, aren't there Jews in Braila?

—He's not Jewish, he's Romanian. He's down as Romanian in all his papers as well. But he's become more Catholic than the pope. He considers himself to be Jewish and he's proud of it! He pronounces his name as if it were the name of a great pharaoh. He even tells us jokes about Jews, to throw people off.

—Maybe he's some inside operative?

—Well, what need would we have of spies? Supposedly he was proposed for jobs in more important places, but he refused, a few times transfer orders came with his name on them and he's still in Censorship. He learned Hungarian too, because he already knew Hebrew and Yiddish, and he would speak with the former director in Hungarian, calling him com. Adler. Not even our Jewish colleagues knew Hebrew and Yiddish, but Zuki did, and they respected him very much. What a learned man! Only once did com. Zukermann have problems. When Roza, whom he set up in the post office, next to the handsome guy from the homeland authorities, brought him the lists of fake addresses belonging to the senders of publications. We suspect that he was behind the plan the whole time and he used Rozalia to find out what he needed.

—When was that?

—Zukermann had been the head of the Import-Export Division since our department was founded, he trained us, in a way. After the scandal he left here to work on a new doctorate. He's in the office of Secret Documents, but he'll come back here after he defends his thesis, that's what he told us. When things settle down.

—I thought that Roza could barely stand him . . .

—She can't stand him, because she was close to being cata-
pulted from the institution because of him.

—She told us stories about her intensive activity here in Foreign Publications, but not one word about Zuki . . .

—Didn't you hear the name Zuki for the first time from
her? Didn't he start coming by your former office only after
she came? I'm sure you hadn't even heard about Zukermann
until Rozalia's arrival. He's following her, he doesn't want to
lose hold of her . . .

My curiosity is completely satisfied, I don't want to know any
more. Nor do I think that Roza is the only one Zuki is following.

I hear troubling news from my former department, a rumor
related to a scandal caused by poorly trained censors (I already
knew this), it's even gotten to the point of manuscripts needing
to be destroyed, yikes, the resignation of some minor bosses is
being discussed, nothing like this has ever happened here as far
as I can remember . . . Though I try to stay out of it, something
still reaches my ears. I'm not too surprised, in fact. Literature
is where you find out what someone's made of, you see what
he can handle and how well he's trained, not in recruitment
or translations. A colleague tells me that they're evaluating my
nomination for section chief, they're thinking of having me
take up the post, at least as interim. I don't think that's true,
but she asks me in a roundabout way whether I'd accept, she
must be spying for some boss, I tell her I don't think I'd be able
to accept. Not that I wouldn't like to be section chief, with a

big salary and the prestige that goes with it, I'd make a good boss, I think, but I don't have people to work with there and I wouldn't be able to answer for everything that the entire section receives, to be the one overseeing all of Literature, when I was barely able to answer for my own manuscripts (and it was still a lot and hard for me!). But as a supervisor, I'd have to count on others, to trust my people, and I don't. It's better for me to stay in the shadows than to perch up on a pinnacle and, with the first storm, be kicked out. I have the example of Sabadeanu, Zukermann wasn't in a hurry to reach the top either, and for me to think I'm better than that! The chief is responsible for the mistakes of the department, those idiots will at most be fined, whereas I risk being fired, due to incompetence! Others who are fired have connections here and there, they're known by the party, they find cozy spots and cushy armchairs for themselves, and they'll remember Censorship like it was a bad dream, whereas I don't want to go anywhere else, I've got no place to go, and I don't know how to do anything else!

We live in tumultuous times (I wouldn't have suspected how tumultuous if I hadn't worked in Export) and it's better to remain in the shadows, modest, well-behaved, and to be about your business.

I went to the appointment with our president, my first time speaking with him alone, I told him politely that it's too great an honor for me and I'm afraid I wouldn't be able to handle it. I don't know the collective well enough (many new colleagues have come in), I've lost touch since moving to Export and I believe that the new comrades might need a longer adjustment period in order to master the assigned tasks, and I wouldn't want to answer for their mistakes (com. president nodded his head sympathetically, we know what's what). I've never been a supervisor and I'm afraid that in the current context, I won't be able to cope, I'm afraid that I don't have the talent for it. While we were talking, the two vice-directors came in as well, they were all very kind. In order to appease them, I told them that, given the very complex situation in Literature, I'd be happy to return to my old department and I promise to take on the hardest assignments, including that of helping my comrades perform their duties successfully. The coms nodded their heads again in conciliatory fashion, they said something formal, we will analyze the situation and your proposals, I got up and left, relieved, happy that I stayed strong, I resisted the proposal and I didn't find myself in a pickle. I'm already getting ready to return to my old office.

But Z.'s reaction to me! Besides him, no one cares whether or not I'm a boss. I've never seen him so angry, furious even, before! It was a key position, do you understand (he seems to me to want to add: you stupid cow!). It was the most important one in Censorship: to have literature under your control! To have the last word, to call the shots, to have your decision matter to the party higher-ups. To educate your subordinates as you see fit! To teach them how to do their job properly! Who, if not you?! So that we'd have our person there (what exactly did he mean by this?). What an opportunity, what a big, important deal! How could you say no? How could you? How did you dare? You didn't ask anyone for advice, you're on your own and you don't care about anything?

I think he was the one who recommended me for this

unwanted "ascension," I think his proposal was analyzed and accepted, and I officially refused with arguments. I understand, in his place I'd be frustrated as well.

I asked him why isn't he a boss, given how smart he is, how much experience he has? I asked him where his good friend Petre Sabadeanu is working now? I asked him what our beloved little Roza's been up to? Who else she's fallen in love with, what lists she's been writing up?

Zuki looked at me angrily, curled his lips as if with contempt, he didn't say a word. I don't think he'll be coming to see me anytime soon.

Our official address:

> Press House no. 1, Sector 1—Bucharest.
> Telephone numbers: 17-60-10—switchboard;
> 17-20-95; 17-13-58.

We have to learn the telephone numbers by heart.

The GDPP had its headquarters on Roma Street no. 32-34, then on March 24, 1955, the institution moved to the General Division for Radio Broadcasting Building, no. 31-35, entrance on Temisana Street.

I can't move in to my office yet, because there's no room. They had brought in another table, you can't breathe with four people in that tiny office. They've sanctioned the two idiots, one will be kicked out (he was already, but he's still in the office, he'll be gone any day now), and the other will remain with us. I'm so happy I can barely stand it! We'll all squeeze in there. And what a meeting, comrades! And Roza in such fine form! The poor thing! And treacherous Zukermann!

Something isn't adding up!

Maybe some people suspected something, but since moving to Export, I haven't been up on the latest news. S. Z. spoke a lot at the meeting and he accused Roza of every wrongdoing, he destroyed her, chewed her out, in front of everyone. At first, I wasn't paying too much attention and I was prepared to be bored, as usual. The meeting had opened with the official part, with reports, analyses, then we got to criticism and self-criticism. I didn't even understand what Roza was being taken to task for. But she was lumped in with com. Nicolae Manciur, accused of coming into the workplace under the influence.

Then, Roza, in tears, as I've never seen her before:

—Lumped in with that com who comes in drunk, he and I thrown into the same basket! All the others are good and respectable, while we, the "worst" censors in the GDPP, are to get our salaries cut, are to be demoted, despised by everyone! I wouldn't be upset if I had made some mistake, if I had let some line slip through, if I had put in something stupid! But to punish me because a volume isn't popular with readers, because no one criticizes it or praises it, a bunch of hard-to-reproduce malarkey, to that I have no reply. To claim that my work is mediocre! Actually, it was so unexpected that even now I don't really understand what it was. And why him of all people? Give me a break, if it were someone who envies me, hates me, but why Zuki? It's obvious, he wanted only to humiliate me, it's part of some plan of his . . . He's ugly! He's old! He's got a belly, he's got a bald spot! He's not even Jewish! Country bumpkin Zaharia from Podunk Hollow! He changed his name to be able to lull those with dangerous sympathies in Censorship into a sense of security! The damned spy!

But what a fountain of ineffability he is! I keep thinking about it and I still don't understand. Maybe he wanted to show me that he doesn't care about her. He punishes her after I reproached him about I don't know what. He didn't look at me at all. I'm still not sure how I feel. I'm a bit sorry for Roza, but I feel a secret sense of satisfaction.

Zukermann left! It's so empty and desolate all around! The Fredericas knew he was leaving and they didn't tell me. He didn't say goodbye. Nothing.

I wouldn't have guessed that I'd miss him so much!

I didn't love him, I don't love him. But how I long for him to come into our office again, to recite a filthy poem to us that he won't censor, to show us where the ineffable is hidden in women and where in men. To corrupt the people! To let a romance novel through from time to time, to brighten up this sadness. To feed literal and figurative poverty with something. Let's think not only of the writer who writes, the potential enemy, but also of the reader who reads, the potential victim. Let the novels get to them! Otherwise their life is a living death! Don't forget, the mission of a censor is not only to cut but also to allow, not only to block but also to clear the way, to keep the literary path open, to let it keep going, oho oho, to not lose control of the direction, hyah, little horse, hyah, hyah, to guess, to bet, who, when, what exactly . . .

It hurts! It hurts!

Why did he leave? How could he abandon me after awakening hope, affection, in my heart, after I believed that the wounds and mistakes were mended, I believed I'd be able to be happy, this time for real, and right when something beautiful, poetic, blossomed inside my heart, he left! I'm the best censor in the institution, but the man who's been by my side, who guided my steps, and who wanted me to be a big boss, got angry and disappeared.

How unjust I was! How quickly I fell into despair! The Lodge exists! The Lodge is powerful and unshakeable. It only moves headquarters and reforms its structure. Comrade S. Z. moved to the Council for Socialist Culture and Education and he's waiting for us, he's laying the groundwork there. He'll take there only those who deserve to be called censors. I've already received indirect assurances that I will get there. An authoritative department awaits you, you can't escape this time! Me—head of a department? After everything I've been through lately, I can't believe it. But my colleagues are already regarding me as a boss, with a kind of respect, so that I can't even talk with them like before.

The Lodge

Darkened hallways, covered faces, a dank and winding path, my anxiety, fear . . . Is this the end of the road for me? It's over now, it's finished?

Actually, it's the beginning of something here. A new Censorship.

I've recovered a little!
    With their masks and air of mystery, I thought I was going to be interrogated. I heard that they put something over your head when you go there, so that you don't recognize the place, the people, and I said to myself: Either they've caught my father or they've discovered some flawed document, like this notebook, for example, or any other thing, because you don't need a lot of evidence to nitpick a censor! Nothing of all that! What joy! What joy to be so thoroughly mistaken! I breathe a sigh of relief . . . Ha, this Lodge might be dangerous, but compared with the scare I just had, it seems like a breeze.

We wear masks, we have our own signs, encoded texts, information on hidden, condemned, protected authors, a special code, a new language, another vision of the creative act. An atmosphere of mystery. Mission. Access. Brisk air. Delight and my overwhelming curiosity.

At the GDPP I'm a level I senior reader, here I'm one of the apprentices. Apprentice Censor! Zuki must be an Officer Censor or a Master Censor. With masks it's better for everyone, yes, our common goal unites us, I've committed to serving the cause of Censorship alone, to not betraying the interests of Censorship, to helping my brothers. I'm a brother, not a sister, and I like that, there aren't any sisters here, and few women (with masks you can't tell anyway, maybe a higher-pitched voice, but that isn't necessarily a gauge). Regardless of our biological sex, we're all brothers here. Brother Didina, brother Filofteia . . .

We're laying the groundwork for a singular literature, a singular sensibility, we're training the Censor for his new mission. Poetry passes through all curtains, even the one made of iron. We're trying to break through borders, walls, differences. The Great Peace and the Great Censorship embrace.

The goal: to educate the Censor inside every thinking human being. To train them to be their own Censor, but to not even suspect it, to not know. To create and to install the ideal Censor, see-through, traceless, without institutions. For there to exist, to live, in every person who thinks and creates, a Censor. The censorship of the future—invisible censorship!

Psychological, prophylactic, philosophical censorship.
   Geographic, institutional, involuntary, ideological, religious censorship.
   Calibrational censorship, self-censorship.
   Editorial, social, moral, encomiastic, military, political,

religious, economic, subjective, discretionary, diplomatic, historical, global, formal, presumptive, original, infantile, conflictual, punitive censorship.

Censorship of correspondence, of coffee beans from personal packages.

Festive, profound, national, sentimental censorship.

Censorship of the Inquisition, of universities, private, state, dictatorial, liberal, insecure, pathological censorship.

Snitching, moribund, criminal, living, murdered, dead, radical, indispensable, cursory, esoteric, mystic, relativizing, cultural, theatrical, total, destructive, selective, legislative, czarist, sociological, pathological, opportunistic, optimistic censorship.

Movie censorship

culinary, poetic

Atavistic, contagious, equidistant censorship . . .

The soul of censorship.

The taste of censorship.

The body of censorship.

The fragrance of censorship.

In the beginning, censorship stinks, it reeks, if you've got a more sensitive stomach that might be a problem, afterwards the miasma settles down, the stench fades, it disappears over time, censorship becomes odorless, the higher, the farther away, the more seraphic, the more vaporous, thin, diaphanous, almost transparent, until even its barely flickering shadow begins to smell like roses. It's a long road to get there.

Wild roses.

What does the ideal Censor look like?

How does the Censor survive in adverse, difficult, threatening moments?

How does he ask for help?

How can I tell whether I have a Censor in front of me?

What is the secret code for censorship?

What conditions must the Censor meet in order to advance within our global Association?

What constitutes the primary activity of a Censor in our Lodge?

The secret, the great secret! There's no wastepaper in any notebook of directives that justifies the existence of the Office of Documents, that's not where the secret lies! The biggest secret is us. A secret in a secret in a secret in a secret, like Russian dolls hidden inside one another . . . And if we don't take care of ourselves, we're the first to go and the most vulnerable to being wiped out. They hate us, the dogcatchers of secrets are hunting us and they want us to no longer exist. They're killing us little by little until the last Censor on earth disappears. So idiots can gloat! The fight isn't fair, but it's motivating and meaningful, we'll fight until our last breath, until we censor the last poem on earth!

The last but not least of the goals of our Lodge is to assure the perpetuation of its own species. Any regular institutional department, I'm referring to the GDPP, can be shut down at any time, if someone imagines something, just as can happen at any moment with any structure that has to do with our kind of activity. Institutions die, but censorship remains. The best Censors have to survive, to carry on with their mission, to fulfill their assignments. To teach the craft to those who come after.

Censorship can't disappear and it won't disappear, as a practice. It has always been protected by powerful state structures, by the important parties. Everyone blames it, they hate it, but they can't live without it. Let's not confuse Censorship with its censors, whom those in power regard with suspicion and hostility, once they consider that they can dispense with their help. The world today is full of censors. Everyone considers themselves a censor, especially since our system is so generous in this respect. Just as any tractor driver can find that he's become a great poet overnight, the party believes that the same tractor driver can also be made a censor overnight. With every change, the new great and powerful one of the day feels more secure if he brings a whole team in with him, which includes his own fresh censors. These ones aren't concerned with the fate of literature, their goal consists of wiping out the old censors, whom they consider, with good reason usually, their enemies. Besides these new censors, there's also the fake censor or the dilettante censor, the censor on their own initiative. A "dilettante censor" should be the biggest possible load of nonsense in our regime based on strict and uniform criteria. Unfortunately, that's not the case. A dangerous opportunism exists, when, through the intermediary of someone who pretends to be a censor, you get rid of an enemy without getting your hands dirty, without getting involved or ruining your reputation. These days Censorship is a far too bureaucratic apparatus; in the institution I come from, many of our brothers work according to a clear, preestablished plan, when you want to condemn a writer, you write up dozens of reports on him that pass through the hands of dozens of people. It's hard to convince everyone to agree with you. Then alleged censors come in who simplify the process and play the game of the person divvying up power and gifts. There's a battle between the fake censors and the real ones, between the new censor and the old one. We here have the mission of identifying those with a true vocation, regardless of whether they're old or new, dilettante or institutional, you don't get here by making your way into the party or by being the mistress of a higher-up.

In generally accepted opinion, writers are, by definition, heroes, and censors—bastards and criminals.

When a writer publishes, he's a hero also because of the fact that he managed to get through Censorship, because of course it's so hard, he makes it past this stage! When he doesn't publish, he's still a hero, because he didn't accept the compromises of vile Censorship, which wants him disfigured and cut down to the bone . . . We've got some of these guys, too, who brag about not publishing, they brag about their inner heroism. They boycott us with their mute and internally self-exiled aestheticism.

Luckily for all censorial creation here, the phenomenon named "samizdat" hasn't caught on in Romania. Our great artists turn a blind eye. I for one wouldn't be mad if writers wanted to publish secretly, without being inspected by us. It's all the same to me. My mission at the GDPP is to inspect what's on my docket and there are thousands of pages, I'm not complaining that I don't have enough to do. For that matter, samizdat can't claim that it's totally free either. By functioning secretly, it's tracked down and punished, even though the texts aren't necessarily subversive. It's not an affront directed at our censorship but at the state, because I'm being paid by the state, the state hires me and trains me for this line of work. It's none of my business whether the writer decides to be published by our state presses or in secret print runs, in private, covertly and illegally. I'd like to see the idiot who runs away screaming from enormous print runs, money, and vacations, just because the so-called censors take out three of his words and five ellipses . . .

Our specialists (Officer Censors) are studying why the spread of "samizdat" in Romania has been so modest. They said there are certain psychological causes, beyond the simple transition from cowardice to courage, from complacency to taking a firm stance. Climate, geography, history, everything has to be analyzed and weighed. One of the members of the Lodge said that all the institutions similar to the GDPP in the countries with "samizdat" should be looked at, so we can see to what degree our activity itself has generated creative passivity and indifference. To what degree we ourselves, the censors, are to blame for writers not feeling the need to write in secret. Of course our limitless kindness and tolerance will be held against us this time. Obviously, if a scrawny little samizdat doesn't exist in Romania, all of Censorship's to blame! I can hardly wait for the moment when some authority higher than Censorship reproaches me for the absence of this phenomenon in our country (to add to the list)!

Otherwise, the idea about other institutions of censorship isn't bad. I've never thought about General Directorates of Press and Publications like ours existing somewhere else as well. It seems logical to me, socialist countries, soviet republics, they're kind of the same everywhere, so it wouldn't be surprising to have similar institutions in all these countries. I've never had time to bother thinking about it. It wouldn't be a bad thing to meet up, to have an exchange of experiences.

Keeping censors everywhere connected to each other was one of the first objectives of censorship brotherhoods, since the time of the guilds. The first brothers appeared alongside the Catholic Church, in connection with the lists of heretical books. Brother Censors traveled widely and communicated these lists, at the same time overseeing the purging of these publications in all of Europe.

Official meeting of the brotherhood of Censors—my first meeting.

After I leafed through a history of the masons, the first thing I thought of was that these meetings resemble mason gatherings, I seemed to feel something of their solemnity. But masons are masons, and censors, censors. And what enigmatic affirmations, and what strange bosses, you'd say that they weren't bosses. They treat us with so much respect, as if we, the novices, were more important than they are. I understand why we wear masks: we come here from all social strata, maybe there's someone coming from the Party, or the Securitate as well. High up there, the master censors know who's coming in, who's going out, but the newcomers, who maybe won't be here for long, what's the point of them seeing everyone? It's a security measure. The mask's a bit uncomfortable and I feel as if I'm suffocating, but I forget about it after a few minutes. What a difference between the GDPP's boring meetings and the Lodge's, exhilarating, I hang on every word, I even forget to breathe!

Is the comrade president of the GDPP aware of these happenings? In principle, he should know about their existence, I assume that he approves of them and encourages them. I assume that the Censor's Lodge operates with the permission of the party and that there exists a well-founded interest in it functioning properly; otherwise, a single institution of censorship, with hundreds of employees, would be enough for us.

What impressed me most was the speech at the beginning:
—As in the fortuitous formulation of the '50s, "let's release love," it's time, comrades, to release the opposition, dissidence, otherwise the system will crumble and, before it does, our institutions will collapse first . . .
That's how I found out that the literature that reaches us (the GDPP) has already been censored to the very limit and the guilt we attributed to editors and publishers is almost groundless. During the course of repeated and thorough inspections and sweeps, our inspectors found that publishing employees performed few censorial interventions. The modest economic state of our literary creators, their desire to put bread on the table, but especially fear, had paralyzed something very important in them. For these reasons, we're below the threshold of European literature and, even sadder, below the level of friendly countries. We're headed toward a devastating fall, if we don't take urgent measures! The ones chosen to survive are also the

only ones who write, but with the help of so many institutions and structures that it makes your stomach turn. They get support from creative organizations, literary circles, specially formed circles of friendly admirers, they're heavily supported by the Securitate, who listen intently for any sound made in their vicinity, they follow them, protecting them even from those who once said, unofficially, that, though they're getting far, their work's rather mediocre. No one's allow to criticize them even by throwing a rose at them. The party supports them, short only of kissing their butts, as you well know, Censorship also supports them by promoting them, casting their competition in shadow, patching up their volumes with lines that the brilliant communist poets could never dream up. Well, and things get all complicated sometimes, when the gentlemen begin to believe that the merit is all theirs, that they're the gods of the universe, that they can give orders and teach others how to live and how to write.

But it's enough for one of these reinforcing links to be missing a replacement part, just one slipup is enough—a more disappointed review in the press, which we didn't receive orders to censor, and the one who wrote it didn't have adequate guidance from the authorities—for our literary god to fall into the blackest despair and he's no longer good for anything, and after so much has been invested . . . Everything's bad, everything's getting worse, etc. He doesn't at all appreciate the effort, expense, investment in him, the time we've wasted . . . Where are our creators, comrades? Where is he hiding, the genius of the Carpathians, the genius of the Balkans, our literary genius, who writes on his own and we don't have to lift a finger?

Comrades, a fish rots from the head down! We foresee the epic downfall of the system! Our most important and influential colleagues are being corrupted by hostile capitalist books and publications. From our branches at customs, the mail, our import-export is sending reports that are increasingly worrying, with coincidences that are strange to say the least. It's dire that our warning isn't being taken into consideration.

Plan of action: to identify contacts at other, similar institutions in our soviet garrison and to try to find out whether others are receiving such publications. Nothing happens by chance, nothing is without consequences.

You don't discover a good poet by reading the best poems he's written, but by reading the worst. Most of them write both good poems and bad poems. That's the most common category of poet and it's close to the bottom of the heap, as far as I've been able to find out. Their good poems turn out that way on accident; if they were good poets, they wouldn't (also) publish so many bad poems. So they have no idea, they can't tell what's of value.

There are poets who, along with their good poems, also have some very good ones, brilliant even, memorable, anthologizable, but even they have had some weaker poems slip from their quill, even if rarely and barely noticeable. You meet with about five or six from this category in each respectable contemporary body of literature.

Some nations are lucky enough to have that singular and unrepeatable poet who writes only well, increasingly well, very well, exceptionally well, wonderfully, fantastically, without making even the tiniest compromise. He is the Poet with a capital "P." He senses when the poem doesn't have that exalted vibration and he doesn't put it down on paper, maybe he doesn't even feel like writing anything other than brilliant poems. By him, by the clear tone of his poetry, you can judge everyone else. We have the Standard. Sometimes, the Standard appears once every hundred years. The man has died, but we'll judge literature according to his perfect and matchless poems for many years to come after his departure, awaiting the following Standard. A Stradivarius violin, in first place, then a Regazzi, for example, then, I don't know, any violin belonging to a respectable luthier. If you study and you're persistent, you can get graceful sounds out of any instrument. But you'll never reach the perfect vibration of a Stradivarius or a Regazzi . . .

If you have a true creator in front of you, then interdictions will stimulate him. A mediocre coward, once you cut out a death from a text of his, will never have anyone else die, forevermore. He'll avoid not only the word, but all its derivatives as well, everything close in meaning. He'll avoid old age too, for fear that death follows afterward and it'll be, heaven forbid, censored!

But cut out a death from a text by a full-fledged courageous and clever author, and he'll come back with depression, loneliness, total fog, illnesses, you cut these out as well, and he brings catastrophes, apocalypses, labyrinths, symbolically negative animals, insane dictators, screams, wars, repeating on top of all that the previous morbidurities as well, all the depression and despair, the entire bouquet of possible and impossible illnesses and forbidden connotations. He doesn't do it specially to give us headaches, the petty official who personifies us in his mind doesn't matter to him. No, for him interdictions themselves constitute an impetus and a primary source of inspiration that propel him toward all negative meanings. For him, a no means thousands of yeses, it means revolving around the interdiction, crushing everything moving around this "no," as if he were cementing it, so it remains, repeats, returns. He's not even aware that, in response to our gaze, his work becomes even more intense, durable, much more powerful, uncontrollable, frenzied, unbridled. He has a kind of inner freedom, unconscious, which we have to channel skillfully. We have to intelligently manipulate the flow of interdictions. For example, if a woman's breast appears in a poem, we'll cut it out, he'll forget about all his morbid states of sadness and death and he'll fixate on the breast. The breast isn't the best option, because we can fall into the sin of eroticism, but the lesser evil is sometimes chosen in order to avoid the greater evil. In general, the most preferred method is to not forbid what should be forbidden and to disorient him instead. Let him find his way without any censorship in this ideologic thicket that's increasingly tangled. It's a simple lesson, but you aren't taught it in the Literature Division. Apprenticize here!

There's literature for children. Yes. Poems with puppies, little pigs, princesses. You, who've reached the age of thirty, can read it, you'll understand everything, certain texts will delight you, others, probably, will amuse you. In the end, you'll be extremely bored.

There's literature for grown-ups. It doesn't matter to us that some children can read it, can understand it. Grown-ups are sensitive in a more variable, more demanding way than children when it comes to reading material. People are equal, that's what the system says. If they're equal, that means, in principle, everyone should read the same way, write poetry, the same kind of stories, everyone. Lenin said: Any cook can be a politician. But he didn't say poet. A politician, yes, you can turn any tractor driver, boot maker, or cook into one, but into a poet, no. By contrast, transforming the best poet into a cook, yes, that's possible in the blink of an eye for our regime.

Literature has an age. If we're to take this even further, it branches off according to many other characteristics, themes, and criteria. When we require the nation to read, we require it to read only what we want. At the same time, however, there's also the attendant requirement of not reading, the injunction against going past the imposed limit. That's why the GDPP, where we work, exists. Education through literature can be done only up to a certain point, beyond that, no. But the limit isn't imposed on everyone, it's not the same for everyone. At first it wasn't clear, it wasn't delineated by population category. Now, it is. The superior reader exists, privileged, intelligent (or considers himself to be), the chosen reader, to whom we can't offer the same novel as we do to a cook or washerwoman (we can, but he has ever-increasing demands). Each category of reader has a certain kind of training, an education more exceptional or less so, different means, expectations, wishes. Factory workers are required to sign up at libraries and borrow books, and tractor drivers might be struck with a passion for reading. But the higher you climb up the social ladder, I'm referring to a few categories of people that reach a higher level of excellence in their field, the more complicated reading preferences become or the more sophisticated they should increasingly become. A new elite has been formed. Those who yesterday didn't even have a high school diploma, even though they occupied important positions, now decorate their homes with antique aristocratic furniture, with books that at other times they themselves ordered to be burned (they didn't burn them all, thankfully) or just purged and hidden from view. They've perched themselves high up and they want to receive something special, inaccessible to other people, they consider themselves better than others and they're sure that the books being offered to them should be different as well. They think that reading the same books as regular mortals is beneath their dignity.

Sometimes, the party elite (official) coincides with the intellectual elite (actual). Writers can also constitute an elite, a true one. And those who enjoy success with publishers and are sold in enormous print runs are true barons, almost like party barons. They're loved and respected. But large print runs are intended for a wide audience, and here's where our elites part ways. It's too difficult and even risky for a writer to combine the tastes (demand) of a wider audience, of regular citizens, with the ever more refined tastes of the privileged few of the system. Usually, this aspect is kept secret. Writers aren't that dumb, they catch on to lots of things, but they prefer money up front over writing in a sophisticated style for three exalted party officials, who today are flying high, tomorrow, crashing, but the other way around too, and the book you wrote made to order today might not be to the liking of tomorrow's bigwig. Writing for the people is safest and you at least have the certainty of dying of natural causes, not scratching out poems in prisons.

We already have small print runs, almost uncensored, for specialists and connoisseurs, and large print runs adapted to the social needs of the common people. To return to where we started: literature isn't for everyone, it's for the chosen. Literacy, the eradication of illiteracy that our people boast of, was done to indoctrinate the masses, to instill in them faith in the party, to bring them around to the new policies. Just as those who were illiterate "read" the drawings in churches and it wasn't necessary for them to know more than that, for the newly "literate" too much literature can be harmful, it can ruin them. If they take reading too far, the initial purpose is lost, because they can become rebellious and resistant. Literature strengthens only the strong, and only they get ahead. But how strong are the chosen ones? How strong is the new nomenklatura?

A lot of mistakes have been made here, we've got our work cut out for us. We're divided into thematic departments. How far literature can spread a message and how much can it influence an individual's behavior, psyche, emotions, etc. How much by theme, how much by essence, content, language, newness, experimentation . . .

Romania has become the center of the universe, the world revolves around it. For this reason, anything that has achieved success in various areas is brought here and adapted to our system, as far as is possible. After the soviet model, when everything was first invented in the USSR, now we're trying to see what we're capable of as well. It's being attempted, in any case, particularly in literature, it should be mentioned that in many other domains it's either exceptionally difficult or impossible. But here, yes, it's possible. We're able to say: You know, there's a South American novel that's enjoying great success, okay, but our native mioritic writer wrote one that blows it away! We're the best, here's the proof. Or about that poet, Spain's prized writer, we've also got some who write along those lines, but much better! If we can't find anyone willing or capable of truly surpassing that imperialist poet, then we find some incapable writer with writer's block who's obedient, desirous of becoming famous overnight, to whom we'll apply some skillful and het-erodentical translations. That's how important literature is! Right now it's vital for us to identify the original idea, the unique one. So it isn't discovered afterwards that the center of the universe could've been somewhere else and that many others are doing the exact same thing as us. And who knows what was applied to the South American, from what unusual source he gets his talent . . . To be the best, we need to know as much as possible, to be able to compare ourselves. The USSR is off limits. They have the right to be as good as us, we read each other, translate each other, and we haven't betrayed each other yet, I'm referring, strictly, to literature.

In general, we don't necessarily want to make enemies, we're interested in forming connections, relationships, we give and receive literature, we initiate exchanges of experience in the area of censorship, studies based on the psychology of creators in order to improve our censorial methods.

A GDPP censor cuts out anything that contravenes the party, reports these hostile outbursts against the ordinances of the system, the current power, to the right authorities, that's what pretty much all the institutional censors of the world do.

A WAC censor pays attention to changes, follows the newest editorial policies, pricks up his ears and sharpens all his senses at any real and meaningful new development. You have to have several (many) special qualities at your disposal in order to be able to see them.

Here lies the paradox and the difference. We don't write reports on what's bad, only on what's unique, original, unusual.

We sell too much literature. It all gets bought up. Tens of thousands, hundreds of thousands of copies and that's what leads to the desire to have something special, something unique, "I'm the most powerful and I want an expensive original painting, a one-of-a-kind palace, a unique novel!" What nonsense, you might think. But only with this kind of an argument could we, the Central European Censorship Lodge, the main branch of the World Association of Censors, survive in a communist regime, where all the secrets and all the lodges (that have survived mostly in name only and have been dormant for decades) have a single parent, in cases where their existence is allowed and tolerated. Our travels are secured exactly with the idea of bringing all that is most original everywhere here and helping our people become the best, they can't be outdone in literature of all things! Their people know how to scribble and ours don't?

There were comparatists before us who, however, couldn't be kept in check, their brotherhood, highly specialized in certain matters, was shut down, their experience proving only too quickly to be a fiasco. They were active before the Lodge was founded and they aren't our brothers. Rotten to the core, comparatists were true devils, poetry thieves. Officially, their job was to identify a number of brilliant works from particular national literatures, but, unofficially, also to identify other, much more questionable things, that are easy to guess. They traveled extensively, maintained relationships with all kinds of ministries, associations, unions, within the country and abroad, many were also secret counselors for certain high officials. For what were they lacking? Attracted by capitalism's shiny little mirrors and lollipops, they began laughing at the citizens of the fatherland, coming up with ideas and actions charged as being outright hostile. They made mistakes. Didn't they think about who was watching them? But their mistakes were our good fortune. We have other goals and objectives, though in some aspects we're replacing them.

As long as we keep our distance from any system, any ideology, we'll be nice and cozy. We won't admire anything, we won't belittle anything. We'll know, find out, be useful, we'll enter into the necessary mechanism and try to guide creation along a coherent path, we won't let the reins fall from our hands, we'll drive the cart, not the other way around. We'll survive.

And connection, connection is essential . . .

Art, medicine, music, astrology, the sciences, all have points of commonality with literature or they stimulate, inspire literature. The connection can occur naturally, on its own, without external contributions, or it can be generated artificially, with the help of specialists, upon our intervention or at the authors' express request.

Through connection you catch, you capture the heartbeat of reason. When they all meet, a spark is produced. Literature, like other arts, is energy. Emotion, love, knowledge produce energy. We desire to centralize it. With our singular party, of course emotion has to be centralized in singular fashion! We capture it, then we channel it, we guide it toward the track requested by specialists (I almost said: socialists). Everything's possible nowadays. We do this to order and we're fully supported.

At the very top, over all of us, is a Writer. He's a writer? The boss of all the Censors is a writer? How embarrassing! But you don't see him, you don't hear him, he's a kind of god! My goodness, how is it possible!

At the very top, our Writer gathers everything, accumulates, burns, and his word changes the world. I harbor the suspicion even now that, the way our superiors describe him, this writer at the pinnacle of our hierarchy can be none other than God. We're not a Lodge, but a religious sect!

A fire toward which all words gravitate, all grace gravitates toward him, all talents are trained on him. He's also the most important reader, thus, everything is gathered up in him and then is dispersed toward others . . . Let everyone rejoice in the divine gift. How he gathers everything, I understand, I contribute to this, but how he disperses it to everyone, how he sends grace back to us, I don't understand, it doesn't seem logical to me. After all, no one's received anything. I don't believe he's a writer. I find it easier to accept that it's God up there. In any case, He's better theorized, constructed and reasoned with so many thousands of words, like grace, like holiness . . . As concerns Him, everything is already arranged, established, and argued logically, logically in comparison with our Writer. With God everything is clear and peaceful. What do you believe?

I'm amazed by what I'm hearing. I don't believe in God, but in an invisible writer who exists in the form of energy and grace, in such abstract forms, it's even harder to believe. At least a bible's already been written about God, has anyone written about ours, has he written something? It's a long road and only master censors are able to answer further questions. We, the apprentices, have more earthly missions.

It would really be crazy to have some God up there! Whom we ourselves take out from all the texts, censor, wish would disappear, when actually . . . ! I'd like less mystery and clearer information about the structure and hierarchy of the Lodge. Why isn't the Censor up there? What's the Writer doing up there?

We've got a ways until we reach the untouchable Clarities.

How is it with our neighbors? Do they have lodges or not?

Not necessarily lodges, but almost everyone has censorship institutions similar to ours.

The statistics of interventions for the annual findings: How many interventions of an ideological, moral, aesthetic nature, how many state secrets. Percentage, frequency depending on the literary genre. We don't handle press. No, others take care of that.

The Great Secret exists! In order to camouflage it as well as possible, we flood it with the small secrets . . .

We identify people who are capable of keeping it and passing it on. Those who wouldn't betray it even under the threat of death. But how can they keep it without knowing . . .

Simple, without knowing.

And further, as far as possible, the arc extends, until you get to the limits of censorship. Where do I arrive? What do I see? A globe. Censorship's a globe, round, spherical. At the North Pole it's day, at the South Pole it's night, it's summer there, here it's winter. There you censored as much as possible and left in as little as possible. Here you leave in almost everything and censor a little bit. The further you go, the closer you get to your starting point.

Central Europe. After World War II, the WAC began following very closely the preparations for the third war, which is inevitable. We're not just following them, we're also censoring intensively. Until it gets to weapons and machine guns, wars are conducted on paper, thus, we can intervene, we can influence, it's our territory, our battle. In general, we don't monitor writers, but rather censors. The battle is between censors.

You should know that the weakest stumble over pornography, the best, ideology. Regardless of regime. But censors with a heightened sensitivity to the theme of war we haven't had yet. You, comrade, stumble over war, which is very important for us. We will take advantage of your intuitions and sensitivities.

We carry out various activities, we've branched out, especially since, thanks to our concentrated efforts, the war is being delayed, we'll hold it off as long as we can.

Today, reality is a well-censored text.

By the skin of our teeth, with superhuman efforts, we're holding off the war, but there aren't any weapons or methods that can stop human foolishness. So, bitter are our hopes, though we fight with everything we have.

The truth is always hidden.
    Everything that's hidden is true, so you have to hide a lie in order for it to appear true.

Instructions, in search of a true censor.

I feel dizzy. When I get out of the Lodge, everything's spinning, all the books, all the principles. Disorientation, a whirlwind. I have to accept other values: from the universal to the specifically national, the universal will win out, the specific, the closed off, the conservative, will lose. I'm taught one thing here, I practice something else there. The Lodge, from what I understand, is on the side of the universal and it will always come out winning. The right camp, with a future, though our Securitate officers beat their chests that they're on the other side . . .

We're putting together the inevitable fall of the regime. It doesn't have to fall right this minute, but we should be ready for it.

We educate praise criticize praise again destroy him; for a writer, the best censor is himself. Let him crap his pants on account of his own courage and do the cutting himself! Let him cut and we'll just look on, condescendingly . . . Yes, like that.
    In fact, we love them, we adore them, we're glad they've written, that they had the courage, the strength.

The regional, national, global thematic plan of the WAC. 1950–
2000, 2000–2050, 2050–2100.
Of course, local five-year plans are also made, usually.

Once a century, women decide that it's time to defend their
rights, they read, they write, then they fall off thematically,
humbled, the virile ones return, the male-female opposition,
national values, what brings us closer, what makes us different,
sex, sex. You encourage some snot-nosed kids, you award some
idiots who describe vaguely debauched scenes they've been
expressly ordered to write, otherwise, poorly depicted passages,
worthless, and for ten years all the youthful amateurs will write
about sex, all of writerdom will have work to do and what
pinnacles of mastery they'll reach! New proposals, diverse,
choose between the potential writers who fulfill the realist-ide-
alist criteria exactly. Women are more successful in the realm
of the real, in prose. Poetry can't be planned, its manipulative
possibilities are much more reduced (I'm not thinking about
propagandistic ones), it's made with images and great talent.
Unpredictable. The planning of literature has proven to be
utopic, in general, there are other much more sophisticated
methods for extracting the expected result from authors.

Just when you believe that every style of writing has been tried,
when you're convinced that it's impossible to discover something new, along comes a voice different from all the other
ones, both fresh and new, leaving all theories in the dust . . .
Otherwise, everything comes under our strict control. No
one surprises us. The new voice is quickly, appropriately integrated, because nothing escapes us. Not a single writer has been

recognized, awarded, paid attention to without our permission and direct involvement.

Contempt. You see one of them go up to receive their award, how disturbed he is as he reads passages from his book to the audience and he doesn't even know whose passages they are, in fact. He doesn't know which poet he's reading. The impostor, the ignoramus, the plagiarizer! To this day, not one has refused the praises he didn't deserve! They haven't thanked Censorship for the auspicious interventions. Now we're doing the work of the disbanded comparatists as well. We've got no choice.

Use fresh, young authors, who haven't studied literature and haven't started copying. We're not referring to plagiarizing, but to the fact that, if you read too much, others' ways of writing get inside your head, you imitate without wanting to and without being aware of it, we might encounter unpleasant surprises. Young people are capable of a great deal of inventiveness and originality, they can birth something that no one else has. Some shouldn't be translated, because they'd lose some of their charm, they'd sound like many others. They all write the same, they all read the same literature and they resemble each other. Look at, for example, European impressionist painting. Czech, Hungarian, Polish, Romanian, etc., you can't tell the difference, only the first one to do something new counts. It would be good to send Danubian poems to Poland, exotic goods, they're not on the Danube and they definitely don't write those kinds of poems there. (And who writes them here? It doesn't matter, we're just theorizing.) Don't send them to the Bulgarians, they're in the same boat. You can give anything to the Soviets, because they're just comparing, verifying, they don't copy even our best-turned phrases. They've got too many authors, more than enough to choose from, they've got a large territory at their disposal. They consider us beneath them and they take inspiration only from capitalists, we know from reliable sources.

Our universal principle: don't take too much if you can't give in return. If you don't have command of a great literature, don't try to create one on the backs of others. You can create the best writer in the country, yes, as a local celebrity, but abroad, no way. Stay in your corner, little impostor.

The themes for export after voting:

USSR—spirituality, the cosmos, psychology

Polonia—resistance, humor, realism

Hungary—history, ?, ?

Romania—aesthetics

China—~~love~~, landscape, punishment

Czechoslovakia—humor, realism

America—democracy, war, family

France—philosophy, erotica, psychology

England—royalty, domination, philosophy

Germany—revolution, mythology, history

India—the male-female binary, feminism, mythological descriptions

Other countries . . .
To be filled in.

Too general, it's done so that you can import and export anything, in fact.

These are the themes for mutual cooperation accepted by the universal Censorship. Meaning we can translate English philosophical novels, about royalty . . . We can observe that, on the one hand, the two blocs are represented, regardless of a country's priorities, while, on the other, the criteria for both blocs are the same if they exist, I for one haven't discovered them. The theme of "love" cut from China means that each country can administrate their own "love" as they wish and may borrow or export it according to requests and needs. This is the plan for the next ten years, 1975–1985, then the themes change, either they're rotated or new ones appear, depending on the times. They say it existed before too, they say the tradition of thematic plans and mutual cooperation has been around for a while, it's over a century old. That's referring just to translations, not to plagiarism, but again it depends on individual needs . . .

The World Association of Censors has a strict rule, they don't accept just anyone and you have to be recommended by at least two full members of the Association (once you reach a certain level, starting with the rank of Officer Censor, you're allowed to recommend new members). Then follows the trial period, that's nothing like the trial period back here, at the GDPP. No one trains censors, not one college graduate will have a clue about censorship and he won't know how to censor, almost everyone's clueless about this occupation. It's often actually a risk to recruit a student, to bring him into the institution and to intuit the future censor in him and prepare him for that.

Two years ago, I, too, was part of the personnel evaluation commission. I didn't go around recruiting people, I never worked in Training-Inspection, but after the instructors brought the quivering fresh meat into the GDPP, very good censors, the best, were needed to shape the novices into the desired form. Trustworthy censors, who'd watch them, help them, open their eyes. I was assigned to the evaluation committee, right from the first stage of their assessment, I was in charge of five and I gave only one a passing grade, I bluntly and categorically declared the other four inept for this activity. Our superiors got all upset, but I was right! The one backed by me is now my pride and the pride of Technical Sciences, sharp, modest, hardworking. After the evaluations, because I wasn't the only evaluator, we were a team that examined the students, three passed . . . Well, the other two left the institution in disgrace, nothing could be made out of them. Not just anyone can be a censor. I remember how harsh I was, I'd even say fierce, the girls trembled, the boys stuttered, they couldn't read the text in question from nervousness, weak, cowardly—qualities, or to be more precise, defects, that are fatal in becoming a censor. You're the terror of the young hires, Hermina once said to me. Afterwards they removed me from personnel evaluation and they assigned me the instruction of already approved employees only.

But in the Association the exams are different. I don't even feel them. I intuit, usually with a delay, that I'm being subjected to certain tests, certain examinations, upon which my fate and future in this organization depend. I answer certain questions I'm not asked, I pass stages, trials without realizing it. I ask myself: who wrote my second recommendation? One was written by Zuki, I'm positive, but the second, who? I wouldn't have gotten here without two recommendations. I can't identify anyone. We're still wearing masks. I like being hidden, but I'd like to know who the others are. Zuki also wears a mask and sometimes I think I've guessed it's him, but I can never be sure. It seems to me either that he's not that tall or his voice isn't that deep, yes it's him, no it's not . . . It's good that this Association exists, I'm proud of being part of it, I don't know what to do to keep going higher up, as high as possible. Now, apparently, it's important to have a subsidiary in each country and to keep in close contact with it, to exchange opinions, to know the authors who matter (from our point of view!) and the newest trends. For example, our GDPP isn't in contact with other GDPPs, not even the ones from friendly countries. I didn't even know if something like that existed. But they do exist and they're almost the same as ours. We work according to the same principles. I know that in the beginning our people were in tight with the Soviets, we'd go over to them, for an experience exchange, they'd come over to us. That was before my time. Censors in Russian exist, the Soviet publishing system hasn't changed, I think, but I know absolutely nothing about their censors and Soviet censorship. Just as I don't know anything about the Bulgarians, Hungarians, who are our immediate neighbors.

Only within the context of the Association can I satisfy certain curiosities of mine. Only here can I find out about all the censorships of the world. The most powerful censorship associations exist in the most powerful countries, the USSR and the USA, and they keep in close contact. We, the others, are barely starting out.

Deep meanings, beyond passions.

Quiet, quiet. Silence means censorship. The most efficient way of censoring.

What isn't written exists.

The initial shock, then you have to keep going, to set your mind to it. They're in a serious crisis, yes, you're right, it can't go on like that. But we are as well, choppy literature doesn't pass here anymore either, you know what I'm referring to . . . Even if it's not visible to the naked eye, our crisis isn't less serious than theirs. We're trying to come up with solutions together, to take from them what's possible and to give what we can. We strongly believe in the future of literature and we're doing everything in our power to ensure its survival. Beyond the state, the party, politics, regime, ideology, which have the same principles and will always be detrimental to our domain. They will always try to utilize, enslave, instrumentalize, slap with fines, buy with money or other means of theirs, blackmail, corrupt, destroy. They simmer us over low heat in the same pot, what's a writer, what's a censor! They're like powerful, influential, aging lovers, often impotent, who choose fresh young wives for themselves, buying love or only the illusion of it. They're buying art. It's not love they want, because they no longer have the necessary receptors, they no longer have the instrument, they want the illusion, we all know what the reality is, but we shouldn't say it. Except that art that's bought goes bad, it stinks and no one in hell would read it!

So we're looking for solutions, don't think that being a censor means only cutting, tearing out, removing something from a book (sometimes something important, something powerful). Being a censor also means healing, supporting, improving, promoting, helping a book. A book or an author, sometimes to the detriment of another one who's just as good. A censor must be cognizant of the author's potential. Value myopia is our most dangerous affliction. We're observing now, we cutting out now, even if we're right, yes, everything we've cut out is correct and well done, we have the list of criteria, we could win an award for our 100 percent justified interventions. Even if, yes, right now we're correct, through our blind and narrow correctitude we can destroy an impulse, a talent, a creator whom we mutilate and who won't produce anything ever again, he won't be able to get over what is for him this supreme slashing and humiliation. He'll publish, in the best-case scenario, two or three more little volumes and he'll end up in literary dive bars, degraded, depressed, an alcoholic. How many such futures were destroyed because of the excessive zeal of some conscientious and ultra-proper censors? Yes, I agree, we censor, we cut. Censors who've never asked themselves what they'll do tomorrow, if they're cutting down to the bone today. Who'll keep writing tomorrow, who'll keep soaring to the upper realms, if today you chop off everyone's wings? Our volume of work keeps growing, they're writing more and more, we're all horrified: Who will be left to read, if everyone's writing? But it's our duty, in this sea, in this ocean of texts in which we're drowning, to find the good and true ones, and to give them a fighting chance. So that literature will follow our course, with the ones we want and the ones we think are fit, so that we'll rule over the literary domain, we, the bosses, so that we won't have to listen humbly and submissively to the orders of a bunch of dilettantes in the field, who aren't any good and don't even care. Who want glorious bricks to prop up their eternal power. You can't stand idly by, you can't not take action. By saving literature, we're saving ourselves, we're saving censorship, in fact. If our readings have refined us, taken us out of dogmatic darkness, helped us to grow spiritually, to be more intelligent and far-sighted, it's only right that we put our shoulder to the wheel and contribute to saving the species when the situation becomes critical. Imagine a field full of flowers and weeds. We pick out the flowers and water their roots, we protect them, so that they'll bloom, be fruitful, so that they'll spread their seeds nicely. It's not enough to let things happen by themselves. Left alone, the ugliest and smelliest weed will conquer everything in its path, it will spread, it will overshadow and destroy all the delicate, gentle, fragrant flowers. The strongest wins, but in art, the most beautiful should win. It's not a boxing ring.

A censor, after reading so much, becomes an addict, a kind of druggie. Not only can he not live without reading, you'll see him walking, holding an imaginary manuscript in his hands, fluttering his fingers in the air as if he were turning pages only he could see, moving his lips as if he were engrossed in following the book's text. Not only that, because that would be a fixable problem (if you want to read, you have enough books to last you several lifetimes, for hundreds of years to come), but he's asking for books that are even more dramatic, even more intense, even more exceptional. Just as you increase the dose of a drug after a while, because you can't feel it anymore, our reader wants to exceed the limits, superhuman sincerity, the skinning of flesh, a book written in blood, he wants the jackpot, he wants what here, but also everywhere, is written in only minuscule amounts. The rhythm of a good author when he's writing doesn't coincide with that of the censor who's reading, especially when his hunger for quality literature reaches limitless, exorbitant proportions. A good book is written infrequently and that's normal. Our censors are becoming increasingly dissatisfied, because no one can offer them what they desire, they can even become aggressive, dangerous for society. We don't accept them into the Association, of course, but we propose to help them, because they, too, are censors, and the progression of the disease is pretty nasty and a far from enviable fate awaits them. They're still people but ones who've taken reading further than what literature could offer. Those who didn't protect themselves against literary temptations and who dedicated themselves body and soul to the profession of censor. We don't even try to heal them anymore, we've looked after them since the founding of the Association in Romania, we've watched them, we've tried a series of methods and not one has proven completely effective. Of course, I'm not referring to the party's methods, when you take disciplinary action against them, you transfer these refined readers to factories and plants, to manufacture equipment or oil parts. We had them write and, up to a point, it works. Some get cut down to size immediately and don't want to continue the treatment, others keep torturing themselves, trying to express their unhealthy craving. We ask them to tell us what exactly they want to read, so that we know what to offer them. They write and write. However, not one of them has turned out to be a writer. But when you put yourselves in the shoes of a writer, you realize how hard it is to get even something simple down on paper, let alone more complicated things. You realize, when you write, how little of what you feel and think you manage to get down, how limited writing is and how modest are the results. Try music, there you can express yourself fully, you can feel fully, there the desire for something more powerful can be satisfied. The yell is more evident. Some go, it's the next and last stage for the refined ones capable of accepting our solution. But reading is not the most condemnable vice, others smoke, drink. Censors are the most exposed and vulnerable when it comes to reading. The reading disease can also affect regular readers, whose health we doubt when they try to hide from their problems in the fictitious universe of a book. In any case, the disease itself isn't contagious. Also, certain books have a greater potential for creating dependency than others, I'm not referring to the love of reading, authors of merit, etc. who depict beauty or our fragile soul. No, we're referring to a psychiatric illness. We're researching it. Us again.

The GDPP censors can't be the ones to do it, the poor things.

The ground zero of censorship! When the author censors himself, dryly, properly, predictably, while the censor poeticizes himself, literaturizes himself, when the author becomes a censor, and the censor a poet. Consensus and complicity are total, the poet increasingly becomes a censor, tragically, inevitably, he feels like a censor, climbs into the skin of a censor, thinks like a censor, he takes out dialogue, lines, words that a potential or imaginary censor, who occupies his being ever more intensely, might cut from his book. Disciplined, harsh, brooding. And the censor, more and more in love, more pierced by the beauty of the words, kneeling before the genius, admiring the beauty of the image, caressing the work. The roles are reversed. Censorship is no longer censorship, literature isn't literature.

Like in the tradition, somewhere in the middle of the river, the two flower wreaths find each other, they embrace and flow down the river together.[18] Toward hell or toward heaven.

The Other Beginning

The note about the Danko "syndrome," his heart, to be precise. I'll summarize just in case:

A noble people was living out its age at the edge of a forest, when, one day, savage tribes swooped in on them and chased them away from their fertile field and into the depths of the forest. The forest was dark, with savage animals, with thick leaves and spikey branches, with poisonous bogs. The people walked for a long time searching for a sunny field, where they could settle, but the forest became thicker and thicker, the rays of the sun couldn't pass through, as for food, they barely ate, they cried and kept walking. From hunger, from fatigue, from dark thoughts, the people perished in droves. Running out of hope and strength, they began thinking that maybe it would've been better if they had returned to their land, now conquered by the enemy, better in slavery than in this savagery . . .

When it seemed the women's wails couldn't get any louder, and their hearts couldn't sink any lower, from somewhere, from out of the crowd, Danko, a handsome and courageous young man, appeared:

—He who never dares always fails! Onwards, my people, no forest is endless, no misfortune is impossible to work through. Wails and dark thoughts won't help us, only courage and the faith that we'll find what we're looking for and deserve! We're a tribe of brave, fearless people and we will prevail!

—Danko, guide us! Get us out of this dark and swampy forest! Save us!

—Follow me!

Danko took the lead and they all began to trudge through the forest again. Their progress proved to be difficult and dangerous, they kept going and going and going, but the forest didn't end, the sun didn't appear. Weakened, more people continued to die. A fierce storm arose, as if all the bad things that had happened up until now weren't enough. Trees fell on top of them, the lightning terrified them, the rain soaked them. All of nature seemed to be against them and want them to perish. Overwhelmed by so much misfortune, the people began to blame Danko. He didn't guide us well, it's his fault things are so bad!

—Where is the end of the forest, where is the salvation you promised? You must die! a few yelled out, desperate and set against him.

There was no mercy, no pity in their words. Danko got angry at first, then he softened. He loved his people and he wanted with all his heart to get them out. He was ready to make any sacrifice in order to save them.

—What more can I do for you! he cried.

Then, suddenly, he tore open his chest with his hands, he ripped out his heart and held it high, above his head. His heart shone like a sun. The forest went silent, illuminated by this sign of love for his neighbor. The people froze in wonder.

—Follow me! Danko yelled.

Stunned and mesmerized, the people stopped revolting and they followed the majestic heart. They didn't even perceive when the forest ended and an enchanting field, bathed in sunlight, laid itself out before their eyes.

Happy, Danko took in the wonderful view with his gaze, he smiled gently and fell to the ground.

The people, overcome with their great joy, didn't even notice the death of their savior.

Only one, who was on the squeamish side, tiptoed up to Danko's body and saw that his heart was still fluttering. Without thinking about it too much, he stomped on the heart a few times, crushing it until it stopped beating.

Everything in this story is beautiful. Dedication. Sacrifice. But the trampled heart ruins everything. Couldn't we somehow cut out this last fragment? It suggests human ingratitude. You die for them, and they stomp all over your heart.

This text was a big headache, a difficult dilemma for our colleagues. In the end, they took out the final fragment, though Soviet literature really shouldn't be censored. The problem is that Maxim Gorky, the great Russian prose writer, wrote it long before the October Revolution (1917). "Danko's Burning Heart" belongs to the cycle of stories "Old Izergil," first published in *Samarskaia gazeta*, 1895 (so, during the time of czarism).

It's an example of how, depending on the context and the

social and political situation, any text can be improved after
being inspected by Censorship.

I've also got my Achilles's heel. When I come upon passages,
descriptions, memories, poems about war, something hidden
deep within me is disturbed. I can't find convincing explanations for it. I feel helpless, I'd like to cut out all the war in
literature, any allusion to it, but I know I can't do that, those
aren't my instructions, it wouldn't be professional, I'd be sanctioned for unjustified interventions.

Is this your fear? What are you afraid of? Of war?

Yes, of war.

Z. advises me: Censor it! As long as we cut out war from all the
texts, it won't happen and peace will reign throughout the world!
Censorship is omnipotent, above warmongering and suicidal
human error. You've never known war, you haven't felt it. You don't
even know what it is . . . Don't think about it anymore . . . There
won't be a Third World War, it's a false alarm, that's what these
writers are like, they need to fear something and they absolutely
insist on freaking out the public as well. But you're powerful and
smart and you don't fall for traps that easily. I mean you don't fall
for their trap. Anyway, any allusion to war and death presupposes a
pessimistic and tragic view of things, so you're covered, you can cut
it out. No one wants war, you're not the only one.

I might not be, but it seems to me that the texts are sum-
moning it, drawing it closer, like a magic incantation, like a
spell that summons the rain and the rain comes. "Rain, rain,
go off to war, sun, return to where you were before!" Why to
war of all things? What's the relation between rain and war? It
chases it away and it summons it.

Everyone has a subject or several subjects that they don't want to look in the eyes, everyone reacts to something, for me, it's war. You have to be a man about it in the end, get over it, ignore it, com. Zukermann encourages me, smiling.

Maybe it comes from my unknown father, maybe it has something to do with my torturous birth in warring times, fathers, one dead in the war, the other as good as dead after the war. If he hid in the forests, kept clear of people, if he's condemned by our regime, you can call that dead. The war and the absence of my father, perhaps? The question eats at me, it tortures me . . . I breathe a sigh of relief when the next thick manuscript has nothing to do with war . . .

Grandma would say: Blast the damned war! It took your father, and your mother! It left you to fend for yourself . . . The worst thing in the world is war, the cruelest and the most unfair. Men either conquer or are conquered. Those who allow themselves to be conquered are killed, usually. Those who conquer treat us like . . . God, I shouldn't be telling you this!

Mom didn't die in the war, but I was sure that Grandma was right. If not in the war, then because of it . . .

From today's meeting, Monday, February 11, 1974:

> Soon after it was drawn up, the collegium's work program became a handbook used daily by the leadership of divisions and services in working with readers and delegates, demonstrating its necessity and efficiency.
>
> Analyzing the main provisions of the program, applied consistently across all our units in the Capital

and the provinces, allows us to draw several conclusions about the achieved results.

Regarding the growth of the professional competence of the work collectives, we find that: a) the increasingly sophisticated materials we inspect (press, book, radio-television, art, etc.) and the complexity of our work have bolstered institution leadership's ongoing preoccupation that all the employees who do specialized work have an advanced degree. As a result of this requirement, currently we have reached the point where, of the 256 readers and delegates, 191 are college graduates who have passed the state exams, 4 are graduates who have not passed the state exams, 18 are currently studying at various colleges, and 43 have a secondary and general education. Among those who do not have the degrees required of a reader, a segment is of an advanced age, while others are not permitted by the state of their health to continue their studies. These, however, have the necessary level of training for their work due to their personal efforts.

Special attention has been paid within the institution to the political education of employees in regard to devotion to the politics of our Party, to the formation of the ethical character of each of us. The provisions of the program regarding the strengthening of discipline in all aspects, a spirit of personal responsibility and initiative, the preservation of a principled work environment, have been achieved, on the one hand, in the work process, on the other, through the ongoing activity of political education conducted by the Party

and youth organization, institution leadership, and the
unit chiefs.

The face in the photograph . . . My picture when I was just a
little girl . . .

At first, I thought that "up there" meant heaven, that my
father, who was with God in heaven, would come down and
look at my photograph, wrapped up in a handkerchief and
hidden in the hollow of an oak tree in the forest. I play back
the scene, it surfaces again now, but differently, with another
meaning. I see myself walking behind my mom. The photo
wasn't the only thing we put in for the father up there, but
also walnuts, apples, bread, and something else wrapped in
newspaper, smoked bacon or cheese. And maybe a little bottle
of brandy? I just now realized that "up there" also might have
referred to the far away mountain, in any case it, for example,
and not just heaven, was up above our house. And father could
come down from up there, from the mountains (not from
heaven), to take the provisions, together with the picture of
his four-year-old daughter. That unknown man who kept the
photograph of a little girl next to his chest. My photograph. I
feel as if I look a lot like this father who's hiding. I was crying
in the photo, I was scared because they left me by myself. Mom
was making happy, encouraging faces. She said that I shouldn't
be photographed beside my brothers, but by myself. I'm a big
girl and I have to pose by myself. I agreed with tears running
down my cheeks.

What a great secret I bear within me . . . Sometimes I want the
Securitate readers of notebooks to go looking. For my father, I

mean. I can't. I have no clues, no trace, I don't even possess a photo of him, not even one of my photos, of the kind hidden in the hollow. I don't know the name of my real father. Mom died without telling me anything, fearing, probably, that it would get me in trouble. She left, taking her secret to the grave. It's not my fault at all that I have a father like that, I've never seen him, I don't know him. But I'd like to see him at least once. I haven't thought about him at all for so many years, but the memory of him comes back to me . . . If he's guilty and he fought against our great and victorious state, let him stay there in prison and let me be allowed to visit him. I want to know if I have his eyes, if I'm this good and this smart of a censor because he was good and smart. My brothers are semi-illiterate, they weren't even capable of finishing night school. While I'm as smart as a whip! Maybe he was an army general, maybe even a writer? He's my biggest secret, the one I censor, I cut out, I want to ignore, but it grows back, it springs up more enigmatic, more powerful in my mind. My father—an enemy of the people? The Securitate officer also has a father and a mother and maybe he understands my situation, my desire. If my secret is ever discovered, if my father were to appear and to declare that he has a daughter and that it's me, with a biography like that they'll deem that I can no longer be a censor and I'll be kicked out of Censorship, as a daughter of an enemy of the people. But it's highly unlikely . . . How many anxieties are torturing me lately . . .

I imagine that he maybe doesn't even know about my existence, he doesn't care that I exist. But the scene with the photograph demonstrates to me that he knows, that he thinks about me, and maybe he wants to know me as much as I do him. Maybe he died already, in the mountains or in some prison, with my photograph next to his chest, maybe he exists only in my thoughts. Too many conjectures, I think too much for a model censor . . .

⚘

—Forgive him, Z. said to me, suddenly, in the middle of a discussion about something completely different. Forgive him and forget about him. Learn from the authors of these texts, learn how to put yourself in the place of someone else. Understand him and forgive him. It was hard for him too, and now, definitely, it's even harder for him. The faster the ascension, the more dangerous the existence . . .

That's easy to say, but I still dream about how we'll meet, how he'll come with our son who will jump into my arms. My husband's holding a bouquet of flowers, my son hugs me . . . The dream is so beautiful, so warm! How can I give it up?

⚘

—Do you like him?
—Yes!
—Do you want to marry him?
—Yes, I answered honestly, smiling dreamily and incredulously.
—Then tonight, when I tell you, you'll climb up into the hayloft and sleep next to him in the hay.

I almost died of fright that night. I was afraid even to breathe, I wanted to run away from him, I didn't even want to get married anymore. When I had finally worked up the courage and was just about to get up and leave, he clung to me, he grabbed my hand and whispered: "Elena!" But I'm Dina, little Didina, my name is Filofteia, even Diana works, but Elena, no, not even close. I'm not used to drunk people, I don't know how drunk he was, how unconscious. I got mad at him, I didn't run away after all, I rode out the entire night there. I'll show him!

With the first rays of dawn, my brothers stormed in:

—Would ya look at our love birds! and they began accusing him, they yelled at him: We brought you into our home, we trusted you! Our friend, when, in fact . . . !

He was sitting there groggy, still sleepy, I, pallid and ashamed, as if I had done who knows what with him that night. My brothers sent me out of the barn, I had to climb down a ladder, I couldn't see anything, overwhelmed by emotions, I don't know how I didn't fall on my head and die right then. I ran into the house and cried, I was bellowing like a cow being taken to the slaughterhouse. I couldn't stop myself. One of my brothers came and told me to quit, because it would end in a wedding, the way I wanted. I blinked my eyes. What wedding? I was really dumb and I didn't understand anything. I think I was over wanting to get married by then. I was crying because he had said "Elena" in his sleep, I was crying because he didn't love me but someone else. I don't know why else I was crying, maybe because I sensed that what was happening to me wasn't right and I felt very bad about it.

I remember our only evening, in fact, night, together. When we were truly husband and wife and we slept together. An entire night! The memory comes back to me with the same shudder, the same heart wrench. I don't forget anything, time doesn't erase anything in my past, good, bad, however it was meant to be. Even now I can see it all, what I wouldn't give for the memory to disappear!

My youngest brother, Pintilie, was together with the woman Calin loved, they were getting ready for a wedding as well. After Calin married me, she must've suffered a lot, she must've lost hope (maybe she had been expecting him to marry her, he'd made her many promises, and there he goes and marries me, out of nowhere!) and when she agreed to marry my brother, in my husband's mind, she betrayed him. That's how men think: he gets married (first) to someone else and she, his former sweetheart, is in fact the one who betrays him. He can get married, but the sweetheart better not find someone else! She has to wait only for him and to love, again, only him, until death, if possible! And she should've understood that he, in fact, loves only her, but as for getting married, he married, no one knows why (we know why), me. But she didn't understand and she married my brother.

I considered that it would be good for my husband to know, see, understand that the Elena who was once his was now with someone else and was happy. I thought that this way he'd be nicer to me, he'd finally notice me, he'd accept me as his wife. My brother's house was on the way to the store and not far from my mother-in-law's house. One evening, we walked together past Pintilie's window and Calin, I mean my husband, heard her lively, flirtatious laugh. Exactly right then! Maybe before she had laughed like that only with him. Maybe he, when he heard her, understood that she wasn't suffering at all and she wasn't waiting for him, she was going about her life and she didn't miss him. She wounded him with her laugh, she crushed him. He was out drinking until late. I returned home, glad that everything had happened exactly as I'd planned.

He came home late, disfigured by pain and cheap alcohol, he slept with me out of desperation, after the alcohol didn't help him forget her. A mountain of unhappiness fell down on me, how is it that I didn't crumble? How is it that our comingled tears didn't flood the house? How were two mating miseries able to beget a new soul, whom no one wanted? I realized then that my husband wasn't mine and never would be.

I felt his hate, his fervor of disgust for me. I felt the sexual act like a vomiting, as if he had thrown up in me, he covered me in filth, he defiled me, he crushed me, left me sticky, dribbling, wounded, bleeding, laid desolate, empty, helpless, lifeless, meaningless. Him, victorious, yelling, jumping around the room like a maniac. He knew he hadn't touched me then in the hay! He was positive! My brothers had gotten him drunk on purpose and thrown me onto him, but nothing had happened between us that night. I was still intact, he, the damned drunk, was the first, but only now! The proof—this night! He looked at me as if I were a cow that's no longer good for anything and you're keeping it for no reason. Now he can leave, now he's free, no one better dare try to keep him here again!

My brothers didn't care about him, or me, anymore. Then I realized that they had used me just to get his sweetheart. Pintilie wanted that woman and he did everything to obtain her. I never heard anything else about Elena, what she did, how she spent her first night. Maybe she felt what I felt too, maybe that's what all women feel the first time, except that for me it was the first and last. How many women do it scores of times, for months on end and they don't get pregnant, as for me—one and done, as if my body knew that there wouldn't be a next time and it seized the opportunity right away.

I can't find any book that resembles my life, I can't find any poem that expresses my feelings. What good is all this literature then? You write about how you cut your pinky but you're unable to think even a bit beyond your own finger, to observe the bigger wounds of others, to intuit them at least, to help them somehow? A bunch of phony, useless whims. A bunch of crappy aesthetes, who've never suffered a single misfortune, and the party coddles them, a bunch of cheap whores, treacherous, opportunistic, ready to kiss the ass of the first aesthetic order passed down and to execute it zealously. A bunch of lascivious jerks who describe asses and hips and expect money and applause for this! Just look how much work they put in, how they struggled to get things down on paper! What effort, how much energy it took! What a sacrifice to illuminate the people! What contempt for the poor people! What an injustice to want to read and not to have anything! They shove so much trash with aesthetic pretensions down your throat. And to be a censor on top of all that—a pure paradox!

Writer, remember, there will also come a time when your weighty word will be full of meaning, when you'll put your blood and singed soul down on paper, but no one will read you, they won't take you seriously, and not one truth of yours will reach a wider audience! You're so full of shit in your books and you've forced others to eat it as well when they read you,

you've sold so many cheap trinkets and forced the world to buy them that one day everyone will get fed up and they'll take revenge, punishing you with complete indifference!

The reader's fountain of patience will dry up (Censorship's dried up long ago!). You laughed at him, you sent him so many false signs, false texts, false alarms, fake values, that when you bring him the True Book, he won't recognize it, he'll reject it, he'll trample over it. He'll have no more use for your values, or your truth. You'll call out for help, you'll try to stay alive, "I'm drowning!" you'll yell and in reply you'll hear: "Go ahead and drown, what's the big deal, what's one more or less, you're not the only one in this position" . . . All will be for naught!

The duty of a censor is to delay the final execution, the final tragic scene, to delay the end of literature, to maintain the current state of things, even through artificial respiration.

I think about it, I'm really preoccupied: Are we making it worse somehow? Is our share of the blame, the censors', somehow bigger than we'd like to believe? Are we somehow contributing to this collective tragedy and the first ones to drown will actually be us? Are we the ones putting clothes on the king when he's in his birthday suit? And if they come tomorrow with the order to dismantle the GDPP, as it's been rumored for a while, will anyone notice our absence, will they be sorry, will there be a change in literature? I'm afraid not. I'm afraid that no one can stop the herd headed for the cliff. No one and nothing. The only thing left for me to do is to fulfill my duties here and now and that's about it. I do what depends on me. The rest is literature . . .

In our relationships with publishers and presses, a series of deficiencies have been eliminated such as: the printing of materials without our stamp, disregarding GDPP interventions, the failure to communicate certain changes made after receiving "imprimatur," the failure to send materials in their final form for inspection. Discussions addressing these problems were had with the leadership of the Academic, Political, Didactic, Technical, Scientific, and Meridians presses, with the editors of Radio and Television, with the magazines *Economic Life*, *History Magazine*, *Literary Romania*, *Hyperion*, et al.

Even with all the measures that have been taken, mistakes caused by the violation of work standards have arisen. For example, the photograph in *Student Life*, pornographic paragraphs in the magazine *Neue Literatur*, granting an "imprimatur" stamp to material that was waiting for a stamp from the relevant ministry.

They wed him to me for the simple fact that his woman was coveted by my brother of all people, who wouldn't give up until he married her. The desires coincided, that's all. There was a series of favorable circumstances, coincidences that changed the fate of so many people. What would've happened if I hadn't climbed into the hayloft? Nothing. My brother would've still gotten married to Elena, and Calin's fate might've been worse . . .

No one cared whether or not we loved each other. We didn't even know each other that well. Given how cruel they were, they handled him with kid gloves, but only because he agreed to marry me, otherwise I think they would've thrown him in jail and he understood this. I didn't object either. But I was sure that I loved him, I remember it well . . .

Does he really not understand that without me, without our meeting and living together, short and dull as it was, his life wouldn't have taken the brilliant and marvelous course it has today? He slammed into me as if into a rock and destiny threw him up so high, so far! If he had married his Elena, he would've remained in the village, he would've loved her and given her an army of babies. He hated me and so, not to have to see my face, not to see my pleading eyes like those of an abandoned cat, he started reading. And he's gotten so far! I still dream about meeting him, I can't think about any other man. I have to, but I'm not able to yet! I hoped for a long time to be able to get him back.

Love isn't the only thing that ties people together. It wasn't because of love that I couldn't let go of him. The more texts I read, the more I realize I didn't truly love him, that I was harsh and mean first of all with myself, not with him. I was angry, I hated him, because he ignored me even after the wedding, we didn't sleep in the same bed, we didn't do what all women, but especially married ones, do, and when that night, drunk, he threw himself on top of me and stuck himself inside me, what pain, what horror, the sensation of being just an animal with holes, who ever said anything about feelings, pleasure, gratification! Only, maybe, his physiological satisfaction, definitely my pain, and his pain. And his eyes, triumphant and conquering and happy that my brothers would finally leave him alone. Look, his wife lied, he was forced into marriage because of a lie. He has proof! Now no one better dare meddle in his life! Would his sweetheart believe him; had she been threatened by my brothers that she'd be picked up in the middle of the night; if if. He must've run to her, to tell her how much he loved her, only her! But either she was nowhere to be found or, worse, she was in the arms of my brother, his former friend. Ah, his regret over having had to spend two months by my side, without touching me, when he could've found out much more quickly what he did on that excruciating night . . . Savage, triumphing over my miserable blood!

Now that's a subject for a real novel, with my husband as the main character! Not like the lousy stories of these craphead writers. What do they know? What have they gone through? And if they have gone through something or other, because during these times we're all going through something, how many have the courage to write the way they should, the way the party asks, from the heart, truthfully? Because life's one thing, literature another.

The girl would've clogged up a prison sooner or later, or just taken a little joy ride to the Baragan,[19] as the daughter of a priest; Calin wasn't far from a similar future either and I saved them both. Given how many relatives of theirs were rotting in prisons . . . And my brother, a valiant communist, nicely took her to be his wife and they both live in our abandoned little village, happy, I believe.

And Calin, how ungrateful!

I don't know how my brothers have been doing and it doesn't even interest me, too few things bind us. I don't go to the village anymore, I don't find any pleasure in it at all.

> However, we cannot overlook the fact that as regards discipline, performance, as well as the organization of work, the overall training and competence of the reader remains fundamental. Not coincidentally, the best readers read at the fastest pace and conclude the entire process of finalizing the item in the least amount of time. This is why the introduction of certain provisions regarding the political-ideological training of readers, their heightened sense of responsibility, and greater personal initiative has proven to be completely warranted.

It was a meeting in which two comrades were criticized—one beat his wife, another keeps cheating on her. I don't know if that's the only reason the meeting was called; in any case, with the adulterer there's nothing you can do. He's not deceiving anyone, but openly living with (at) another('s). Condemnable, of course. They threatened to kick him out, remove him from the party (I think), and nothing. He's still living with his mistress. It's none of my business. The girls discuss what's preferable: for him to beat you or to cheat on you. They arrive at the predictable conclusion: neither. Both, I think, but I don't say anything, I refrain. I censor myself.

You're young, beautiful, healthy and, suddenly, you realize you've gotten old. That you're now on the side of women with wrinkles, respectable, dried up, faded, when gray hairs can no longer be hidden. You're getting old and the saddest thing is that you haven't taken from life everything it offered you, while what I wanted to take, I couldn't. I'm in the prime of my life, a flower in full bloom, yes. But the petals of a flower fall and my life is spent reading, correcting texts. I'm so close to all these writers, all the artists, their world. And so far away.

Our geranium has bloomed again. Hermina tends to it with such dedication, even gently blowing on its leaves. Maybe she even kisses it secretly, when we're not looking. Then she says to us: This flower doesn't bloom where there are bad people, so we all have good souls (the idea delights us, it doesn't even matter whether it's true or not). And if it hadn't bloomed? Well, something must've been wrong with it, it wasn't getting enough light. And we would still have been good people.

"I'll cut my hair, darling. I'll get fat, I'll become a party member, darling, if you don't come over tonight.

The water wheel goes round! click-click-click."

It's so relaxing refining texts, this line works, this one doesn't. It's calming, it's important. It's as if I worked at a medical station: you, sir, off to war, on the front lines, you, sir, home, you, sir, are not of age, you, sir, are over the limit! As with Aristotle's bed, where, if you're too tall, he'll cut off your feet, and if you're too short, he'll stretch you.

I'm back: The bed belonged to Procrustes, not Aristotle, but when I asked Hermina what this Procrustes wrote, she didn't know. I prefer Aristotle to Procrustes.

Sometimes I feel punished by fate, that I have to deal with all this wastepaper, then I resign myself and, after a while, I like it again. I think: If not in Censorship, then where? The idea of going somewhere else doesn't excite me at all, of all the professions in the world, I don't like any of them and I don't think any of them suit me.

Censor! and everyone around trembles and not one of them escapes my vigilant and patriotic eye.

> The words that come close, that envelope you, that dress you, aren't faithful to you.
>
> The words that only he feels, he subjugates them, because he's king of the vocabulary!
>
> With wives, lovers, and slaves, like the pharaohs . . . words love him . . . But they escape me, run away from me . . . (me too, sometimes!)

Women censors. In fact, they're women like all other women, they put on airs in the beginning, at first contact with the outside world, and potential suitors think they're Securitate, then they're rather disappointed after they find out the truth.

I was on the trail of my husband, I wanted my man back, to chain him up, put him under my thumb, I couldn't accept that he had abandoned me, even despite my three savage brothers, in the face of whom he was a puny and powerless little mouse, with his tail trembling from fright. He ran away, leaving me with a small child, we being officially married. No, he ran away a long time before that and he didn't even know that he had gotten me pregnant. I'm sure he found out somehow, but he still never came back . . . Men need to be held tight, tied up, shackled, otherwise they run, they slip through, they seep out, escape. I was like a giant whose treasure had been stolen.

A giantess! The kind whose mouth is so big it reaches from the heavens to the earth. I'll catch you, I'll dig you out of the ground, you can't escape me even dead!

I think that when they recruited my man, that's when he was the happiest he's ever been. I think he would've quickly and joyfully accepted to serve Scaraoschi himself, with his entire party of demons, on a single condition: that they save him from his beloved wife! I'll do anything you ask, on one condition—I don't want to hear about her, I don't want to see her, I don't want to meet with her EVER AGAIN! And they kept their word. I've never seen him again, I heard something about him only last year, by accident, when he became a big boss in an embassy. From some colleagues in Press, there was a story in the paper about him. I couldn't even believe that it was really my husband!

And how naïve I was! How stupid! When he left for college, off I went, running after him. I lost two years because of the child, but during that time I crammed like a crazy person, with my healthy origins, I got in as well, I became a student. I didn't know anything about my husband, but I was sure I'd run into him one day. There were spaces he had passed through too. For example, I felt he had gone to the library, because he had become, since marrying me, a great reader. I had hoped to run into him, on accident. It wasn't meant to be. The child remained in the care of some relatives and I didn't bother about him at all.

College was much harder than I had expected and hoped it would be, and with every failed exam, I risked being kicked out, so I studied, without noticing how quickly time was passing, and before I knew it, I was in my third year. I know now why the censors chose me—then, however, I hadn't even heard about their GDPP and when they invited me, discreetly, mysteriously, I was positive, just like many others before me, that they were calling me to work for the Securitate. Finally, I exulted, he can't escape me now, I've caught up with him, it's over, I've captured him! He'll be all mine, the damned fugitive! I wanted to see him humiliated, pitiful, powerless, weak, unhappy. For him to say sorry, to ask for forgiveness, possibly on his knees. And for me not to forgive him, but to take revenge for all the tortures I've endured, for all the exams at which I've trembled, for all the loneliness and humiliation . . . Almost a year went by before I figured out where I really was. I kept hoping that the General Directorate of Press and Publications was a department of the Securitate organization. I remember how baffled (and angry) my bosses were when I said to them, almost yelling (the first and only time I've yelled), that I want to work for the Securitate, not Censorship! But no one called me there. They didn't choose me, they hadn't noticed me. If I really didn't like it here and I couldn't handle it, I could agree to leave and nicely finish college, waiting to be assigned to a dead-end village and to commute through sun and snow. So I accepted my fate and became a censor. I didn't really have a choice.

My hardest exam in Censorship was when I had to censor my professor. I was already in my final year and my section chief in the GDPP knew he was my prof. Of the scores of people working in Censorship, they decided on me, of all people, they assigned his book to me. His travel journal, full of praise for hostile and bourgeois museums, enthusiastic about everything putrid in Europe, about who knows what wonderful decadent fellow writers, I tore into it, capitalist sympathies and butt-kissing and all. The esteemed professor's book will appear when tulips bloom in December or whatever plant doesn't really bloom then. Afterwards I was a bit ashamed and it seemed as if he was staring at me a bit longer, as if he knew I was a censor and it was me specifically who had censored his book. Maybe it just seemed that way to me and the professor never suspected anything. There were always two or three eminencies hovering around him, looking at him as if he was the supreme god. Never mind, never mind . . . As for me, he barely gave me a passing grade. He could've been nicer to me or at least as neutral as he was with everyone else, but no, no. I felt he didn't like me. He looked at me as if I were a peasant profiting off the regime; in other times, my place would've been up on some hill, with a hoe in my hands—that's what he thought, and, look, I'm a college student too. And the intellectual gentleman, slender and refined, condemns me, has contempt for me, to him I reek. I'll show you, filthy bourgeois rot that you are!

This year, our young colleagues arrived as ready-made censors, set to take literature by storm, while for us, the transformation was a longer, harder process, a second college education, we didn't know anything, the ones with experience taught us, they tested us. One of the tests was the book by my professor. Which I've even forgotten, both him and his lousy travels, with the state and the Securitate footing the bill, make no mistake. They told us to draw blood, not to look at the name, reputation, everyone must be subject to censorship. We liked this. They must be subject to censorship, and Censorship was us. They must be subject to us, everyone, no exceptions! Ah, what importance, what authority! Then we snapped out of this power-induced stupor . . .

But these young people arrived as ready-made censors, as if they had sucked from the same bottle or teat as censorship itself, ready to slash everything in their path, to criticize us as well, the censors with seniority and experience, for maintaining an unhealthy attitude in the institution. Behold, thus, the long-awaited new man. Behold the new censor! They're young and powerful enough for us, the others, to feel useless and outdated. They've never even known other times, never in their lives have they seen kulaks or landowners or bourgeois intellectuals. I hadn't started working in Censorship yet when a colleague of ours had to censor her husband. Her husband committed suicide when he found out, from the shame and pain of it, and the wife quit. I think it was some ordinary text dealing with agriculture, what's the big deal! But to be a censor was something disgraceful, and now it's a competition, they're fighting over a cushy and privileged spot, they've lost all shame, if they ever had any, our young wolves! Who are ready to kick us all out, to bring in their own people, trusty colleagues, just like them, and they brag that 25 percent of GDPP employees are younger than twenty-five years old! I stay away from them. They're dangerous, arrogant, they think they're better than us and nothing's holy to them. They point fingers at everyone and they're such stool pigeons that the bosses can't even keep up with their gossip.

Comrades, it is well-known by all of us what special care the Party and the government have given to the young generation, we know—and the majority of us have felt directly—the efforts made by workers to create all the necessary material conditions for the growth and education of healthy youth, armed with Marxist-Leninist ideology, unencumbered by bourgeois mentalities and prejudices, youth who will be diligent builders of socialism, ready to devote all their capacity and understanding to the triumph of the cause of the working class, the cause of our Party.

Hermina shows up dreamy and glowing, smiling mysteriously. A man, we thought, and exchanged meaningful glances (Roza and me). A man who turns any woman into a flame, a joy, a flower in bloom.

I remembered my own wedding. The disgust with which the groom was looking at me, his hate and resignation, hitting up against my victorious stubbornness: He's mine! I caught him! I've tied him up!

I was so happy and triumphant, it was as if I had just won a contest and they were handing me the prize. Little did I care about his faces and whims, his unhappiness or powerlessness. I caught a look in my grandma's eyes. I had ignored it then. Now I'm unpeeling it, like an onion, unpacking all its meanings. My grandma accused me, mumbling through her missing teeth: It's a good thing your ma can't see you now, because she would've died a second time! The man's out of your league, he doesn't want you, you can't force someone to live with you. At the time I rejected any thought that could've stopped me, any hesitation! And now, if I had my handsome hero by my side, I'd shine just as I did then, on my wedding day, even if it took an army of brothers to keep him from running away from me.

I notice how working with texts is having a positive effect on me, I'm more literary, more poetic, I can express myself increasingly well. I even understand what's going on around me better. I think that because of this effect some of us, the smartest, most talented ones, disappear after a few years of working here. And no one hears of them again. Com. Z., our walking encyclopedia (he likes that we call him that), assures us that the best censors are promoted, not exterminated, and they end up in such high positions that we're not high up enough to even imagine them, they receive better jobs, they're sent on important missions. That may be the case or not . . . But I want to stay here. I want to die censoring texts. If you're a bit on the stupider side, if you're not sparkling with intelligence and political sensibility, you stay here. No one kicks the stupid ones out, being a bit dumber works fine for me, if that's the condition for not disappearing from here. They can go ahead and punish me for insignificant mistakes and oversights. They'll point to our blonde as an example for me, I'd like to see that! The stupid ones float, the smart ones sink to the bottom, because of the weight of their gravity and mind.

"Mirroring reality *sine qua non*!"

"In books they're writing about me!"

Some authors have the gift of writing so intimately, it's as if I'm hearing the voice that blames me for the death of my mother, abandoning my child, and all the other sins you can blame a person for in our times. This happens very rarely and I ask myself whether there isn't somehow someone who knows me, who knows who I am, knows where I work. After reading books like these, I begin thinking about my life more.

> You feel the need to burn. To burn me, so I'll disappear, you feel me as a threat.

> While I turn up like a Phoenix, every day more persistent in your life, pouring more and more words into the same wound.

> Words that are more acidic, and more searing.

> When you thought it was done, you were over it, you'd wiped that past clean, the words came back. You hang on fighting through the smell of smoke of burnt pages.

> Of burnt wounds.

Roza adds more fuel to the fire, when I was certain that this happened only to me:

"The texts in which I see myself as if in a mirror give me the creeps. I'm reading, I'm reading and, suddenly, I realize that someone's writing about me! I thought my life was unique and it wasn't like anyone else's." If so many people have the impression that authors are writing specifically about them, it must be some special authorial talent. Writers mean to do it.

I dream that I'm holding a volume in my lap that I'm about to censor, to write a report on what's good and what's bad in it.

The volume is full of texts about me, about my own life, childhood, adolescence, youth. Everything, everything, on every page, full of biographical details that I remember only as I'm reading them, that had been lost from my memory. I'm alone in the office and I'm crying. I suspect who could've written it. I'm afraid of never meeting her. In those texts, a mother who wasn't a censor like me (that would've been cut out anyway), it doesn't say what she was, she worked somewhere, hard, lost her child, taken by her husband who was a Securitate officer and she was left alone, unhappy, without her only child. I've got such pangs of conscience! It was logical that this would happen, I mean that I'd suffer, but I'm suffering only now, years later, and only in my dreams! For years, on rare occasions when I remember that I have a son whom I haven't seen, also for years, I think that it ought to make me suffer that he's not with me, that I ought to miss him a little . . . I abandoned him without a regret so I could go to college, and I was a bit resentful when my husband picked him up during a visit to relatives. My aunts told me afterwards, with accusatory insinuations, how threadbare, how scared and wild my son was (I didn't have money to send them for his upkeep!) and how my husband, who had never loved us, neither me nor his own son, was moved with pity and took the boy with him.

That's how it was in reality, but in the text it was far more beautiful, it was sad, heart-wrenching. A helpless, loving mother who fights for her son. Sadness, loneliness, the loss of hope, and deep love were ascribed to me and described so expressively, so generously, that I couldn't have put it better myself. I cried reading it. The pages trembled and were wet with tears . . .

Then other scenes. All presented heroically, romantically, with the woman who loses an unfair fight. I liked the point of view, it defended me. The author who forgave me and upheld my cause was none other than his wife, who was raising my child, taking care of my husband. With comforting compassion and understanding. I went on reading and cried again. It was the woman who seemed to be saying: I'm raising your son, but I know he's yours, I'm sorry that I can't do more for you. My heart softened while reading these texts that pitied me, that were completely on my side. I understand, after all, I put my handsome Calin into her arms and she became the wife of an ambassador thanks to me. If I had been able to keep him by my side, if I had (re)discovered him in time, she wouldn't have seen the inside of a single embassy and she wouldn't be expressing her gratitude.

Then the words change, pity and compassion disappear. I felt that the author had more than one face or that there were two authors, in fact, maybe more . . . Next, the poem with a child who stares past the fence and waits for his mother to return, but no mother on the horizon. Instead, a man and a woman appear, who look at him with great compassion. They're gentle and they don't want to harm him, they get closer, they caress him. The child dares not believe that an unknown woman is hugging him lovingly, he retreats, he's scared, the wild, hungry, unhappy child. The woman tames him, she takes care of him, and he appears happy again, well-dressed and clean, he plays, laughs, runs around. But, this time, not one kind word for the mother. It's fair this way. It's just. What kind of mother is that? Strangers took the child with them, accusing her of not caring about him and keeping him as a weapon for revenge. The man was the child's father and he was angry with his mother—namely, me. With his heart of gold, he takes the child to raise him and take care of him. While you, cruel soul, the poem says to me, are a liar. Through deception you forced the man to take you as his wife. The only moment of truth led to this child, the result of our mistakes. I'd have dozens more children and I'd need thousands more moments of truth (nights spent with my dear husband!). Was that the only truth you needed? I ask the man, but the poem doesn't answer me, it keeps going, as it chooses. That single night, our only happy night, was written by him, seen from his perspective. Not an ounce of pity for the smitten girl I was. As if he'd never made a mistake in his life, as if my entire body and my entire soul weren't also in pain then, while he, while he . . . In an even more malicious, even crueler, even more reprehensible tone of voice . . . My tears dried up, my face stiffened. The pen transformed into a knife, I began striking the manuscript, blood was flowing from it, I heard it moaning quietly, but I felt no pity at all, I kept striking, striking without stopping, striking it with a certain sense of enjoyment, then, just before waking up, I remember asking myself: How am I going to be able to write the report if the manuscript doesn't exist anymore?

After I woke up, I thought that I hadn't left out a single detail, I even had a pen in my strange dream. It's true, I can't read something without holding a pen in my hand. In my dream, it seemed to be a pen from somewhere else, a far more beautiful pen than my own. But it was my pen. Now, with a manuscript in front of me, I wave it left and right, as if it were a sword, as if I were rehashing the scene from my dream with the pen transformed into a dangerous weapon. The girls look on with suspicion at the way I'm handling the weapon during work hours.

I'm so glad it was only a dream! To be honest, I'm positive that my son is better off with my husband and his current spouse. The wife must've been someone as well, the daughter of a communist from some ministry, otherwise you don't end up at an embassy just like that, I hope she's kind, educated, and that she doesn't beat my boy! What could I have offered him? Meanwhile my husband's already a consul at the embassy, he's got everything, the child is living a sheltered life . . .

Although, if he were here with me, how I'd snuggle him, how I'd caress him . . .

To touch him lightly, discreetly, to ask him, as an excuse, for a pencil and for him to shake off your tenderness as if it were dust, like a mosquito buzzing around him disagreeably, irritatingly, landing on his hand. Rejection. I dream that my husband rejects me. I withdraw, unhappy, I shrink, I curl up, I go inside a seashell that's so small, smaller and smaller, like the head of a pin . . . The rejection nullifies me to the point of disappearing . . .

Where are these strange stories coming from? It's someone else's life, some other woman's. They're dreams . . .

I also dream of Elena the beautiful, whose sweetheart I stole and who got married to Pintilie. I dream she's dead. First unhappily married to my brother, then dead. I feel her death weighing on my shoulders. In this dream I'm not reading any manuscript, no book could recount this. It's just the pure dream. So loaded with guilt that I'd feel better in jail, but there's nothing I could be charged with. I don't dream of myself in prison. My brothers told Calin: You got our sister pregnant, you slept with her. But Calin had slept with Elena and gotten only her pregnant. I feel from my mother a kind of disapproval, I also feel the gaze of my grandma, who raised me, everyone condemns me for coming between them. And Elena's relatives have come to plead with grandma, they said their girl was with child, that the boy had asked her to be his wife, that I'm very young (I was in elementary school, the relatives said, but I had just finished high school and was ready to get married) and that I'll find other boys, that my brothers had beaten him up and threatened to kill him if he didn't marry me. I remember that in the dream, as in real life, nothing and no one could've stopped me.

I dream about the love between the two of them, that miracle, that liquid light that passed through them whenever they met, whenever they kissed. They kissed thinking no one could see them, but I saw them! I've never felt that, neither before nor after I got married, I intuited a kind of peace between them, a peace I had never known, and I wanted to stop everything. If he isn't mine, then I don't want that light to exist either! And I succeeded. He was mine! Grandma begged me, she said it cannot be, she crossed herself, your mother will turn in her grave when she sees who she gave birth to. But I was laughing, I was dying of laughter. Get thee behind me, devil! I told her she was embarrassing me with her God, because any day now I'd become a member of the Communist Party.

How I wish I knew whether Elena's still alive, whether she

has children. People were saying that she had, indeed, gotten pregnant by Calin, but the rumors stopped when Pintilie married her. How much is dream in my dream and how much reality?

Heavy weights on my heart.

Where's the giant, the mighty one who could at least move them a bit farther off, a bit farther off.

For college, my healthy origins mattered more than my learning. There were definitely many people smarter than me who didn't make it in. I became an activist there as well, very respected, no one dared contradict me. Whoever didn't behave could be kicked out. I knew all kinds of surefire methods.

After he married me, my beloved husband, from such overwhelming joy, began reading. So he didn't have to see my loving face, so he could forget where he was, to confound fiction and reality. I never even heard him speak, or breathe, all he did was read. So much so that he astounded his professors at college with how much he'd read, considering the dumpy village he came from and what a smooth-cheeked dossier he had. I'm sure he was recruited from his very first year in college, not like me, only in my third.

My husband's career has been a meteoric success. My husband, a misnomer. We were officially divorced very quickly and without my even catching a glimpse of him, without a loving goodbye. I don't know how it was possible, so he must've already been with the Securitate, because only with them is everything possible. His greatest wish was to never see me again, I'm positive, and they took it into account! Save me from this scourge of a woman and I'll start working for your Securitate tomorrow, just keep her away from me. And they kept me away, what's more they also found him a suitable woman, one with whom he could be promoted easily. And the child didn't figure into his life plans. Being from the same village, however, he went to see his parents, his relatives, during a visit or a vacation, whatever, what does it matter anymore?! His parents suggested that maybe he go see his son, he went, his son didn't recognize him, he'd never seen him in his life, he lived with my grandma, his great-grandma (or, if she had died already, he lived with one of my mother's sisters, I believe), in rags, hungry, I should've paid closer attention to him, as his mother, checked in on him, helped out somehow, at least with some money, because I was already working and I had a good salary. I lived with an old lady almost for free. During weekends I went with the girls to dances, I didn't go home, to my relatives, to my child, no one from my group, then none of my colleagues, knew that I had been married and that I had a child. I was tired after work, I'd say to myself: next time, next week, next month, during vacation . . . and I never went. Then I was told he had taken the child and I really didn't have any reason to go or anyone to go see anymore. Grandma died, I said I'd go to the cemetery. Maybe I'll get there someday. He took the child and looked for a mother for him, that's what I think. Or he already had someone and he went to the village with the love of his life and she became fond of the child. Because she had no choice. He looked like him. Andrei. Born two days after Saint Andrei. Grandma came up with this name, it was all the same to me. At least I remember that.

I've changed now, now I regret my behavior, my indifference. But then I was young and stupid and, especially, unfair. I thought, if I'm a communist (I had joined the UCY and I was getting ready for the next step up), everyone should listen to me and obey me. Do what I want. My husband, first of all. That's what I saw with my brothers whom everyone was afraid of, everyone was also afraid of the four puny communists who had arrived in our village under who knows what circumstances. Thin and slight, but everyone was scared of them and didn't make a peep when they were present. I wanted to be the same, listened to, powerful. I wasn't beautiful, I wasn't loved, but at least I could make everyone fear me, tremble and obey!

I accused my classmates of being enemies of the people, I had learned this language from my brothers whom I admired. I abused, as we'd say today, my power. I was so virulent that the mothers of the accused would come to our gate and plead with Grandma to plead, in turn, with me to at least let the children finish school, because they're wretched, the poor things, with half their family in prison, what kind of fate awaits them if they're kicked out for being enemies of the regime? They'd come with an apron-full of fruit, with a chicken, some corn, with whatever they had, because they were poor. But their corn couldn't soften me up. Eleven kids were kicked out, five later went to prison. Already without my personal involvement.

I was proud then and I considered myself a heroine, expecting my name to be added to the wall of fame. I even asked my homeroom teacher why it wasn't, because I'd contributed so much toward the prosperity of the fatherland and the detection of hoodlums. My homeroom teacher said I'm still in school and they only put grown-ups on there. I think she was afraid of me too. I was young and stupid, but not that stupid. I didn't think the children I denounced were really the enemies of our country, criminals, etc. They were my competition, they were better dressed, better looking, better, they had their parents by their side, while I was an orphan, and I wanted to show them that I was the best, the most powerful, I was at war with the whole world and I wanted to win. Why I was at war, I don't know. I think I was born with war inside me, smoldering, bubbling up, with an endless desire for conflict, difficult to extinguish. There were girls more beautiful, nicer, more educated than me. Almost all of them were more beautiful. But I was smarter, more intrepid, more more . . . and I caught the most desirable and best-looking boy in the village and he was mine! I stole the most wonderful boy, whom everyone was secretly in love with, from under their noses and I married him and the idiots were left standing there with nothing, that's what I thought back then, probably. If I didn't like someone or they didn't obey me or, worse, insulted me in some way—me, a poor orphan with communist brothers who hunted partisans—I declared them an enemy, a landowner, a tick sucking the blood of the people! Away with him, to prison with him! In the end I won! This life is a battle and the strongest win!

Only after growing up a bit more, after I had left that closed-off environment in which I had taken over everything, after I had read a thing or two in college, had gotten divorced, had

started working, only then did I understand that I was neither the ugliest, nor the meanest, nor the poorest, nor the most
powerful. A bit late! My logic had been simple: I thought I
was the ugliest and I took revenge on the most beautiful, I was
the poorest and punished the richest, I was the meanest and I
took revenge on the gentle and kind, I also hated the people
who gave us sweetbread for Easter, us, the poor ones, me, the
orphan, I'd take it and feed it, offended, to the dog. My older
brothers would always say that they had an ugly, stupid, disgusting little sister and I took them at their word. Grandma
had stopped talking to me, she avoided me, she prayed secretly
for my wicked and hardened heart, my classmates avoided me,
out of fear, I didn't have any friends nor did I need any, same
as now.

I don't know what has happened to the kids who were thrown
out of school back then. My brothers, after long quests in
search of enemies and partisans, got married and now have
kids, future communists with impeccable dossiers. We don't
really communicate, especially after the whole story with my
supposed father ended in Mom's death. They figured that I
was born after their father died in the war, so Mom must've
had me with the partisan whom she secretly gave food to, an
enemy of the people whom my brothers had been trying to
catch for a long time. Mom died of a broken heart when I
told my brothers where she was and to whom she was giving
food. I don't remember this moment, I was too little. Meanwhile they still didn't catch my so-called father. After Mom's
death, I stayed with Grandma, and my brothers would come
by only sometimes, when they needed something. They turned

up when Pintilie got it into his head to get married and then they decided to kill two birds with one stone. To see that stepsister married off, and their beloved brother united with his chosen one. Pintilie stayed in the village, while the others settled in neighboring villages, so there wouldn't be competition between the brothers for important social posts.

Death sneaks up on you, so much poetry until then and afterwards, but death itself isn't at all poetic. Little worries, illnesses, pain, stuff.

I wonder how Mom died?

I wonder how Grandma died?

Grandma raised me, I could say, but I remember Mom really well too. Thin, sad, with a kind of pain in her eyes, that seemed to spread throughout her whole body, I was afraid to touch her, so as not to hurt her. I wanted her to pick me up, but she was so fragile, and I was too big and heavy, I understood that it wasn't possible. At the age I am now, Mom already had three grown sons, from her first husband, and me, illegitimate, a love child, with who knows what man . . . My brothers told me later, after they were older and had stopped to figure it out, I had never suspected for one second that their father, a hero fallen in the war, wasn't my father as well. They would say among themselves, proudly, that he was a hero, but I never saw a medal, heroes have medals, even if they die. I thought that, if they beat me, if they always made me be the donkey or the sheep or the prisoner in their games, if they took the apple or pear from my mouth, they'd kick me in the butt and I'd fall down, while they laughed, they'd lift up my skirt in front of other kids and so many other things, I thought all this was happening to me because they were boys and I was a girl, they were big and I was small. I'd forgive them and I was proud of my brothers, I didn't really get mad at them, except rarely. But did they already know then that I was their step-sister, with a father hidden in the forest, an enemy of the people, because no one hides for no reason? Who stopped to calculate in what year my father died in the war and at what date I was born, though it's not hard to calculate, because Stalingrad didn't last forever. They say that Mom's second husband also fought at Stalingrad, but he survived, he came back and they had me. I don't know anything about this.

If it had been known! They would've kicked me out from work. No one would've taken me. They would've sent me to be an exterminator, to do menial work, like the prisoners who got released in recent years. I would've secretly done translations and some luckier colleague with a clean dossier would've signed their name to them. Maybe I would've even censored for others, because that's what I know how to do well. But my brothers didn't betray me when they found out, and the date of my birth very likely isn't the real one . . . Maybe I'm a few years younger, and my brothers didn't care for having blotches on their dossiers (a small blotch, it's true, but if it can be done away with . . .), so they never betrayed me.

A father who isn't with you and whom you don't know is like a useless object. The very memory of him darkens my existence. But without him I wouldn't have existed. Few men made it back from the war and those who did were probably in great demand, even if they were hiding in forests. The women found them even there. But my mother, with three children, harassed by worries and hard work, no longer in the prime of her youth, how was she able to find him? What did that fugitive, or whatever he was, like about her? They say he organized the resistance in the mountains. Though I hate this unknown father, I'm a bit proud of him and I hope he doesn't get caught. Let him keep walking through the forests, in the fresh air, if he's alive, because the prisons are full anyway . . .

In their books some describe what exactly the enemies of the people are like (a bunch of monsters, negative characters) and I wonder: Is my father like that as well or is he different? My enemy, my father.

So, they knew and they searched for him in the forest, to kill him, while mother loved him. She'd secretly take him food and in those times of poverty pastries didn't grow on trees, and she would take him pastries. She'd give me a little corner of a pastry, but to him, the entire pastry. Mister enemy also liked jam. And a little chicken stew. When the best bits of meat disappeared from the stew, Mom would apologize guiltily and say that she ate them. She didn't feel well, she felt weak and she ate them. But she never even touched them, never tasted them, that's why she became a shadow of herself, just skin and bones. My beloved father drove her into the ground. I hated this gluttonous father, always hungry, hidden in the wooded mountains. But my mother loved him. He could've secretly brought me a toy, and given it to mother, I would've known it was from him, I would've realized. He could've made it from wood with his pocketknife, since he was whittling away time in the mountains anyway and didn't have a job. But I never received a toy from him.

I wonder how Mom died?

I know about Mom more from what Grandma told me. She (Grandma) had been alive during the time of the noblemen, the good times, she said, but that's not true, I know how hard life was then, but if I contradict her, she won't go on with her story, so I keep my mouth shut. She was a servant in a noble family. But how wonderful it was to be a servant! Grandma would say (I keep my mouth shut). And the dresses she used to get from the noblewoman and her daughters! It was good that someone cut them down to size a bit, they had gotten to be too grouchy and thought that only they had feelings. But many were like manna from heaven, they helped out whenever necessary and they had a heart of gold, like the nobleman where she served, for example. The noble family came to her wedding, they were also the ones who had found her a groom, a good boy from the village, the most handsome one in the village, after her own heart. They didn't force her to get married, as was said happened sometimes. Some ignorant people today claim that the noblemen would ruin young girls, that they slept with them and, when they got tired of them, they married them off. I was an honest girl when I married my dear Petru. Neither before nor after him did a nobleman go up my skirt! He didn't really even tug on the noblewoman's skirt either. He was a good and learned man. And they didn't have me get married when I was green either, at fourteen, like others. But like their girls, at eighteen. They said that was exactly right and they asked me what I thought, because their little ladies had been eighteen too. And I wore the beautiful daughter's white dress, because we were about the same height and just as slender. Thank goodness they left in time. Now what's become of the manor house, a complete disaster and a ruin. A Cultural Center, ugh! That's a joke! Thank goodness they left the church alone, because they closed them down in other places. Small, on the outskirts of the village, it doesn't stand out, maybe that's why. Sometimes, whatever's tallest falls under the scythe, while the little things survive. That's how it is with our tiny church. And dear Petru, what a good man, never came back from the first war. Thank goodness I had three children, two boys and a girl, your ma. In the second war I lost the boys, and my girl also lost her husband. They all perished. What times, what times . . . I thought the worst had already happened, not by a long shot! My grandsons told me that if I want to die of old age, I should give Joiana to the farming collective. It's a good thing I did . . . because woe to those who didn't want to . . . And just as I was crying for Joiana, she was crying for me too. All the cows were crying and mooing and the women were crying and wailing. But it's a good thing I gave them away! Lord, Lord, it's a good thing I gave it all away! Your will! As long as we've got our health! Now, at least I can die of old age on my stoop, with my corner of sky, no one swallowed up my land, you can see it, you can pass by there. Thank goodness I had only a hectare, there, and half of that was ditches and holes. Life's more valuable, the kind of life we have, that's the kind we live. Better here than in prison. Our men died in one war, our children in another. And our grandchildren don't seem to come from us, but from the old cloven-hoofed himself, how can they be of our blood, what times, what times . . .

I don't really cook, because I'd stink up the old woman's kitchen. I don't care as much for cooking as I used to, anyway. I don't have anyone to cook for. I eat at work, I'm content. I don't invite boyfriends or girlfriends over, because they'd make noise and bother the old lady, in fact, I don't have boyfriends or girlfriends. I don't buy myself too many things, so she won't think I'm too rich and raise my rent. I'm saving up my money and waiting to receive a place to live, like everyone else!

Com. Mirare, who knew the dearly departed husband of my old woman personally, recommended that I rent a room from her, because it's not appropriate for a young censor to live with curious students. I don't know what she told her and how she convinced her, but I'm positive the old woman's afraid of me.

I even see the little curtains at the window. I feel how he tenses up, how he freezes. He suffers when he hears her laugh. How would she have known, how could she have guessed who was listening to her, who was walking under her window? I didn't understand everything either, young and stupid, too much had landed on me all of a sudden, married overnight, a husband I never could have dreamed of, I had never even kissed a boy, they were all afraid to get close to me, also I wasn't exactly gorgeous. Maybe I had loved Calin in secret, like in romances, but I was certain, like everyone else, that he and his beautiful sweetheart would get married . . .

But things change sometimes, everything becomes possible, I don't even want to imagine how they convinced his sweetheart to marry Pintilie, because it didn't take much to convince me at all. Actually, I know: she waited for him until he married me, until our wedding, maybe she came and secretly watched us, maybe she cried, maybe by her side, protective, was my brother, consoling her and stroking her long, almost blond, soft and silky hair (mine is short, black, and stiff as a broom!).

When I left the village, I held a grudge against my brothers, I was very angry with them—I blamed them for my husband's leaving me. They had beaten him up once and forced him or however they convinced him to marry me, but then they abandoned me, they didn't care about me anymore. What I wanted then, I know, I remember, was for them to bring him back, to force him somehow, to convince him, like the first time, to beat him up again and to bring him back to me, so I could comfort him, take care of him, so I could have a man by my side, humble and obedient, my husband. How dare he run away, escape unpunished? To leave me pregnant at not even nineteen years old and disappear? And my brothers didn't care at all. Now that they had gotten their hands on his sweetheart, the fate of their little sister didn't interest them anymore! I wanted him back submissive, obedient, like a lamb, faithful and dutiful, like a dog. I left the child and went after him, to find him, to punish him, to get revenge. My womanly heart hadn't even awoken and it was already frozen before springtime.

My ex-husband is now an important figure in an embassy, he has a wonderful wife, the daughter of a minister, of course, who am I, a peasant, he climbed up the ladder and he wouldn't look at an ordinary mortal like me anymore. I can't compete with ministers. I observe that even the most stuck-up colleagues are stunned into deep respect mixed with sincere admiration when I tell them. This is what they're thinking: this ugly thing, who you'd think had never even been kissed, can you believe she was married, and to whom, and she also has a child . . . I tell them more, skipping over some episodes, how I don't know anything about my son anymore, that I haven't seen him for years, how often I dream of him at night; I buy him toys and I imagine how I'm going to give them to him all wrapped up, but he's abroad, he's receiving an elite education, he'd turn his nose up at my modest and ugly toy. He's got his own bedroom, full of teddy bears and stuffed-animal puppies, beautiful and soft . . . Their tears trickle down, even I get emotional. It's almost true. That's almost what I do. The truth is the thing you believe and I believe, here and now.

Not one woman in Censorship hates me, not one man loves me. Com. Zuki sometimes points out that I need to lift up my left shoulder when I walk, and my head, because I walk as if I were looking for lost coins on the ground. I walk as if I were bearing the weight of all of Censorship on my shoulders. Hmm. For a beautiful gait, balance a book on your head. You'll see that it helps. An uncensored one? A comrade from Documents, when she was about to retire, gifted me a jacket. Maybe she also gave others a thing or two, but I felt like I was the worst-dressed one here, not only the ugliest. But I'm the best censor! Returning to a previous thought: Have I really never exchanged a loving kiss with anyone? Really never, really not once? I search for some memory on this subject and I don't find anything.

∽

I've got my more difficult moments as well. I read and read, and either I'm tired, too exhausted to process anything anymore, or the text really is too cryptic, complicated, and I can't understand a thing. I go over the letters, I trace them with my eyes, but I can't manage to catch the meaning, as if I were looking at a drawing with meaningless marks. In moments like these I ask myself, unsettled, whether I'm well enough prepared for a mission as hard as this, if the text really is that difficult or if it's my fault. There are moments when I consider all books the result of a total madness, generalized, and, worst of all, contagious. Authors seem to me a bunch of lunatics fit to be tied up, put away in a hospital, and I doubt and fear for my own mental equilibrium. Who could tell me whether I'm healthy or not after so many years of reading and reading? Out in the country, where I'm from, the old women would cross themselves and recommend who knows what.

Sometimes, at night, I dream of my mother. I can't remember her that well anymore, her face seems blurry, erased, I don't know whether that's how I saw her or whether her face imprinted itself on my brain like that from some misplaced photograph. Fragments of movements, gestures, appear to me the way you sprinkle salt between your fingertips into a steaming pot, bits of dialogue that I can't manage to fit together, to reconstruct all the way. I dream certain scenes so often that I begin thinking they're actually real. The scene at my mother's death, when Grandma points me out with a finger to an aunt, as if to say, look, she's the one guilty of my daughter's (my mother's) death, I don't understand the gesture, I think Grandma's calling me over, I come closer to her, but she as well as the person she's talking to look at me with hatred and they turn their backs to me, I stay there alone and don't understand. What if that scene didn't happen only in my dreams? What if something from my dreams really took place? If I told my partisan-hunting brothers that Mom makes pastries and stew, but not for me, for Prince Charming in the forest? And my brothers would've said to Mom: We're going to go catch Prince Charming, we've been searching for him for a long time! She got really scared, and she realized that I, being a clueless child, betrayed her, and the life of her beloved husband was in danger. Her tortured and tired heart finally gave out. Maybe that's how it was, but I don't remember these details, however it is quite probable that I let something slip to my brothers, who knew that the people in the village were helping the partisans . . .

Then the dream changes. I've grown up, I'm not a child anymore and I say something cruel to my mother, painful, hurtful, I accuse her of something, something very spiteful, I accuse her unjustly, my words frighten her, she backs away, we're both sitting on a long, country-style bed in a dark, cool room, Mom shrinks back from me, she breaks, she doubles over from the pain, from the injustice fallen on her shoulders, too heavy, she almost faints, she gets small. I realize what a terrible thing I've done, I really regret it, I come closer and hug her, she's so helpless, light, absent, that she can't resist me, I'm crying bitterly, I realize my shoulders are shaking as I hold her tightly in my arms, that it wasn't me who hurt her, but someone else, who was also sitting in the room with us, and I want to defend her, to protect her, I love her, I'm hugging her and I want to keep her with me, I feel that she doesn't want to live anymore, she doesn't have the strength or will to stay here, with me, she's leaving, she accepts death, I squeeze her tightly to revive her, she's hanging like a rag doll, her body limp, inert, drooping, neither alive nor dead. I don't say anything, I feel that those spiteful words have crushed her, there's no way to revive her, she doesn't even know who's holding her. But I feel that embrace so vividly, so fervently, I feel an enormous need to have my mother with me, I hold her in my arms and I feel how painful her absence will be, even as unconscious, sick, fragile as she is, I need her, to hold her hand, to hold her close, I'd like for her to caress me a bit too, to hold my hand. I feel how she's slipping away slowly, how I'm losing her, how she's dying in my arms, while I can't do a thing, I can't ease her suffering, I can't stop the speed at which death is stealing her from me.

I wake up crying, but with such a vivid memory of the embrace, so needed, so warm! I close my eyes and I struggle to bring it back, to feel it again. I'm not dreaming anymore, I'm awake, but I imagine I'm hugging her, I'm touching her weak and weightless hand. My whole body warms up, I touch my mother's hand, I want to stroke her hair, it's gray, but her face is young, it looks the same as I remember, her short hair, neither too soft nor too dry, Mom stays there, well-behaved, without moving, like a child, and she lets me caress her. I'd very much like to hear her voice, but she doesn't say anything, I don't remember her voice.

I know that she called me little Didina, little Didina, I say quietly, maybe my mother's voice will mix in with mine. I'm like a sick, abandoned animal, left for dead, prey to loneliness and suffering. My mother leaves me, she dissolves in my arms until I'm holding just air, thinner, thinner, a smoke that disappears. I miss her so much! I realize, in these moments, how much warmth exists between people who love each other, how many things escape me, how much I still have to learn, how many things she would've taught me if she hadn't left. Only with her in my dream, when we touch, do I have the intimation of an unbelievable happiness, which, when I wake up, doesn't exist anywhere. To stop the pain, I start working. I furiously read the texts and I still feel my mother's embrace. Cold, abstract texts. I read and push away that illusion of love. The texts kill the embrace. They censor it.

I fear the passage of time, not because I'll get old and always be alone, nor because they'll kick me out of Censorship. No, no. Time passes, just as seven years have passed in the blink of an eye, just like I went from being twenty to thirty, I don't even know when. I'm afraid that's how I'll turn forty as well, and time will give me back my child. My son will come of age and he'll search for me. He'll find out I'm his real mother. He'll find me and ask me: Who are you and why did you abandon me? I'll have to lie to him, but I don't know if I'll be able to, I'll have to tell him the truth, but I don't know if I'll be able to. I'll have to avoid him, to hide from him, to hide the nature of my occupation, but will I be able to? I'll be ashamed, I'll be afraid. My child will be a tall man (Calin and I are both tall), he'll probably grow a moustache and a beard, he'll fall in love, he'll get married, he'll have children. I'll become a grandmother. No! Maybe he won't search for me. Maybe they told him I died, maybe they never even told him he has any other mother than the wife of his father, hiding the truth from him. Maybe he won't wish to know me when he finds out about me. He won't search for me. Every one of us has a secret they wish to hide. Everyone should keep their truth to themselves.

I'd like to know when it's his wedding, so I could secretly go and watch him. Without his seeing me, without his knowing who I am. My heart tells me he knows about me and will search for me. I'm afraid of that moment. I really hope he'll forgive me. I'm guilty! I'm guilty of not having loved him, of abandoning him, of not thinking about him. Young and stupid with a heart full of hatred . . . I can't even imagine how his father found him. In what state the unloved child must've been . . . I hope his fate is better now, better than it would've been if he had stayed with me. I would've been able to offer him things too, I would've offered him everything, I would've been able to have him with me, I would've hugged him, I would've bought him toys. I'm thinking of it only now, after so many years . . .

Books are the cheapest and most effective form of contraception. At least they protect me from any danger from men. I'm not that old yet, until I hit forty I'd still be good for something. But you don't get pregnant from books and all I have around me are books. At least I had a child when I was younger. Now, as time passes, it's getting harder and I still don't want anything or anyone in my censorous life.

I'm positive I won't have any more children.

If I live another ten years, I'll be as old as my mother when she died.

So many books, so many books, more and more of them, more and more beautiful, more complicated, more attractive, published in greater and greater numbers. People fight over books, they wait in line for them, buy them at inflated prices, on the black market, under the counter, the people who love books adore them, they devour them. They can't live without them. Addicted to books, weak, vulnerable, almost drugged up on literature. They don't know what it is to love each other like they used to, nor do they value simple words anymore, nor do those few steps needed to get closer to a person mean anything anymore, they don't count anymore, literature has changed the standards. I feel this, me, here, from my censor's office! You're subhuman if you haven't read the latest author. It doesn't matter that you have a more spacious home, a car (a new one, even), if you're a stupid unread person. Girls go gaga if you recite something to them from a couple contemporary lechers! How language has puffed itself up! How full of self-importance it's become! Like a giant balloon and, when I say "balloon," a needle immediately appears in my mind: "Pop!" and no more balloon! Or a soap bubble, beautiful, multicolored, that pops by itself, without any outside effort. Can it be that books are as fragile as soap bubbles, as impermanent?

I'm an addict too, ahead of these poor souls. I read Sundays as well, I'm reading constantly, nonstop, I'll die bending over manuscripts and, if we're reminded, every now and then, that we're not allowed to take documents out of the institution and I don't take anything with me to read on Sunday, I sit around on my only free day and it's as if I'm missing something, I can't get comfortable, I feel an intense need to be bending over some sheets of paper, to be reading . . . A bunch of sickos, that's what we are, both the readers and the writers—all jumbled together. When we were kids, we'd run through the hills, we'd play in the middle of the street, we'd steal away to the pond, the forest, we'd climb steeper hills or trees, jump over deep ravines . . . But now we all read. And those who neither read nor write are no longer good for anything, a bunch of brutes, animals, cockroaches . . . Degenerates who want to get as far ahead as possible and rule the world.

When I work on a heftier manuscript, I need about two days of reading at a brisk pace and I ask myself: How long does it take a normal reader, who has a job, a family, basically some definite responsibilities and occupations, to read a book like that? Too long, far too long, so the person, the citizen, will ignore their professional, familial, personal obligations, they'll steal time away from work or the time dedicated to their family, they'll abandon their children, husband, wife, parents, and they'll read. Mothers who are readers letting their children go on screaming. People who read working less, caring less about their loved ones. By reading you become smarter and more rebellious. Reading is an antisocial, antisocialist activity. I don't understand why the state encourages this pastime. We, censors, have everything to gain. Writers are invited to write, readers to buy books and read them.

A new generation is growing up with their head in the clouds, delicate, sensitive, vulnerable, tearing up at even slightly dramatic pages. But you can also become insensitive, like me: when a scene that wants to break my heart gets in my way, I think of the author picking his nose, ripping a fart, eating a piece of bread with bologna, and then writing another page, proud of himself because look what he's let out, and I should bawl at his scene? Yeah, when hell freezes over! Or some drunk lecher squeezing his bottle or girlfriend, panting (over the bottle or his girlfriend), and smacking his lips like a pig . . . Or some woman writer gasping from debauchery of all kinds and, in between, jotting down a thing or two. However beautiful the text might be, the act of writing remains a physical, physiological one, by authors—advanced mammals, already entering, some of them, a state of degradation or decomposition. Most of them are past the prime of youth—the ones who, by writing, want to stop time. I don't intend to cry reading them and, no, I really don't cry. But the number of readers is far greater than that of censors. We're in the minority.

A second possibility in reading, a more frequent one, is that you become more sensitive, quivering, you cry along with the book's characters and are caught up in the moment in a way that maybe not even the author intended. That's not my business as a censor, but I'm afraid that it's more dangerous these days to read all the time than it is to hardly ever read. Writing illuminates and darkens. Awakens and puts to sleep. People have written things before, we have a literary tradition, but nothing like what's happening now. Everyone's writing; the entire country, collective, is reading. A country of readers and writers. When is there time to work, to think, to love? What's the point of reading? I feel I'm being used, in my capacity as a censor, forced to participate in this collective, general readorgy. The situation's beyond me.

Why do these writers write so much? Maybe to heal themselves . . . Difficult times, many temptations, sins, compromises. To get safely past existential nausea, life transitions. Writing, you get over things more easily and it doesn't hurt as much. Why write? I've never stopped any of them to ask: Did you write what you wrote and you're better now? And do you think, if I'm in pain over something, that I'll feel better by reading your book, that I'll forget about my pain?

Yes, I'm in pain, but the more I read, and I've read a lot, for years, a lifetime, my pain gets deeper, it becomes acute, like cracks in a dry field, the harbingers of future ravines and chasms . . . At any description of a beautiful relationship, and that's the majority of them, because you can't describe things as hopelessly black, it's recommended that they be optimistic, healthy, I ask myself why wasn't it the same for me, why wasn't my husband a real husband, why wasn't my marriage a real marriage, even a short one. But if, in some line in a subplot, less visible, in the background, two or three lines down, less happy relationships are mentioned as well, scenes from my short and strange marriage appear with miserable intensity on the television screen of my imagination.

If an angry man in a novel doesn't want to eat or even taste the food cooked by the woman he no longer loves and if he feels like throwing up, it disgusts him, he can't stand it, I remember, with painful clarity, as if it were yesterday, I remember that my husband didn't eat at home either. Was he disgusted by me, by my food? Once he went out and bought bread, salami, and yogurt from the store and that's all he ate. Meanwhile, I was always cooking, that's what I knew wives did, the kitchen smelled of delicious food, but him, nothing, salami and yogurt. Since he didn't eat, I'd call the neighbors or I'd throw it to the pig. At first, I thought he was secretly nibbling it, I'd leave the pot steaming on the stove and I'd go out, so that he'd have some.

I'd come back late and look in the pot—he hadn't touched it, he hadn't even put his finger on the lid. His having a bowl of soup or whatever was in there cooked by me would've compensated for the nights spent alone, it would've been the most tender declaration of love, an important step for the continuation of our marriage. But it wasn't to be. And I don't think this memory would've come back into my life with such intensity and so insistently if I hadn't read so many novels, all with more or less truthful representations of reality.

Manuscripts with men and women who meet, stare at each other, reject each other, hate each other, have contempt for each other, get closer, connect, love each other passionately. I read, and my life is reflected as if in a mirror in everything I read, as if everything I've lived were a page in a novel. Or several, disjointed. Composed of scenes, words, but no one's written it out from beginning to end. But I'm afraid to take a pen to my life, I get the feeling that it would be very painful. Maybe that's why novels are pure fiction, imaginary, with incredible incidents, incredible loves, incredible pain, tragedies, and suffering. He never ate my food, I had been cooking since I was little, I helped Grandma after Mom's death, I knew how to make everything, I had become a real homemaker, ready for marriage. Even if at the beginning, right after the wedding, I was scared, nervous, I could still cook so well you'd lick your fingers, not only the bowl. But he never ate anything I made. Is a more total, more limitless, rejection possible?! But back then it didn't hurt me, I wasn't conscious of it, I didn't have time, one thing after another happened to me, the days flew by. It hurts me only now, only now do I feel his rejection like a hole in the middle of my chest, my stomach, my hands, my entire body. It hurts and I feel like weeping, howling, and I'd like to no longer remember anything. It's as if it happened not long ago, maybe even yesterday or this morning. I cry over the past, because then I didn't shed a single tear, I didn't cry at all.

The other kids had taken my ball and he asked me why I was crying. He appeared before me like a hero, handsome, magnanimous, ready to save my life. My brothers will beat me because I went outside with their ball (stolen from some manor house, it occurs to me now). They beat me even for no reason, there's no sayin' what they'll do if I go back without the ball. He said: Wait here. He went over to the kids, he said something to them and, in a little while, he returned with my ball. Did he smile at me before leaving or not? From that moment I loved him wildly and I wanted to marry him. When I saw him again, I don't think he recognized me, he must've forgotten that miraculous incident. But I didn't forget. I remember the ball, I remember his voice, I remember his shorts, he was barefoot, like me, all the kids walked around barefoot during the summer, a bit tousled and so handsome, so handsome and so kind to a girl he didn't know who was crying, miserable, in the middle of the street! It's my only tender and beautiful memory of me and my husband . . .

The Trojan Horse

"In antiquity, the Greeks, after unsuccessfully laying siege to Troy for ten years, decided—as Homer tells us—to conquer the city through subterfuge. Under the pretext of a religious offering, the Greeks built a giant wooden horse, inside of which were hidden five hundred soldiers; then the rest of the army pretended to retreat. The Trojans then brought the horse into the city. In the dead of night, the Greek soldiers left their hiding place, opened the gates to the city, and, thus, Troy was conquered through a stratagem that became famous throughout the centuries and is known under the term 'the Trojan horse.' This expression characterizes those who use trickery to sneak into the enemy camp; it denotes an enemy disguised as a benefactor." (I. Berg, *Dictionary of Famous Words, Expressions, and Quotes*, Scientific Press, Bucharest, 1969, p. 60)

On a day like today, on April 24, but not 1974, rather 1184 before Christ, but what does three thousand years matter for our ageless censorship!, the Greeks are preparing a giant wooden horse, at Ulysses's suggestion, out of dogwood from a forest sacred to Apollo, and they bring it to the gates of Troy.

In the form of a respectful offering, they're coming now with their herd of horses to our gates, they're no longer satisfied with their little lizards.

More devious, more deceitful, the enemy with many heads is by the walls, hidden in the convincing wood.

But who hears it, who can make out the clanging of dangerous weapons, who can foretell the death, the precipitous murder, the exodus, the repeated plagues, and the misery that's to come?

A loyal patriot with a healthy mind, the censor Laocoön had saved his people from many adversaries, he'd set fire to many enemies.

Carloads of books have burned, thousands and thousands, the flames have reached up to the sky, but the enemy hasn't stopped advancing.

With a valiant spear he strikes the too generous belly of the horse, to convince the people to believe him, but the people are fascinated by the majestic animal and the gates of the city are impatient to let it in. Laocoön manages to cry out: "Don't allow the horses to enter! Don't allow the fierce enemy to take advantage of our trust! Why would they give us gifts now of all times, when they hate us the most?" The worthy Laocoön isn't able to finish his speech, because the mighty serpents wrap themselves around him and his family, taking them far away, to the provinces, to menial labor, to assemble screws.

"Oh, great powers, you who guard the truth, I refuse my spotless beliefs to hide! Ward off Apollo who cast his curses and fruitless made my prophecy be! What great punishment to have to witness the death of my people and not one theocre to heed me!" Cassandra, our sister, cries, and how right she is think we who long reports write about the wiles of the enemy, but no one to us attention pays, the enemy enters the city.

On her knees, Cassandra prays, somber predictions she

brings, but the haughty Trojan ignores her: "Away with her to apiculture! Let her number the lazy bees, construct more optimistic statistics, and stop bothering us with decadent and sad prophecies!"

And, behold, the gates trustingly open. What can be more innocent than a book? What gift more pleasing to the hearts and souls of the Trojans bereft by sickness and wars? Awestruck, the gentle people read, without suspecting the force of the devastating gift. How majestic, how voluminous, what dedication and sacrifice, what genius! What inventiveness, what deceitfulness! They swallow the poison without knowing . . .

Until midnight the Trojans celebrate, then they go to sleep. At night, from the belly of the horse a multitude of armed soldiers escape and open the gates of Troy to the other soldiers outside. A great massacre, while for the trusting and naïve vanquished people only one final hope remains: that along with them, the final hope would die as well . . .

What greater punishment for the censors hidden on Mount Ida than to witness the total destruction of millennia-old cities?

More and more books now, and enemies, as I've said—a herd. Not just potbellied horses, filled with armed enemy soldiers, but also dangerous, impetuous nags, who, if you let them out of your sight, will reproduce like rabbits in the attractive pages, making the entire un-cloven-hoofed clan harder to catch. They even send an adorable, playful colt to our gates sometimes. That's dangerous too, beloved immediately by readers, but he's still a Trojan horse, a colt today, tomorrow, a steed.

Do you see, my far-off son, what a difficult profession censorship is! How many words keep disguising themselves and hiding, how many meanings change from one day to the next, how many layers of clothing the truth puts on until it becomes a lie or the other way around. Everything dressed in words can be a lie, because the truth is naked, as we know.

Estrapade—I can't find what it means anywhere. Zuki found it in a foreign dictionary: 1. A form of torture consisting in lifting the condemned to a certain height by means of a rope and then letting him fall brutally almost to the ground repeatedly. 2. Movement in gymnastics consisting of hanging from a strap with both hands and making the rest of one's body pass in between both arms.

When I arrived in Censorship, we didn't carry dictionaries around with us! Maybe you could find one in the library, but no one consulted it. Whereas now, without them we're as good as dead, we can't live without them! We drag around the entire whopping four-volume Encyclopedic Dictionary! And not even that helps us every time! From where do these writers pull out such words? At first, I brought a dictionary from the library and kept it hidden, so no one would laugh at me for not knowing the language and automatically looking up words. Then the girls brought themselves one too, and we didn't hide them from each other anymore, in any case, there was nothing funny about it. The problem was officially brought up and it was decided that dictionaries needed to exist in all the Literature, Press, Social and Technical Sciences offices, they bought them for us in the necessary quantities. With Sciences it's understandable—they come into contact with specialized terms, you're allowed not to know some species of frog or have no clue what a "heliopterix" is. But what in the world are such words doing in a delicate literary text? Why clog up your poem with medical, juridical, technical terms so that it makes your head spin, in totally unexpected and even inappropriate contexts, in our opinion, words that neither I nor anyone in my entire family tree had ever heard in our lives, words impossible to pronounce, enough to twist your tongue in all directions, real perils appearing in the text like so many delayed-action bombs? How can I censor what I don't understand? How can I realize how dangerous a word is or how subversive it becomes in the given context?

It's the final and cruelest method of mocking a censor: these incomprehensible, encrypted words that you have to search for so carefully in the dictionary and, oftentimes, you can't even find them there. They're so perfidious! Some writers invent words, they put them in innocuous contexts, we get used to them, accept them, then boom! They throw in a torpedo right when we've let our guard down. Greek, English-Romanian dictionaries, dictionaries of archaisms, of neologisms, old and tattered from back in the age of knights or more recently released, the one from 1966.[20] Colleagues are working on a comprehensive explanatory dictionary that they're racking their brains over, if only they'd come out with it faster, it would help us so much!

Mykterismos—sarcastic, defiant attitude; sarcasm . . .

Floritura isn't in there, we have *florigen*, *florivory*, *flosculous* . . . all related to flowers.

Maybe *fioritura*? In context: "delicate floritura, a caress for the ears."

Fioritura—a musical embellishment consisting of a note or group of notes, commonly indicated by smaller than usual musical notation, which is added to the main musical phrase to adorn it. From It. *fioritura*.

Crenel—1. Each of the narrow openings, spaced out, on the upper part of a parapet on a defense tower of a medieval castle or fortress, through which projectiles would be thrown at the enemy. 2. Narrow openings in the walls of a blockhouse, a shelter, or the parapet of a trench, through which enemy movements can be detected and shots from portable automatic weapons can be fired.

Spatangus—sea urchin, heart-shaped, in muddy coastal sand . . .

Absession isn't in there, *abscission* is—the shedding of various parts of a plant, such as leaves. Easy as pie!

Encomiastic—of a laudatory nature, eulogistic. I've heard this word before, but it sounds rather pejorative in an official context. Instead of: "encomiastic tone," they can say, for example, "a sober tone."

Mesmerism—theory of animal magnetism; treatment based on this theory. It's not hostile, I'll leave it.

Jocum—does it come from joke? Big whoop of a word!

To parrot—to repeat mechanically, like a parrot, the words or opinions of someone.

Endemic—that which has local causes, specific to certain regions; that is of a permanent nature in certain regions.

Can't they be any clearer?

I'm positive that just as we're sitting here with dictionaries to decipher their words, that's how they're writing too, all with dictionaries in front of them. We should ban dictionaries! They should be kept only in the Reference Collection with limited access.

No, not only do they want to show that they know the language they're writing in better than others, they also want to demonstrate that they're smarter than censors and that they can rub it in our faces like this! They're hiding behind words! Editors don't bother looking for them and saving us the hassle, they leave this "noble" task to us. A regular reader might skip over these words, but we can't, we're not allowed! Who knows what might be hiding behind some regular "jocum"!

The word "polymelmelia" isn't in there, there's only *polymelia*—congenital malformation consisting in the presence of an excessive number of legs . . . Spiders and octopuses!

And then it's not enough just to know the meaning of the word, which can have several meanings. What about the context? The context matters too! We're all buried in our reading, what silence, each one of us with her nose in a manuscript, and someone, Hermina, this time, who's the quietest and most reserved one among us, distinctly enunciates in an astonished voice: *Menarche!* Me-nar-che.

We look up from our manuscripts, wrinkle our noses, we don't know, we've really never heard of it! Hermina looks it up, then she tells us too, because it interests us: the first occurrence of menstruation. In context: "a young woman on the threshold of menarche," hmm, nothing hostile, any young woman could be on the threshold of . . . it would've been wasting words to write everything out. It's a case of an unknown word in an appropriate context.

If "estrapade" has a subversive meaning and, in context it's very difficult to substitute, a rarer and less often effectuated (meaning used), but still correct and efficient, method would be to change a letter or two. To transform a real word (if it's real) with a concrete meaning into a fantastical, nonexistent, poetic one. The reader is accustomed to moving on—in any case all the words he doesn't understand seem fantastical and made up to him—and not looking things up in dictionaries. Just let anyone try to take issue with our vigilance! Give me a break, are we supposed to wait on writers hand and foot? They can toy with us however they want and we're supposed to search through dictionaries like idiots? They can create words that don't exist anywhere in the universe, and we can't? Hermina and Roza are inexhaustible in that department. What beautiful and original words they invent! Many authors wouldn't be clever enough. What talented girls I have in my office! I'm really lucky to have them. Thus, in addition to the pleasant operation of extracting words, we also substitute others sometimes.

I'm in such a hurry, such a hurry! Just like our colleagues who smoke, when, shaking, they light their cigarette and, frantically, fervently, bring it to their lips, close their eyes, and inhale, inhale deeply . . .

I smoke the difficult manuscript and it relaxes me. Everything becomes peaceful and calm. My hands are almost shaking the first few pages, the first pages are shaking, the first lines of dialogue, the first characters, I can't concentrate. I close my eyes, take a deep breath, pull air into my chest, I also pull the pages toward my chest, I hold them there tightly, I establish first contact, I try to guess whether I'm embracing an enemy or a friend, is it a snake I'm squeezing to my bosom or an adorable and innocent little kitten, a friendly and worthy manuscript or a secretive and dangerous one? With my eyes still closed, after the embrace, it's my nose's turn. I smell the pages . . . What do these pages filled with letters contain? Before I use my eyes, before I read per se, all the other senses have to be put to work. What do my fellow censors think? How do you approach a book and understand its essence so quickly and so well? It's an entire array of habits . . .

Then the hunt begins. You tiptoe, carefully, without a sound, without a trace, you don't have before you a simple forest with three hedgehogs, five boars, two deer, and a fox. The book is a much more deceiving jungle, fatal if you're not careful and make a wrong move, haunted by lions, tigers, fierce and poisonous snakes, hyenas, panthers, and other predatory beasts, they all want to attack you from behind, they all want to strangle you and kill you. What does it mean to be vigilant? This is what it means. This is it. To defend yourself, to anticipate the danger, to cut, to bear your claws and fangs, to annihilate the enemy before he can knock you over. That's the only way you can come out victorious and get ahead of the author. You immobilize him just in time and you don't take your eyes off the threat for a second. Lowering your guard for even a moment, loosening up even a bit, can be deadly.

If I don't write, then I don't think, I don't progress, I don't evolve in my profession. I feel that writers are always a step ahead, more talented, more refined, smarter. Fine, it's in their nature to be talented, but other than that, we shouldn't be outdone by them. Stupid censors shouldn't exist. If I censor them, I don't become better, smarter, I become more tired. The talent of others, scattered generously throughout a whole book, genius, perfection—they exhaust me. A page I've written, filled with banal events or impressions, is to me more important than a hundred masterpieces put together. Wonderful books crush me, undo me, I feel like an impostor who's trampling a beautiful garden. A wicked incubus who sullies the purity of a work, entering it before it comes out into society and deflowering it. I feel I am its enemy. A miserable dwarf who hacks away mercilessly left and right. I feel the work directed sharply and hostilely at me, defending itself and ready to attack me from behind. I feel that the simple readings we're accustomed to and the simple cutting of words aren't working anymore, things are more complicated, the role of cunning hunter who has to attract his prey is replacing the role of the implacable inquisitor. I have to pretend to love it. I'm its ideal reader, in fact, I'm its first great love. Its bride, its groom. Declarations of love, as sincere and substantiated as possible. So it doesn't suspect the great abandonment and the great loneliness to which it will be condemned at the end of the reading. Then I expel it from me, sometimes I leave something inside it, a trace, a correction, a seed, a syllable and I walk away, I leave, I forget about it, I don't care about its fate anymore, like men who can't remember the women they sleep with.

Book after book, book after book. And the same loneliness, identical, like a steppe, without hills, valleys, knolls, without anything to vary and liven up the landscape. I offer it its first reading and its first love and no book ever forgets this. They're left with imprints, with marks, with memories, blood, pain, amputations, even spontaneous abortions or curettages. Very rarely, the first love is also the last, but that happens too. None of the readers who follow know how to lick it with their eyes, to soothe the tormenting wounds of the first reading. The trickles of innocent blood . . . No book can forget its first reading, just as no girl can forget her first love. The experience is harder or easier to get over, but you can't avoid it. The book! I open it and possess it. It's mine. It's my great blessing, sacrifice, love, life, death. I'm not bluffing. I don't think I was bluffing with my first and only husband either. I'm honest through and through. I give it everything, I belong to it completely. I convince it. I even serenade it under its window. I poke and examine each letter from all sides, I tug on each punctuation mark. So that it opens up. And my manuscript bride allows itself to be convinced, my sincerity wins it over. It opens up its pages, heart, secrets, intimate places, coded language, symbols, mysteries, and I take advantage, I rummage through all the recesses of the candid novel, I search for potential dangers, enemies disguised in diaphanous shadows, poisonous lizards painted in warm and friendly colors, other devious animals or words with unclear intentions. I find them, I extract them, carefully and gently, so it doesn't hurt. I write the report, I turn everything in and bye-bye! I don't know you, I don't love you, I don't even want to remember you! You don't exist!

It's another maiden's turn in my fragrant bed.

I'm the best censor! If someone were to read what I'm writing now, they'd kick me out. I think that in the deepest part of my being, in my most hidden subconscious, I want to abandon this work, I want to run away, to begin a normal quiet life somewhere, free of all these risks and responsibilities, it's not too late for me to start a new family, to find myself a job that won't steal my life and heart away. So I'll have some time, some emotions, left over that I won't have to give to anyone. To have some time all to myself, to live out an emotion, even a banal one, related to the sunset, but for it to be mine, and not read somewhere, taken from who knows what censored book. From books I find out about wondrous life, fog, clouds, loves, farewells, who else has died, who has traveled where else. I read, I read. All these years all I've been doing is reading constantly. Listen up, esteemed readers of forbidden notebooks, I'm talking to you, because it's impossible for you not to steal such a notebook! It's impossible for you not to read what censors secretly write! It's impossible for you to be so indifferent and apathetic. I haven't told you before, but I was aware that it might be read, even if we're required to keep the notebooks, together with the secret documents, under lock and key. How many times have I left things unlocked on purpose, just pretending, in front of my colleagues, that I'm locking up, so that maybe, just maybe, someone will steal my notebook or at least someone curious will flip through it! I even placed strands of hair, and other small and invisible signs, that I found untouched. No one's reading it. Sick to death of reading and secrets, our censors should be required to read out of their own initiative, how else could they be made curious about it? I even feel slightly disappointed. Fine, fine, I understand the censors. But the Securitate officers who check up on us? I understand them too. With how many enemies there are out there, how much there is to do, to read, to listen to, it seems that the Securitate are also sick of texts. What's the point of reading the personal writings, bound for the fire, of a trustworthy comrade? She can write what she wants, nothing will happen! It's not as if she has the ambition of publishing it, like the rest of the texts. I write and I don't censor myself. That's something. It's hard, it's new, I don't even know what to write . . . Most likely, this notebook won't be stolen, it won't even be flipped through secretly. I need to be realistic. How many censors have notebooks like this one? I think around a hundred. Who has time to read this hundred, when there are so many suspicious, hostile individuals, whereas we belong to the party, we're the most devoted and upright readers. For us to expect to be read as well would be utopic. We're readers, not writers. This notebook is like a bone thrown to a hungry dog, to ease its hunger. Therapeutic, so we don't go crazy from reading so much, for a change of activity. Probably the only reader of this notebook will be the fire from the paper factory or the wastepaper shredder.

It seems like nothing, it seems banal and suddenly it appears. It stops your breath, you're fascinated.

From reading so much some censors develop a crucial flaw that could even cost them their job. It happens when it seems to them that something's missing from certain texts and so they fill it in, they improve it in an exaggerated way, they change sentences, titles, some, granted, are maybe inappropriate, but others don't have to be changed. There's no reason for the intervention. The censor feels a sick need to bring it to the state that he considers to be perfection, he won't rest until he finds a more fitting rhyme, a more melodious line for a scrawny poem.

When you reach this phase, you're capable of writing an entire poem and sticking it in, just like that, among the others in a volume, as if it were the most natural thing in the world.

You don't see anything unusual about this. Adding two or three colorful epithets to a rather drab landscape seems too little to you. You feel as though you can write better than any author. It's an illness, you have a problem and you don't realize it. Sometimes even your group of colleagues don't realize, because the reports are normal, with two or three indications, and the manuscript is sent back to the press and who has time to look over all the censor's observations and, especially, to analyze how warranted they are? When suspicions are raised, double readings are introduced, which require several of us to work on the same manuscript, to compare our different ways of looking at a text . . .

I was here back when we were criticized and even punished if we substituted the honorable and important work of a censor for that of a simple copy editor, meaning we straightened out spelling mistakes. The people in Press especially fell into this ready sin, but we, those who had longer texts, did too, because it's easier to find a comma missing or an extra letter, than who knows what ideological mistake, that wouldn't have existed there even in the most innocent intention of the demiurge . . .

The second report—a joint report. I'm afraid of doing joint reports. It's been years now since they've given up this practice. Any collective censorship activity is a headache for me. Censorship is a solitary occupation, in its essence. Now I'm thinking: Is something up with the volume? Do they want to bury one censor through the intermediary of another who'll identify the mistakes that the first one didn't see? Does someone have a problem, are they exaggerating somehow? And by any chance is it me, because it's not out of the question for me to be the one they're targeting!

So I'll do the joint report on this shitty novel! I'll go through this as well. I'm not stupid, I know how to get by, I'll move my butt along all sides of the fence, it'll turn out to be neither fish nor fowl, neither publishable nor unpublishable, neither valuable nor valueless, neither outdated nor too current . . . I won't commit myself to anything! It's a lousy novel and I don't understand why they're carrying on about it, of all things, so much.

Z-mann showed me the memorandum put forth by the party and the list of those who were to receive housing. My name was in the memorandum, but not on the list! I'm furious! Some have only just arrived in Censorship and they're all set up in new apartments, while I'm still renting a guestroom, and I've been working here for seven years!

> . . . Out of the total of 45 requests for housing from the state fund, submitted with the purpose of drawing up new charts, 18 represent serious and very serious cases. A significant portion of readers work by rotation in different work shifts, including at night, which increases intellectual and physical wear, influencing, in not a few cases, their work capacity and health. In this respect, it bears mentioning that, according to the database at the Al. Sahia Polyclinic—which provides medical assistance to the employees of the institution—for the past several years a troubling increase of a morbidities among readers, especially of nervous conditions, has been noted.

434 THE CENSOR'S NOTEBOOK

One category consists of the requests of 5 employees who, together with their families (3–4 persons), occupy a single room each, oftentimes damp, in the basement, without direct sunlight, and which, because of the crowding of multiple persons into such a limited space, do not permit the necessary resting conditions for even a regular job, let alone for the restoration of work capacity after an activity fatiguing to the nerves.

Another comrade who has been working as a reader in the institution for over 18 years lives with his wife and 15-year-old son in a single room in an insalubrious state. In the same situation are comrades Stanescu and Rosemberg, readers active for 18 and 11 years respectively, who also occupy a single room with their three-person families (in the first case with a wife and mother, and in the second with a wife and 10-year-old child).

Com. Rosca is a reader of foreign languages (including Chinese) and for several years also has been living in a single room without a bathroom or a kitchen together with her husband and her mentally ill sister. The comrade is seven months pregnant. Another example is com. Kulcsar, a reader of foreign languages, who occupies a single room with her family (4 persons).

A case that requires urgent resolution is that of com. Trifan who, together with his family (5 persons total), occupies one room and a kitchen, both damp. Of the 5 members of the family, the 2 children and the wife suffer from TB and are under permanent medical treatment.

There are 4 more employees (Moldovean, Ternios, Naumescu, Tompa) who do not have any kind of housing, living as tolerated guests or renting rooms from private individuals.

Taking into account the numerous still unresolved inadequate living situations and the fact that under the working conditions of the General Directorate of Press and Publications, the provision of satisfactory housing acquires particular importance for the work capacity and health of employees, we urgently request that this year our institution be allotted a housing quota of 500 sq. m., which can be used to resolve the requests of employees who live in the conditions described in the examples above.

This is the memorandum, after that is the list that my name isn't on! When push comes to shove, I have a child too, and, if I had an apartment . . . Everyone has housing problems, everyone is living in improper conditions, in rooms that are too small, dark, damp, inadequate. What about me, having to live with an insufferable old lady? As if that's how it should be! And if the old lady comes in my room and reads my manuscripts? I think they have a network of grannies, and all kinds of beginner censors and other sensitive directionless provincials are distributed among them, to be kept under control.

Mine is the widow of a brave communist, the former editor-in-chief of a magazine, who died of a heart attack. The big house is full of souvenirs, a well-traveled man, with a library, a well-read man. The old lady has never opened a book in her life, she was a nurse in a hospital, and how a communist this intelligent met her and asked her to be his wife is unfathomable, though she keeps telling me the story. The old lady is definitely getting another pension in addition to her own in return for monitoring me. I think she writes down somewhere even how long it takes me to pee. No way I'd ever invite a man over. She'd put a glass to the door to eavesdrop on what we're doing. However often I might tell my bosses that any day now it'll be ten years since I started working here and that I still don't have a place of my own, however small, it's no use! Lists are written up, each year censors receive housing, only I never get my turn. I'm told that I'll be at the top of the next list, but married couples, families with mothers and grandmothers, come out of nowhere and they always get priority. While I, young and single, have to keep waiting.

Not everyone here knows that I was really married, that I also have a child, whom I gave birth to, who was in my belly for nine months, I breastfed him . . . Before, I had the small chest of an unmarried girl and, after breastfeeding, they got bigger, stretched out, and even sagged a little. I was positive that they would tighten up again after I weened the child, but I'm still wearing a number three even now, I'm full-chested, voluptuous, as the poets would say. Then my son took his first steps and I held his hand. He grabbed on tightly to my finger. If I'd known I'd lose him, that those would be my last moments with him, I would've held him in my lap, I would've hugged him, I would've kissed him. I don't remember occasions like that. Instead, I pushed him aside so many times when he reached out his little hands for me, when he wanted to be held, when he wanted his mama, but his mama left for college, leaving the small child with great-grandmothers and other relatives. I felt that I would lose my husband if I didn't go after him and I told myself: I'll follow him at all costs, but I never for one second felt that I was losing my child. What little maternal instinct I had back then! Maybe the fact that I lost him was a punishment for not really, barely, appreciating him, for not showing him love? Without a husband by my side, the child was no longer worth anything to me and I abandoned him without regrets, without suffering at all. I'd almost forgotten about him. And when certain scenes come up in my memory, they're so faded it's as if I dreamed I had a son, as if he existed only in my imagination. I transform him into censored literature, he's the intervention for which I'm thinking up justifiable arguments, so I can take it out of the text and go on living peacefully.

—When we hired you, we really didn't know you were married and had a child. But think about how you want to raise the issue. Usually, the child remains with the mother after a divorce. So it's obvious that, if your son is with your ex-husband, he must be a big shot. See how everyone handles you with kid gloves, you've got nothing to complain about. But they're afraid that, if you ask for the child, they'll come into conflict with more powerful entities. Meaning you might not receive housing precisely because someone doesn't want to create unnecessary problems for your high-up ex-husband.

You can claim that you want to start a new family, that you don't have adequate working conditions, but not that you have a son . . . Think about it when you bring up the right to housing next time. It's possible that, if you bring up the issue of your son, you might not get something very soon or even ever. That's what I'm guessing. I was in the commission and that's what it seemed like to me.

—Even Roza got one!

—She got one when she was working in Press, she had the night shift. They're usually at the top of the list. Literature doesn't work in three shifts, the way Press does. That some can't handle it is another problem. Yours is a different can of worms. I gave you a piece of advice. You can take it into consideration or not. Do what you want.

Advice! I piss on your advice! What do you all know?! My husband didn't kidnap my son and I don't believe my son would come to me now even if I had three apartments. I did think, however, that if I invoked the fact that I have a child, I'd receive an apartment more quickly. But they think exactly like Zuki! He's right, why didn't I think of it too? Just between us, what a bunch of liars! They didn't know I was married! How is it possible for them to lie to my face so blatantly?! The files that Censorship compiles, not even the Securitate is more thorough, and the comrades didn't know! That's why I haven't received an apartment all these years! How stupid am I! How did I not realize?! It's a good thing that at least Zuki told me the truth. I have to consider things more carefully next time . . . So they're afraid that I'm going to ask for my son, that I'll fight for my rights as a mother. I don't have these rights, I don't. I wasn't a good mother . . . "And if you write a note in which you give up your rights to the child, you'll definitely receive housing, even faster than you might expect . . ."

An important aspect of the activities carried out among personnel has been the education of all employees in the spirit of staunch work discipline, of deep attachment to the political duties of the institution, the cultivation of the characteristics befitting communist ethics, qualities absolutely necessary to the job description of a censor, who has been entrusted with a task of great importance.

The conclusion we can draw is that all members of the collectives must demonstrate a great degree of precision, of decisiveness, and not tolerate any instance that could lead to the weakening of the unity of the collectives, to liberalism and lack of discipline, to the weakening of a spirit of vigilance and—in the end—to a decrease in the quality of professional work.

The specific nature of the activities of our institution has necessitated the formation of a collective of devoted readers, well-trained from a political and professional standpoint, with an appropriate makeup and healthy moral conduct.

After spending several months together without him touching me, he came home and, almost crassly, reeking of alcohol and half asleep, motioned for me to get undressed and get under him. I remember that singular night and I feel like crying and screaming just as I had back then. I was sure that he'd begin snoring the moment he lay down in bed. But the man was determined to do great things and decided to fulfill his obligations as a husband (finally!). The only other time he had been this drunk was in the hay, maybe. In any case, I was as scared as I was then. When my husband pushed into me the first time, I thought I'd die of pain! When he pushed again, my nails went into his flesh and tears spilled from my eyes. Suddenly, my husband, woken from his stupor, shocked, scared, asked me:

—What is this, it's your first time?

—Yes, I whispered, asking for mercy.

—But didn't you say that something happened between us that night, when I woke up in the hay with you, you were dressed, and I didn't remember anything!

—I lied, I wanted you to marry me. I had heard that other girls had done that too and had gotten married.

I didn't tell him my brothers told me to lie down next to him, there was no point. In any case, another night of love never followed. I know that he ran to the love of his life to tell her that he loved only her, that I had lied and he, what an idiot he was! He ran to my brothers to tell them too, that they had beaten him for nothing, they had made him get married for nothing, because he hadn't touched me, that their sister was a liar, a liar, etc., etc.

I read and no love tears me apart inside, nothing in my chest, nothing between my legs. In my heart, nothing.

When Hermina, with the voice of a saint being led to her death, gave her opinion that if a man gets a woman pregnant, he'll definitely marry her, I laughed and told her: a man is even more disgusted by a woman he doesn't love when she becomes his wife. She asked me whether I knew this from personal experience. Since it came up, I told her that I had been married for three years (three years and four months, I was with the child in the village for two years, and in my first year of college I signed the divorce papers), even if I didn't always have my husband by my side, I didn't bother saying exactly how much time we had spent together, there had been something between us, if we even had a child together, so I know something about life too. I can't say much more to this airhead, who wouldn't understand a thing. Actually, she's not quite as naïve as she might appear, though this innocence appeals to men and it suits her. The way she is, white, fragile, like a love poem struck down by the overpowering wind. And I don't know what's gotten into Roza: she complained that she doesn't like going from man to man either, all of them feeling up her skirt, instead of inviting her to a movie, a café, then nicely marrying her. She wants to get married too, like all the girls. They're so different, but they both want the same thing. They all want to get married, the good and well-behaved ones, as well as the easier ones who wave their boobs around.

There the motors rumble.
Here the rivers babble.
There the factories hammer.
Here the sparrows clamor.
I sit on the grass and listen to the sounds,
I shake off a stray spider and trace the shape of a cloud.
There are words, songs, arriving on tiptoe, undulating,
    to your old house.
I knock, the door's locked, waiting.
For me to open it, to turn up in galoshes, at the gate.
We'll meet again in the next world.
We'll die together.

The last moment of wind, the first of monsoon.
The last ray of sun, the first ray of moon.
Life will be gentler, life will be better.

For a thing like this, a colleague won an award! And how many of these "brilliant" lines do I find and no one gives me any award? It seems unfair! That this guy, Ludovic Turcu, a beginner, still pretty shaky at the job, needs to be encouraged, I can understand. But don't I need to be encouraged? When there's some devious text, come on, Didina, you're the only one who can figure it out, you're the best, only you've got a nose specially made for this and you know from the first words where the mistakes are hiding. But when it comes to awards—always someone else! Because I'm conscientious no matter what and I'll do the work. How unfair! But just let me make one small mistake, even the slightest oversight, and immediately they'll jump all over me triumphantly!: "You messed up too, you're the same as us! They'll criticize you as well, they'll tar and feather you!" and all the good-for-nothings and idiots in Censorship will rejoice. They can hardly wait to see me taken down a notch, crushed, humiliated. I wouldn't hold my breath if I were you!

If I were crazy, I'd say: in front of a manuscript, I am God! But I'm not crazy and I affirm that in front of a manuscript, I'm almost a god. One on whom depends the fate of the manuscript, the fate of the author, and the fate of the many people who read the book before it got to Censorship, and all those who will read it from now on. No one will ever understand how much satisfaction reading and censoring a manuscript gives me, identifying the mistakes, correcting them. This occupation makes me drunk with an unparalleled feeling of triumph! Of fighting and prevailing. I'm above everyone, somewhere impossibly high up, majestic, victorious! I'm in this state of euphoria each time I figure out everything a book could be blamed for, not just the mistake, but also its intention. I blocked it, I cut off the branch. I did it! What supreme bliss!

If I get this sensation just by inspecting and reading, how much more do the authors who create worlds out of nothing feel?

Comrades,

It is a well-known fact that the successes achieved by our workers in the professional and public arenas are, to a great extent, the result of the permanent efforts of institution leadership, of the branch organization office, of all our party organizations, in educating our personnel in the party spirit, to be devoted to their work, disciplined, vigilant, combative, both in their professional work and when faced with any unhealthy displays that might arise around them. This process of education was begun with each worker from the moment they entered the institution. We only know that along the years young comrades have been hired—20–21 years of age, who were given support and guidance with the aim of cultivating their well-rounded training, their political maturity. Opportunities were created for them to complete their studies, to earn a higher degree, all this for the benefit of the institution's work and, at the same time, their personal benefit.

Thus it results, comrades, that the vast majority of our workers have grown concomitantly with their work. For them, the professional activity carried out within the institution, inextricably linked to the study of Marxist-Leninist teachings in the different forms of party education toward which they were guided, has constituted, as each of them recognizes, a true school.

At the same time, young personnel, competent, with a well-developed party sensibility, were confidently promoted. Leadership of units was supplied by party members and candidates. Along the same lines of strengthening the work of the units, of strengthening party combativeness, recent organizational measures, applied in the same way to each unit, have been taken. All these, comrades, are nothing other than a reflection of the practical application—of course, on the institutional level—of the instructions of our party regarding care for personnel, their development and advancement.

One Sunday I discovered a black skirt made of good fabric, quality material, rather snug. I had put it aside, because it was too tight on me, but the idea popped into my head to take it to the seamstress, it had extra material at the seams that could be let out. I knew a trustworthy seamstress on Lipscani Street, I went there, she altered it for me the way I wanted, the chatty comrade advising me to rub the area where the stitches had been a bit with water and vinegar so it couldn't be seen that it was once narrower. I left there satisfied and, when I headed out, I didn't take the same way back on Lipscani to reach Victoriei Avenue faster, instead I went down Smardan and took a street parallel to Lipscani, on I don't know what side street under construction. I spotted the little church. I don't believe in God, I don't think about him and I don't observe religious holidays, I don't pray, I think I did when I was a child, when I prayed together with Grandma, she taught me prayers, she took me to church, but times have changed and I've forgotten everything.

I'm a pagan, in the conception of the people from the village I left. I've paganized myself, they'd say. I don't have a religious education, it's impossible, it's improper. But I have an excuse, several actually, if I think about it. Sometimes I'm searching for something, sometimes I feel like there must be more. I don't know whether I've found what I'm looking for or I'm just imagining I found it. I think I hid something somewhere, so what was deeply planted, in my first years of life, wouldn't die; my grandmother, being very devout, taught me many things. Because I didn't want to upset her, I wouldn't tell her what they taught us in school. Excusable, she wouldn't have come over to my side in any case, she was old, and sick. But I'm young, I still want to get into the Securitate, to my husband, and I've gotten rid of everything inside that could stop me from reaching my goal. And He would've gotten in my way! So there's nothing there, he doesn't exist. I won't read your worn-out bibles! I'm not tempted to go inside your churches, I don't go inside, I don't . . . I could say that censors censor not only others but also themselves. But here I was, right now something, someone, was tugging at me, calling me, my legs walked that road by themselves, while my head wasn't thinking of anything. And I found myself right in front of the church.

I looked to my left, to my right, to make sure I didn't see anyone I knew. At the end of the day, you're allowed to study a

beautiful old building. But still, it's not the beauty that interested
me . . . I don't know what exactly . . . I was afraid that someone
might catch me, a full-fledged censor, going into a church! No
one, deserted, not a person in sight. I felt like going inside the
church, though I could've just admired the building from the
outside and continued on my way. But I felt like going inside.
I was amazed by this impulse of mine and by my own courage
(or madness, stupidity?) and I went in. I looked around again.
For some, it doesn't matter who might see them in a church, it
doesn't threaten them at all. For me, not only is it risky, because
I'd lose my job, it's also very shameful. What business do I have
with a god whom I take out of all the texts? No one was in the
church. Alone in the church. I was amazed again. I took a few
steps and heard the clear sound of my own footsteps. In the
silence all around I heard their distinct echo, the footsteps rever-
berated. The church was small and the images were faded, in
the semidarkness I could barely see anything at first. Then my
eyes adjusted and I began making out the pictures on the wall. It
wasn't at all a bad thing that there was no one in the church, no
one could see me, I could stay there as long as I liked, looking
closely at the walls. I was expecting to find at least a pious old
lady, at least one soul sitting and contemplating in some corner.
Really no one! When I would go with Grandma to church, it was
full of people, you couldn't move, your headscarf could catch fire
from the lighted candles crowded in too closely. It was hot inside
from too many people. Whereas here, how empty, how cool, you
could catch a chill in your back.

I stopped to gaze longer at a saint on horseback, St. George,
I recognized him and discovered, surprised, that instead of
fiercely aiming his spear at the dragon, he was aiming it at a

large open manuscript. In the upper-right-hand corner of the page that the saint's spear had just ripped out, a dragon was meticulously drawn in bright colors and gilded. I looked more carefully at the walls and I saw that all the saints were holding large, gleaming books in their hands, out of which they were ripping and tossing pages. One by one, the pages left the icons and floated softly through the church. Threateningly. Frowning, stern, the saints of the church were tearing pages from books, in a distinguished manner, elegantly, with their right hand, with delicate, long fingers, while they held the books in their left hand. I went through all the saints, row by row, I rotated through the empty church, maybe, just maybe, I'd find at least one who had nothing to do with books. I searched for an icon painted without a book. I sounded out their names, I stopped next to each one, I got closer so I could see better, maybe I was imagining things, I was having visions or hallucinations. The figures depicted in the icons looked at me maliciously, pulling out a page at a time with two or three thin, dry fingers and throwing it right in my face. I protected myself, I ducked. All around me pages were floating. The fires of hell flickered with flames in which burning books were visible, hell was full of sinful books, heaven was illuminated by large, white, gleaming books, so heaven's full of books too and of angels reading. Every which way, pages floating, like so many wings punished to carry out their last flight. I got scared and hurried to leave as quickly as possible. As I exited, above the church door was God himself, probably, with a giant, heavy bible. He could barely hold it and I was afraid that he'd drop it right onto my head when I passed under him. It seemed as if pages were slipping out from the big book as well.

Vast is Your garden, Lord! And full of censors!

I got out and breathed a sigh of relief, for a while I still felt like a ripped-out page had gotten stuck to me, and St. George was aiming an arrow behind me . . . I can still picture his fight with the manuscript dragon! I'm writing it out and leaving it here and forgetting about it! Let it remain just a memory in a notebook that will also, in turn, be burned! I'm never going to step foot inside a church again! It's more peaceful in the Press House.

If I really stop and think about it, I censor myself in all the important areas of my life, love, faith, freedom. When it comes to "Life or death!" I don't know what to say, I couldn't find any argument, any proof that I censor myself in these areas. I don't have life or death . . . I have so little time during the day, while on Sundays or on vacation I don't know what to do with myself. I almost always miss my job, this occupation that consumes my entire day and my entire life. I like my office, I like the Press House. When I come to work in the morning and, off in the distance, I see the wonderful and imposing building, the most beautiful one in Bucharest, I think to myself with pride and satisfaction: I work here! Yes, my life belongs to Censorship, it belongs to my people. I try to serve the fatherland to the best of my abilities, with great love and complete devotion! And if our most important leaders say that religion is an opiate of the people and it must be eradicated, that's how it is, we'll eradicate it, we'll yank it out of ourselves with pliers and throw it into the fire. We must believe in the radiant achievements of the people, in our beloved leaders, in this we believe and we don't question, we don't doubt! But I went inside a church. I saw the saints and gods ripping up books, the pages were flying through the entire church, the books were burning on the walls, I felt the danger, I was disturbed, I had visions that were scarcely communist . . . which are the fruits of my backwards education, I come from peasants who believed in God and went to church their entire lives, they went with God at their helm, just as we, the younger ones, now go with the Party. Well, did they have such a loving party during the difficult feudal-bourgeois times? Such a beloved leader, a radiant future? No, just a stern God and many unforgiving and scowling saints, who await the smallest mistake so they can slam a book on your head! They definitely must have sprayed that church with something, with some super-powerful holy water or something, and that's why I had unpatriotic hallucinations. It had been a long time since I had gone inside a religious establishment (when I think about it, since I came to the Capital!) and you won't see any sign of me there in the near future, nor in the far-off one. If I do go in again, I really will find myself with a bump on my head from the books they're throwing around. How uncivilized and what a lack of respect for precious incunabula! But I can't not think about this, I feel an uneasiness that won't leave me alone, I can't escape it. Fine, in other times, when there were censors, like me, but communists didn't exist yet, were those censors religious, might those from the XIXth century, for example, have been believers? I don't dare ask even Z. something like that, because who knows what he might think. If I ask these kinds of mystical questions, next thing you know they'll get it into their heads to transfer me to some apicultural association . . .

Why didn't I call out inside the church, if I was alone anyway:

God, if you exist, why did you make me a censor?
Maybe I would've gotten an answer . . . A book to the head would've been, likewise, an answer . . .

Full of hope, with complete admiration, with utter eagerness, that, finally, this is the quintessential book, the best one in my entire life! That's what happens to me in the beginning, but already by the middle of the book I realize that I've fooled myself again, that this isn't the perfect, ideal book either, that it has many flaws, shortcomings, ineptitudes . . . After I finish reading it, I'm overcome with a feeling of sadness, a sense of the uselessness of reading and censoring . . . Poorly written books shouldn't exist, useless books, wastepaper filling up the heads and souls of readers. The enemies are in our heads. The enemy begins by attacking the head. It's becoming increasingly conventional to discover something "hostile" in a book, when in fact there isn't, there isn't. But mediocrity, yes, that's hostile, yes, it should be banned. It will lead us to our doom. Wastepaper will destroy the world. It envelopes the world slowly, it suffocates it. Nothing tragic, nothing painful, nothing subversive, just tons of it and mediocre. Wastepaper and its ever-increasing number of authors, its numerous devotees, mediocre readers. With all these pessimistic thoughts, I continue to hope for the ideal book. We haven't yet all started producing wastepaper. There's also the criteria, which change more and more quickly. History's racing onwards. I pick up a book and think: Why didn't I read this three years ago? Then my tears would've spilled onto its pages, it would've fascinated me, turned me upside down, now it leaves me cold. We've got other expectations, I realize I'm changing, I'm evolving, and with the passage of time, my expectations are also changing, transforming. I'm growing, most of the time. I realize that the ideal novel will always be one step behind me, I'll always have tastes and expectations that are more complicated and harder to satisfy. Maybe if I stopped watching and searching, if I didn't think about it, I'd have a better chance of coming across it. It would search for me, it would fall into my hands, unexpectedly. I'd recognize it immediately, I'd love it, our meeting would thrill me. I wouldn't regret the lost time, the effort of searching. But I'm a censor and I can't stop. I'm always reading, always searching, I don't have the right to sit and dream the way an ordinary reader does.

Glomerulus—particle formed from several granules in a soil, conglomerated with humus, clay, calcium, or different salts and having the properties that derive from the characteristics of these components; an organelle formed through the bundling of capillaries or lymphoid tissue. *Renal Glomerulus.*

A tiny, disobedient monster is born inside my head. Someone carefully, insidiously, planted something that sprouted. I opposed it, I resisted, I fought, I did everything in my power. Words I don't know, meanings that escape and baffle me, begin to move, like the first living cell at the bottom of the ocean that will give rise to the future sea monster, gigantic, hideous. It can be nothing other than a murderous and vengeful monster. I couldn't stop it anymore even if I were to quit reading. The monster I feel inside me and which I hide thinks thoughts with my brain that I wouldn't think, that I don't want to and shouldn't.

Your poisonous books, your murderous books! Useless interdictions and murky verbosity!

Pathetic, theatrical, throwing around flowery, bloody words, shooting out and splattering meanings and truths in all directions, that's how the monster's born . . .

While I'm writing, I hear Hermina pronounce in a seraphic voice: "I waited for Roza to step out to tell you: that hairstyle looks great on you! You're so lofty and beautiful. You're exceptional!" Instead of being happy, I felt like crying, and I still do. Already being born are you, you abomination? See, delicate Hermina immediately felt the change. It's transforming me, the devil, it's shaping me. Me, beautiful? Me, exceptional? Hermina's sincere and smart. More than probably I can agree with her, believe her, that's how I am, that's how I've become after so much reading. Increasingly beautiful and exceptional books lately. But that's not it, it's not just that! A stranger, another me, a new Filofteia is being born, she emerges from the former Didina. A doubling, a multiplication, schizotude. One is good, worthy, an honorable citizen, an exemplary and trustworthy employee, the other is rebellious, dangerous, beautiful, and what else? What else is she like? Suicidal—here's the proof. The written proof.

Whoever reads will kill.

I've come to this, butterflies and other animals in my head, graceful or aggressive, etc., monsters, just by reading. That's all I've done, all this craziness stems from me reading! But any censor is, before all else, an almost ordinary reader, one that reads a bit more carefully, but lots of people read carefully. Why couldn't monsters be born in their heads as well? In each of their heads, a monster, according to their level of culture and literacy . . . It's plausible, isn't it, more than possible? Maybe others didn't resist the temptation (they didn't want to, they couldn't) and their process of schizoidization happened more quickly and vehemently, who knows? Maybe we all have a tiny monster inside our heads and keep it hidden? A monstrous country! Who knows what or who exactly lies inside the darling little heads of literature lovers? All of us are dangerous. And readers are even more hostile and more subversive than authors. The reader drinks in each word, analyzes it, comments on it, enjoys it, criticizes it, gets into the mood of each book, falls in love with a poem, learns it by heart, loves the author. He cannot be controlled. He doesn't care about censorship. He's free! We arm him to defeat us. The author can't get to the reader without us. The reader, without us, is just fine! We don't have the right or even the option to ban everything, or everything we'd want to. Nor to sound an alarm. We offer weapons to our enemy. Who is the reader, not the author. He slips through our fingers . . .

In the Royal (State) Kitchen, we taste the dishes, the foods, to see whether they are by any chance poisoned. If they're poisoned, we die and no one misses us, no one cares. What a thankless job! The censor and the poisonous kitchen of books!

"You're mutilating my heart!"

I'm not mutilating it, the excrescence, I'm breathing into it, I'm giving it life, I resuscitate it often, so that it'll live, so that it'll enjoy a long life and the admiring gaze of readers.

You brought it to me mutilated, I'm healing it, bandaging it, I'm a doctor, not a murderer!

The monster inside me is also a censor, what else! The ideal, quintessential, absolute censor. Thirsty, hungry, in its essence. I feel it waking, moving slightly, getting up. Literature! it shouts. Literature! Gobbling up manuscript after manuscript, spitting out, quick as a wink, mistakes, lizards, and other animals harmful from an ideological point of view, which give it slight indigestion and make its stomach hurt. After all it's our monster, from the same camp as us.

What is censorship? What does censorship mean? A privileged way of reading, when you can change what you don't like. A prereading-reading-postreading-omnireading-transreading. Just as our operations are divided into three stages: pre-inspection (preliminary inspection), inspection, post-inspection (the inspection of already published books). Keep going, don't stop here. It's the reading that obligates me to think, to awaken and feed the monster. Don't you understand? Reading is for people who are strong. Reading is a war against idiots. Those who are able remain standing, the others fall on their hands and knees and stay like that. I've been fighting my whole life. But you don't feel it, you don't see it . . .

I, the censor, am in the middle, with one hand outstretched toward the writer and the other toward the reader. I stay there between them, I'm the scale that balances, the equilibrium. When I like a writer and do him a favor, turn a bit of a blind eye, the reader suffers; when I squeeze the writer in a vise, violently, punishing him for real or imaginary faults, the reader, on the other side, is doing great, nothing hurts him, he reads between the lines or turns the pages bored, indifferent. I have to keep them all on their toes, to keep all of them in mind.

I, the censor, am the arbiter of all battles, emotional or ideological, strategic or contextual.

The world's going downhill, it's going to pot, in a systemized way, marching to the beat of poetry, with rhyme and meter. A march with approval from the top, with all the necessary authorizations. Like a herd led by a sheep with a cowbell or jingle. The sheep recites sweet and passionate verses, the herd, mesmerized, follows it. We can do nothing, there's nothing we can do. We should at least anticipate the change, announce it ahead of time somehow. Not enough is being done in this direction. We don't consider the consequences enough. You publish a lot, you read a lot. But who studies the adverse effects? And if they're worse for a regular reader than they are for me, a censor, well-read and experienced but powerless? Who knows what effects a book can have on an entire nation?

Before, only educated people read, cultured aristocrats, in very small numbers, not just any factory worker or peasant out in the hay, urged and required to start writing plays or poems about the radiant future overnight, to establish literary circles on top of that. They would send us out to places conducive to healthy origins to discover poetic geniuses. I'm not saying there isn't some old man Ion who's a talented storyteller or some aunt Marioara who sings heartfelt carols during the holidays. But to turn the entire country into writers and readers can be more harmful than our much-maligned illiteracy and more dangerous than bringing in armies of spies and evildoers. Books are weapons and, if you don't know how to handle them, they can turn against you and hurt or kill you. Reading transforms a person, that's already clear. Too much reading is bad for you, especially if censorship's just a façade, for show, as it is in our communist regime.

We should learn from the example of our predecessors, from those with experience in the field, who practiced true censorship. We're picking our noses and cutting out two commas and we're done. You call that censorship? Meanwhile authors are crying and screaming as if we had cut out that pathetic comma not from a miserable poem, but from between their nimble legs, thus creating the illusion of a real censorship, harsh and very active. Only we know how mild and, especially, how ineffectual our censorship is. We're the only ones whose hearts are breaking over the poison we're serving the poor nation without being able to do anything about it. We should learn from religious censorship. The oldest and the most efficient . . .

There's so much I could say, but I'm wasting my time . . .

Back to the manuscript, then!

Communism will fall because of reading, they're all becoming smarter than the smart ones, they ask too many questions, they have more and more desires and requests, constitutional rights, written and unwritten rights. We can barely keep writers under control. No censorship exists that can resolve the problems of the entire world, all the readers.

Sometimes I feel like a scarecrow in a cornfield. When I first appeared, all the crows took flight, they scattered, scared, then they begin growing accustomed to my presence, they convince themselves that I can't really harm them, they stake me out from a distance, then they get closer, the bravest among them land on my shoulder and with great satisfaction deposit some droppings on me wherever they might fall. All I can do is wait for the wind to blow, so I can helplessly flutter a moth-eaten sleeve of my old jacket in the hopes that they'll leave. The main role of censors has become like that of a scarecrow in a field overrun with impudent crows. When the birds get used to it and it no longer has a reason for being, our censorship will disappear. It will become useless in that scenario.

I need an actor! One who's smart as a whip and who'll understand your game from the first couple words!

> The great hunt. The hunter is devious and cruel. He says to us: I'm going to go hunt a duck tail or a pheasant wing, a stag horn or a pig liver. He catches the pig, takes out its liver, then lets it go. It doesn't matter whether it lives after that or not. A feather or two, plucked from its tail, doesn't really affect a peacock and it goes on its grumpy way, but how can a swan fly without its wing? Or how can a pig survive without its liver? We all go on living, scared that the next hunt will be even more merciless. Thinking that maybe we got off pretty easy, we survived. I paid with a feather, this time.
>
> Ode to the lizard!
>
> Who can understand that the lizard is the only one not suffering in this context, the only one running around happily, the only healthy, cheerful one among us, the sick and scared hunters. That doesn't mean it isn't hunted, but it drops its tail and leaves, it grows another one, it has one body to give to us hunters and

another body of its own. We hunters and the other beasts don't grow back our tails and other organs whenever we lose one. The lizard keeps growing it back, it and its regenerable tail! It's caught and uncaught. It's the animal we hunters hate the most.

Just between us: all their withered beasts and all their lizards can kiss my ass! You'd have to be a real idiot to believe that we censors will end up high and dry. Whoever thinks that they'll find even one person who, after ten poetic years, still cares about all the poetry filled with ugly, poisonous lizards is deceiving themselves. Whoever is expecting for there to be at least one person who will write a very useful dictionary of lizards for future generations is deceiving themselves even more. Only a censor could do something like that and not one of them will do it, mark my words! In a short while, no one will care about lizards anymore. They'll prefer a classic conceited lion or a painted crow. Go ahead and pollute literature with this reptilian species!

Roza is suffering from her latest disappointment in love: "He answered my letter, but he didn't say he kisses me, he didn't say he loves me. Me to him: my love, him to me: just baby." How stupid! Censors shouldn't suffer because of love, they shouldn't suffer anymore at all. All these trivial passions shouldn't gnaw at your consciousness. If it happens, it's a sign of immaturity, you haven't grown up yet, you're not smart enough nor prepared enough for difficult tasks.

A censor is one who understands! You don't cut something out just because a word, a sentence, or some passages seem subversive, hostile, to you. Everything you don't understand can be hostile. Ignorance itself is hostile, dangerous. You have to understand.

And if I'm dumb, what do I do?

Understanding can't be borrowed, it can't be received, it comes with time.

It comes to some, to others, never.

And literature can't be understood by ordinary means. You don't memorize it like multiplication tables. It's like love. You love a beautiful woman, you don't keep trying to figure her out. You love her, you feel her. You don't keep trying to find out what she thinks, what she wants, what where why. Something that isn't made up of words attracts you, something ineffable . . .

What?

Ineffable?

?

It lies, look, here.

And how tenderly he put his palm on his chest, up high, in the middle, slowly sliding lower, caressing as if without meaning to his bosom, just because it happened to be on the way, descending optimistically toward his stomach, then, too quickly, flying back home.

Ineffable? I murmured in the hopes that he'd apply another ineffable for me.

You intuit, he said looking off in the distance and ignoring almost completely my thirst for that ineffable, which I couldn't have expressed except in a banal and incomplete way. If that's what literature means for com. Zukermann, I think I don't know him at all, though we've been around each other often for a while now.

I want another ineffable! A short one, closer, please, for better results, for greater vigilance, better performance, optimization of outcomes, I wanted to say to him, but I didn't dare. He would've gotten the wrong idea . . .

You feel literature, you love it.

The creator can induce his drug out of thin air, out of anything, and he lives intensely. Be careful, he can take advantage of us, use us, he can be very dangerous. You have to feel his trance, the climax, you have to go through what he's going through and divine, beyond words, the ineffable. All this necessitates experience, time wasted, and a great deal of suffering.

Suffering?

You have to hit up against life too, you have to put yourself in the place of those who write, in order to understand what supreme reasons make him say his creed and at what cost . . . And to always look at things in perspective. What does the line you'd cut mean for him? If the entire meaning of his life fits into a few words that you cut out, only because they don't edify optimism and the radiant future, because they bring to mind something cosmopolitan, pessimistic, or mystic, meaning you're defending yourself with empty and abstract concepts, applying empty theories to a living and suffering being, acknowledge that you could be likened to a murderer and take responsibility for your deed. You're cold and just, but you kill the spirit. You kill today, tomorrow, the next day, until the person is ruined, one person, two people, a nation. Who, if not us censors, understands the cost of killing this spirit? How many lives has it cost us up until now and how hard was it to raise this new generation, and now the new generation is also in danger.

Well, let the new generation disappear too! Let the nation disappear! So that all that's left are ruins and censors! Too much, too much. No ruins and no censors, let it all perish! I wanted to answer him, but I didn't dare. He would've gotten the wrong idea . . .

Such a warring spirit in me! I want to fight and there's no one to fight with.

We also talked about the fact that nothing can be achieved on your own. A team. Party. Group. Collective Association.

He also told us about the rabbit that walked on water. While it was hopping across a river, the rabbit remembered you can't walk on water, it began to swim, kicking its little paws, and then it remembered that rabbits don't know how it swim and it drowned. Moral of the story: Forget!

If you keep everything you read inside you, you're going to run into some big problems, forget, forget everything!

Face to face with a book, I'm always sitting and taking a test. Another test or the same test. You pass, author, I pass too. I safely pass through your book, I find a way though the thicket of traps, snakes, lizards, and other aggressive and poisonous animals, that you throw at me in each line, each paragraph, and you pass into the visible part of the world, the publishable part. I arrive at the end of your forest of signs and meanings, and you arrive at the end of the process required for a volume to appear. Tied to one another, without either of us really wanting this, running away from or heading toward the same prison, always together with the book that unites us.

Where are the poems full of emotions, where's the streaming blood, where's the life pulsating with dramatic events?

I've come to understand how weak the alcohol is, how diluted the text I have in front of me. Watered down, plain water. I'm not too stupid to catch on. I want a real text! I need more and more, more powerful, I need life and death on a razor's edge! I don't know what else I need, but what I have in front of me is too little, too little . . .

Why do people say: Your nose is always stuck in a book? As if we read with our nose? To take this idea a bit further, the first ever reading since reading existed on earth was done by a censor. The censor reads with their nose, meaning they intensify the process of reading, in order to sense more than can be read with the eye, to smell and to understand what doesn't appear at first sight. Meaning it's an allusion to the idea that the first ever reader, the first reader of the first book, was a censor! Maybe they didn't even know how to read, they just sniffed the paper and by scent alone could they tell, as we do, whether the book was good or not.

The first reading belongs to the book's author, he's the first who cuts out, adds in, so the first censor is the author.

A book, however thick, is nothing but a page from a long, interminable reading, you finish it and begin again. I don't even realize when I'm beginning a new manuscript and finishing the old one, but what does it matter . . . The book is eternal, like life, it never ends! Just as life repeats itself over and over, day-night, good-bad, beautiful-ugly. We get by however we can. What would it be like if one day nothing were to arrive at Censorship? There aren't any more manuscripts! No one's writing anymore. Everything's been written, now you can rest, esteemed censors!

No party ideology helps me. Nor can I truly regulate a book! How can you regulate a book? Who can regulate the emotion, talent, genius, suffering, surprise, fear, pain, laid down on paper? You can't stop it, you can't restrain it, you can't control it. We can instill fear, but only in the cowardly, the brave laugh at us, they play along, they understand our thankless role and they understand us, they forgive us. I want to experience that long-awaited pleasurable moment, when the writer of a good novel will invite me out to a restaurant, bring me flowers, thank me for everything I've done for him and for his book. I'd even allow him to ask me to marry him.

Isn't there at least one thing in this world, something small, insignificant, that isn't Censorship's responsibility? Do we have to be responsible for absolutely everything that moves in this country, the river, the bough? Everything's on our shoulders:

birth, death, creation, divinity, power, thought, humanity, love, doubt. Everything! And some say we're not important.

This is how it is here: high-level comrades ask for permission to hunt Carpathian stags, maybe also Carpathian bears, ones lower on the ladder hunt rabbits, quail, and little foxes, while we, ordinary censors, hunt mice and tiny bugs in damp basements, where we're getting moldy for weeks on end searching for rare books that are in a more or less acceptable state . . . It's our turn next; after the books were purged by the jackass cultural councilors of the former minister of propaganda who, terrified of the soviet councilors, hid them in attics and basements—that is, if they didn't burn the books on the spot—so that we, too, would have something to keep us busy. Not that the Carpathian go-ers were struck by a pang of academicism or bookish pity, yeah, right! All sorts of suspicious characters from abroad are asking about our expensive, old books. We're serving imperialism, I mean, how shameful! We look for books in moldy basements that our stag-hunting higher-ups then sell!

I'm tired of hearing that we censors are a bunch of criminals, that we have to hide, take our noses out of the air, heads down, guiltily, humbly. But I'm a true censor and I'm proud of it! I'm not a reject from the party or someone kicked out from somewhere else, downgraded, demoted three ranks and punished by being made a censor, frustrated, bitter, resentful until retirement and afterwards. I'm not the mistress of some higher-up, brought somewhere cushy, paid, and protected from harsh words and danger. We have bimbos who don't know how to read a book or write a report, sent to arrange newspapers on the left and books on the right, at customs, at the post offices, with the same salaries as ours. They don't know how to do anything else, but you wouldn't believe how much importance they ascribe to themselves, what an air of superiority about their duties! What ideas about responsibility in the workplace, about confidentiality and political sensibility! Without their vigilant and fundamental efforts not only would Censorship collapse but half the party would as well, they whom we spoon-feed the results of all our work! They sit around and discuss what gifts their lovers in the party have given them lately, comrades with wives and children at home. We turn a blind eye, what can we do!

I'm sorry that the institution operates in secret, that it requires us to lie to others regarding our place of work. People aren't stupid these days, they don't believe everything you say anymore, like they used to, people have gotten smarter and, at any small hesitation regarding work details—you say you're a proofreader at a newspaper and you run into someone who works in the same area, you get tripped up, you become shaky—the other person doesn't insist, charitably, but in his mind he now thinks you're a filthy Securitate officer who listens in on phone calls and writes intelligence reports. Your interlocuter will avoid you, quietly, disdainfully. I'm not Securitate at all! The old lady I'm staying with also thinks I'm Securitate. She doesn't so much as breathe when I come home, she never asks any questions about work, as if she weren't at all curious. What, as if I don't know that she gossips about me with all the old ladies? As soon as I leave the house, she's already starting to backbite me: Look, there goes the Securitate officer!

Comrade Zukermann's dream:

"I seemed to be attending something that could be called a ball, with wonderful music, aristocratic, in a hall decorated exceptionally artfully, everyone was wearing masks like during carnival, they had on lavish, brightly colored costumes, large wings, crazy tails, hats, airy cloaks. Then I understood that the people weren't wearing carnival costumes, but that these were their regular clothes, that's just what they were like, more eccentric, dressed garishly and over the top, but not wearing special costumes for that event. And their outfits, as I later observed, had been mangled. A wing disgracefully trimmed, a pantleg cut asymmetrically, making the wearer look ridiculous, a dress unstitched in indecent places. Some were really mangled and they looked horrible, for others you had to really search to see what had been cut, but you couldn't see the modification and I didn't think it ruined their appearance. Then I realized that the attendees of the ball were censored texts in human form. Though I was walking among them, they acted as if I were invisible, they completely ignored me. Maybe they thought I was one of them, I can't tell. Even with the décor and the fine music, I began to get bored there, nothing was really happening and I moved on.

"I went into the next hall, austere, fallen on hard times. Here music wasn't playing anymore, there were no more masquerade costumes. There were naked texts, in agony and with blood streaming from them, what was mangled wasn't their outfits, but their bodies. I also saw internal organs on the ground, guts spilling out from wounded bodies, puddles of blood, the hall was full of cadavers and the mortally wounded. A heart twitched not far from its owner, organs were moving around, all kinds of body parts were trying to do something to stay alive, to remain active; at someone's orders, they tried to gather together, then they scattered, a morbid atmosphere reigned, of helplessness and pain. Like a battlefield after the attack, filled with the wounded. I felt nausea, fear, and something else unpleasant as I passed through this hall, yes, also their hate and powerlessness, that they couldn't destroy me, they couldn't turn me into a ball of guts and bones, same as them. I couldn't leave that place fast enough.

"I think there was another room. Yes, I kept going. Here there was neither singing nor moaning, but still it appeared to be the most important hall, how can I define it?, it was dominated by a great and invisible danger. You couldn't see anything, everything was in a fog, but you felt that a presence was stalking you, that it would come out from behind a corner and strangle you, you began to hear quiet steps, you looked in their direction and you woke up, scared, gasping for air. That's it. I can only guess what that last hall means. I think it was a space of revenge, in which the censored work (or its author) strangles its censor. You could no longer walk through as an impassive witness, as I did in the first two halls, you had to fight and the fight wasn't fair. I, the censor, wasn't the one who survived. I remember that, at first sight, when you entered the last hall, nothing was out of the ordinary, but you immediately felt afraid, you began quaking with fear and you were sure you couldn't avoid the great danger, that in that perfect silence someone would kill you and there would be no escape, mercy, forgiveness."

A censor's dream. I sometimes dream too, but not like that! I'm better off.

Literature means freedom, the only freedom accessible to us.
    Oh, give me a break, for real!
    Censorship is freedom too.
    Censorship is the freedom of freedom!

Today a book made me cry. It was perfect, exactly how I imagined and how I had hoped it would be for so long. About a
mountain and a bear. About love transforming and purifying
us. About death, about forgiveness. Almost all books are about
this, but I've only cried now, for the first time. The other girls
in the office were curious to read the pages that made me cry.
They picked up the pages after me, they scanned them quickly
and said, elongating the vowel: Yeeees . . . Meaning they agreed
that pages like these would make anyone cry, it's understandable. With respect for my feelings and tears, the one who always
claimed that nothing impresses her, she doesn't like anything.
This doesn't indicate that I'm a weak censor, that my senses
and powers of attention have gotten worn out. No, in the conception of my girls here, only now am I real censor, meaning a
living and empathetic being. A robot that never cries and never
has any feelings has a longer expiration date, but it, too, rusts at
some point and it's only a machine. People can evolve, understand more, their work gains in quality, if they don't ignore
their emotions.

Hundreds of pages. I can't say that they're about absolutely
nothing. But the essence is so diluted that the something that
remains suffocates itself, it slowly disappears, it vaporizes.
Book-forest, book-landscape, an ecosystem of meanings.
    I'm the wolf that stalks the sick, weak animal and cleans up

the forest. The censor-wolf that cleans up.

I dream of myself as a white she-wolf, pure, beautiful, with melancholic blue eyes.

How dare you waste your life away without writing something truly important? Highlighting your failure with every line, every word. Why do you punish others with your inability?

Literature humanizes. Here we get a bunch of boorish faces, freshly hired employees with impeccable dossiers and the expressions of anthropoids who've just left the cave, and, after a while, some look like Greek philosophers. What piercing gazes, what intelligent smiles on their faces . . .

Roza was born in a small town, me, in a village, and I melt with delight when Hermina, a city girl from Bucharest, tells me that, between me and Roza, I look more like the city girl, and Roza, uneducated, uncouth, seems pulled out of some godforsaken backwater.

I had a revelation. Or an important discovery of my own. The ideal censor doesn't exist. You can't remain a good, true, upright censor all your life. Z.'s right and he recommends the benefits of moving from one place to another, from one direction to another, as happens to some censors, the better ones. If you're a living, breathing, and more or less normal person, the texts you read and work on influence you at some point. You close off everything and resist, like a fortress, like a medieval citadel, but a small window remains a fingerbreadth open, and the texts slip in through there, like smoke, like a poisonous vapor, and they ruin you, corrupt you, change you. You begin thinking differently, you have doubts, you lie, you fool the system, you fool yourself, you, a censor and citizen. In questionable complicity with authors and texts. In every person, censorship exists either in a more visible and intense form or in a more hidden, harder to detect form. But we're the only ones doing this as a profession, we use up resources that under different conditions would last us our whole life-times. If you wish, you can compare it to the sperm of males: you can't produce it your entire life, unless you expend it in moderation, according to the affirmations of scholars. If you tax it ten times a day, you put not only your capacity for fer-tilization and reproduction in danger, I'm referring to sperm, but also your life. You exhaust yourself if you practice it in exemplary fashion, even if you don't get too involved or you try not to get too involved, now I'm referring to censorship, I've moved past sperm. We're getting off topic. So, censorship can exhaust its resources as well . . . I'm not a man so I can't develop my theory further from my own experience, nor am I in close and intimate relations with any of our male censors, to see if censorship affects their potency directly (Roza giggles, Hermina stands upright), not figuratively, as I have in mind, me, the female censor, a woman censor. When I see how my colleagues evolve, in just a few years, only those who are really dense remain the same, but they're also the weakest censors, who, oftentimes, either leave or reach retirement without truly knowing what censorship means. For the others, who are even just a bit more advanced, Censorship transforms them, they turn into new people, formed by hostile lizards, capitalist temptations, the rebellious and noxious courage of certain

individuals who have nothing to lose and who splatter their
so-called truths onto us, at the risk of their life or liberty. And
where do these truths end up? They fall on our robust, powerful
shoulders—but we're people too—however much the Party or
the Personnel Department might want to transform us into
a bunch of docile, impassive, and robotized brutes—they'll
never succeed (except if they've already hired such brutes)—all
the documents, all the doctrines, all the bureaucracy and the
stilted language are blown to bits by a deeply sensitive poem, a
wise, eternal sentence, by simple beauty dressed in words, like
a living flower breaking through the middle of the pavement.
The censor's heart is also assaulted every day, from all sides, by
flowers and not only. I'm amazed that our institution is still
functioning! That we're still getting our paychecks. By 1971, I
had already realized that they're going to shut us down. I don't
have to look too far or get to know my colleagues, I can tell
from myself. I don't tell anyone, but yes, I'm in danger, I'm in
danger. I think, criticize, see, know. And that's no thanks to
the party, who'd crush us as if we were a bunch of bugs if they
found out about us and understood us. It's thanks to the texts.
Even the most naïve and stupidest ones, which aren't even
dangerous or hostile, even they humanize, educate, change.
Literature is a danger lying in the path of any type of state
structure. It is, in general, incompatible with the state and any
power structure. While all types of power throughout history
have avoided it, have kept it at a distance, when it was possible, have set fire to it, our kind and generous regime sets it
at the head of the table. I'm holding a snake in my bosom. It
will overturn the system! We'll all disappear off the face of the
earth because of it. Poets are our rulers and theirs will be the

kingdom, as it was for Jesus Christ and for kings. To them belong the future and true religion, and they're the ones who hold power in their hands!

Is there a God of all our texts . . . Or a devil? A good spirit, a bad one?

A supreme power—but this kind of substitution is even more inappropriate, God belongs to the mystic category, which is more forgivable, but if you say "supreme power" without meaning our party, that's the worst thing you could do, you want to upset power, though that's exactly the poet's idea—that his poetry (flimsy even if the volume's thick) is above the party.

A judge of all texts?

But what is there?

A censor of all texts—this goes without saying.

A life like a long day, without seasons, without bad weather. In the office, the same constant temperature, the same tempered texts, always the same occupation. Back home, in the country, we have spring, when everything comes alive, the ice melts, we have autumn, when we bring in the harvest, summer, with blazing heat and plenty of work, gathering hay for animals, winter, with darning, sewing, weaving, pickles, a warm oven. Here—a room where winter and summer are the same, a job with texts that don't care about the changing seasons, they only care about changes in the political wind. I've distanced myself from normal life, when even city-dwellers enjoy, after all, the first snowfall, the snowdrops blooming in Cismigiu Park. I don't feel like I'm a real city girl, I don't know what it's like to be a peasant (peasant woman) anymore, I've pretty much forgotten, I only know what it's like to be a censor. I feel I'm living an irreproachable censor's life, a somewhat clandestine life, where I'm allowed to walk alongside people, sit next to readers in the tram, but no one knows who I am or what I do. No one's allowed to know. I can't detach myself, I can't pull away, I can't and I don't want to. When I go to sleep, my comforter becomes a giant manuscript page. I fall asleep wrapped up in texts. I dream solutions to problems in the manuscripts, in the texts I read during the day, the words I couldn't find turn up, answers—interpretable, suspect—more delicate fragments, which didn't catch my attention on the spot, whose hostile potential escaped me.

On my sensitive white body, banned words appear. I dress to hide them. I can't wipe them away, if I wash myself forcefully and scrub them, they still won't go away, I can only cover them up. It occurs to me that they could also appear in places I can't cover, on my face, forehead, cheeks. I look in the mirror, scared.

On my forehead, in big letters: "Communist piece of crap!"

I wake up from the job-related nightmare, I conscientiously rub my eyes and forehead.

I'm in a hurry, you understand, in a hurry! I barely start a novel and I already want to be done with it, I want to finish it faster! Everything that takes you five hundred pages to write can be said in just three hundred, and a three-hundred-page book is far too sprawling and it can be painlessly and unceremoniously transformed into a decent one-hundred-fifty-page volume. Now you shouldn't think that one hundred fifty pages isn't a lot, don't you see how much is being written everywhere, even trees are writing, and houses, and the sky, and the flowers, voices ring out from every direction with wonderful stories, everyone's writing, so one hundred fifty pages is also far too long, have some decency and allow yourself to be convinced that a real, complex, complete, multitudinous novel shouldn't run over seventy-five pages. A novel as long as a person's life (the life expectancy of a man!). Seventy-five pages—what a long novel, you read and read and it never ends, a page for every year of your life! That's the only way I'd read with pleasure. I read six hundred pages of wastepaper because I have to, because I don't have the power to ban it, out of obligation, duty, necessity.

Who listens to me? What am I to this world that it should listen to me? Who am I to you? A censor? In your conception—everything most worthy of contempt and hate. If that's how things stand, then you have there the cause of our reciprocal relationship. You definitely, definitely hate me, but you sincerely and in all honesty expect for me to love you. Does that seem fair to you? If you could love me just a bit, a teeny tiny bit, maybe my heart would stir a little. It might melt a little.

What message are you sending? Why do I have to ruin my eyes over your mounds of letters piled up in a jumble, brilliantly, according to you? If only you had to dispose, as we do, of so many piles of semantic garbage, texts that mean nothing, many of them noxious, polluting, you'd think differently. You, too, would reek of rotten, expired meanings, your stomach would hurt from the unnatural, extravagant combinations that you're so proud of right now, you'd find out what foul winds your so-called superbissimus verses produce and you'd learn, you dirtbag, to write!

I feel that state approaching, sneaking in, undulating . . . I try to avoid it, to ignore it, I look for something to do. I'll write it out, put it down on paper, put it into words, exorcize it. That's what you do too, isn't it? Authors! It's like a wave that rises from your whole body, it gathers itself up, becomes big, like a snowball that transforms into an unstoppable avalanche and it reaches your chest but it doesn't fit inside there, it's too big, it's too much. Should I cry, thrash around, yell, call for help? I try to define it. To see what it wants and what I could do to make it go away.

Censorship isn't found in censorship. I'm not your censor! I'm not the one who constitutes the essence or the object, the way you keep saying. In vain you pick on me and won't give me a moment's peace as long as I live. What I cut out is superficial censorship, for show, it's not at all important what I do. Censorship lies in some other place. In the other place. Usually, wherever we're not.

Censorship is a part of the system, and the system doesn't mean three institutions, a party and a few other adjacent structures, it's not a hierarchy that limits and bans, censorship is somewhere inside us, in each of us, and not on the institutional level, but somehow personal, individual, unconscious, mechanical, it moves ahead without us, cutting, modifying, adjusting without our volition. The reins have fallen from our hands. As if a too heavy rainfall had destroyed the dams and now the water is drowning us, invading us. We wave our arms, our pens, we struggle, we try cutting something from some pages, we try different methods of salvation, but no, what's the point in lying?, any attempt at survival is useless.

I'm conscious that everything I'm doing is superfluous, inefficient, it doesn't save anything. It doesn't help me, the one who's cutting, or him, the one being cut. We're both suffering pointlessly. Censorship is very, staggeringly, important, but not here, not at this level. It's not the cutting of a word from a book, it's much more than that. A core, the core of censorship exists somewhere, the nucleus that keep us all tied up, prisoners. Censorship means a word put into a book, not taken out, all the words and all the meanings, not cut out, but written in. You, who throw your written work at me, you assault me, I feel all your cruelty, the barbarity of your meanings that censor my options, my free time, my right to life, my right to love, and my right to what you're screaming at the top of your lungs you don't have, my right to freedom! My rights in your hands. You're killing me, you writer! You're forcing me to die with your open books on my table!

At least if you were intelligent enough to understand that, of the two of us, the real censor is you! You spoiled brat! Hypocrite! Filthy censor that you are!

Translator's Note

Separating fact and fiction was one of the challenges as well as part of the pleasure of translating *The Censor's Notebook* by Liliana Corobca—real specialist in the study of censorship under the Romanian communist regime, real novelist, fictional character in her own novel about censorship. The completely plausible frame story of a communist-era censor's notebook that is donated as an artifact for a new museum of communism sets the tone. The novel incorporates fragments of government documents written in the same style as those actually found in the archives; it includes historical names as well as fictional ones. Oftentimes the dutiful government censor narrator, Filofteia Moldovean, is trying just as hard as the reader to decipher the intentions of the regime. All of this contributes to a vivid experience of the banality and surrealism of the era, allowing its darker aspects to lurk just under the surface.

During the totalitarian regime, the list of things restricted for Romanians was long—ranging from traveling abroad, to making jokes about party leaders, to being religiously observant—and the state conducted an incredible amount of surveillance to keep the people under control. The Securitate, the Romanian secret police during communism, was tasked with creating and maintaining a vast network of informants in addition to its numerous employees. Informants could be coerced through threats or torture, or offered personal advantages, or simply convinced it was their patriotic duty. To keep citizens in line, phones were tapped, people followed and photographed, friends and relatives questioned, instilling a general atmosphere of fear and paranoia, and producing an immense archive of paperwork.

As the novel makes clear, the institution of censorship, which surveilled texts through its own networks as well as worked in tandem with the Securitate, was shrouded in even greater secrecy. It did not exist officially. While I had become familiar with Securitate files by being able to access the files held on my grandfather, the structures and procedures of Censorship were fairly new to me. I had known, as the novel mentions at one point, that every typewriter in the country was registered so that any typewritten material could be traced, but I hadn't known that censorship involved adding things in, not just taking them out, or making entire texts and writers unavailable to the public. I also hadn't considered how the shift in Romanian communism away from Russian influence, in addition to all other foreign influences, toward an intensely nationalistic stance would affect Censorship as well in the form of changing directives and personnel replacements.

Filofteia unwittingly reveals these secrets and more as she writes about her life in Censorship. Her tendency to "talk shop" about an extremely bureaucratic institution forced me to track division and department names very carefully, especially as they tended to be restructured. Corobca's patient responses to my queries were especially helpful here. For example, the Foreign Publications Division later became Import-Export Publications and I decided to signal that in my translation of the preamble, since both terms later appear. I also had to track the terms for all the types of paper circulating in the institution in addition to the notebook itself, including: provisions, directives, reports, summaries, charts, memos, records, notecards, scratch pads, statements, declarations, bulletins, informant notes, briefings, lists, synopses, studies, announcements, etc.

In translating the language of bureaucracy in which the transcribed government communiques are written, I had to walk a fine line between preserving a sense of their opacity and making sure they sounded intentional and weren't completely incomprehensible. The same applied to the stilted language of communism. If terms like "radiant future," "healthy origins," and "hostile" sound slightly awkward, that's because they do in Romanian as well. For the communist-era term *multilateral dezvoltat*, the literal translation "multilaterally developed" seemed too awkward for how commonly it was used and I relied instead on the repetition of "well-rounded" to convey a sense of the era's obsession with the concept.

The censored literary fragments, written in different registers by Corobca, posed a similar challenge. They are frequently opaque both because they lack context, being snippets of a larger work, and because they often employ hyper-literary language. As Filofteia complains, certain writers might have written in this style on purpose to evade censorship, others because it seemed more elevated. On the opposite end of the spectrum, a few fragments are humorously lowbrow. Here I tried to match the rhyme scheme and rhythm to create the same effect in English.

Most importantly, I wanted Filofteia's voice in English to convey the same qualities I experienced when reading it in Romanian. She's old-fashioned but perceptive, proud but vulnerable, and sometimes dangerously petty. Part of her has bought into the relentlessly sunny picture the communist regime has painted of itself and another part of her is hopelessly skeptical and even sarcastic. She's funny but no one around her knows it. When Filofteia is transferred to the Import-Export division, she encounters foreign texts for the first time and is scandalized, but also intrigued. Given the cultural insularity Filofteia has experienced up until that point, I decided to omit, paradoxically, special Romanian characters such as the "ş" in "Ceauşescu" or the "ă" in "Bărăgan" to make these names and places seem less foreign to an English language reader, but to include them for other languages, such as the Polish "ł" in "Gomułka." Her censor's notebook, which Filofteia increasingly treats as a personal notebook, is a space where contradictions are allowed. It annoys her when writers make up words but she does the same thing on occasion. At one point she claims that she correctly punctuates all her writing in her notebook though she's not required to, and then often doesn't—as if intentionally contradicting herself. These and other contradictions make her real, memorable, and relatable.

Ultimately, it was impossible not to become self-reflexive as I translated *The Censor's Notebook*, a novel that so deftly complicates what censorship means even as it expertly exposes the mechanisms of Romanian communist-era government censorship. How much was I unwittingly censoring as I translated? How much was I trying to control what shouldn't and couldn't be controlled? Any creative act, and translation is clearly one, is an interpretation of reality that inevitably will leave out certain aspects, twist some, and add in others. The questions remain—to what end and for whom? I believe my goal in translating aligns well with Corobca's goal in writing: to convey what I experienced as true in my reading while preserving the ambiguity that gives the book its vitality. Without excusing moments when I fall short of my aim, I can only hope for as much understanding as Filofteia surprisingly elicits.

—Monica Cure
Bucharest, November 2021

Notes

1. The Iron Guard (also called the Legion of the Archangel Michael or the Legionnaire movement) was a militant fascist movement in Romania founded in 1927. Though outlawed as a political party in 1938, it came to power in 1940 under Marshal Ion Antonescu. They wore green uniforms and were also known as green shirts.

2. Communism in Romania was installed after World War II through the presence of the Russian army. The first phase of communism was heavily influenced by Russia after which Romanian communist leaders sought to distance themselves.

3. Romania became a constitutional monarchy in 1881 with the crowning of Prince Karl of Hohenzollern-Sigmaringen as King Carol I, and it lasted until 1947, when King Michael was forced to abdicate and the Communist Party came to power. The interwar years are popularly considered to be a golden age in Romania's past culturally and economically.

4. Greater Romania refers to the borders of the Kingdom of Romania in the interwar period when Romania gained control over Transylvania, Bessarabia, and all of Bukovina, regions with historically large numbers of Romanian-language speakers. Romania lost Bessarabia and the northern part of Bukovina to the Soviet Union after World War II.

5. The Dacians were an ancient people group in the geographic area that is now Romania who were conquered by the Romans. During communism, the dictator Nicolae Ceaușescu encouraged the trend of "researching" and writing about an idealized Dacian past that would glorify Romanian national identity.

6. "The Little Ewe" ("Miorṭta" in Romanian) is an old pastoral ballad popularized by the poet Vasile Alecsandri in 1850 and is one of the touchstones of Romanian folklore. In the ballad, a ewe foretells her shepherd's death at the hands of two fellow shepherds. The term "mioritic" is often used interchangeably with "Romanian" in the context of folk identity.

7. "Morsd" here is the narrator's misspelling of the word "Morse," as mentioned in the preamble. In the wave of persecution after the communist regime came to power, large numbers of political prisoners were often kept in conditions meant to exterminate them. This overcrowding of prisons, however, led to close contact between intellectuals and to a subculture where inmates would hold lectures on different topics or recite poetry they had written. These and other messages were sometimes communicated to other cells using Morse code.

8. During communism, trips abroad were usually reserved for party elites, hence a work featuring a traveling cow could be considered equivalent to calling a party leader a cow.

9. Mihai Eminescu (1850–1889, pseudonym of Mihail Eminovici) was a Romanian Romantic poet. Under communism's semiofficial advancement, Eminescu was extolled as national poet.

10. The concept of the "five-year plan" originated in the Soviet Union in 1928 as a method of economic planning and growth through the use of quotas, and was later adopted in other socialist states including Romania.

11. In order to promote desired authors and approved topics, books were sold in bundles of usually at least three in which less popular books were mixed in with highly anticipated ones.

12. The many shortages during communism included toilet paper. It was

a well-known fact that the population improvised as best they could with any kind of paper material.

13. While not subversive in themselves, the film titles added after the names of the movie theaters seem like insults. Theaters were named or renamed after important communist figures or events: Vasile Roaită (railway worker shot during a strike in 1933), Tudor Vladimirescu (leader of a Romanian rebellion in 1821 during the Ottoman empire's rule; considered a progressive by the Communist Party), Constantin David (communist activist assassinated by the Iron Guard in 1941), Alexandru Sahia (1908–1937, communist journalist and writer), August 23rd (main national holiday during communism, commemorating the 1944 coup against the fascist government), Grivița (railway yards in Bucharest that became a focal point of the labor movement in the interwar years, including as the site of the railway strike of 1933).

14. In Roza's wordplay, Moldovean goes with Ungureanu because the last names refer to families from two regions of Romania, Moldova and Transylvania (Ungureanu derives from a term for a Romanian from Transylvania). Iancovici and Johnson both mean son of Ian/John, but a Johnson would clearly come from a forbidden Anglo-Saxon space whereas the Slavic origins of Petrovici allow it to be a more realistic match. Toth and Vass are both Hungarian names but it's unclear whether they have anything else in common, leading to the speculation that Roza simply has her eye on someone with the last name Vass.

15. A reference to Pushkin's poem "Exegi Monumentum," which in turn refers to the line from Horace in Odes III claiming that with his poetry he has built "a monument more lasting than bronze."

16. "Clinic" here is an allusion to an illegal abortion "clinic." Abortions were banned by decree 770 in 1966 in an effort to increase the population, and hence productivity, of Romania.

17. Lucrețiu Pătrășcanu was an early leader of the communist party in Romania but came into conflict with the newly installed regime due to his disagreement with Stalinist tenets. He was imprisoned and executed in 1954.

18. A superstition of the sort practiced during the midsummer folk celebrations on June 23 by young women to discover whom they will marry. In this reimagining, if a young woman places two wreaths, one for herself and one for her beloved, into a river and they join up, they will soon be married.

19. In the 1950s, an alternative to prison for political undesirables of the communist regime, especially those living near the Yugoslavian border, was deportation to the Bărăgan plain in southeastern Romania. In more extreme cases, they were dropped off far from towns and left to fend for themselves.

20. In 1966, the fourth and final volume of the Romanian Encyclopedic Dictionary was published, with a total of approximately 3,700 pages written by over four hundred authors.

ABOUT THE AUTHOR

LILIANA COROBCA is a writer and researcher of communist censorship in Romania. She was born in the Republic of Moldova and is the author of the novel *Negrissimo* (2003), which was awarded the Prometheus Prize for debut fiction by the Moldavian Writers' Union. She is also the author of the novels *A Year in Paradise* (2005), *Kinderland* (2013), and *The Old Maids' Empire* (2015). She has received grants and artists' residencies in Germany, Austria, France, and Poland.

ABOUT THE TRANSLATOR

MONICA CURE is a Romanian-American writer and translator, and two-time Fulbright grant award winner. Her poetry and translations are widely published internationally. She is the author of *Picturing the Postcard: A New Media Crisis at the Turn of the Century* (University of Minnesota Press). She is currently based in Bucharest.